WED TO HER ENEMY . . .

Ruthless Lord Jackson Rushford forces Mairey
Faelyn into a devil's bargain: to come work for
him or lose her livelihood. Trapped, Mairey
moves onto his estate—where she sees that
despite Jack's wealth and power, he guards his
heart more strongly than any treasure. As they
kiss in the moonlit woods, she knows that he
is the one man she should never marry. But
then she is forced to do so.

OR TO HER TRUE LOVE?

Mairey had plotted to lead the dark, thunderous lord astray from the start—for the key to
the treasure he seeks is a secret only she
knows, passed down through generations.
And now the fiercely loyal Mairey fears that
she'll be forced to betray either Jack or her
vow. Is their love just a fairy tale—or could it
be forever?

LINDA NEEDHAM

THE WEDDING NIGHT

An Avon Romantic Treasure

AVON BOOKS ◆ NEW YORK

This is a work of fiction. Names, characters, places, and incidents either are products of the author's imagination or are used fictitiously. Any resemblance to actual events, locales, organizations, or persons, living or dead, is entire coincidental and beyond the intent of either the author or the publisher.

AVON BOOKS, INC.
1350 Avenue of the Americas
New York, New York 10019

Copyright © 1999 by Linda Needham
Inside cover author photo by Expressly Portraits
Published by arrangement with the author
Library of Congress Catalog Card Number: 98-93888
ISBN: 0-380-79635-X
www.avonbooks.com/romance

First Avon Books Printing: April 1999

AVON TRADEMARK REG. U.S. PAT. OFF. AND IN OTHER COUNTRIES, MARCA REGISTRADA, HECHO EN U.S.A.

Printed in the U.S.A.

WCD 10 9 8 7 6 5 4 3 2 1

This one's for you, Micki.
Thank you.

Chapter 1

⌒◯◯⌒

Northwest Lancashire, England
Summer 1858

"It's an elf bolt, miss! A real and truly
one!"

"An actual arrow, made by an elf?" Mairey
Faelyn gave a properly astounded gasp, then oooed
grandly. The children scooted in closer to her as
she studied the barbed flint arrowhead in little Orrin's coal-begrimed palm. "Amazing!"

"Found it myself, I did!" The boy was perched
with elfin lightness on a bale of moldering wool-
sacks in the abandoned fulling mill, a changeling
if ever there was one.

He was wearing Mairey's hat—her father's, really—a tweedy, sagging-brimmed relic of his folklore field-collecting. It was dear and dilapidated,
and reminded her of the wonderful years she'd
spent following him into hip-narrow caves and
weeping catacombs, collecting folktales and mar-
vels from every part of Britain.

1

"Hey, *I* got three of 'em, Orrin!" Geordie leaped into the center of the pack, plucked back an imaginary bow string, and shot an equally imaginary arrow into the sagging rafters. "Yep, the sky cracked open one night during a storm and 'n elf bolts fell right out of the clouds."

"Imagine that!" Mairey had seen hundreds of such arrow flints; had a very fine collection of her own in her library at Galcliffe College. And although she knew they had been hewn by ancient human hunters—not by elves and witches—she loved the folklore far better than the facts.

She loved the children's tales most of all. "Where did you find this very fine specimen, Orrin?"

"In the barrow field, last winter."

The Daunton Barrow. She'd heard of the ancient burial mound but had never seen it. This was a coal town; the sacred site was probably a slag heap by now, but worth a visit.

"Is the barrow field far, Orrin? Will you take me there?"

"Oh, no, miss!" Orrin slid off the bale, shaking his head gravely. "We can't go there. It's a dragon's barrow!"

"A dragon! Here in Daunton?" She'd never heard of a worm tale this far west of the Bleasdale Moors. "Does he have a name?"

Orrin glanced around at his fellows and their smudged faces, looked past them to the open door with its afternoon glare, and then blinked back at Mairey. "Balforge."

Everybody gasped in delicious dread and then

wrestled each other for a closer spot, primed for a whopping good story.

Orrin opened his mouth to continue, but Geordie, ever the brinksman, thunked a stone onto the floor, startling everyone and missing Mairey's toes by an inch.

"This here's one of his fangs!"

Orrin snorted. Everyone else oooed, Mairey loudest of all, though Balforge's fang was, in dull, scholarly reality, a primitive flint axhead. The wonder was that these children called it a dragon's fang. That was certainly worth a footnote in the book she was compiling on folk beliefs.

She picked up the axhead by its blade, and the boys tumbled over each other to get a better look.

"Careful miss! Could be poisoned! Just like his scales!"

"They shoot out of him like quills when he's angry!"

"His wings are as wide as the sky!" Geordie wedged himself and his part of the story into the space beside Mairey. "And when he roars, he scorches the forest—"

"And when he gets hungry," Orrin said, eyeing Geordie and nodding sagely, "he eats virgins."

Mairey bit back a laugh, her fingers itching to write this all down. "Which are? . . ."

"Oh, very much like onions, my gran told me."

"Ah." Mairey rescued her notebook and stub of a pencil from under the dragon's fang and quickly wrote, *Balforge: fire-breathing, poisoned-scaled, foul-tempered virgin-eater.*

"And he lived right here!" Orrin stomped his

foot on the planking. " 'Neath our village. For ten-hundred years, way long before the mine came."

Mairey's chest filled up so fast with red-hot anger, her next breath was a billow of steam.

Bloody coal barons and their bloody mines.

Balforge was the product of Daunton's despair. A wicked, relentless beast with a heart as hard and black as the outcropping of coal that had bred Daunton's voracious mine.

She wanted to hug Orrin and Geordie and all the other boys gathered around her, but they would find no dignity in her sympathy, and might even run from the meddlesome stranger.

"What do you suppose gave Balforge such a foul temper, Orrin?"

"Treasure, miss," he said, spreading his arms to encompass the whole of the mill. "Had a heap of shiny gold and stolen silver and pirate's jewels that he was guarding—"

But then Orrin's tale seemed to dry up on his tongue, and exited his small chest with a rasping gulp and a whispered "Bleedin' cockles!"

Suddenly every child had gone silent, their gazes fixed with Orrin's on something behind her. Something huge and terrifying, by the wide-eyed, gape-mouthed looks on their little faces.

She began to feel a niggling fear of her own, a compelling coldness catching at her ankles, a pin-point of prickling heat between her shoulder blades. She rose slowly from the clinging tangle of boys, then turned and tucked them behind her skirts.

"Balforge," Orrin whispered.

Sweet silver acorns! The towering shape in the

timbered doorway could truly have been Daunton's dragon—it was tall enough by half again as he stepped out of the afternoon sunlight that blazed crimson across his massive shoulders into the colorless shadows of the mill.

"Just a man, Orrin." Though Mairey wasn't altogether sure what sort of man she was looking at. He lacked barbed scales and poisoned fangs, and his wings were only a black greatcoat that draped to his calves, but that was demon fire dancing in his dark eyes as he swung his gaze across the trembling huddle.

Not a breath stirred, nor a muscle, as each of them, Mairey included, waited to be roasted and eaten.

The man made a sudden, growling grumble in his throat, sending the children screaming with the shooshing scatter of feet, like frantic wings beating against the sides of a cage.

Then the children were gone, and safe, and the mill tomb-quiet again, leaving Mairey alone to confront their poison-toothed dragon.

A wild-game hunter who had lectured at Galcliffe College once said that when facing down a fierce-eyed tiger in the jungle, it was best to stand stone-still and not to breathe at all. And that one should never, *ever* look the slavering beast in the eye, for that signaled a deadly challenge to him.

Well, she'd cut her teeth on dragons and manticores and hoary trolls; had translated the *Bestiary* from its twelfth-century Latin before she was ten. So she knew her monsters. She would easily be rid of this one—who was surely just the cantankerous landlord, here to banish the children from his property. Then she'd round up Orrin and the others, finish collecting her stories from them, and be off to the next village.

"You're exceedingly good at frightening children, whoever you are." Mairey swept her father's hat off the empty grain cask where Orrin had thrown it and crammed it onto her head. "Have you any idea how long it took me to gain their trust?"

"Have you any idea how long it's taken me to find you, Mairey Faelyn?"

Mairey stared at the shape in the doorway—at the dragon who knew her name. Before she could demand to know why or who he was, he was bearing down on her in a gait that thundered across the planked floor.

And there she stood like a stunned rabbit, a thousand and one questions knotted up inside her brain. She couldn't move at all, and just when it seemed the great beast would overtake her, he shifted his weight and coursed around her in a lingering circle, brimming her lungs with his startling scent of bergamot and saddle-leather, making her think absurdly of Sir Thomas Browne's observation that serpents copulated in slow, sinuous spirals, length against languid length, turning and turning against each other . . . just as Mairey was doing with this Balforge-incarnate, countering backward until she bumped against a strut and was forced to stare up into his coal-dark eyes.

"Who are you, sir?"

She'd never felt quite so much like a curio, so

thoroughly and keenly appraised as his flinty gaze touched every part of her face: brow and lashes, the edge of her nose, her mouth. Then his jaw flexed and his frown deepened.

"Rushford," he said. His hair glistened midnight to his collar; his gaze was darker still. "Viscount Jackson Rushford."

Why would an imperious viscount named Jackson Rushford be looking for her? Something to do with Galcliffe College? Surely not a colleague of her father's: he didn't seem the scholarly type. More like a smuggler or a Barbary pirate.

"I've never heard of you, my lord." And yet something about his name seethed in the pit of her stomach, some murky and roiling thing that made her certain she ought to know and fear him. That she ought to run home and shield her family from him. "I don't know what you could possibly want with me. And I certainly don't appreciate you standing so cl—"

"I *want* the Willowmoon Knot, Miss Faelyn." He closed the short distance between them, eyes glinting sharply. "And you're going to find it for me."

The Willowmoon.

Mairey's heart stumbled, thudded, and stopped. A clanging like an alarm bell began to ring so loudly inside her head, she could barely think.

Hold fast, Mairey! Hold fast!

Hold fast to what, Papa? He'd told her that no one else knew of the Willowmoon—no one but the Faelyns! Certainly not this thieving dragon who had curled himself around her and was stealing the air right out of her chest.

Mairey took an amazingly poised breath, considering the violent rattling of her heart as it chugged to life again. And, against the big-game hunter's dire warning, she looked up and into the beast's eyes.

They were fathomless. Blazing crimson and licking yellow.

He must surely have heard her gulp.

"The Willow . . . *which?*" she asked in a little squawk. It was safer to look at the fiercely square line of his jaw and the deadly muscles flexing there than to stray again to his eyes, where the flames danced so hotly.

He raised her chin with his gloved finger—not sharply, with nary a hint of violence—but causing her heart to rattle around in her chest again all the same.

"The Willow*moon,*" he said evenly. That very short, very rumbly 'moon' brushed past her eyelids, made her hitch in a long breath that filled her lungs with his exotic scent. "You know the piece very well, Miss Faelyn."

Dear God! She wanted to run for the farthest hills—but running away from a wild beast only made it give chase. And, pinned between the solid post and Rushford's even more solid chest, she wouldn't get any farther than the reach of his powerful arm.

I'm going to lie through my teeth, Papa—deny ever having heard of the Willowmoon Knot!

"Sir. Lord Rushford." He still had her chin

caught up by his knuckle, was still staring down
and deeply into her eyes—a tyrant used to having
his own way. His intimidation only raised her hack-
les and sharpened her senses. "I wish you all the
best in finding your Willow Knotty thing. However—"

"However, madam?" All that earth-rumbling
converged in her chest and settled low in her belly,
a provocative terror.

"However, I—" Mairey faltered, but thought of
her father and her promise, then boldly stated her
unshakable position. "I can't help you."

There! The simplicity of fact. She couldn't *possibly* help him find the Willowmoon Knot. No
chance in the world.

"Mmmmm . . ." A growl which he must have
perfected underground, best suited for shaking
mountains. His eyes took on a deadly, narrow
gleam even as he straightened and gave her a distant but oddly approving appraisal.

"You are clever, Mairey Faelyn."

She knew better than to take compliments from
dragons. "I'm nothing of the sort, sir."

"Oh, yes—and worldly-wise to guard your precious treasure with your life."

"Treasure?" She laughed—"Ha, *ha*!"—having
no other defense at hand. Now the man was talking
of *treasure*! Could he mean silver? Please, God,
no! "Sir, I have a train ticket, three pounds-ten in
odd coins, and a Gladstone full of sticks, stones,
and feathers. Hardly treasure—unless you're a rag-
and-bone man."

Which he didn't look like at all.

"Now, now, Miss Faelyn." His tsking scratched at her nerves; his smile frightened the life out of her. "You can drop your pretense."

"I'm not pretending—" She stopped because he had fit his finger to her lips, a searing brand.

"But you *are,* madam, protecting your knot of ancient Celtic silver."

"My—"

"But it isn't necessary with me, Miss Faelyn. Your secret is mine now, and I will guard it as you could never do."

"I have no secrets, sir. Not from you or from anyone." Mairey's fingertips had gone cold as ice, though all the steamy heat of hell seemed to be pouring off the man, working its way through her jacket, through the too-flimsy linen of her bodice and her camisole, to the cleaving of her breasts.

"You've no secrets from *me,* certainly. I know that you are Mairey Faelyn of Galcliffe College. Daughter and heir to Erasmus Faelyn. I know, madam, that you are an antiquarian. That you've been flitting around the countryside for the last two weeks on some inexplicable mission—"

"Collecting folktales, sir!"

"Carrying *that* traveling case and wearing *this* remarkable hat." He slid his fingers along her jaw and through the hair at her temple until her hat came loose and fell to her shoulder.

Mairey made a feeble grab for it, but he held her pinned and paralyzed as the hat fell to the floor.

"Your *father's* hat, I'm told." That dark, unreadable gaze lingered on her face, searching out her secrets. Knowing too much already.

Impossible. Where could he have learned of the Willowmoon? The jumbled legends of the silver lode rarely surfaced—every page of research on the subject was in her private library at Galcliffe; every fact was in her head. How did Rushford know? And how was she to turn his interest elsewhere?

"You've caught me, Lord Rushford: I *am* a scholar of Celtic folklore."

Rushford raised a brow but said nothing, sending her careening thoughts into even larger, more useless circles.

"And I don't mean to be rude to you, my lord, but I travel alone, collecting my folktales, and as a woman I must be wary of strangers."

"Indeed." He nodded, an almost gracious tilt of his head, though triumph and a galling amusement shimmered in his eyes.

"Especially strangers who, for no reason at all, seem to know my name."

"Ah, but I've given you my reason, Miss Faelyn. We have a common interest: the Willowmoon Knot."

"And as a scholar of Celtic history and art and literature, I can assure you that you've gone to a lot of trouble for nothing." Mairey took a chance and ducked beneath his arm, past the warm, clinging folds of his greatcoat, then slipped behind the pole and collected her hat, before dodging to her travel case.

"*Nothing,* Miss Faelyn?"

She had escaped him but not the sensation of his gaze, which she could feel through her back as she retrieved her Gladstone from the floor.

"Absolutely nothing, my lord—because I've never in all my studies heard of your Willow Knot. So, you see, we have no secrets between us. No common interests. Nothing. But I do wish you well on your quest. Now, sir, I have a great lot of evidence to collect from those children you frightened away, and all before night falls. So if you'll excuse me—"

Without a whisper of warning, Rushford was behind and above her, closing his hand over hers around the handle of her travel bag.

"Enough of your prevaricating, Miss Faelyn," he said too softly and too close to her ear. "We will discuss the Willowmoon Knot. And we will do it now."

"Please sir, I have nothing more to say to you." Mairey tried to pull away, but she met Rushford's chest in the curve of her back, her hip against his. Oh, but the underbelly of this poison-barbed dragon was steamy warm.

"I've come too far and too long for this charming dance you're doing. It won't dissuade me. You and I are going to strike a bargain."

"If you don't let go of me, sir, the only thing I'm going to strike is *you*!"

"And you, my dear, have underestimated my intentions." Rushford turned her sharply. "I've searched for you these two weeks, traveling mudded byways and goat paths, through sorry mining towns like this one."

"Chasing your fancies—"

"Chasing *you*, Miss Faelyn. And a crest of silver knot-work, no larger than my palm." He held out his hand between them, a powerful and sinuous scape of dark glove leather, clutched round an imaginary shape that caused Mairey's pulse to rise and her skin to prickle. "Ancient, struck in the Celtic form—or so I'm told. But *you* are the Willowmoon scholar, Miss Faelyn. I know that for a fact. You're the only one in all the world who can find this treasure for me. And you will."

Mairey felt exposed, stalked by a shadow who seemed to know her most sheltered secrets. She tucked her courage into the deepest part of her heart and then looked up from the broad fist that Rushford had now made of his hand. He was watching her from beneath his savage brow, waiting as a wolf awaits an unwary hare.

Rushford. Why did that name terrify her even more than his knowledge of the Willowmoon? She felt blinded and dizzied, confused.

"Are you an avid collector of Celtic antiquities, Lord Rushford? Is that why you're so willing to believe in your fanciful bit of crestwork?"

"Hardly that." He pulled off his gloves as though he planned to stay to tea. The afternoon sun had tracked through the mill's clerestory windows and across the floor like a druid's clockwork, and now branded its blazing brightness onto the fine broadcloth of Rushford's shoulder.

A man who tamed fire.

"Are you an archaeologist?" she asked, drawn by his broad, work-bronzed hands, his able fingers as they fisted his gloves. "Are you looking to pillage treasures closer to home, now that Egypt's have all been plundered to near extinction?"

"You know very well why I want the Knot, Miss Faelyn." His gloves went into his pocket. "The very same reason that you want it."

He couldn't possibly. "Then I wish you luck, Lord Rushford."

"I don't need luck, Miss Faelyn." He was smiling like a dragon with a belly full of virgins. "I have *you*."

That simple statement of possession, with its immutably present tense, nearly felled her.

"Sir, if the Knot does exist—if it ever has—and *if* it should miraculously find its way into your keeping, what could you possibly gain from it?"

"Silver, madam."

The glade of the Willowmoon. Mairey closed her eyes and was there among the willows, her village tucked safely below, her sisters playing in the fallen leaves, her father's grave and her mother's.

"You must be deep in debt, my lord, if a few ounces of silver can add so very much to your coffers." Mairey tried to be glib, but her words clung in her throat. "Melt down your auntie's silver sugar basin and save yourself a lot of trouble."

"I could care less about the Knot's history or its meaning, Miss Faelyn—only that on its face is a map that will lead me to an even greater treasure. A network of silver veins so pure that it glitters from its bed in the forest floor."

Dear God! Mairey suddenly knew with terrifying clarity why the man's name had rocked her off balance.

Rushford Mining and Minerals. Tin and coal.
And silver.

Jackson Rushford was a mining baron! She knew the name as she knew the devil's. A spoiler of willow glades and villages. A thief of souls and childhoods.

He must never have it—not the Willowmoon Knot or the vein of silver, or her village that nestled in its shadow.

"Mere legend, my lord Rushford," Mairey said evenly, surprised that she could look him so plainly in the eye when her world was spinning out of control. "Smoke and shafts of light, nothing more."

"And where there is smoke and light, Miss Faelyn, there is always fire." He was too close again, his eyes too dark and smiling. "And we shall walk through it together."

Chapter 2

❛❛**M**y lord Rushford, I wouldn't walk through a slight breeze with you.'' The brash young woman sniffed at Jack and went back to her battered Gladstone.

He allowed himself a large measure of satisfaction from her angry frown. Though truth be told, he would have preferred prim-faced outrage and eyes that were pinched and bespectacled, as befitted a scholar. He'd been searching for a pasty-cheeked, hollow-chested girl with limp hair pinned tightly to her pointed head, expecting lank-boned shoulders hunched from overlearning, and an arid wit turned in upon itself.

Instead, he'd been dancing with dappled moonlight, trying to trap its beams with his fingers, coming away with only the heady scent of peaches and dogwood.

He spent a silent curse on Dean Hayward and the man's shabby college. The blackguard hadn't had the sense to tell him that Mairey Faelyn was as breathtaking as she was brazen. That she wore her stubbornness like a shield.

16

His patience with the woman was gone—he had no time for hedging or petty negotiating. There was too much at stake here, a fortune in silver, the very least of it. He would have her cooperation in this venture. Hayward had given his word; plans were in the works. She would carry out the terms to the letter.

"I'll brook no more delays and deceptions, Miss Faelyn. The deal has been struck. You will work with me in the matter of the Willowmoon."

"Are you entirely mad, sir?" She pried her Gladstone open, glaring at him all the while. "You and I have made no deal."

"*We* have not, madam." He stepped between her and the doorway—she would not be pleased. "However, Dean Hayward and I *have*."

"Hayward?" She paled, all that dusky pink anger washing from her cheeks, leaving her voice unsteady, with a dread that betrayed her fondness for the treasure. "The dean of Galcliffe College? You discussed the Willowmoon Knot with *him*?"

"I'm not a fool, Miss Faelyn. As I assured you, your secret cache of silver couldn't be more safe than it is with me."

"Your assurance?" Blushing color returned as bright spots of outrage. "What sort of agreement has Hayward made on my behalf?"

"Your cooperation with me on my *unnamed* project, in exchange for a sizeable annual endowment to Galcliffe College."

Her lovely mouth fell open, damp and glistening, obviously awaiting speech. It arrived with a half snort.

"Then you're both mad, Rushford. I refuse."
She tipped her nose and turned away to stuff a map
and a small book of much-abused paper into her
case.

Jack had never in his life browbeaten a woman,
and he was trying his damnedest to temper his
threats—for that's what this erstwhile meeting with
her had become—with reason. She was no taller
than his chin, as lean as a fallow doe, and would
probably outdistance him in a sprint. Once he'd
released her to flit about the mill, her defiance had
seared him. And he hadn't been able to keep his
thoughts or his fingers off her all the time he'd had
her pinned against the pole. In truth he'd been
roundly aroused by her scent, by her softness and
the silver-gold of her hair; had taken foolish lib-
erties and had only let her go when he had regained
control.

A dangerous associate for this venture—but he
needed Miss Faelyn and her resources, needed
them now, before one of his competitors found her.
Whether the silver turned out to be legend or fact,
a waste of time or a limitless fortune, she was the
only one who could lead him to the truth.

"It isn't your business to refuse me, madam.
Your salary is paid by an endowment to the college."

"Little you know, sir. The endowment was my
father's bequest; he willed everything he owned to
the college."

"But the funds are managed by Dean Hayward
and a Board of Endowments." An ill-advised, ide-
alistic arrangement on the father's part, but it had

provided the perfect opportunity for Rushford Mining and Minerals.

"My father set up the endowment so that I might carry on his folklore research after him. The trustees would never break my father's will. Not unless they've made a deal with"—the young woman's opinion of him had bordered on distaste from the beginning and an unreadable fear for a while; it now changed to open loathing in a single breath—"a devil like you. No. I refuse to believe they would do that to me."

"For the opportunity of a limitless endowment?" Jack drew closer to her furious packing. "For a library to rival the Bodleian, for a museum that would put the Ashmolean to shame, an endowment for a Geological Chair? My dear, such a fortune would tempt the angels themselves."

"I'm not a bondswoman, Rushford, nor a slave." She retrieved a pencil from under a bench, grabbed up the cloud of hair that had loosed itself from its bonds, gave the mass of it a twist, and then stuck the pencil into the resulting nest. "My time is not yours to buy, let alone Dean Hayward's to sell."

He'd been foolish to look for innocence in all that beauty. She was devious and resourceful, crafted to the marrow in stubbornness: a formidable adversary.

But she had a price. Everyone did.

"You'll be handsomely provided for, Miss Faelyn; your salary plus a substantial royalty for your cooperation."

"A royalty?" She laughed deeply in her throat,

as though he had offered her a piece of green-molded bread. "You can sit on your royalties, Rushford, and hope they hatch into fat diamonds for all I care. Let Hayward do what he wants with my father's endowment. I won't help you."

What the devil did she want with a silver mine, this wispy girl? Not money, not security; neither had tempted her. Yet, her desire for the Willow-moon and its riches blazed so brightly that it burned him; was so unyielding that it disappointed him to his soul because it felt so much like greed.

He'd come upon her among the flock of children, had heard their ringing voices and her laughter even before he'd stepped into the mill and found a mother bear and a den of cubs.

What moved her to such fierceness: blind loyalty, love, commitment to a cause? Her dreams for this Willowmoon were impossible, whatever they were.

"You're quite foolish, madam, if you think you can keep an entire silver mine for yourself."

She threw up her hands, then fisted them against her slender hips. "You've found me out, my lord," she said, catching him straight on with her glittering gray gaze. "I have a huge, aching need to find the silver before anyone else does. I want it. It belongs to me. I plan to pit-mine it with my bare hands and become grotesquely wealthy beyond all my dreams."

"Absurd."

"Why? Scholars have grand dreams, just as mining barons do."

"Have you a pick, my dear? A shovel?"

"No." That stubborn chin went into the air and stayed.

"A cart to carry the silver ore to a smelter?"

"I'll *find* one."

He nearly laughed at the image: Miss Faelyn strolling across the village green to the train station with her single load of ore, cart by cart.

"Have you enough capital for augers to drill into the earth, for the sledges to haul the ore out of the shafts, for rails to carry the coal to market?"

"I will find all that, too."

"Enough for the great steam engines, enough to house two thousand workers and their families?"

"Of course I do, Rushford." She stooped to collect a handful of rubble off the floor. "I've at least that much hidden here in my shoe."

"Dammit, woman! How do you expect to turn a profit on your discovery?"

"I have my ways, Rushford." Into her satchel went stones and feathers and sticks; items he would have tossed into a hedge. "And it's none of your business."

"The Willowmoon and its silver *are* my business, madam." He met her, nose-to-nose, as she stood. "I've a royal warrant from the queen herself, and a grant from Parliament to find and exploit the mineral worth of the Commonwealth. All of which supersedes any claim you might make on anything you find. You cannot remove a single ounce without my permission."

"Well, then." She crammed her ridiculous hat on her head and raised the brim in a mock salute. "My very best wishes to you in your search, sir.

Do write to me in care of Galcliffe College and tell me of your progress.''

She turned a rounded-bottomed hip to him, hitched her sagging Gladstone over her shoulder, and started away as though he'd let her go.

"Stop right there, madam." Two steps, and he had hold of her arm and turned her. "We are associates now."

She sighed with great drama and cast her defiance to the timbers above. "I'm not in the least interested in helping you find your next breath, sir, let alone waste my time helping you look all over hell and gone for a mythical piece of Celtic knotwork. I've got my own work to do, including another week of field-collecting."

"A week. Today is Saturday. Good. Then I'll expect you to report directly to me on Monday next at ten in the morning, at Drakestone House, London, where you will commence your work."

She blinked up at him, settled on a scowl that winged her brows. "Oh, do you, sir? And just what is it you envision I would be doing at this Drakestone place?"

Jack knew better than to take the woman's question as a change of heart—more a change of direction, another of her diversions. That she had the interest to ask at all was as significant as hell. "You will be conducting your investigation into the whereabouts of the Willowmoon Knot."

"Ah." She nodded, gave him a cheeky perusal that licked along every nerve. "How would I go about doing that, sir?"

The amused bluntness of her question caught

him broadside, exposing a weakness in his plan.
He hadn't the slightest idea how to begin such an
investigation. He opened mines, not museum
vaults. That's why he needed her, damn it all. Yet
he couldn't very well admit that.

Jack shrugged as though he knew the how of her
work as well as she did. "I'll provide whatever you
require for your quest, Miss Faelyn."

"What do you mean?" Her question was quick,
incisive.

He could only guess at the needs of an indignant
lady antiquarian with sun-silvered hair and lumi-
nous eyes. Antiquaries usually liked dusty darkness
and cubbyholes.

"I will see that sealed vaults are open and available to you." He was pleased to see the quirk of
her brow and the bob of her hat brim—here was a
clue. "That records are exposed; that contacts are
made with anyone, anywhere, anytime. Ask me,
my dear, and all the resources of the kingdom shall
be yours."

Confusion softened her brow and lit her eyes
with a flash of possessive anger. Her breathing
came more swiftly, raising her chest and parting
her rose-damp mouth.

Desire. Hope.

Ah, yes, Mairey Faelyn. There was the fault in
her stone-walled defenses. Resources. She needed
resources.

She needed *him.*

Jack held back his smile for the damage it might
do to his credibility, as well as to his strategy, and
yet he felt the smile—and a long-forgotten rush of

happiness—deep in his gut, like hearthfire and a warm brandy.

"Well?" he said instead, mortally satisfied when her anger flared again with a clear-eyed vengeance.

"No, *thank* you, sir." She yanked at the brim of her hat, tipping the front upward so she looked like a field-lass in a blowing wind. "Let Dean Hayward sell my soul to the devil; let the queen issue her royal warrants; let Parliament grant you the moon and all of its cheese, sir—I don't need anyone. And, my dear lord Rushford"—she shook her head gravely—"I certainly don't need you."

Jack watched as the woman dodged her airy way through the bedraggled mill, watched her skirts catch on a rusted gear, and finally allowed himself his chest-stuffing smile at her grumbled "Great sizzling toads!" as she yanked them loose.

A moment later she was gone from his sight— but not in the least from his senses. She was the wild, heady rose in his nostrils, peach down and heavy cream against his skin. Though she couldn't have meant to, she'd left him something of herself: a single, sinuously long strand of her hair, caught up near his shoulder in the dark nap of his greatcoat.

Pale, precious silver.

"I need you, Mairey Faelyn."

And soon you'll know just how much you need me.

Mairey escaped through the mill door and out into the blaze of afternoon sunlight with an utterly amazing amount of grace, considering the terror pooling in the pit of her stomach.

"Brimstone-hearted dragon!" She was breathing like a blast furnace, hot nerves and sizzling anger all caught up in a conflagration that made her hurry away from the mill.

Curse and bury the man! He'd known everything. As though he'd searched through her heart while she wasn't looking.

Museum vaults! Church crypts! *Oh, Papa, just imagine!*

Her father had shown her every secret known to the Faelyn family; how to interpret every resource stored in his library at Galcliffe College. She had studied his crumbling manuscripts and the sketches of Celtic drawings; she'd learned about ancient silversmithing and mining, learned also that the Willowmoon silver had passed into history more than a millennium ago, leaving behind just a few faded references to its worth. How the Knot had turned up in London, no one knew, but it had last been seen in the treasury of the first King Charles.

The Faelyns had been tracing it for the past two hundred and twenty years, trying to return it and its dangerous map to its rightful place in the glade. But they'd long ago come to a sturdy, impossibly high wall: their resources were exhausted. And now Mairey was alone with the burden of finding it.

The agencies of government were unwilling to open their doors without an explanation—and that was impossible without giving away the location of the glade. The family had long ago scoured all the scholarly resources; the Church campaigned against the ancient pagans; and most museums were reluctant to reveal their own secrets.

Still and all, partnering with Rushford was impossible, no matter what doors he could open for her. She had successfully escaped him and his beguiling temptations; the Willowmoon and its secret were intact.

For the moment. That skin-prickling thought sent her flying through the coal-rubbled streets of Daunton, past the forlorn-looking train station and down a winding country road. Balforge would have to wait to have his folktale collected from Orrin and his friends; Mairey wanted to be miles from the beast by sundown.

She would confront Dean Hayward and his indiscretion next week, letting her temper cool. His threat to sell her services was as ridiculous as it was barren. She was a grown woman and owed nothing to the college but a token rent on the dismal old chamber that housed her library. She had no intention of interrupting her trip just so that she could skin Hayward's ears for his foolishness. The sooner she finished, the sooner she could be home in Oxford with her three sisters and Aunt Tattie.

Besides, Mairey knew Hayward well enough to recognize one of his sentimental but wholly unsubtle attempts to lend a hand to the children of his old friend and colleague.

God save her from such good works.

But if by some horrible chance the trustees *had* stolen her father's endowment and she needed ready cash to house and feed her sisters, there were plenty of marketable items in the Faelyn collection of artifacts and oddments. Treasures enough to sell to museums and collectors; all moderately valuable pieces of art, but not in the least sentimental.

Her father would understand and applaud.

At all costs, Mairey, but for the family.

Her heart and all her hopes for her sisters were housed in the ceiling-high shelves of the Faelyn library.

Knowledge. Wisdom.

She'd never known just how precious—and how dangerous—a bit of knowledge could be until she met Jackson Rushford.

She made the next village just as night fell. She dropped into a sagging bed at the Greenleaf Coaching Inn and slept fitfully through the night, her dreams tangled in the exquisitely amorous coils of a dark-eyed dragon.

Chapter 3

Mairey spent the next week coaxing folktales from irascible cotters and reclusive crafters, until her Gladstone was brimming with field notes and bits of village folklore.

A blessedly full week with not a sign of Lord Jackson Rushford—curse his blighted soul.

His image trespassed at will, though—that awakening sensation of being so completely surrounded by him in the dim light of the mill. His scent of danger, and the touch of his breath drifting through her hair, his untamed largeness, his fingers tracing the edge of her ear. She'd had no place to run then, and, she realized now, no real thought to do so.

But she hadn't backed down—and in the end, Rushford hadn't followed.

Which should have reassured her. But the man's conspicuous absence, his easy acceptance of her final rebuff, only caused her to watch over her shoulder every minute, guarding against the dragon at the door.

By the time she returned to Oxford she was exhausted, her nerves wrung dry and her heart aching from missing her sisters.

The broad, comfortable lawns of Galcliffe College were a ruddy orange in the midsummer sunset. Just ten minutes in her library to unload her Gladstone and sift through her mail, and then she'd return home to her family.

"Miss Faelyn! You, Mairey!"

Dean Hayward. Not now! She wasn't ready to raise her sword and do battle.

But she turned toward his familiar warbling hail and watched him padding down the gravel path toward her, his polished shoes winking out from beneath his dusty black robes, a cheery smile on his leathery face. He was more than three times her age, twice her weight, with all the power and prestige of an Oxford dean—and the coward had crumbled like a shortbread biscuit the moment Rushford had pressed him.

"Mairey, my dear, dear Mairey!" Hayward beamed at her as though he hadn't a notion that he'd nearly ruined her life. "Your travels have pinked your cheeks."

"And I shall tweak yours clean off if you dare betray me again." She dropped her Gladstone at her feet.

"What is this, my dear? What have I done?"

"Rushford!" Mairey focused her glare past Hayward's spectacles into the injured hazel of his eyes. "Does the name sound at all familiar?"

"Ah, yes, my girl! Quite an arresting development, eh?" Hayward reached into the pocket of his robe and took out his ever-present flower snips.

"Arresting, sir? You nearly stripped me and my father of our life's work—took the food from my family's table."

"Nonsense, Mairey." He carefully deadheaded a rose that had bloomed and crinkled to pale brown in the time that Mairey had been away. "I would never do such a thing to you or to your father. I loved Erasmus like a brother—love you like a niece."

"Dean Hayward, you set a barbaric industrialist on me. That isn't love."

Hayward shook his head. "Mairey, Mairey, you misunderstand. Lord Jackson Rushford is a very wealthy man. Your father spent his life and his fortune looking for all sorts of fanciful things. I could offer Erasmus little help in all the years of our friendship. He wasn't the most companionable of our lecturers. Reclusive, I would say, until he needed something. He complained to me unendingly about the resources that he lacked, that he wished he had access to. I could do little; Galcliffe College is not a Merton or a Balliol. Research money has always been granted to loftier ventures than his: science and manufacturing, exploration. And after your father died—"

"It became my turn. And I'm doing just fine with his endowment. And if it comes to it, I'll do fine without it!"

"Yes, my dear, but the trustees thought it best to, well—"

"The trustees thought what?" Mairey felt a wobbling roll of fear in her stomach as the flush on Hayward's cheek brightened to well-defined blotches.

"Galcliffe is in a sorry state, Mairey. You know that. Rushford's first payment for your services will keep us open for another ten years, at least. Maybe longer!"

"My *services* are not for sale, Dean Hayward. I will leave the college if I must!"

"But Rushford is expecting you to—"

"Let him rot." Mairey's smile came easily, triumphant and at peace with the simplicity of it all. The Willowmoon was safe. She'd never see the man again, never again be tempted. "Now excuse me, Dean Hayward"—she started up the short walk—"I've been gone three weeks and have a lot to catch up on."

She took hold of the door latch, but the handle wouldn't budge.

"Mairey? . . ." Hayward's voice had become wheedling and whiny.

She ignored him and tried the door again. Still nothing, though the entire mechanism looked as if it had been polished quite recently.

"You can make up for your great gaffe, sir, by having the door planed to meet the jamb." Mairey wedged her shoulder against the panel, gave a shove, but came away with an aching arm and a colossal misgiving.

"Mairey, I couldn't stop him."

"Stop whom?" Mairey didn't like Hayward's ashen pallor any more than she liked the prickling chill that lifted the hair at her nape.

"Rushford."

"You couldn't stop him from what?" Yes, *Rushford* was the misgiving, and the anger that grew hotter at the tips of her ears.

"He wanted . . ."

"He wanted *what*?" She'd been privy to the power of Rushford's wants but was having difficulty finding sympathy for Hayward's fear.

He sighed and handed her a brassy new key.

She kept back a sailor-blue curse. "He's locked me out of my own library?"

"Well . . ."

"May the man find adders in his marmalade!" Mairey grabbed the key out of Hayward's cold fingers, crammed it into the lock, and yanked down on the latch. She shoved hard, and the door flew open to a vast, echoing emptiness.

Stunned, Mairey stepped inside, her heart gone hollow.

The orange light of the nearly spent evening spilled in from the tall, barren windows, painting soft stripes across a floor stripped of its carpets and the threadbare tracks her father and her grandfather before him had paced into their delicate patterns.

The towering shelves that had once held thousands of books were empty. Gone were the cluttered curio cabinets and the gouged, ink-stained worktables, her father's leather chair with its caressing imprint, and the partner's desk they had shared.

Gone.

A sob filled her chest and found voice in her throat. Tears slid down her cheeks.

Rushford.

"He came a week ago, Mairey." Hayward clung to the door handle. "With a half-dozen men and three lorries."

She swabbed away the tears, cursing them, too. "You let Jackson Rushford steal my father's library!"

The Willowmoon!—he had it all! Every word. Every letter. Drawings, maps, runes!

"Rushford promised me that he would pay you well, my girl."

"Pay me?"

He dipped his chin and shook his head. "Oh, Mairey, I'm a wicked man."

You're a fool, she wanted to say. But she knew that wasn't true and would only hurt him more deeply. Hayward wasn't privy to her father's secrets, and certainly not to hers. How could he have known the havoc he would cause? Better that he didn't pry.

"Never mind, Dean Hayward." She slid her palm across the windowsill. Clean. Stripped bare. Sterile. The room was cleaner than she'd ever seen it, from ceiling to floor. Not a trace of the Faelyn family remained. "I'll go to London in the morning. I'll find Drakestone House and rescue my library, or Rushford will pay dearly."

"How?"

"A thief is a thief. I don't care who he knows, God or the queen."

"Do you mean to call down the police on Jackson Rushford?"

She couldn't risk the authorities—too many questions.

"I have no choice but to confront the dragon in his lair."

And not a clue as to what she would do when she got there.

Her temper still charringly hot, Mairey let herself into the little house in Holly Court wanting nothing more than to see her sisters, to hold them and never let go. But it was nearly ten, and they would be fast asleep and not expecting her until tomorrow. She could hear Aunt Tattie's nickering snore from above stairs, her day's work accomplished and her three "baby ducks" snuggled down safely to their dreams.

God, how she loved coming home to them. Home, where even the playful shadows and the creaking silence seemed a fond welcome, where the scent of tomorrow morning's bread cooling on its rack made her stomach grumble.

Tomorrow.

Tomorrow was Monday. *Rushford's* Monday. Damn the man!

Mairey sat her satchel on the hall chair and was about to make a foray into the kitchen for a cup of tea when she heard familiar whispering curling toward her from abovestairs. Three ghostly little figures in glimmering flannel appeared on the landing. One by one they glided down the steps, their small hands clinging to the rail, but not very well to their giggles.

Mairey knew these errant spirits as she knew her own heart and loved them as she loved life itself. They were the joy in everything she did, her hope

for tomorrow, her sacred promise to her parents—
and the reason she would defend the secret of the
Willowmoon and the glade from men like Rushford.

She stood as still and unnoticed as the spriggy
wallpaper, biting hard on her tongue to keep herself
from giggling as her sisters descended the stairs.

First Anna, almost regal at ten, her pale hair
veiled by what looked like the sheer lace curtains
that usually hung in Mairey's bedroom window.

"Shhhhhhh—hush your squealing, Caro!" she
said none too quietly herself. "Aunt Tattie will
hear you."

"Then wait for me, Anna!" Caroline whispered,
her earnest, ghostly, eight-year-old gait hobbled by
a pair of Mairey's boots. Her best and newest!

And then little Poppy, dragging Mairey's bed
pillow behind her—barely six, but quick to study
mischief from her sisters.

Three little whirlwinds—her chamber was no
doubt turned topsy again. Poor Aunt Tattie.

The scamps thundered into the dining room and
headed for the kitchen.

Mairey let the door to the butler's pantry close
softly on its swinging hinges; waited until she
heard voices rising in the kitchen, the clinking of
the honey crock, and the rattle of the spoon drawer
and the plates. She made her way quietly through
the pantry and leaned against the kitchen jamb.

"I'll cut," Anna said, the bread knife already
halfway through the first inch-thick slice. "Do keep
your fingers out of the way, Poppy."

"They're hungry."

"So's this knife. You best hurry and get the butter. The honey crock, Caro!"

Caroline only grunted around the fingerful of honey she'd just stuck into her mouth.

They were so busy raiding the bread keep that Mairey was completely unnoticed as she drew her coattails up over her head, hunched her back, and stepped into the kitchen.

"Ah, me tasty little morsels," Mairey said in her best wicked-old-witch cackle. "You'll give me tea with my bread and honey, or I'll eat you all up!"

There was shocked silence, then in the very next tick of the kitchen clock, three terrified little voices rose up in a single, glass-shattering scream, rattling kettles and pie tins, and making Professor Martin's old spaniel bark two houses down.

They screamed until three pairs of eyes found her, and then three smiles lit her heart.

"Mairey!" Their screams of delight pierced the night again and brought on another howl from the dog.

Mairey was tackled full-on by her sisters. They fit perfectly into her arms, and she knelt to collect and kiss them all.

"You're home a day early! Hooray!" Caro planted a honey-smeared kiss on the side of Mairey's nose, then danced off in a melody of "hooray, hooray, hoorays."

"You should have told us!" Anna hugged Mairey, her face flushed from her raiding, the lacy window curtain forgotten in a pool beneath the worktable.

"Only a half-day, sweet." Mairey slid her fingers through Anna's hair, wondering when its baby-fineness had thickened to ropes of silk, full of sorrow that she hadn't noticed. "But if pirating is what I'll find when I return unexpectedly, I think I'll keep my comings and goings a secret."

"You're going away again, 'Ree?" Poppy had fastened her arms like warm shackles around Mairey's neck, and rubbed her cheek against Mairey's. "Please, stay! Pleeease!"

No thanks to Rushford, she'd be gone again in the morning. "I'll be away for only another day, Poppy. I promise."

"Ducks, ducks! My baby ducks! I heard screaming!" Auntie's voice found them well before she came through the pantry, wielding the poker from her bedroom stove. "Anna, what is this? What—well."

· The lanky woman stopped at the door and shook her head gravely, sending its white blossoms of cloth-tied curls waving.

"Mairey Faelyn, you're as naughty as your sisters!" Tattie bent down to Mairey and stuck out her cheek to be kissed.

"Haven't I always been?" Mairey gave her a quick peck and laughed as she got to her feet with Caro's sticky-handed help, though Poppy held on like a cat clinging to a buoy in a raging sea.

Tattie nuzzled Mairey's cheek and then Poppy's. "Mairey didn't say she was comin' in tonight, did she, my Popper?"

"My plans changed suddenly." Radically. Unalterably.

"Changed how, dear?"

Mairey hated to dodge her aunt's question. But Tattie was her mother's sister, as unaware of the Willowmoon and its secrets as anyone else in the world—except a certain dragon. The woman was as possessive as a lioness when it came to her nieces. Widowed since Waterloo, when she'd lost her handsome young groom, the woman had never had children of her own but had made up for it in the last six years.

"I'm going to London tomorrow—"

"London?" Anna grabbed Mairey's hand and held it tightly. "Can we go with you, Mairey? Can we please? I want to see Kew Gardens again—the orchids."

"The zoo! The zoo! The zoo!" Caro threw her arms around the lot of them, jumping and making monkey noises.

Poppy's grip around Mairey's neck tightened, and the girl climbed higher in her arms. "I just want Mairey."

"I'm sorry, loves. You can't come with me this time."

"Next time then?" Anna laced her fingers together in girlish prayers, bouncing on her toes, nearly as tall as Mairey.

"If it's at all possible, sweet. Don't I always keep my promises?" Especially to little girls whose hearts deserved a daily dose of wonder. She tried; oh, how she tried.

Anna kissed her. "You're the best sister in the world, Mairey."

"What's in London, Mairey Faelyn?" Tattie had perched her spectacles on the nub end of her nose, great lenses that turned her nondescript hazel eyes into piercing inquisitors.

A battle to the death with a thieving dragon. "My work," Mairey said, turning to Anna to avoid Tattie's glare. "Would you light the kettle for me, Anna, please? I haven't eaten since noon."

"I'll get the honey!" Caro said, dashing after her sister.

Tattie persisted, both eyebrows arched, eyes narrowing their focus. "Going to London by yourself again?"

"Yes."

"For how long?" Titania Winther had an unnerving genius for knowing when something was bothering one of her nieces. And, adult or no, Mairey was included in that incisive sweep.

"I'll be gone no more than a day," Mairey answered, her toes crossed against the possibility of a white lie.

"And a night?"

"Possibly." If she wasn't put in jail for murder or mayhem, or both.

"If I didn't know you better, Mairey Faelyn, I'd swear you were skipping off to London to see a—" Tattie paused in her whispering and studied Poppy, whose nose was buried against Mairey's neck. "A man," Tattie finally mouthed.

Mairey couldn't help a belly laugh. How simple a bit of sinful cohabitation seemed in the light of Rushford's infamy.

"There's no man in my life, Auntie. I'm skipping off after research material." Mairey nuzzled her nose against Poppy's. "Nothing more."

Anna and Caro were clattering dishes and whispering in the pantry. Poppy finally succumbed to the lure of conspiracy, flung herself out of Mairey's arms, and followed after them.

"You and your father, Mairey! I don't know what drives you to wander so. Gone two weeks out of every month, from spring till fall."

Mairey sighed, and, as usual, her aunt heard every shade of her regret. "I don't wander, Auntie; I collect stories and publish them in books. But it seems the girls change overnight. Another year and Anna will be a young lady. Poppy will be as tall as Caro. And Caro will be as wild as a country hare."

Tattie laughed. "An affront to every hare in the county, I think. Oh, dearie, I nearly forgot!" Tattie fingered through her recipe box, past the tattered, food-stained cards, finally handing Mairey an elegant, unadulterated envelope. "This came for you. I didn't want to lose it."

The envelope bore a bristling crest emblazoned with an ornately decorated R.

"Rushford," Mairey said, a familiar uneasiness clutching at her heart. "Did he bring it here himself?"

"What does 'himself' look like?"

"Very tall, very dark, and very, very—" Mairey caught herself before she could utter the word *handsome*. He wasn't at all. Not in the standard meaning. He was . . . compelling, coercive, insidious. Any one of those words would cause Aunt Tattie to bar the door against Mairey's leaving for London; she had to speak carefully. Auntie's eyes were blinking, at their most perceptive.

"Very . . . insistent," Mairey offered, hoping the word was bland enough.

Tattie shook her head. "It wasn't 'himself' then. Could have blown this one over with a sneeze. The letter came a week ago today. Sunday."

The woman hovered as Mairey stuck her finger into the flap, popped the sealing wax, and fumbled with the contents of the envelope.

A railway ticket. And a note written in a strong script.

Drakestone House. Monday, ten o'clock. Drakestone Crossing.

"Who is this Rushford fellow? One of your father's antiquarian friends?"

"A collector."

"He's the man you're going to see in London?"

"Yes."

"I see."

So did Mairey.

"Welcome home, Mairey!" Anna was standing proudly at the pantry door, flanked by both of her grinning sisters. She held up a neatly arranged tray, its snug landscape complete with a steaming teapot, Mairey's favorite cup and saucer, and a bread plate spilling over its edges with the honey that Caro must have soup-ladled onto the stack of three fat slices of bread.

A poxing curse on you, Jackson Rushford.

Chapter 4

"I tell the tale as 'twas told to me."
Jack doubted that very much. Still, he leafed through Mairey Faelyn's book of untidy scrawlings, barely making sense of the words, let alone their meaning. It seemed nothing more than a collection of falsehoods and gross exaggerations—which made him wonder again if he were placing his trust in a crackpot.

Albeit a *stunning* crackpot—one who should have arrived here at Drakestone House hours ago. He shut the lid on the box of scrap paper and shelved it beside its corner-worn twin.

Erasmus Faelyn's name had been painstakingly inscribed in the *ex libris* of nearly every book Jack had removed from the open crate on his desk. He shook his head as he glanced around at the maze created by the one hundred and forty-three other crates he'd shipped to Drakestone House from that ramshackle library at Galcliffe. He'd only had time to open two. And they had only puzzled him more with their diagrams and drawings of rain-faded stone faces and crumbling ruins.

Lunatic woman and her accursed hedging. He felt blind and extraneous, though he stood in the midst of his own vast library—one of the grandest in all Britain, with its two-storied arching windows and a mezzanine that ran three sides of the room; books, ladders, high-backed reading chairs, and a hearth that he could stand inside. Miss Faelyn's entire library would fit into one corner of his— roof, windows, battered furniture, and all. Anyone else in the world would be pleased with the opportunity, but Jack had a strong suspicion that she would not.

He lifted out another book—or what was left of its tattered binding and brittle pages. Ancient hands had been at work on the wood-bound manuscript, its ownership proclaimed in faded ink and a more florid script than today's fashion. The next book and the next were inscribed with the same name, one Joshua Faelyn.

A very odd legacy of scholarship, a bred-in-the-bone penchant for antiquities. There were years, *ages* of other Faelyns besides the prolific Erasmus and the very unpunctual Mairey.

Even as Jack thought her name—fully prepared for that hot stirring of air in his chest whenever she danced blithely across his mind—the marble clock on the library mantel wound itself into a clanging frenzy of gongs. Four of them.

"Devil take the woman!" Jack shoved another of the noteboxes onto the shelf and started for the foyer, only to find his butler standing rigidly at the partially open door.

"Tell me, Sumner," Jack said, tidying up his

temper so he wouldn't misuse it on the man's wiry shoulders. "Tell me that you found Miss Faelyn at the station and that she's waiting in the foyer."

Sumner cleared his throat and shifted his gaze to somewhere beyond Jack's shoulder. "Miss Faelyn wasn't on the 3:38, my lord."

"Great bloody hell! I explicitly instructed the woman to arrive this morning by ten. I told her personally, I sent her a ticket and a note—"

"The rail lines are somewhat flexible in their timetables, my lord."

"Damn it, Sumner, you've met every train from Oxford since before ten o'clock; it's past four now, and not a word from the woman!"

"Perhaps I missed her, my lord." Jack had known Sumner since they were both pitmen in Labrador, and the man's abiding patience and even-toned voice had always been his most irritating flaw.

"You could not possibly have missed her, Sumner. I have carefully cataloged Miss Faelyn's most striking features three times before; I needn't again."

"Silver-gold hair, you said, sir. And long, to the waist, if I recall. Gray eyes. Not quite clearing five feet and two inches." Sumner blinked his attention back to Jack, his unsubtle opinion showing through his butling. "Shall I try again for the 4:57?"

Silver-gold and *long* was a bland and truncated description of the woman's hair. But Jack couldn't very well ramble on about how its silky fragrance had roused him like an untried schoolboy, or how the trailing wildness of it had impelled him to wind his fingers through it. He'd be damned if he would give the man an excuse to go sniffing at Miss Faelyn's hair. Nor did he wish to detail the *exact* color of gray in her eyes: frosty, with flecks of blue and aqua, lamplight on silver.

"My lord, the 4:57?"

"Yes, all right. But this time I'll go with you."

"Yes, my lord." Sumner gave the stacks of crates and barrels a disdainful arch of his brow, then left the room, no doubt bound for his greenhouse and orchids.

Jack went back to the bristling crate on his desk and shelved more of Mairey Faelyn's books. Requisitioning her library had been a necessary maneuver, though she would likely denounce him as a thief. Which was exactly his plan. These books were more than paper and ink and desiccated leaves. They were her memories, all that she had left of her father.

He knew how compelling memories could be. How they could rise up and become indistinguishable from one's hopes.

She would come to him. And she would stay. If he hadn't been watching her so carefully, if her eyes hadn't been so fascinating and gray-glinted, he might have missed the wonder in them and never have known her heart.

He pried open the lid of another crate, then lifted the bowl end of a pot from the tangle of fine wood shavings.

It was broken, most of it gone.

"Damn!" This was a hell of a way to embark upon an alliance of trust with the woman. She would think him a careless clod. He rescued another broken piece from the shavings and tried to fit it to the ragged edge of the bowl.

Not even close. The next piece fit—sort of. If he had a smaller wedge to put in the corner . . .

Perhaps he could glue the bowl back together before Miss Faelyn arrived and set his ears afire. No need to add fuel to the conflagration. He gingerly sat the bowl on his desk, picked through the shards until he found a few promising pieces, then sat down on a stool to begin the puzzle.

"Your pardon, my lord."

"Not yet, Sumner. Can't be time." Jack steadied one of the shards against the broken edge of the bowl, unable to spare the man a glance as he tried still another place. "Oh, and find me a Cement of Pompeii, will you? The kind with a brush in the stopper."

What he really needed was a shard that looked like a fish wearing a large derby.

"She's here, sir."

"Who is?"

"*Me.*" The voice was silken and sultry, and fit for one hell of a fight.

Jack looked up from the fractured bowl, across the maze of crates and stacked furniture, and directly into a pair of eyes that leveled him with their clarity.

She *had* come. The redoubtable Miss Faelyn, framed by the tall, dark, mahogany doorway, and dangerously more beautiful than he'd remembered.

Silver-gold. Yes, he'd been right about her hair, though just now its thick plait looked well-used by the wind. She was dressed simply, clutching her huge, sagging Gladstone in front of her, and glaring at him from beneath the slouching brim of her hat. Outrage sat high and pink upon her cheeks; her chest rose and fell rapidly beneath the green wool of her traveling jacket.

"You're late," he said finally, swallowing hard as he stood up from his desk, unable to think of a single other greeting that wouldn't have been taken for bluster or relief.

"And you, Rushford, are a bloody thief."

The heat of her glare was a beam of summer sunlight focused through a magnifying glass. If he'd been a dung beetle, he'd surely have been charred to cinders by now. Sumner knew enough to vanish.

"No, Miss Faelyn, I'm a businessman." Jack tucked the evidence of the broken bowl into a cubby on his desk, then made his way toward the door. "The sooner you learn that, the better off you'll be."

"I know all that I need to know about your kind of *business*, Rushford. Consider yourself lucky that you haven't yet unpacked my library. It'll save you time sending the lot back to Oxford by morning. If it isn't there by ten o'clock, I promise you, I'll call in the authorities."

"I doubt that, Miss Faelyn." Jack leaned an elbow idly against a crate and studied her.

"You're not above the law, Rushford. I don't care who you know. You stole my library—"

"I merely arranged for your books and papers to be packed and shipped here to Drakestone. It would have been done sooner or later, and the end result is the same. You are here; your library is here.''

''Of all the arrogant toads!'' She came two feet closer to him. ''I told you, Rushford, I'm not interested in your project. I will *never* be!''

Jack let her statement boil the air between them, delighting in the anticipation, in the awakening that would come when she learned of the bounty he could put into her hands.

''Madam, have you ever read the *Dyrgel Gofarian*?''

''The—'' Jack felt her incensed huff more than he heard it, and the soft sound filled his gut with an unexpected heat. Her back was straight, and her chin, high, her head tilted slightly as though she were listening for an echo.

''We're talking about my *library*! Not some fanciful—''

''Have you read it?''

Her white teeth worked at her lower lip, sorting unthinkable decisions, it seemed, deepening the rose hue in the process. All the while charting his eyes, breathing as she might if he'd just kissed her and she was deciding whether or not she approved.

''No,'' she said finally, spitting with anger, dropping her bag to the floor and her hat onto the nearest crate, wishing him dead if her scowl meant anything at all. ''No one has read the *Dyrgel Gofarian*. It's the mythical writings of a fourth-century Welsh silversmith-turned-monk. But there is no such thing, Rushford.''

''Are you sure, Mairey Faelyn?''

She took another sharp, passion-heavy breath,

too obviously battling her belief in wonders. "The book is a legend, sir. Any scholar of the Celts knows that."

Her face was haloed by flaxen curls that frayed from the plait hanging from her shoulder. She smelled of the outdoors, of the wisteria hedge that clung to the stone wall containing the grounds of Drakestone House. She must have come cross-country from the station, walking off her outrage or summoning it to its full-blown fury.

He fought the urge to wind a strand around his finger and stuck his hand in his jacket pocket instead. "There are many ancient secrets kept from the secular world—or so I understand."

"Which has nothing at all to do with your absconding with my library."

"Oh, but it does, my dear. It has everything to do with it."

"How, Rushford?" She was a tight bundle of indignity: fuming, curious, prepared to deny that the winter sky could be quite blue at times.

"The *Gofarian,* madam. Which, by the way, was at one time a scroll, but is now pressed flat between wooden covers to preserve it. Ordinarily kept in a vault in the minster at York."

He was close enough to see her pulse shifting just above the low-buttoned collar of her dark shirt-waist. She feathered a loose spiral of hair into place behind her ear.

"I suppose you've seen it?" She tossed her head and the strand came loose.

Jack shrugged for effect. He truly couldn't fathom the value of the fragile, decaying artifacts

he'd seen this past week, but he knew that antiquarians and scholars like Mairey Faelyn would
have approached the minster's vault in reverent
awe.

"I saw mildew-encrusted rolls of old lambskin:
the *Dyrgel Gofarian* and other manuscripts in bad
repair, kept just as secretly. They all looked alike
to me—"

"You're lying." He'd never seen such bright,
beautiful intensity. So protective. So provocative.

*I have you, Mairey Faelyn, just where I want
you.*

"I couldn't read a word of its Latin, Miss Faelyn. Nor could I decipher its other scratchings."
The moment of truth, the crux of this unlikely partnership, had arrived. "But *you* can, my dear."

"Can?" Mairey felt as though Rushford had
caught her up in a stumbling trance, tempting her
with his impossibilities. "How?"

"Come," he said, smiling in that sumptuous
way. He held out his hand to her, his broad palm
bare and exposed, dreadfully inviting, as though if
she touched it he would lead her somewhere she
shouldn't go. She resisted, balling her fist into her
skirts and standing her ground in his unparalleled
library.

His eyes brightened in his conceit, never shifting
from hers as he left her for a small table near the
soaring windows.

"Vaults, madam, museums, the archbishop's
ear—just as I promised you." Rushford swept
aside the red velvet cloth, revealing a square-

cornered object nestled in the center. "My credentials."

He was good, this mining baron, surprisingly theatrical. But she wouldn't be swayed to his side—not even tempted.

"You're wasting my time, Rushford."

"I doubt that, Miss Faelyn. Come, see for yourself."

There was something deeply stirring about the object, about its weight as he lifted it to show her, and the faint ornamenting across its broad face.

It wouldn't hurt to look. Setting her heart and all her hopes against him, she indulged the wicked man and approached the table.

In the next instant, the room began to reel.

A legend come to life—the *Dyrgel Gofarian;* the secrets of the Celtic silversmiths. Most antiquarians doubted it had ever existed. And this marauding heathen had it here in his library! Mairey could hardly breathe, could barely hear for the maelstrom of hope and terror.

"Where did you get this?"

"It was delivered to me yesterday under guard from the archbishop of York, at the behest of the queen herself."

"Impossible."

"Nothing is impossible, Miss Faelyn." He reached down to touch the page with his bare fingers.

"Not that way!" Mairey caught his hand in hers, felt the glance of lightning in his fingers. "A kerchief, please."

Without a word Rushford set the book gently on

the table, then proffered a kerchief from his breast pocket. "Madam."

Mairey whipped it from him, wanting more than anything to find the book fraudulent, an elaborate hoax to trick her into joining him.

But this *was* old lambskin, old tanning, evidence that it had once been laced and scrolled. The ends of the stiff parchment were bound by thongs into two strips of oaken heartwood, and those were bound to flat covers, front and back.

"This cover isn't the original." Wonder and habit made her speak aloud. "Nor the binding."

"It had damn well better be original! How the bloody hell can you tell?"

"The gilding, for one. A thousand years old, no more than that." History be damned—this was legend come to life!

"A thousand years? Blast it, woman! Isn't that old enough?" Rushford shook the table with his weight as he leaned over the book, his hands resting hard on the tabletop.

"The cover missed the *Gofarian* by five centuries."

"Damn the man! The archbishop swore to me this book was authentic."

"I didn't say it wasn't." She prayed that it was, for it was a miracle. Mairey opened the cover to the parchment, and the first words of Latin took her breath away.

> As the Willow shall race the Moon
> On footsteps bright with silver.

Begetting of sorrows,
Begetting of joy.

Tears rushed to Mairey's eyes, so very hot and incriminating if Rushford ever saw them. Here was magic—a priceless sword dangling above her head, held there by a man who had the power to destroy her village and the people she loved. The same man who could open doors so long closed to her.

"Well, madam?" His voice came rumbling from behind her, and frightened a sob from her chest. The blackguard must know for a damning fact that she would have crawled on her knees from here to York just to catch a glimpse of the *Gofarian*. And now here it was, inside Rushford's library. He was a sorcerer, a piper whose music was meant only for her, and she was helpless against his enchantment.

She could almost feel the weight of the Willow-moon Knot in her hand, feel the cool silver turn warm. It was as near to her as Jackson Rushford.

"Well, yes," she managed to say, though too softly, as she wiped a stray tear off her cheek. "The book is *interesting*."

"More than interesting. I can see it in your eyes." He was leaning so close, he might have seen inside her heart.

"A scholarly surprise then."

"Ha! Private museums, Miss Faelyn," he said evenly, giving a wicked crook to his brow. "Gilded invitations into restricted archaeological sites, sacred books, crumbling manuscripts, sealed vaults, tea at Windsor with the queen—they are yours for as long as you associate yourself with my search for the Willowmoon Knot and the secret of its silver.''

Oh, Papa! What should I do?

''We're an impeccable fit, Miss Faelyn.'' He was impossibly tall. Impossibly dark-eyed and handsome. ''Offer your skills to me, and I shall give all this to you. A simple, profitable business relationship.''

Not simple. Terrifying. Impossible.

And as perilously tempting as gazing over the side of a cliff and believing with soaring certainty that she could fly. This man, this predatory beast, was offering her a precious set of wings and making her fly over the mouth of hell.

He was offering the Willowmoon.

''But if you're truly not interested, Miss Faelyn. . . .'' He offered his open palms. ''I will engage someone else.''

The threat was so blatantly idle that Mairey snorted. ''Who?''

''There was a young man recommended to me. Brawlings, I believe.''

''Arthur Brawlings.'' Mairey knew him well. A despicable charlatan who would boil his own mother's bones and salt an ancient barrow with them, if he thought it would bring him an ounce of glory. Yet Brawlings was also a scholar of the Celts and treasure hungry. With all the resources that Rushford was offering, the man would soon be on a trail that would bring sorrow to everyone Mairey loved.

Rushford had thought of everything.

As always, the man was watching her every

move, had probably seen the teary redness in her eyes and would make the most of her weakness.

"Should you refuse me, Miss Faelyn, I will put these same resources at Brawlings's disposal." He folded the cloth over the ancient text, one corner and then the next, until it was gone from her sight. "We will surely lose precious months of research while he catches up—a year or two, perhaps. But I am a patient man, willing to search the world for what I want, if need be. The Willowmoon Knot will eventually be found, and its clues will lead me to the silver."

She couldn't take that chance.

She would have to make a pact with the devil. Yet not on the devil's terms.

Deception, half-truths, sleight of hand . . . the secrets of the Willowmoon still belonged to her, and the truth could be as blinding and deceptive as any lie. Let the man believe that she was as greedy as he, that they were after the same glittering prize. Mairey's heart was raw and her head ached.

"You've left me little choice, Rushford. I want the Willowmoon Knot as much as you do. A fortune in silver is difficult to deny. Very well—I'll join your project."

He raised a dark brow as though he were surprised that he'd won. "Done, then."

"Yes. Done." Mairey felt as though she'd been flogged and thrown out on a rock. "Now, sir, if you'll point me in the direction of the nearest lodging house, I'll return to Drakestone in the morning to see my library properly packed and sent back to

Oxford, where I can conduct my research properly."

"No." The word was plain and clipped, but as powerful as a blow. "You work for *me* now, Miss Faelyn. Your library stays here."

"I can't afford to ride the train back and forth to Oxford every morning and evening." She couldn't leave her sisters and her aunt. And if she was to keep Rushford from learning too much, she needed to conduct her research safely distant from his prying.

"And I can't afford the time to have you on that train. You'll live here on my estate—"

"I'd rather sleep on a park bench! Good day, sir." Mairey got three steps toward the foyer before Rushford got a fist-hold of her skirts.

"Be still, girl!" His momentum propelled him against her before he easily hauled her backward into his chest.

"I'll not live alone with you, sir!" He was wrapped around her like a winter coat buttoned up against a cold wind.

"I'm offering you a private lodge here at Drakestone," he murmured against her ear.

"No."

"I assure you, Miss Faelyn, that if I had improper designs on you I would be forthright about it."

"What the devil does that mean?" The man was forthright enough with his shimmering heat and the fierce banding of his arms, a cocoon as ravishing as she remembered in her dreams.

"It means that you and I have contracted a business deal, which satisfies both of us in equal measure.''

''As I measure it, Rushford, *you* got the bucket and *I* got the hole.''

Rushford was silent and still for the space of a heartbeat, then Mairey heard a rumble and realized that he was laughing softly, the sound coursing through her like another pulse.

''Indeed,'' he said, freeing her from his grasp but blocking her retreat. ''Drakestone is large and the lodge is separate, secured behind as many locks as you find comfortable. But you will work with me in the main part of the house. My hours are long and unreliable. The sooner we find this Knot and its silver the sooner we'll be quit of each other, and the happier we both will be. Agreed?''

She looked up over his shoulder. His library was enormous, with two full stories of books and polished mahogany, and a mezzanine ringing the room. And a quarter of the shelves on its lower floor were empty but for a few of her field note boxes lined up together.

She could build an impregnable fortress against him here.

''Whose desk is this?'' Mairey slid her hand just under the edge of the desktop, following the undulations of the mahogany-cabled carving. ''Have you a clerk?''

''It belongs to me.''

''How often do you use it?''

''Rarely. This is my library. My office is through that connecting door.''

''Your hours?''

"Vary, as I said, as required by my business concerns."

"Your *mines,* I assume." She endured the bitterness, offered him a smile.

"Yes. As well as my forges and smelters, my foundry—"

"So you're busy most days?"

"And most nights."

Busy stripping hillsides of ancient trees and defiling gentle waterfalls with coal slag. Like any busybody dragon, he'd soon tire of sniffing round his new bauble and leave her to the wonders of his lair. Hiding her work from him would be simple if she built her walls of dancing mirrors.

Oh, Papa, the possibilities.

"May I see the lodge?"

He led her silently through the clipped shadows of the formal garden, past an afternoon-gilded greenhouse, over a low footbridge and its crystal stream, and into a remarkably unspoiled willow woods. He was single-minded in his long stride, constantly looking back to make certain she was following.

And when the lodge appeared beneath the heavy canopy of oak and hornbeam, Mairey thought they had accidently stumbled onto a storybook house.

It had a thatched roof and round-topped windows, three chimneys and a winding path of pearly gravel that seemed to sing as she followed it to the front porch.

Rushford held open the door, and Mairey found herself as charmed by the inside as she had been by the outside. Big, bright rooms freshly furnished, the homey smell of woodsmoke caught up in the timbers.

The girls would love it here!

"I trust it meets with your approval, Miss Fae-lyn."

Rushford was waiting for her in the wide hall as she came down the stairs. He'd been oddly puritanical in staying below while she explored the bedrooms, this feral-forged man who had thought nothing of pinning her to a post in an abandoned mill and fondling her as though they had been hungry lovers.

"The house is very unlike you, Rushford."

"An old royal hunting lodge. It was the first building on the property, some three hundred years ago. And as I promised, a full five-minute walk from the main house, with plenty of locks and a sturdy bar for the door. It's yours to do with whatever you wish."

"Are you married, my lord?" Mairey hadn't meant to ask that particular question, and never so bluntly, but it seemed important if she was going to be tied to the man indefinitely.

She'd have thought the question a simple one to answer, but Rushford just stood there looking at her, frowning.

"I only ask, sir, because a wife might object to having another woman living on the estate." Mairey's heart beat wildly under all that glowering. "*I* certainly would."

"You'll have no trouble on that count, Miss Fae-lyn. I've never had a wife."

Her heart took a crazy thunk, a little too relieved, a lot too giddy. She hurried the few steps past him into the parlor. "Do you plan to take a wife any time soon?"

"Why?"

Because the idea didn't set well with her. A wife in the offing—a wedding at Drakestone. She couldn't quite look at him, so she inspected the hearth and its damper, rattled the handle and came away with sooty fingers.

"Because, Lord Rushford, although no one hopes to conclude our pact sooner than I do, my father spent his entire professional life looking for the Willowmoon Knot. He was a much more experienced scholar than I am, and after thirty years he'd made little headway. We can hardly expect success after only a few weeks."

"And?"

She faced him, glad for the distraction of rubbing the soot off her fingers. "And if, sir, three years from now you should find a wife and you and I are still . . . associated, she would doubtless want me to conduct my research elsewhere than on your estate."

"Would she?"

"*I* certainly would!"

"Well, then, my dear," he said, leaning too close with a badly tucked-away grin, "I'll keep that in mind should I ever go looking for a wife."

"You'll warn me if you change your mind?"

"Absolutely."

That set off an entirely different set of fluttering in her stomach . . . bubbles of profuse contentment.

Absurd—it was the lodge. She liked it too much.

"Good. In the meantime, if I'm to live as well as work here at Drakestone, I want to be assured that I may have the run of the lodge as you promised."

Rushford leaned easily against the arch. "As long as you don't add a wing onto the place without my permission."

"I won't even paint."

"Paint the lodge in yellow stripes, if you wish. Raise geese and goats. Just don't go inviting anyone onto the grounds who might pose a threat to the security of our project."

A threat? Though Caro and Poppy were liable to run wild, given the pond and the stream, and Anna was an unrepentant flower thief, they were hardly a risk to Rushford's security. Nor did he need to be a part of her private life.

"Of course."

"So, Miss Faelyn. I'm offering you the use of the lodge, a hundred pounds per month in salary, and one-tenth percent royalty on the net profits of the Willowmoon Mineworks in exchange for your cooperation. I can offer no more."

The Willowmoon Mineworks. The words slammed into the backs of her knees and her heart grew cold. She saw thick gray smoke where her village had once nestled against the hillside, and a dark-eyed dragon curled up on a heap of glittering silver.

Staying close to the beast seemed the safest way to govern him. Yes, belling the dragon. Heel, Balforge!

"I can hardly turn down such an offer, can I, my lord?"

"Well, then, Miss Faelyn." Rushford offered his hand, and Mairey took it without thinking, never expecting his to so fully enfold her own. It wasn't a handshake, it was a binding. And she could only watch in bewitched anticipation as he slowly lifted her hand to his mouth—so very warm and well-shaped—as he left a grazing kiss in the furrow between her fingers.

"To the Willowmoon, Miss Faelyn."

"Oh, yes." Her breath wobbled out of her chest, leaving her powerless to object, and wondering irrationally what his kiss would taste like—

"My lord?" Sumner was at the door of the lodge, clearing his throat in short rattling bursts.

"What, Sumner?" Rushford kept her gaze as steadfastly as he held her hand, his fingers having separated hers to fit between them, as though he believed he had gained possession of her in the bargain and planned to explore her byways.

"There are three gentlemen to see you up at the main house, sir. I showed them to your office."

"Who?"

"The Messrs. Dodson, Dodson, and Greel."

Rushford straightened, and Mairey thought she saw a despairing confusion soften the flint of his eyes, a weighty sorrow that half-rounded his broad shoulders and drew down the corners of his fine mouth.

"I'll see them now, Sumner. Settle yourself here, Miss Faelyn. Make a list of what you'll be needing and give it to Sumner. Firewood, food, blankets—''

"My clothes will do for a start."

"Ah." He frowned, distracted, and she felt illogically abandoned by his abruptness. "Send for your things—for anything you might need to get you through this."

She needed Anna and Caro and Poppy, and Aunt Tattie. And a magic potion that would put this disturbing dragon to sleep for the next hundred years.

"I'll send word this very afternoon, sir."

"Yes. Good." Rushford gave an abbreviated bow, then left the lodge as though his coattails were afire.

Oh, how easily she could imagine the stench of sulphur curling toward her as he set off to ravage the countryside. Yet it wasn't brimstone she smelled but the exotic spice of the kiss that he had lingered over, the very same kiss she'd done nothing at all to discourage, that still jangled in her veins.

A dangerous way to begin building a fortress against the man.

Rushford had been right about one thing: the lodge was large and entirely self-contained, with a small kitchen, five bedrooms, a dining room, a parlor, and a large sitting room. Five times the size of the house in Holly Court. She explored her new home from the attic to the root cellar, noting all the crannies and hidey-holes, should she need to use them in her campaign against her new collaborator.

Rushford was foul tempered and imperious, but

she had never once felt in physical danger. His touch was resolute, insistent, but never harsh. The girls would be safe, but she would keep them away from the main house—keep Aunt Tattie busy with their schooling when she couldn't, and send them on outings.

Mairey smiled as she thought of the terror her sisters would bring down upon Rushford's sensibilities should he ever venture out to the lodge. Anna had become properly shy in recent months, but Caro and Poppy still had no sense of shame, and thought bathtime was playtime. So the sight of naked little girls squealing down the hallway— their auntie fast on their heels with towels to dry and cover them—was everyday normal in the Faelyn household.

It was good that her family would remain distant from the rest of Drakestone House. And if things didn't work out, she could always send them home to their village and its ancient peace.

She'd never been allowed to live there; she'd been exiled by her father's research. She would miss the girls fiercely, but they would surely thrive there.

Heaven alone knew how long it would take to find the Willowmoon Knot, or how long Rushford would persist in his search before he gave it up and let her go. The Willowmoon had been missing for two hundred and fifty years; she might be bound to the man forever! The quest stretched out before her as bleak as any prison sentence: Anna and Caro and Poppy grown and moved away, with families of their own. Mairey's hair gone gray and her heart lonely as Jackson Rushford tore up the countryside looking for the glade of silver.

She found a pen, a pot of ink, and a pad of letter paper in the parlor desk.

Dearest Aunt Tattie,

I have found lodgings near my work and wish you to join me here at Drakestone House, as soon as you can pack the girls and all their things.

And may the dragon beware.

Chapter 5

Dodson. Christ, he'd forgotten. Had another June come already? This one had crept up on him, forgotten in his quest to find Miss Faelyn and her silver mine.

No, not altogether forgotten. Never that. It was an everlasting echo in a heart gone hollow.

Jack made a detour into his private office, not yet ready to face Dodson and his partners. This meeting took more and more out of him every year, sapped his strength for days afterward.

It had become a dreaded reckoning, an acrid accounting of his failure. He had a file drawer packed with reports and assessments. Eighteen years of searching for the family his father had left to him.

Protect them, Jack. The girls, your mother. They'll need you, son.

But he hadn't protected them: he'd never seen them again. Not after the savage violence of a miner's strike gone horribly wrong. He had lost track of his family even as his father lay dying in his arms.

He'd been sent away that night, exiled to Canada, with the law on his heels and a price on his head. He'd spent his first shilling searching for his family; he would gladly spend his last if he had to.

Dodson and his lot had found little trace of them—only rumors and unverified sightings. Eighteen years was a lifetime of waiting, of stark loneliness and phantoms.

And hope was a heavy burden.

Jack emptied his chest of the pain, of his fury, and dimmed his memories so that they wouldn't flare up and overcome him in the midst of his meeting. He took a steadying breath and then shoved through the adjoining door into his office.

"Your report, gentlemen," Jack said sharply and without preamble, because he'd never found any other way to begin this annual farce. Every year it grew more difficult to talk through a tightening throat. "I haven't time to waste."

The firm of Dodson, Dodson and Greel, attorneys at law, had been sitting like undertakers around the conference table, and now they scrambled to their feet, all chattering at the same time.

"Well . . . sir . . . my lord Rushford—" The youngest of the men struggled to right his chair, his fingers creasing an already folded sheaf of stiff documents.

"Speak up, boy!" Jack stood fast at the end of the table, looking down its cold expanse of mirror-glossed mahogany. "You've had another year, Dodson. Have you added anything at all to my very thick but very empty file?"

"No!" the young man said, casting a pleading

glance at the elder Dodson. "I mean . . ."

"What my son means is nothing explicit." Dodson punctuated his findings with a bow. "I'm sorry."

Sorry. That answer still slashed as deeply through Jack's defenses as ever, made his throat close over and disabled his fury. He turned away to the windows and the green woods beyond the garden, where Mairey Faelyn was settling her brightness into the lodge.

"Detail your report, if you please," Jack said, hearing the shuffle of papers and the whispering as though they were close-kept secrets. A scheme to keep him from his family, to expose his shame.

"Um, sir. We . . . our operative, that is, he . . ." It was Dodson's son again, and more whispering.

"Your operative did what?" Jack turned, his anger patched over thickly enough to shield his heart from the blows that would come.

"Our operative searched the usual sources, sir, focusing this time on the parish records in Cornwall and Devonshire."

"You've searched both counties three times before."

Greel wagged a patronizing finger. "But not for years—"

"*Seven* years ago, Greel. I have the report in my own file, compiled by a Mr. Wilfred Rainey." He'd memorized every item, sorted and analyzed, hoping Dodson had overlooked some fact or an idiosyncrasy that only Jack himself would notice. Nothing. "Why do you waste my time looking in places you've already examined?"

Greel lowered his finger. "Mr. Rainey no longer works for Dodson, Dodson, and Greel. We thought that our new operative—"

"Tell me, Dodson, why I shouldn't fire your firm and find another."

Dodson bristled and blinked. "We are the very best at these issues, sir. We've found many a lost relative, united heirs with fortunes—"

"But what have you done for *me?*" Jack's righteous anger made him feel whole and in control, made him feel as though his mother and sisters were waiting for him at Southampton or at the shore in Brighton, eating frosted cakes, their hands and faces scrubbed clean of coal dust. He need only take the right train.

"The 1842 Devonshire assize, my lord," Greel said quickly, sliding another page out of the report and across the table toward Jack. "As you can see there, a woman named Claire Radforth was fined three shillings for stealing eggs from her employer."

Jack picked up the paper, tasting venom on his tongue. "And I see that the same woman served three months in the Female Penitentiary in Exeter. What has this creature to do with my mother?"

Greel's face paled to match his ginger frizzled hair. "Well—we just thought—"

"My mother's name is Claire *Rushford,* not Radforth."

"Yes, of course, sir. But mistakes are often made when the illiterate speak their names to a court official. Rushford quite easily becomes Radforth if one—"

"Claire *Rushford*, Mr. Greel." Jack came slowly around the table, grateful that the man was backing well out of his reach, else he might take him by the throat and squeeze too hard. "My mother was a collier's wife, not a street-corner slattern. She taught *me* and all my sisters to read and to write. She damn well knew how to spell her own name."

"Yes, yes, of course she did, my lord. However—" Greel sat down hard, and Jack followed after him.

"Nor was my mother a thief. You are looking once again in the wrong place."

"There is the graveyard accounting, my lord," Greel said, shuffling wildly through his papers, thrusting one between Jack and himself. "Here."

The graveyard accounting. The page crumpled against Jack's chest.

The writing was a blur, as it always was at first. That startling fear of finding a name that was too dear, and with it a spiraling pool of emptiness. His hand shook as he went to the window with the report, where the light was better and the air was sweetened by the wisteria.

"You'll see, sir, that our operative has singled out a number of possibilities." Jack could hear the fear and hesitance in Greel's voice; relished it because it matched his own. "Odd spellings and such, as I said. Collected in potters' graveyards only because they were connected with the appropriate dates and locations. The unclaimed body of a woman your mother's age."

A body. Jack grasped again for his anger and found plenty of the sort bound up in helplessness.

It would do; it was heavy enough to weight him to the spot.

"What else have you got to show me, Dodson? I have three sisters: Emma, Clady, and Banon."

"We know their names, sir."

"They would be twenty-eight, twenty-six, and twenty-one, respectively."

"We know their ages."

"Then why haven't you found them? I pay your firm thousands of pounds annually, have done so for nearly two decades—long enough for your father to die, Dodson, and your own son here to have grown out of knee breeches and take his bloody place as a partner—and in all that time you have yet to turn up anything of consequence. Not a single word. My family did not vanish from the earth!"

"It isn't easy, my lord," young Dodson said from behind his chair. "Perhaps if you could give us a bit more information."

"There must be a very hot place in hell for lawyers, Dodson. I've told you everything I know."

"Yes, yes. Without a doubt, sir," the younger man stammered, though Jack had spoken his curse to the senior partner. "Perhaps if you'd repeat it again. I'll check our notes."

"Do that. Check your damn notes. I last saw my mother the night my father died. I was on the deck of a smuggling ship that was sailing out of a dark cove off the coast of Furness." Sightless darkness, the sting of salt in his nostrils. A fatherless son. The sea had smelled of desolation and betrayal and untimely farewell ever since. "It was the twentieth day of June, 1840."

Young Dodson's nose was buried in the file. "Yes, my lord, as it says here. When again did you last see your sisters?"

Jack swallowed the clod in his throat, tossed the report onto the table, and looked to the enormous map on his wall, the breadth of his domain. Lead, tin, copper. And for what purpose?

"I saw them that morning at breakfast, before they crawled back into the mines for another twelve-hour day of dragging coal sledges to the surface. That was the last I saw of them." But their faces still gleamed each night in his dreams, haloed in golden curls.

Young Dodson was still searching his notes. "That was a full two years before Parliament enacted the law prohibiting girls and women from entering the mines. Perhaps your sisters met their ends in an accident. If that were so . . . I mean . . ."

The young man inhaled sharply and raised his eyes, wary, obviously waiting for Jack to strike out. But Jack had never allowed himself to think of a cave-in or a fall, or the skull-cracking swing of an iron donkey.

Was it time to begin thinking that way?

Had his family's silence been so immutably real all along? Had he been alone from the beginning? He cleared his throat and steadied his hands on the back of his chair, wondering if he would ever be ready to hear that kind of truth.

"I suggest, Mr. Dodson, that if your operative hasn't thought to research mining accidents in northern Lancashire between twenty June, 1840 and the autumn of '42, perhaps he *should*.''

A spark lit the young man's eyes. ''Yes, my lord, immediately. I shall oversee the project myself.''

Jack should have been grateful for young Dodson's enthusiasm, and for this new direction, but there would be harrowing pain in such success. A molten hotness pricked the backs of his eyes.

''That will do, gentlemen.'' Jack walked away from the stinging heat and found his anger again. ''Leave your report on the table, Dodson.''

''My lord, we've not finished explaining—''

''One more season, Dodson,'' Jack said, holding open the door to the breezy foyer. ''That's all I'm giving you. Then I shall terminate our association.''

''But, sir, we—''

''Good evening.'' Jack waited while the men clucked and eyed each other gravely as they gathered their ruffled dignities and left.

Jack listened to Sumner's balmy tones as the man let the Messrs. Dodson and Greel out into the twilight, and he wondered if he could ever act upon such a threat. Terminating his relationship with Dodson's firm would be admitting that hope was lost, that he had abandoned his pledge to his father. A trust betrayed. He wasn't ready for the shame of it; would never be.

More than that, he wasn't ready to be alone in the world with no other blood of his heart but his. He battled every night to keep the memories from fading to fog, turning them into dreams where his parent's small cottage was larger and brighter and warmer than it had ever been. Where his father told stories of his soldiering, and his mother combed the tangle of twig and bramble out of Banon's hair. Where Emma read the month-old *Times* aloud and Clady wrapped Jack around her finger, and his heart around hers.

Jack bit the inside of his cheek and tucked away his grief. He couldn't risk losing them. Not yet. He would give Dodson a year, perhaps longer. After all, the man's son seemed to have taken a real interest in the case. New blood. Yes, that's what was needed.

Just as he needed to give Mairey Faelyn free rein to find the Willowmoon Knot. If its design truly was a cryptic map to a vein of silver hidden in some forgotten part of Britain, he would find it as surely as he had found the glitter of silver in her eyes.

Granted, the woman was ill prepared to conduct a prudent investigation. Her library had resembled a squirrel's nest and had had just as much security.

She would need a key to the Drakestone library.

Jack unlocked his desk drawer and fished out the extra key. He kept his own deep in his pocket, but for some reason he would never understand, women rarely had such conveniences stitched into their garments.

A piece of twine would do nicely.

Jack left the house through the rear door, relieved at the head-clearing mission, and traversed the graveled garden walk to the toolshed. He found only bailing wire there—strong, but hardly suited to hanging about a woman's neck. He tried the stable and the laundry and finally located a thin length of hempen cord in the cook's pantry.

Jack let himself into the library, lit the lamp at his desk, and noticed the broken pot, sitting like an indictment. Beside it was a brush-stoppered bottle of cement.

"Thank you, Sumner," Jack said to the bottle, "you've just saved my hide." He would glue the bowl back together in no time, and Miss Faelyn would be none the wiser.

He sat down at the desk and found a shard that looked as though it would fit perfectly—well, almost perfectly—in the space near the lip of the bowl. He unstoppered the cement and was about to dab the sharp-smelling goo against the first piece when the library door opened.

"What the devil do you think you're doing, Rushford!" Miss Faelyn was on him in the next blink, a cloud of peach-scented fury as she grabbed the bowl out of his hand and cradled it as though it were a baby chick and he were a slavering wolf.

"It's . . . broken," he said, feeling foolish as hell for stating the obvious.

"It isn't *broken*, sir. It's Pictish!" She held the thing up to the lamp, inspecting the finish as though suspecting he had bruised it.

"Pictish?"

"*And* irreplaceable. What were you going to do?"

Jack felt like a child confessing to roughhousing in the parlor. "I was trying to repair the bloody thing."

"Repair it? Sweet blazes!"

She clutched it tighter, abject horror on her face. This wasn't going well. He'd best confess all.

"The breakage must have happened in the course of shipment from Oxford. Look for yourself, in here." Jack pointed to the shards still tangled in the shavings, prepared to ride out her displeasure and then buy her another pot or two. "Shattered in two dozen pieces."

She obliged him by peering into the box of rubble, then stared up at him as though he'd grown a second nose. An airy, indulgent smile bloomed in her eyes and made them twinkle like the evening star.

"Which is exactly the state in which my father found it thirty years ago."

Inscrutable woman. She was testing him. There would be a lot of that between them; she hadn't come to him gently.

"Your father found the pot shattered?" he asked, willingly walking into her trap to best learn how she set them, how they could be sprung.

"Yes, shattered. Imbedded in clay, in a burial mound near Dundurn in Scotland."

A plausible trap, and utterly absorbing, this antiquarian of his. "Your father kept all these pieces of a broken bowl? Why?"

"Not a bowl, actually. A bevel-rimmed cook pot. Papa kept and cataloged the pieces because he was a scholar of antiquities, just as I am." As thorough and forbearing as a mother lion, Miss Faelyn gathered up all the pieces that Jack had spread out on his desk and replaced them one by one in their nest inside the crate.

"How, madam, do you know this cook pot was Pictish and not Wedgwood?" She smelled too much of the woods and his own roses, too fine to keep him from peering over her shoulder into all her nesting.

"The pot is red slipware, imported by the Romans from the Mediterranean. But the painting is"—she held up the rounded end and drew her finger along a series of black slashes as though she were lecturing to a room full of twelve-year-old boys—"here, Rushford, this raven design is Pictish. Third century, A.D."

Yes, a fine trap. An even finer fragrance. He sighted down her arm, up the curve of her wrist to her hand. "Ravens are Pictish then?"

"One of their most common designs. The raven was thought by the Picts to give power through omens and sneezing."

"Sneezing?" There were limits to his gullibility. He'd been willing to believe the Picts, the broken pot, the burial mound, and the omens. But sneezing ravens? "Not bloody likely, Miss Faelyn."

"Think what you will, Rushford. But considering your inexperience in the preservation of antiquities, you'd best leave the unpacking to me."

Mairey heard Rushford blow a curse from under his breath and fancied that she could feel it on her neck as she dug in the nearest crate and retrieved a bundle of eighteenth-century guides to county antiquities—one of the first purchases she'd ever made with her own money. She'd been twelve at the time, and proud as cinnamon pie.

"I'm more concerned over the matter of security, Miss Faelyn.'' He reached into his coat pocket and dragged out a double length of bristly twine. A key dangled from its center.

"Security for what? Hey!'' He abruptly turned her away from him, then stepped in so close behind that his chest and all that heat met her back like a caress. Before she could protest he surrounded her completely with his arms, his broad hands holding the loop of twine out in front of her.

"You'll wear this always, madam.'' The weight of the key and the twine fell into place over one of her breasts, a buoyant pressure that could have been his caress. But his hands were busy behind her, wrestling with her hair and the knot he was tying.

"So you're trusting me with a key?'' She centered the loop, trying to sound unperturbed, but the key matched the thrumming of her heart and echoed it in a pulsating swing.

He took her by the shoulders and turned her, frowning down into her eyes.

"This is not a game. Nor is it a scholarly grant where you can wile away the hours with your nose so deeply buried in a book that you can't tell midday from midnight. I've made an investment in you—''

"As I have in you.''

"Exactly. I am what is known in the world of British finance as a mining baron.''

A devil. A dragon. "So I understand.''

She hated them all and appreciated his reminder, but not the intensity of his dark gaze and all the shards of crystal color she could count there.

"Investors and adventurers watch me closely in everything I do; they follow when my viewers appraise a coalfield. If my competitors or anyone else discovers that Viscount Jackson Rushford is looking for Celtic silver, every barrow and stone circle, every museum vault and private collection in the country, will be swarming with treasure-seekers. Holding *my* silver for ransom! Where would that leave us?"

His silver. Mairey exhaled. She had never imagined this kind of threat to the glade and to her village. The vestiges of the Willowmoon legend were still whispered in the hills of the northern marches. Scavenging scholars like Arthur Brawlings would beat the woods for its mysteries. Rushford might just as well hire a circus parade and reporters from every rag in Fleet Street to tag along behind them.

"If you'd left me in Oxford, where I could have continued my work in secret—"

"In secret, Miss Faelyn? Where this collection of pot shards and rabbit pelts and untold treasure was housed behind a paper-thin door, which was hanging badly on pig-iron hinges and secured by a lock that had rusted open eons ago?"

"We never once had so much as a bottle of ink stolen." Yet she had never given much thought to thieves.

"Until someone like me, with a large enough wad of bank notes, came along to tempt the impeccably ethical Dean Hayward and his trustees?"

"You are the exception to every rule, my lord."

"Think what you will. If rumors should arise about our little enterprise, this library—bloody hell, this entire estate—will become a target for robbery. We need locks and we need privacy. I'm having a cupboard safe delivered tomorrow.''

Rushford went to his desk, stripping out of his jacket—a wholly improper action, given the late hour and the fact that they were alone. But Mairey's objection never made it past her admiration. The man's shoulders were broad enough when bound by the sturdy seams of his jacket, but they grew massive and straining under the stark white of his shirt and silken waistcoat.

She grabbed a breath. ''A cupboard safe, for what?''

''For locking up your notes when you're not with them.'' He studied her from under his brow as he unlinked his shirt cuffs and pocketed the studs. A thoroughly intimate sight, made of bed-chambers and rumpled counterpanes . . . his male scent on her pillow, on her breast.

''Rushford!'' He'd rolled his sleeves to his elbows, past his corded forearms, and had taken up a pry bar. ''What are you doing with that?''

''Unpacking.'' He thunked the bar into place under the lid of a crate and yanked downward. The nails came away with a squawk. ''I'll open and you can put things away.''

Rather than fling herself across the crate and demand that he stop right there, Mairey smiled with as much gratitude as she could muster. ''I'd rather unpack myself.''

''And I'd rather help you. Here.'' He eyed her pointedly and handed her a bristly armful of wood shavings out of a crate marked Desk Drawers. He

nodded in the direction of the enormous hearth.
"For the firebox."

The nosy beast was going to pick through everything. All her notes and private papers from her
father, exposed to his questions. She deposited the
wad of shavings. Erecting a fortress against the
man was going to be more difficult than she had
imagined.

"I'll take that, Rushford." Mairey scooped the
small desk drawer filled with letterhead and enve-
lopes out of his hands.

"And while you do, you can tell me how your
father came to have such an interest in this Willowmoon Knot."

She'd already planned the answer for that most
unanswerable of all possible questions.

"He just fell into it, I suppose." She fit the
drawer into the desk and then scooted past him, on
his way with two drawers stacked together. "He
heard about it somewhere and liked the idea of
finding a vast treasure of silver."

Knowing with complete certainty that her father
would approve of her defaming his character in this
instance, Mairey shoved the drawer into its place
on the right side of the desk and noticed that the
lock had been pried open with the point of a knife.
Her life and her destiny had been exposed without
her permission. Would the man search her laundry,
as well?

Rushford stood up from his muttering at the ill-
fitting drawer full of pens and clips. Mairey backed
up as he rose, but he was still as tall as the sky

when he looked down his long, slightly crooked nose at her.

Cedar and citrus, she thought absurdly.

"Your father heard about the Willowmoon somewhere? From his own father, perhaps?"

How could he know that? "Possibly."

What else could she say? The man was a mind reader! Mairey slid out from beneath his heady scent and returned to the open crate before Rushford could dig around in it. She hurried back to the desk with another drawer, careful to hide its cache of pocket notebooks that her father used in the field. He hadn't been the neatest record-keeper, and she often found a stray note about the Knot in them.

Rushford was waiting for her, and snagged one of the books as she was shoving in the drawer.

"What are all these little books?" he asked, fanning the pages hard enough to ruffle the hair off his forehead. "You had one at the mill."

Mairey knew better than to grab it from him, though she dearly wanted to. "Field notes," she said.

He walked toward the lamp, blessedly distracted. "Yours?" he asked, frowning as he turned the pages. The book looked like a toy in his hands.

"Mostly." Mairey used his distraction to carry another drawer to its rightful place in this oh-so-wrong library.

"What the devil is a 'can-wall gorff'?"

A harmless enough question. It would be good practice to answer him, if she was going to learn to dodge the man's curiosity without him noticing.

"Canwyll gorff," she said. "A corpse candle."

Rushford raised a brow at her in reply.

"A sourceless light that foretells a death. It's a Welsh term. Also called a fetch-candle in Scotland."

"And Nekha lights by the people of the Mekong River."

Mairey couldn't have been more surprised. "Truly?"

He nodded lightly, looking vastly proud of himself. "Truly."

The ends of Mairey's fingers began to itch to write it down. Nekha lights. Mekong River. She found a pencil and scribbled Rushford's definition onto a stray shred of packing paper, folded it, and stuffed the piece into her bodice.

She looked up and into Rushford's stark curiosity.

"What's that you've written?" He came toward her, his gaze as warm as ladled honey on the place she'd just stuffed the note.

Mairey covered her bodice and the gathering heat with her hand. "I wrote down your Nekha lights for my folk studies."

"Show me." He seemed immovable.

Mairey plucked the note from her bodice and unrolled it for him to read. "As I told you—it's what I do when I'm not hunting treasure."

He took the note, read it twice, looked on the back, then drew the piece beneath his nose as though he were tasting her scent. "Most glad to be of service to your science, Miss Faelyn."

"Thank you." Mairey took the note back, her

ears surely flaming. But instead of replacing the paper in her bodice—a habit she'd have to break immediately—she stuffed it willy-nilly into the nearest notebook.

When she turned back to her unpacking Rushford was leaning an elbow on a crate, chewing on a smile, all the drawers in place and Mairey feeling rifled from bodice to stockings.

"Now, my dear, why don't you enlighten me about the Willowmoon. Tell me all you know."

No, she thought, her heart thundering high in her chest. "Well—" She would inundate the man with historical accuracies, bore him senseless with an austere lecture. "The item of antiquity known as the Willowmoon Knot was first recorded in a pamphlet published in 1589 by the Elizabethan Society of Antiquaries."

"Published?" Rushford came toward her with quiet intensity, planting his hands on the partner's desk. "Do you mean to tell me that those dust-witted scholars published a map to this pot of silver we're after? For all to see?"

"You needn't worry on that count, Rushford." Mairey stood fast against his bottled anger, relieved that he was standing safely on the other side of the desk, praying that he would stay there while she gathered her thoughts. "My fellow antiquaries in Elizabeth's time knew nothing of the silver, knew nothing of the clue that the knot-work might reveal. As students of ancient history, they were interested only in the Willowmoon's Celtic design."

"You're certain of this?"

"Positive." She couldn't very well tell him the

full truth: that only one man had known of the silver in the glade at the time—Joshua Faelyn, the first of her family who had tried through the years to rescue the Knot. Unfortunately, Joshua hadn't recognized the significance of the odd knot-work until it was too late to rescue it from the wrath of the king.

Rushford looked unconvinced, but he cleared a spot on the desk and sat down on the edge, closer now and leaning toward her. "Continue."

Which wasn't as simple as it had been when he was across the room, when she could better ignore his eyes and their constant seeking. She reached into a crate and pulled out an armload of note cases, which she began to sort on the shelf behind her desk.

"It was next seen, or rather next described, among an inventory of other antiquities that were confiscated in 1614 by James the First."

"There, you see, madam! The king knew something of its worth! He wanted the silver!"

"No, Rushford. King James knew nothing of the silver in the—" Dear God, she'd almost said "in the glade"! She steadied her thoughts. "In the time of his reign."

"If not for the silver, then what would a king want with a piece of ancient metalwork?"

Mairey's heart was still clinging to her ribs, but Rushford hadn't seemed to notice her near slip. She turned from him and added another notebox to the row on the shelf.

"The king took 'a little mislike,' as they termed it at the time, to the Society of Antiquaries, suspecting that it was a political organization conspiring with others to do mischief to his reign.'' She turned from the shelves to fetch more boxes, but Rushford was there beside her, his arms loaded to his chin.

"There's a fool for you,'' he said, setting the boxes on the desk, "to see a threat in a society of scholars.''

Let him spout his prejudices; let him believe that she was as ineffectual as her predecessors.

"Exactly, my lord.'' Mairey slid the boxes one by one next to the others. She'd sort them later; build her walls against him while he wasn't looking. "The king ignored the priceless stone axheads and bits of bone, but like any right-thinking pirate, he took the gold and silver into his personal treasury.''

"And then?'' Impatient, the man began to pry open the lid of crate after crate, as though he smelled treasure nearby. She watched him carefully.

"The Knot next appeared in a royal inventory following the king's death in 1625. It was recorded once again in 1642, when Charles the First went to war against Parliament. It was listed among the treasury items that left Windsor coffered and disguised in various carts, accompanied by a caravan of Cavaliers.''

"On its way to where?''

"To Charles's queen, Henrietta, who had already sailed to Holland and was awaiting payment for arms. When the caravan arrived at the Aylmouth quay in Northumberland, one cart had disappeared.

Stolen, or waylaid—history has been absolutely silent on the subject.''

''And then?''

Mairey sighed sharply, reminded of why she had agreed to his blackmail. ''That, Rushford, is exactly the question we need to answer before we can take another step.''

''What do you mean, madam?'' He stopped his noisy work and stared at her.

''I mean, that's the last we know of the Willowmoon Knot.''

''The last?'' He dropped the pry bar on the crate lid, looking more a pirate scorned than a mining baron. ''Hell and damn! Then how the devil do you know that the Knot still exists?''

''I don't.''

''You—''

''I made that perfectly clear to you from the first, my lord.''

''Bleeding hell!''

It did Mairey a world of good to watch him rake his fingers through his hair, watch it curl and then fall back into place, a little awry. The poor man was exasperated. Good. *Excellent*. Now he'd be better inclined to listen to anything she wanted to tell him, grab on to it with both hands, and call it truth.

Which was exactly what she'd been telling him: the bare, untraceable truth, but fully in her control.

''So, madam, this trail of silver goes stone cold way back in 1642?''

''Not entirely cold, my lord.'' His ears pricked, this wily dragon, and his gaze fixed on her as she braved the open crate nearest to him. "Many of the items which were cataloged in that wayward cart have reappeared over the years, returned to their rightful place in the royal treasury, or mentioned in probate inventories. So the Willowmoon Knot is out there somewhere."

"What does this knot thing look like? Was there a woodcut made or an engraving?"

"Not even a sketch." Here she would have to tread more lightly. "Only a vague description of the moon's cycle and a knot-work of Celtic tracings." Mountains and a serpentine river, a chevron of geese pointed northward, an arrow nocked and aimed directly at the heart of her village. "Meaningless to the modern age."

His eyes were on her, as though he'd discovered some truth of his own that he didn't plan to share. "To anyone but a scholar of Celts."

"Hopefully."

"So where do you begin, Miss Faelyn?" He leaned close to her, peering into her eyes. "Which door do you wish me to open first?"

Impossible man—improbable wizard. But oh, the vistas she could see from here!

"Tell me what great sources are available to me, Rushford, and I'll best know where to begin."

"The *Gofarian,* of course." He nodded to the cloth-wrapped treasure on the worktable.

"I'll start it in the morning."

"And then report to me."

"That *is* the charter between us, Rushford." But she expected to learn nothing from the miraculous manuscript beyond a hint at the Willowmoon's history. Dear stuff, and heart-singing, but not helpful because it had been written too early, and she already knew it all. "What else can you show me?"

Rushford nodded, unlocked his desk drawer, and pulled out a folder. "Beginning with the most obvious, the Royal Archives at Windsor; the Chapter House at Westminster Palace; the Court of King's Bench at the Lord Chancellor's Office. And, of course, the Public Records Office, which has begun moving a few documents from the Wakefield Tower. Deputy-Lieutenant de Ros and the Keeper of the Records have been notified that I may drop in."

Ah, yes. His commission from the queen. Her father had been a mere scholar, not a mining baron with a title that was probably as old as God's and pockets as deep as the seas. No wonder he'd gotten nowhere.

"What else have you in your arsenal, Lord Rushford?"

He looked up from his page of miracles, dreams of silver plunder alive in his dark eyes. "Far too many to list, and I am no judge of their significance. Of all the resources of the Empire, which would you pursue first? What would be your fondest wish?"

To be done with this business, she thought fiercely; to be free of the burden of the Willowmoon. It had become unbearably heavy in the last days, and more than a little confusing.

"I would like to see the personal papers of Henrietta, Charles's queen."

"Why?"

His directness always startled her, made her stop short and weigh every word before she spoke it. "The queen's personal guards would have supervised the shipment of her treasury under her express instructions."

"Of course. Done. I'll look into the matter in the morning."

Just like that. The Faelyns had spent two hundred years knocking on locked doors, and Rushford was able to open them with a wave of his hand.

"What the devil is this?" Rushford was staring into a wicker basket he'd pulled from a crate, his nose wrinkled. "Another of your mummified squirrels? Gad, woman, it reeks!"

He stuck the basket and its fusty ripeness under her nose. The offending item was green and withered, and Mairey couldn't help her laughter.

"It's a meat pie, my lord. Your cloven-hoofed pixies packed up the lunch I threw away three weeks ago and shipped it here to Drakestone House."

He looked so thoroughly disgusted that Mairey took the basket from him and set it outside the library door.

They worked well into the small hours, stopping only to eat from the tray Sumner had set on Rushford's desk. Like a boy at Christmastide, the blackguard opened every crate himself. Mairey had to run to keep up with him, nearly throwing the books into the shelves so that she could be back in time to keep him from reading too deeply.

He seemed to be everywhere at once, and always with her; steadying her on the wobbling footstool, chiding her for risking her neck, and then bearing the task himself.

Her father was there too, in everything she touched. His hand, his script, his philosophies. The Willowmoon and all it meant to him. His body was buried in the churchyard in her village, on the breast of the hill beside her mother. But he was also here in the library, in her heart, and so very much alive.

His field notes rang with his voice, and she couldn't help but turn the pages, remembering their travels through the countryside.

Finally, in the deepest part of the night, when the shadows clung heaviest to the vaulting mahogany, Mairey's yawns became noisy. She flopped in the chair at his desk, bone tired but unwilling to leave Rushford alone in the library with all of her research unguarded, and prepared to stay till dawn two days hence if the man was so inclined.

"To bed with you, Miss Faelyn." He was studying her from the hearth, his eyes as old as the earth.

"No, thank you, my lord. Not without you."

Dear God! The string of words had made perfect sense inside her head, but now that she'd launched them into that crackling space between her and Rushford, all she could do was ride out the flush that scorched her from her toes to the ends of her hair.

"A tempting invitation, Miss Faelyn," he said softly, moving toward her, his face planed in the flame of his desk lamp. Then he leaned across her shoulder, tipping her backward, and turned down the wick. "But ill-advised, considering—"

"Considering, sir, that I misspoke." She scooted

the chair out from under him, stopping abruptly when the wheels caught on the carpet fringe. "I meant to say I would stay here in the library and work as long as you were staying. That's what I meant."

"I believe you, Miss Faelyn," he said calmly, letting another lamp gutter out, leaving the library dark but for the gas-lit sconce by the door. "And I applaud your diligence. But the day has been long and we both need sleep. We'll finish this tomorrow. Come, I'll walk with you to the lodge."

"I don't need you to coddle me, Rushford."

"I wouldn't dare." The sconce hissed, and the room darkened completely, shadowing him against the pale light from the foyer.

"I've walked the heathlands alone in the dead of winter, sir, and I've rowed myself across the Menai Strait in a carrack that I constructed myself. I can surely find my way alone through the woods."

"Not through mine. Not until you know them better. I have no intention of losing you in the duck pond."

"I can swim."

He laughed broadly. "I'd have bet my last farthing on that, Miss Faelyn, my very last."

Mairey fumed all the way to the lodge, blazing a trail ten feet in front of him.

At the lodge door Rushford lifted her hand, turned it, and kissed her palm. "Sweet dreams, Mairey Faelyn."

But sweet dreams were no longer possible, for a stone-hearted dragon had just overrun her life, and it seemed that he planned to stay.

Chapter 6

"The Wakefield Tower is an impossible mess at the moment, Lord Rushford."

The assistant to the Keeper of the Records offered his apology to Jack as they stood in the inner ward of the Tower of London, but the man's gaze was fixed on Miss Faelyn, who seemed completely oblivious to anything but the stout, stumpy tower rising out of the massive main guard wall.

"I mean to say, sir, what with the Public Record's staff in there twelve hours every day, sorting and cataloging, preparing for the transfer to Chancery Lane, it's rather like an enormous spring-cleaning. Wouldn't you say so, Miss Faelyn?"

"No need to explain further, Mr. Walsham," the woman said, dragging her gaze from the tower and cutting Jack a precisely pointed frown. "Lord Rushford and I are very familiar with spring-cleaning, aren't we, my lord?"

Her hair was drawn off her lovely neck, its pale curls caught in a loose plait and wound beneath the brim of that god-awful hat, which she had to clamp down with her hand to keep it from falling off as she stared up at him with those sparkling eyes.

"Indeed," Jack said at last, refusing to be baited in front of the meddlesome keeper. "Proceed, Mr. Walsham."

Miss Faelyn took off after the man, her sensible beige skirts flying in her wake.

An ordinary woman would have taken Jack's arm and begged his guidance down the grassy slope and around the flotsam of irregular stone blocks that marked the remains of the Tower's ancient, innermost ward. But he was fast learning that there was little about Mairey Faelyn that was ordinary.

Least of all that she didn't wear stays beneath her shirtwaist—a fact that had raised a callow sweat and a bullish erection that morning when he found her shelving more books in the library. She wriggled where a proper woman shouldn't, at least not outside the bedchamber. She bobbed. Swayed.

Holy hell, she was a good deal of marvelous.

It had taken two days to arrange this visit to the Tower. He had chafed at the delay, but Miss Faelyn had used the time to nest herself into a corner of his library—a process that she claimed would take another week. He was useless to her, useless to himself when he tried to simply read while she was in the same room. He did a lot of staring.

Jack followed after Miss Faelyn and the Keeper's assistant at his own pace, and caught up with them as the woman stopped to admire a vine of just-blooming roses that had affixed itself to a crumbling wall. Walsham cut a flower with his penknife and shyly handed it to her, a schoolboy pink blushing his already sunburned face.

"When was Wakefield Tower built, Mr. Walsham?" The woman brushed the furled petals past her nose and sniffed, a gesture so simple and yet so provocative that Jack felt it like her kiss across his mouth. The shock of it traveled like a bolt of lightning to his groin.

"Some historians say William Rufus began it back in 1093. But recent theories—my own included—lean toward 1220, about the time Henry Three began redesigning the entire complex." Walsham seemed to be in his element now, guiding a lovely woman on a personal tour of his tiny kingdom. He spread his weedy arms and legs like a stickman, then crossed the width between the grass-bordered stones and the nonexistent walls. "By the end of Henry's reign, he had rebuilt the Great Hall on this very site."

Miss Faelyn listened to the fatuous little fellow with every part of herself, leaning toward him on her toes, smiling, those clear eyes catching every nuance as though she were committing the entire performance to memory.

Jack knew a courting dance when he saw it. Walsham's was ridiculous. Misplaced entirely. Miss Faelyn couldn't possibly be interested in the dullard.

"You are a font, Mr. Walsham." She blinked back at Jack. "Isn't he, Lord Rushford?"

She was bobbing, or would certainly be if he could see beneath her jacket to the linen. He could only stare, as much a mooncalf as Walsham, who continued his gamboling.

"Henry next connected the hall to the Wakefield Tower, which he then used as his apartments. In fact, the upper floor, where the Public Records are now stored, was his privy chamber."

"How long have the records been kept there?" She was still bright-eyed with interest, still making maddening love to the rose and its copious petals.

"Since the first Edward, we believe. Thirteenth century."

Miss Faelyn's face fell, and she gazed up again at the tower. "That's a lot of paper."

His patience at an end, Jack scooped the woman's fingers through his and fixed them into the crook of his elbow. "And we've so little time."

She scowled at him but held fast around his arm as Walsham scurried ahead of them to the thick door. He unlocked a massive lock with a key from a crowded ring that must have weighed a full stone.

"Here we are, then." Walsham shoved open the door, and Miss Faelyn followed the sunlight into the round room as it spilled onto the floor, leaving her rose scent to swirl around Jack's head.

The room was scattered with tables piled high with wooden file crates, loose-sheeted books, and safety lamps. In the middle of the room, a thick post strained under the weight of whatever was pressing down on the floor above.

"Well now, my lord, if you can tell me what record you're looking for, perhaps I can point you in the right direction."

"Royal letters written in the autumn of 1642." Miss Faelyn spared the man a patient smile, but she was already eagerly leafing through the papers in the boxes. "You see, Mr. Walsham, I'm the one who is looking for a record. My father's family has always claimed a blood connection to Charles the First, through his queen's cousin."

Jack nearly laughed at the baldness of the woman's lie.

But Walsham's eyes grew large and his voice conspiratorial. "Ah, and you're looking for proof! Is that it?"

"Indeed." She lowered her thick lashes, then proceeded to unravel her impossible story. "Though I am sure I'll find that proof on the . . . well, on the *wrong* side of the bedclothes."

The man looked scandalized. "How dreadful!"

"A royal peccadillo."

Preposterous woman. She was a practiced mountebank, and Walsham was falling for her sleight of hand. Jack would have seen it from twenty paces—at least he hoped he would—but the defenseless little man was beguiled.

"The woman in question was the daughter of the king's chamberlain. Once her transgression began to show itself—" Miss Faelyn demurely mimed a bulging belly, and Jack's heart skipped, then barrel-rolled. The splendor of filling that space with himself struck him like a ball of blue thunder.

Walsham's jaw was hanging loose.

Miss Faelyn was oblivious to the head-butting that was passing between the two men in this very crowded room.

"As you can imagine, Mr. Walsham, the poor girl was married off to a yeoman of the guard, a man whom, according to family legends, the queen

trusted with the transfer of the royal treasury whenever the king's army needed weapons. If I could
locate the name of that yeoman, then perhaps I
could discover where the young woman went, and
follow her branch of the family to my own.''

Jack's head was spinning from lack of air.

''Fascinating.'' Walsham's cheeks were blazing.

''Indeed, Mr. Walsham. To that end, I'm looking
for Queen Henrietta's private letters here in the
Tower, where I might find mention of the names
of her guards.''

''Queen Henrietta?'' Walsham clicked his
tongue and scrubbed at his chin. ''Not good. Not
good at all.''

''Why?'' She stopped her paper rifling, a ruthless cant to her brow.

''William Prynne, to put a pinpoint on it. One
of my predecessors. A staunch Puritan: hated the
queen and her papist ways.''

''Do you mean that he destroyed her papers?''

''More wretched than that—he purposely ne-
glected them when he took office. 1662, it was.
Cromwell's papers were protected to the fullest, but
according to Prynne's logbook, he dropped Henrietta's into a barrel and sealed the lot with tar.''

''So her papers *are* here?''

''Possibly.'' Walsham rolled his eyes skyward,
to the sagging ceiling of the floor above. ''Up
there,'' he said. ''What's left of them.''

He motioned them to follow and disappeared up
the curl of stairs.

Miss Faelyn grinned at Jack, obviously pleased,
or at least used to this labyrinth of shifting fortunes.

He preferred looking for outcroppings of coal. It was there, or it wasn't.

"It's going very well, my lord." She stuck her nose in the middle of that damned rose. "Thank you."

"You're welcome, princess."

She gave Jack a mocking curtsey and hurried up the stairs in a flounce of skirts and trim ankles.

Jack followed and emerged in the darkness of an octagonal room that smelled sharply of damp rags. The ceiling was vaulted and ribbed, and the plaster was cracked, its paint long ago flaked off. The floor sagged dangerously and was indeed supported by the timbered post from the story below.

The rest was a rabbit warren of iron-bound chests, crates, and barrels. Miss Faelyn looked right at home amid the clutter, smoothing her hands across every surface as though she could read its history with her touch.

She was in a windowed alcove, staring up at the water-stained ceiling, her hat in her hand, her hair twisted and fastened as always by a pencil.

"Henry Six was murdered right there where you're standing, Miss Faelyn," Walsham said as he lit a sconce lamp beside the door.

"Here?" A proper woman would have scurried away in fear, but Mairey Faelyn knelt and spread her fingers against the planking. She closed her eyes. "Does he haunt these rooms?"

"Never heard it said. I hope not. As soon as all these records are gone, the plans are to fix up the Wakefield to display the crown jewels to the public. Can't have a ghost scaring off paying customers.''

''Where do you keep the queen's barrel, Walsham?'' Jack asked, done with the man's endless tour.

''A very, very good question. This quarter of the chamber to the left of the stairs would be about right for Charles the First. I'm afraid it's all badly labeled, and of course, not all of it's here.''

Jack glanced at Miss Faelyn, and his heart gave a sharp thud against his chest. Tears were starring her lashes with bright points, and there was an unsteadiness about her chin. Changeable woman.

''Leave us, Walsham.'' Jack caught up the man's elbow and turned him toward the stairs.

''But, my lord, I was told to be at your service for the entire day. To see that you got whatever you needed—''

''I need you to leave us. Immediately.''

''Well, all right. Here's a key which should fit nearly every lock. But do come for me should the lady ask. I'll be at the White Tower.''

Jack listened to the man scurry down the stairs, and stayed to hear the door close before he turned his attention to this partner of his, who was swabbing tears from her cheeks. Great puddles of sorrow, and he could do nothing about them. He had felt just as helpless whenever his sisters had cried, and even more so when his mother had. He didn't need this from a business associate.

''What the devil's gotten into you, madam?''

She snuffled and touched her finger to the softly arching bow of her lip as she looked around at the

mass of records. There was a smile there, too, rue-
ful and turned inward.

"Treasure, Rushford. Piles of it."

Jack snorted and handed her a kerchief. "If
there's treasure here, Miss Faelyn, you'll have to
point it out to me. I see broken-down chests, sprung
barrels, and damn me if I don't smell a . . . Christ,
I don't care to know what that is."

"I'm a weeper, Lord Rushford." She pocketed
his kerchief. "Pay me no mind."

Like hell. "What now, my dear?"

She paged through her field book, passing the
rose stem that now stuck out from the binding. "I
brought a map."

"Of what?"

Her eyes met his, and she paused momentarily
before sighing. More hedging. "I told you that a
number of items from the stolen treasury have
turned up over the last two hundred years."

"I remember." Jack held the lamp as she spread
out a map of Northumberland on a chest. "What
are these red numbers?"

"That is a bejewelled sword pommel known to
have belonged to James the First. It was recorded
in a will here at Bowton in 1729. And in 1817, the
Whitehall Firedog was found hanging over a dart-
board in a public house in Todhorn. This number
seven is the churching brooch of Joanna, wife of
Llewelyn Fawr. There are at least a dozen other
historically significant pieces known to have been
among the royal treasury as late as 1641. Notice
how they concentrate around Donowell?"

"What I notice, madam, is that you knew about

all this two days ago, and yet told me nothing."

"The information was meaningless without full access to the records."

"I want to be informed, madam. Completely."

"That's what I'm doing now, sir. My father suspected that whoever waylaid the caravan lived in the area where the booty turned up. He combed the parish records in each of these towns, and this is all he found. Once we find the name of the men in the treasury detail, the next step will be to scour the records of Cromwell's Court of Probate."

"Why those in particular?" Jack still felt as though he was being danced around the Maypole.

"Probate includes the inventory of the deceased's estate, his debts and duns, and also records how those goods were distributed."

"Yes, yes, I know."

"But few people know that during the Interregnum, Cromwell's probate court had jurisdiction over the entire realm. Nothing was kept in the parish records." The woman began unbuttoning her high-necked scholarly jacket as she spoke—one small, round button and then the next, in a long line of gray pearl. "So if the Willowmoon Knot came into the possession of a man in Northumberland—as the other items from the stolen cart seemed to have done—then when that man died, his last will and testament would have been probated here in London, not in his home parish. That's where we'll find his name. I hope."

Jack had managed to follow her logic even as his eyes had followed the progress of her unrelenting unbuttoning.

"Miss Faelyn, how many men do you suppose died in Northumberland between the years 1642 and 1660?"

"Hundreds at least." She shrugged out of the jacket, and left Jack to stare at her finely pleated shirtwaist. And beneath the white, nothing but a vest of some sort. And all that buoyant swaying. Her breasts were small, barely a handful each, but God bless them, they were perfect handfuls.

Jack's palms itched for them. He cleared his throat. "And how do you propose to sift through that many records?"

"Word by word, my lord. It's the only way."

"That could take years."

"It already has." She closed her fingers around his in a startlingly unexpected intimacy, then lifted the forgotten key from between them—a caressing brush, a flash of eye—and then she was gone with her map.

Years. Years of clearing a path for the woman, of watching over her shoulder as she deciphered faded documents, as he waited for her to unearth his vein of silver.

Waiting. He'd spent the last eighteen years waiting for his life to begin, waiting for joy to replace the ever-present dread, the loneliness. The prospect of waiting for his nymphish partner to lead him to a silver mine should have pressed hard upon him. But she had clambered over a chest and disappeared through a thin opening between two iron-strapped wardrobes, and he wanted desperately to follow after her.

"Prerogative Court of Canterbury, local to London,'' she said from somewhere in the room.

"Is that good?" He tried to locate her from the sound of her voice.

"Not particularly. But the labels look recent. If I can just move this"—she started shoving at something, which caused a tower of crates to shudder.

"Watch it, woman!" Jack took a shortcut over the top of a chest and landed just in time to keep the crates from falling onto her.

She seemed startled to see him standing so near her in the small well created by the labyrinth, his arms filled with an iron trunk like Atlas holding up the world.

"Thank you, sir. But I've already opened that one." The exasperating woman gave him a placating smile, then turned away and leaned forward across the top of a chest, apparently trying to read the label on the far side. Her perfectly rounded, wriggling bottom was shaped in spectacular detail beneath the pull of her skirts, which lacked the fashionable, copious crinolines.

No wonder she wore plain, practical clothes and no stays; she was an acrobat. Jack shouldered the trunk onto another, thankful for a place to put his hands. They wanted to be up her skirts.

"Just more Prerogative Court records," she said, righting herself so quickly that she would have bounced off Jack's chest if he hadn't caught her around her waist—a two-hand span of warm, curvaceous flesh, hinting at the soft cushion of her breasts, the gentle flare of her hips.

"Have a care, madam." As he must, else he'd

soon be ravishing her here in the Wakefield Tower.

"It's very good to have you with me, my lord."

"You're welcome." Jack did his best to seem indifferent, but in the next moment she used his shoulder for a hand support and hoisted herself to the top of the nearby crate, putting him eye-level with her backside. She rose on her toes, reaching toward a box on top of a locked cabinet, and teetered off center.

He had no other choice, and no better grip, than either side of her hips to steady her.

Jack expected a well-placed kick in the chest for his impropriety, but the woman not only accepted his aid with a "thank you" but used him to reach even higher, until her skirts fell away from her pale-stockinged calf.

A hot bolt of desire surged through him and lodged itself in his groin.

"Got it!" she said, dragging the box toward her and handing it down to him. The lock popped easily, and she laughed when she opened the lid.

"Quills," she said, shutting it again. She was cobwebbed and dusty, and glowing pink with exertion.

Jack could only sweat.

She continued her search, undeterred by dust and dampness and lack of light, accepting his aid when he was near enough to help, and forging on alone when the passages grew cramped and excluded him.

He had accompanied Miss Faelyn to observe her methods, fully expecting to find flaws and inefficiencies, fully prepared to institute changes for the sake of the project. But for the moment she seemed to know far more about this business than he did. It was an inscrutable maze, and all he could do was stand and hold the string while Miss Faelyn looked for the way to freedom.

He wouldn't always be around to escort her. He would make random forays with her, but the job was really hers. Though she spun silk-webbed stories as tightly as a spider in springtime, he had to trust her research—though he would keep guard against her equivocating.

As he would keep guard against the meadowy scent of her skin and the tempting display of her legs.

Jack spent the next three hours bridling his passion for the eccentric woman, unlocking chests for her and unscrewing parchment presses, while his agile partner passed judgment on the contents. She touched him often in her enthusiasm, unconscious of its effects on him. It was only when they reached the end of a corridor of chests stacked nearly to the ceiling that they found a stash of barrels, and finally the one they had been seeking.

"Henrietta!" she shouted.

Queen Henrietta Maria of France. The label was burned unceremoniously into the side of the barrel.

"Success, madam."

"Oh! You can't know how much, Rushford." Tears again, huge and streaming. And then a great wracking sob that she clutched against her chest.

It seemed the most natural thing in the world to wrap himself around her, to fill his arms with the funny sobs that he felt so responsible for. She was much smaller than he'd expected, her fierceness belying her delicate bones. He wasn't at all certain what this was all about, but he planned to ride it out with her.

It wasn't until he was pressing his lips against the top of her head, where all that sweet, golden hair grew wild, that he realized he'd been wondering what their children would look like.

Chapter 7

"**G**ood God, woman! Sumner told me you were hanging paper in the conservatory. I thought he meant wallpaper!"

Mairey smiled up at Rushford and his familiar scowl, and she clothespinned another mildewed page of Henrietta's personal letters onto the waist-high maze she'd constructed from table and chairs and twine. He looked every inch the mining baron this morning, in his long black coat and gray trousers. He was Hades in hard male flesh, the giver of riches, the author of this particular miracle of musty history. A feat her father could never have wrought.

"The barrel was delivered this morning, by Mr. Walsham himself."

Rushford snorted and entered the web of twine. "I'm not surprised, Miss Faelyn, the way he flattered you without end."

There was something wildly erotic and inexorable about him as he prowled his way toward her through the maze. "I'm not interested in Mr. Walsham."

"He was very interested in you." Rushford painstakingly followed the rickety, winding path she had laid out, when he could have so easily carved a swath through the forest of chairs and knocked it all down.

"Yes, I know, my lord. I'm not blind." Though she was having some trouble concentrating on her work. "I grew up in a college town, surrounded by randy young men who had only one thing on their minds."

"Not mathematics." His eyes were darker in the morning light, but clearer and questing.

"Definitely biology." Mairey stooped and pinned up another page, letting its cheerful mustiness flutter away in the warm breeze that came in from the pair of doors that opened onto the garden.

Rushford reached her at the center, and gazed intently down his long, straight nose at her, nostrils flaring. "Do you have a young man of your own in Oxford?"

Mairey met his frown, wondering where its fierceness had come from so quickly. He smelled of bergamot and soap; his hair was still wet from his bath.

"What are you asking, sir? If I've ever succumbed to the sweaty charms of an undergraduate? If my maidenhead is intact?"

All that towering masculinity went crimson, and stammered, "I—I—damn it all, madam, I would never ask that."

Men. So easily threatened by a little honesty from a woman. She was a social scientist. However unmentionable the subject was in polite society, human sexuality was the key to human behavior. She'd had many a discussion with her colleagues about fertility rites, sacrificial virgins, ritual circumcision, and polygamy. She wondered what Rushford would think if he knew she kept a collection of carefully cataloged phallic artifacts in a box in the library.

"Not that it's your business, sir, but I am *virgo intacta*. Qualified to tame unicorns and tend the vestal fires should the need arise."

The man was near rattling, his breathing gone ragged, but his chest was taller than a tree. "Madam, that wasn't my question. I only wanted to know if you have a young man in your life."

"I don't."

That made him frown more fiercely. "Well, then," he said, finally. "I've been called to Cornwall today, Miss Faelyn. An emergency at one of my foundries. I'll not be home until very late tonight."

Mairey searched for relief at the prospect of being free of the man, but found only an alarming disappointment. He'd been almost—well, *very* charming at the Tower, despite his impatience with Walsham, despite the thrill of having his large hands wrapped round her waist a bit too long. They had walked in the garden twice, and had taken meals together in the breakfast room. He'd become a perilously agreeable presence in the library, reading the *Times* or studying one of her books on antiquities. She wouldn't miss him—exactly.

"Lord Rushford—" She opened her mouth to tell him that her sisters would be arriving this afternoon, but the words just wouldn't come. "Do have a safe trip."

"Thank you." He left the conservatory with too much arrogant grace.

An emergency. She could just imagine it: miners striking for better pay, for safer working conditions, for schooling for their children, for food and clean water. A cave-in, an explosion—Rushford trying to minimize the loss to his profits.

As soon as Mairey finished hanging the queen's musty letters in the conservatory, she went back to the library and set about raising her defense against the pillaging dragon. She had already faced her side of the desk to the center of the room to keep him from peering over her shoulder. She mislabeled noteboxes, and created false bottoms inside them so that she had a safe place to store any evidence she uncovered that might lead him toward the Knot. She had two sets of journals—one to show to him regularly, the other, written in the oghams and runes of the green world, to hide away from his prying.

She even wrote a short report for Rushford, making suggestions for sources and listing items she needed, then put it on the top of the desk in the adjoining office.

By midafternoon, with a bit of help from Sumner and his assistants, her father's chair was tucked up against her desk, and the two gouged and stained worktables separated her part of the library from Rushford's.

A very small part, indeed. His sumptuous, overly male furniture sprawled across a meadow of woolen carpets, a rival to any library at Oxford.

But so comfortable, scented with the honey warmth of beeswax polish and leather, and the drift of roses from the beautiful windows that opened to the garden.

A lovely place to raise a family.

A family of her own. Children and a husband. A fairy tale of ungainly proportions, but one she longed to have come true. Of course, it could never be. Mairey had long ago decided that she would never wed, *could* never. She was pledged to the Willowmoon, which left little enough room in her life for her sisters, let alone a husband and children of her own.

She shoved away the terrible yearning; marked it off to the fact that Rushford was, without question, the most compelling man she'd ever met. The compulsion to reproduce was unstoppable; what woman wouldn't want to mix her blood with the very robust Jackson Rushford's?

Biology. That's all it was. Resistible and finite.

And he was her enemy.

"Your pardon, Miss Faelyn." Sumner was standing at the library door, his usually starched exterior wrinkled around the edges. "There are three young ladies here and a—"

"Maireey!"

Pandemonium broke around Sumner like raging water rounding a boulder. Crinoline and squealing and shouts of joy flowed toward her as Caro and Poppy and then Anna tumbled into the library.

"My loves!" Mairey met them in the midst of the furniture-stuffed room. Poppy launched herself into Mairey's arms and snuggled into an embrace.

"Are you a faerie princess now, Mairey?" Caro asked, squeezing Mairey around the middle.

"Not even a mortal princess, I'm afraid."

Poppy turned Mairey's face with her sweat-sticky palms. "Caro said we shall live in this castle for ever and ever afterward. But how can we, Mairey, if you're not the princess?"

"Is there a knot garden, Mairey?" Anna had already purloined one of the yellow roses that grew in profusion along the foundation of Drakestone. "The grounds look big enough for three."

"Come here, Anna! Look!" Caro had bolted away from Mairey and was standing on a chair at the window, pointing wildly. "A giant's garden!"

"Ah, there you are, Mairey, my girl." Aunt Tattie brushed past Sumner, throwing the stunned butler an irritated glance and handing him a hatbox. "A bit showy, don't you think?"

"You're a brave woman, Auntie. You made it here in one piece with these three little baggages."

"And all our belongings. Which are still outside in the cart." The woman dragged her spectacles to the end of her nose, glared again at Sumner. "What's this all about, Mairey Faelyn?"

"Miss, if I might speak with you a moment?" Sumner was still standing at the door, crooked forward from the waist but apparently fearful of actually coming inside and being drowned.

"Ah, yes. Sumner, this is Mrs. Titania Winther, my aunt."

"Madam."

"Mr. Sumner." Tattie sniffed her suspicion.

"The young lady who plundered the rose is my sister Anna." Anna had already found the water cruet, but managed a bobbing curtsey—not exactly the correct salutation to offer a butler.

"And this is—Caro, sweet, *please* don't rock so hard in Lord Rushford's chair. My sister Caroline." Mairey kissed Poppy's wind-tossed mop of curls. "And this is Persephone—we call her Poppy."

Sumner hadn't moved a muscle, save for the un-Sumner-like slackening of his jaw. She'd seen the same look of disbelief when one of her folk-study subjects was telling her of their first sighting of a commune of fairies cavorting in the midnight mist. The eyes played tricks in the moonlight.

Rushford's reaction would hardly be as guarded.

"Will Mistress Tattie and the young ladies be staying for dinner tonight?"

"I like 'snips," Poppy said, "an' carrots."

"Parsnips," Mairey explained to Sumner.

"And carrots." The man closed his mouth and nodded. "I shall inform the cook, Miss Poppy."

"Mairey, there's a pond!" Caro was rattling the locked latches and would have thrown open the door if Tattie hadn't grabbed her around the waist. "And ducks!"

"May Caro and I go out to the garden, Mairey?" Anna had poured water from the cruet into Rushford's empty crystal inkstand. "Can we, please?" She dropped the rose into the vessel.

They were home. For good or ill, dragon or no.

"Soon," Mairey said, gathering her sisters into her arms.

"Then they *will* be staying for dinner, Miss Fae-lyn?"

"Actually, Sumner, my family will be staying with me in the lodge. We'll manage dinner there."

"Through the week's end, miss?"

Through eternity, she wanted to say. "Indefinitely."

"Ah!" Sumner cut a wide-eyed glance toward the foyer, as though Rushford's hearing were superhuman and reached all the way from Cornwall. "Does his lordship know about . . . your plans?"

"Not yet."

"I see."

But settling her sisters into the lodge proved as difficult as squeezing cider back into an apple. Tattie took command of the lodge kitchen and settled into a bed-sitting-room, while Mairey helped the girls unpack. Anna had her own room for the first time in her life; Caro and Poppy shared the garret next to Anna, just below Mairey's own bedroom. She prayed that the ceiling plaster would hold with all their stomping, and made them promise not to bounce on the beds.

By the time they returned from exploring the duck pond and the creek and the fairy woods, there wasn't a spot on anyone that wasn't matted with mud, or leaves, or feathers.

And Mairey was as happy as she'd ever been.

Welcome home, my loves.

Jack climbed the stairs to Drakestone in the blue-gray invisibility of the spring twilight. He didn't particularly like Cornwall; hated the noise and the heat of the foundry, and the bellowing furnaces most of all. And yet the process of coaxing iron and tin out of bare rock fascinated him; it had done so since he was a boy.

He'd spent the day in an interminable meeting, moderating the safety issues between his engineers and the men who would run the newly designed forges. Jack had worked all sides of the process, from sweating at the furnaces and shoveling coke to engineering better fuel consumption systems. All of which made him aware of whom to invite to the design table when changes were needed. Those college-bred engineers who balked at sitting across from a good furnace man didn't last very long in Jack's employ.

Today had been long, but productive. He was disappointed not to find the gold-rimmed glow of lamplight spilling from the library. Miss Faelyn had been in the fore of his thoughts all the way home. And all the way to Cornwall, and no less than a dozen times an hour through the day.

Virgo intacta. She'd ambushed him with that— left his head spinning and his blood sizzling.

He could have stayed the night in Exeter as usual when he was called away, but tonight he'd wanted to come home to Drakestone. To Mairey. He'd been so long without anyone to come home to that he hadn't recognized the pull until he was halfway to London.

He'd imagined finding her sorting through Henrietta's papers, ready with her odd stories and her laughter. He needed no pretense to seek her out tonight in the lodge; he had a perfect excuse tucked in his coat pocket: an invitation to visit Windsor whenever she liked.

Jack caught himself whistling as he dropped his attaché on the desk in his office, scattering the stack of mail.

He picked the top letter off the pile.

Rushford, it said. The writing was familiar, and he touched it to his nose, sniffing the whisper of her scent. Lilac and—he sniffed again—rose. His heart pounded absurdly as he went round the desk, wielding the letter opener like a sword against the seal. He bent his knees, prepared to sit down for a leisurely read.

His butt hit the floor just before he noticed his chair was missing.

"Bloody hell!" Jack dragged himself, cursing, off the ground and stared at the empty space behind his desk. It was always there! Designed for him to fit perfectly in the foot-well of his desk! Where the devil—

The library. Miss Faelyn had probably absconded with his chair and was using it for a drying rack.

He unlocked the library door, expecting to find the familiar labyrinth of crates, but all was neat and orderly. Miss Faelyn's corner looked particularly stalwart, prepared for a battle.

But his chair was nowhere to be seen.

However, there was a yellow rose plucked from his garden, floating in his inkstand, water dribbled in a ring around his blotter. Next she'd be using his shoes as coal scuttles and his necktie as a lamp wick.

And the door to the garden was standing open! A blatant breach of security. Jack grabbed the latch to pull the door closed and came back with a handful of stickiness.

Honey! A great gob of it.

Had the woman gone mad? He washed his hands in the kitchen, then set out for the lodge.

It was lit like Christmastide, a candle blazing in every window, the front door standing open to the breeze and to every fiend who might pass by.

He couldn't have her living here alone. He'd convince her to move to the main house. Hell, he'd move her there himself! He should have knocked, but he heard a commotion at the rear of the house—shouting and screaming.

"What the hell?" Fearing the worst, Jack tore down the hallway toward the sitting room, his heart in his throat.

He threw open the door, ready to charge in, but time stood by for a moment and filled his heart to bursting.

His sisters were playing there in the hazy lamplight, unaware of him, draped in fanciful too-big-for-them gowns, pale-haired and lovely, their little voices chattering like field mice.

Emma, so near young womanhood; Banon, with her unforgettable smile, and dear Clady, who had loved to ride upon his shoulders.

He'd found them.

The scene blurred and stung his eyes.

"Clady . . . ," he said to the littlest of the ghosts, afraid to take a step into the room for fear of frightening them away.

But three pair of startlingly clear eyes found him. "Oh, look, Anna! A dragon!"

And then they were screaming in terror. Jack was rooted to the floor.

Emma picked up an apple and heaved it at him. "Away, monster!"

Jack took one apple in the shoulder, and another on his knee. They didn't understand. Didn't recognize him.

"Maireeeeeey!" Banon was shouting as she brandished a fire-poker; Clady was throwing pillows.

They came at him in a cloud of nightgowns and streaming hair, still screaming like banshees, and calling for Mairey.

Jack felt warm hands around his waist from behind, and the scent of apples, and then Mairey was standing in front of him, her back warm against his chest, intercepting the attack.

"Anna, stop that right now!"

Anna. Not his Emma at all. Not Banon, or Clady. No, of course not. His sisters would be older. Years older.

Mairey was looking up at him, a magnet for the little girls, who had lunged at her and were tucking themselves into the fullness of her night robe.

"I'm very sorry, sir," she was saying, lifting the one he had thought was Clady into her arms. "We weren't expecting anyone. You frightened them."

Jack couldn't find any words, couldn't spare a breath of explanation.

"Is he your dragon, Mairey?"

"No, Poppy." Mairey smoothed her fingers

through the little girl's wispy hair, and set a kiss against her temple. "This is Lord Rushford. Our host. You must tell him you're sorry."

"We're sorry!" The chorus of little voices wounded him, made him angry.

"Who are these children?" he bellowed, instantly ashamed to see the little faces fall.

Mairey was frowning fiercely at him, as though *he* were in the wrong. "They are my sisters."

Hers.

"What the devil are they doing here?"

"No, Auntie, don't! It's all right." She was shaking her head at someone behind him, waving them off. "And this is our Aunt Tattie."

Jack turned slightly and caught sight of an older woman wielding a large iron kettle.

"Your lordship." The woman ducked him a curtsey, then went to stand beside Miss Faelyn.

They were a wayward sight, the five of them. So out of place and so familiar. Hiding from him. They couldn't stay.

"Come with me to my office, Miss Faelyn." He turned to go, but the children were clinging to her.

"No, Mairey! Don't go! We just got here! A story, Mairey. Please."

The angel voices rose like a hymn.

"My lord, I believe this matter will wait till morning." Bright smudges of color pinked her cheeks. "I haven't seen my sisters in a long time, and then only briefly. We've missed each other."

They couldn't stay. "Then we'll talk now, madam. Here."

She must have seen that he meant it. "Tattie,

will you please take the girls upstairs—''

"Mairey, nooooo!" The littlest of them clung tighter. Jack felt a raging rush of guilt when those fawn-brown eyes peeked out at him from under a fine spray of curls.

So like his Clady. His heart lurched, and his stomach roiled with shame and sorrow. And all those memories.

No. He couldn't have them here underfoot. They would get in the way. He had his own family to worry about. He didn't need someone else's.

"I'll be up soon, girls. And you'll each have a story."

" 'Little Red Riding Hood'!"

" 'Gwynella and the Enchanter'!"

"One each, I said. Now go with Auntie." Miss Faelyn managed to funnel her brood through the narrow door, then leaned against it as it closed behind her scowling aunt. The sounds of footsteps echoed above them.

"You didn't have to shout at them, Rushford." She held her place at the door, as though he would break it down and devour them. "They're only little girls."

"Damn it, woman! You said nothing of this family of yours."

"Did you once think to ask me if I had a family?"

"You should have said."

"And then what? You've decided for me that I must make my home at Drakestone House. Home to me *is* my family. And here they will stay."

"Not when it means a full-scale invasion of my property."

"They are children, Rushford, not an army of locusts."

"They are a risk to security, madam."

"Ballocks! They are three little girls and a war-widow who would lay down her life for them."

"I'm not interested in your family."

"That, my lord, is the *only* thing I'm interested in. I'm sorry if you can't understand that."

Dear God, how well he understood; it was the gaping hole in his heart, wide and lonely, aching for the family that he'd abandoned.

"They can't stay."

"Then neither can I, my lord."

A stone thumped against his chest, the empty sound of his heart beating in a hollow drone.

"We've made a bargain, madam. You and I and no one else."

"You knew everything about me, didn't you?" She came away from the door, her long hair falling to her waist. "You knew my schedule, my library, my desire to find the Knot. How can you possibly have overlooked my family?"

"I would have forbidden them in any case. Drakestone House is not a place for children."

"Nothing in the world could have persuaded me to come to live here if they can't stay. I'll keep them away from you, my lord, away from your house. You need never see them."

"Impossible." He remembered his own sisters. As unmanageable as smoke, slipping through his fingers like water to bedevil him and make him laugh.

"Despite what you saw here tonight, sir, my sisters are well behaved and respectful."

A cloud of giggling poured down the stairs and slipped under the door, wrapping his heart in aching wonder. The woman who was standing guard against him, wearing no more than her robe as armor, glanced fondly at the ceiling. He knew the indomitable love in her eyes and envied it in deep, dark waves.

"You won't see them, Rushford; won't hear a peep. I promise to hide them away."

The giggling came again, irrepressible and without guile. And crowded with memories. Dear, soul-flooding memories. He turned away from her, from the mist blurring his vision. He cleared his throat to speak.

"My desk chair is missing."

He felt her relax; knew that she stooped to pick up an apple.

"Ah, well, yes. For that I must apologize. Caroline saw that it had wheels and tried to use it for a pushcart for our bags. The wheel broke as the chair rolled down your stone steps and is now in the carriage house under repair."

Memories. The wagon he'd made for Banon, whitewashed with paint he'd stolen from the pit boss. How could he let these children stay and not feel the loss every day?

"Also, there's a rose in my inkstand and water all over the blotter."

"I'm sorry. That was Anna. She loves flowers. I'll take care of it."

His blossoms. *Where are you, Emma? Are you happy? Are you loved?* He could see Miss Faelyn in the window's reflection, at peace and so steadfast in her care.

"The window latch is sticky with something sweet."

"Poppy. She loves honey. On everything."

"She took honey from the hives in my apiary? She could have been stung."

"She wasn't." The woman's gentle laughter was so forgiving, and soothed him when he preferred his anger. She was too close behind him, touching his elbow as if to make him understand what was so very clear to him. "There were no bees involved in the incident, sir. Cook gave her a spoonful from the kitchen crock. I'll clean it all myself. I'm just sorry you don't like children."

What other opinion could she have of him? "I don't like deception."

"That wasn't my intention. They are my sisters, left to my care when our father died. I love them as I love my life. I will not desert them for you, Lord Rushford, or for the Willowmoon Knot, or for anything in the world. I pray you'll understand someday."

Jack swallowed back the searing shame that had hold of his throat. "Just keep them away from me, Miss Faelyn. Far away."

He started for the door and would have been well gone from her, but the woman tugged him back with her gentling question.

"Why did you come to the lodge tonight?"

To see you, Mairey Faelyn; to sit with you in the hearth light and tell you of my day.

He was dizzy for lack of breathing, unable to avoid her too-wise gaze. "It will keep till the morning, Miss Faelyn."

He left the lodge and didn't slow his stride until he was well down the wooded path, away from the softly glowing windows, away from the laughter that spilled from the garret.

But not nearly far or fast enough to outpace the ghosts or the dismay in Mairey Faelyn's eyes.

Chapter 8

M airey watched Rushford stalk out of the lodge and down the path, wanting to be blazingly angry at him and his conceit—for breaking down her door, frightening her sisters, and then trying to turn them out! Anger would have served her best. But while he'd been raging at her, she'd looked a little too deeply for a flaw, and had seen too much: his beastliness bore the unmistakable mark of a raw and painful wound. It had made him shy from her and the children, the way a lion might with a thorn in its paw.

"Is your dragon gone, Mairey?" Poppy had escaped her aunt and was sitting on the landing above, a crooked frown creasing her brow.

"That's not your business, Persephone Faelyn. Up to bed with you!" Mairey swept Poppy into her arms and tossed her into bed with the other two.

Poppy was asleep long before the wolf had eaten Riding Hood's grandmother; Anna and Caro lasted just long enough for Gwynella to refuse to marry the prince and run away with the enchanter.

126

Tattie was snoring softly in her own room a few moments later, leaving Mairey to clean up the sitting room where her sisters had pitched their battle against Lord Rushford.

She had arrived in time to see him standing unarmed against the onslaught of apples and Caro's poker. He'd done nothing to defend himself, Goliath allowing Mairey's three little Davids to do their worst against him. If she hadn't stopped them, Heaven only knew what injury they might have inflicted on the man.

She had never seen a more vulnerable sight in all her life, all that mighty brawn so achingly disarmed.

No wonder he'd ordered them to leave Drakestone House. They'd made a mess of his library, had broken his favorite chair, and had nearly disabled him.

The mess in his library would still be there to greet him in the morning, a further reminder of the Faelyn sisters' invasion of his precious privacy—surely a breach of security, as well. It would be best to clean it right now and not have to face him in the morning.

Mairey dressed and hurried through the moonlit woods to the main house, letting herself into the library with the key that she kept meaning to restring on a ribbon.

She lit a small fire in the hearth and set the thick desk blotter to dry nearby, then washed honey off the window latch and the back of a nearby chair, discovering more of it on a dozen other surfaces that Rushford would have bellowed about. They would have to live more lightly on the estate, keep to the woods and the shadows, and out of Rushford's sight.

Waiting for the blotter to dry and finding herself restless, Mairey collected some of Henrietta's papers off the lines in the conservatory and returned to the library. She rolled her father's chair to the fireside, then sorted the still-musty letters by date, setting aside those written after September of 1642.

Thinking just to skim some of the faded passages, she soon found herself caught up in Henrietta's letters. Most were passion-filled missives to her dear Charles, written in the woman's native French, having little to do with the war except for her diatribes against the Roundheads.

Henrietta's personal letters! *Oh, Papa, imagine!* She had the key to the Tower of London, to all the vaults and collections in the kingdom. She'd sold her soul to Jackson Rushford to gain entrance, but so far the price hadn't been too high.

Some of the ink on Henrietta's letters had washed away, leaving them readable only with a bright light behind the page and a little guesswork. She was holding up a particularly badly faded letter when a latch clicked and the door from the foyer opened to a silhouetted darkness that she would have known anywhere.

"My lord."

"What are you doing here, madam?" He was in a fine midnight mood, was her dragon.

"Working," she said, holding up the letter to the fire, hoping that he would leave her to her task.

"Damn it, woman! Is that the way it is between

us?'' He was on her in the next moment, his wall of heat overwhelming the fire in the hearth as he leaned his weight and his fury so fiercely against the chair arms that she rocked backward on its gimbals, making it impossible not to look up into his blazing eyes. ''Have I so insulted you and your family that you're burning evidence to spite me?''

''I've burned nothing except wood. It's cold.''

He snatched the letter from her, tipping the chair further backward. ''Then what is this?'' He thrust the paper into the small space between her nose and his.

''It's a letter from Henrietta to her husband. I would never destroy it.''

The man growled a curse and straightened to read. Her chair rocked upright abruptly, yet he kept his knee between hers, pressing it against the edge of the seat so that her entire field of vision was made up of his woolen waistcoat, the gold-fobbed watch chain bridging the line of black pearl buttons that marched down his broad chest to the tapering of his stomach, and the front of his trousers.

Her heart took off on a zithering flight and strung her pulse along behind it. She wanted to reach beneath his coat and shape her palms over his hips. But Rushford was scrutinizing the offending letter as though he suspected that it contained the alchemists' secret.

''It's blank,'' he said, and loomed again, bending her chair backward so that their noses were nearly touching.

''Blank, except when it's held to a backlight.'' Mairey snatched the letter from between his fingers. "May I rise, sir? Or do you plan some other mischief with me?"

Dear God, he was handsome, and wild-hearted again in his passions.

"The mischief is yours, Miss Faelyn. You and your sisters."

Dew glistened on his hair and across his shoulders; he smelled of the night, of the blueness of the moon.

"Have you been out walking, sir?" Some bit of lunacy made her touch a bead of water that clung to a dark curl at his temple. It slid off his hair and ran down her finger.

"Hunting the moon with my fellow wolves, my dear. Just like the bloody tales of the bloody beasts you tell your sisters." He dipped his head, his breath almost a kiss. "Whatever you think of me, I don't eat grandmothers or little girls."

"Aha!" She pointed her finger between them, amazed at his confession and utterly charmed when she ought to feel spied upon. "You were listening at our window! Why?"

He had the courtesy to look chastened. "I was waiting."

"For?"

"You."

That made her heart leap to all sorts of conclusions that it ought to avoid.

"Well, then, sir, if you were at the lodge, you saw me leave there a half hour ago. Why didn't you say something then? Were you lurking?"

He chewed on his lip, straightened and walked to the window, then confessed quietly, "I . . ." He glanced back at her, a wryness in his tone. "Fell asleep."

Mairey knew that she shouldn't laugh, knew that the slightest whimper in that direction would set the man's pride on end. But even after clapping her hand over her mouth, she couldn't keep the giggling noises from escaping her.

"Thank you, madam."

"Oh, my!" Crispy leaves and bits of loam clung to the back of his coat. She went to him and started brushing him off, then handed him a good-sized maple leaf, complete with a winged seed pod attached. "You should have stayed with us, sir. You could have slept on a bed with the other cubs and not in the briars."

He watched her from over his shoulder, his eyes tracking hers like beams of pure sunlight. Her lashes felt sun-warmed when she lifted them.

"They can live here at Drakestone," he said quietly. "I won't fight you."

"Good. It would have been very uncomfortable for all of us. I wouldn't have stayed."

"I know." There was finality in those two resolute words and a nuance of approval.

Unnerved, Mairey made her way around the brute, almost certain that she had no ulterior motives for stroking him repeatedly—quite apart from the hard-packed brawn. "I'll do my best to keep them away from your house. But I cannot absolutely guarantee that you won't find honey on the greenhouse door."

"Drakestone will survive, Miss Faelyn." His

voice rumbled against the palm of her hand. "I had young sisters of my own once."

"Did you?" Ah, then he was used to the changeable fancies of little girls; he would have learned patience under their constant disruptions. "I have just the three, but they often seem like twice that. How many do you have?"

He shook his head and left her for the hearth, giving a dry laugh as he crushed the maple leaf in his hand. "Three. Imagine my surprise when I found *yours* in my lodge. I thought for a moment—"

But he stopped there, on the very brink of something that Mairey couldn't see beyond. He seemed altogether tame now, curled up in defeat. Weary to his soul. And for some unfathomable reason, she wanted to wrap her arms around him and put his head against her heart. It pained her immeasurably to think of him asleep outside her window when there had been so much room inside.

"Your sisters must be grown and married by now."

He nodded, staring at the flames, but offered nothing more.

"Do you see them often?"

"I haven't for a very long time." He tossed the wadded leaf into the hearth and turned to her. "Look, Miss Faelyn, I . . . I waited for you outside the lodge because I didn't want to interrupt the felicitous scene I had leveled with my earlier outburst. I was going to knock as soon as you'd put your sisters to bed. So I listened and waited—"

"And fell asleep."

He nodded, sighed with the breath he'd been holding. "It was a long day."

She wanted to ask more about his family, but he'd obviously closed the subject. "What was it you wanted of me?"

"This. What I'm trying to say now. That I over-reacted and I'm sorry for it. That I won't gobble up your sisters or your aunt should I come upon them in the garden. And that I won't fall upon you in a rage thinking that you're destroying evidence. That would be absurd, when both of us are chasing the same thing."

"Yes. Well." A little snake turned in Mairey's stomach, cobalt blue and glass-eyed. Deception wasn't the most ennobling skill, even when prac-ticed against one's greatest adversary. "Come, then. I'll show you what I was looking at just now."

Mairey knelt in front of the hearth and added a handful of kindling. The fire brightened and snapped as Rushford joined her on one knee.

She extended the page of washed-out ink. "I read at least a hundred letters today. I'd just begun to read this one."

"There's nothing on it."

"So it seems, until you hold the paper just so against a—Dear God!" Mairey's heart slammed up against her throat. She brought the page closer, and then back again so the runny blue coalesced into sharper lines. "Adam Runville! It's him!"

"Who?" Rushford squinted closer and closed his hand over hers to keep the page steady. "Where do you see a name?"

Oh, Papa! Just like that! First Henrietta's papers and now the keeper of the woman's treasury! And here she was, blurting out his name with Rushford looking on, holding her hand, letting her pulse run wild with his. She'd grown too comfortable with the man, forgetting to temper her excitement, to shield her successes from him. There was nothing to be done now.

"Here," she said, pointing to the first line in the letter. "Adam Runville—the captain of Henrietta's guards."

"I see blurred blue. And I don't read French. You'll have to read it to me."

Of course! She'd forgotten—another artifice to employ against him. She sniffed away the blink of guilt. It didn't matter that the man was unwavering heat, or that he had fallen asleep under her window, listening to her fairy tales—he was her nemesis. There was no other word for his relationship to her. And no hope for anything better between them.

"It says, 'Dearest husband of my soul, our favorite Runville de Donowell left Windsor this night with ten carts, and under God's good grace, should make Aylmouth in a fortnight.'" Mairey still couldn't believe their great good fortune, couldn't have predicted Rushford's part in these miracles.

He handed back the page and studied her face. "You're certain this is Henrietta's infamous shipment of the treasury?"

Mairey always felt borne up off the ground when he watched her, as though her hair were lighter, and her eyelids kissed.

"Of course I'm not entirely certain." All that

lightness made it a little difficult to breathe, and whenever she managed to do so, his scent thrilled her. "But here Henrietta writes that the shipment was bound for Holland. The very place where two similar transactions happened in the course of the war. Runville is one of the few who could have stolen an entire cart from a caravan without anyone suspecting."

Rushford rasped his knuckle along his jawline, across the midnight sheen of his day-old beard. "There's a Donowell on the coast in Northumberland. It was on your map of items already recovered."

"Yes." She knew that, was already planning a secret excursion without him. But not until she'd found Runville's will, and she needed to do that without Rushford eavesdropping. "The evidence piles up against our Baron de Donowell, doesn't it?"

"So it seems." He was still on one knee, the other bent firmly, his fine leg collecting hearth light along its length. "What next, madam?"

It was difficult to think of ways to outflank him while he was tangling his fingers in the ends of her hair. "If Runville died during the Interregnum, then his will was probated in London and will hopefully be in the Tower. I'll go back there tomorrow. And the day after. . . ."

He laughed lightly. "You're quite marvelous, Mairey Faelyn." It was a simple statement made breathtaking when he began to trace the line of her cheekbone with his hand. "Softer than I imagined."

A week ago she would have scorned him; tonight she dammed up an immodest sigh and braved the alluring pleasure, looked up at him and into those flame-brightened eyes.

"*Do* you imagine such things, Rushford?"

His answer was to touch his fingers to his mouth. "Honey," he said.

She wasn't sure she'd heard him right—surely not an endearment. "What?"

He smiled down on her, catlike, indulgent.

"You have honey on your cheek, Miss Faelyn, and here on your lips—" Because he'd put it there with his fingertip, and now followed after with his mouth and then the tip of his tongue—a grazing of lightning that dazed her, made her take hold of his lapel to keep her balance.

"You taste of honey, madam."

"Do I?" *Are you sure? Please do try again.* Mairey's heart was a scramble of thumps and pauses, made useless by the man's utterly ravenous smile.

"Far sweeter than my imaginings, my dear." He was breathing unsteadily, a sheen of dampness gilding his forehead. "That being so, Miss Faelyn— and my manners sorely lacking—before I take you back to the safety of the lodge, I'd like to know of this Princess Gwynella person—"

"From the fairy tale?" Mairey's head was spinning; he was still so close, still tracing her mouth with his fingers, as though he might sample there again.

"Tell me the woman doesn't take up with the prince. He was an ass."

Mairey's heart swelled; she nearly kissed him. He hadn't heard the end of the story. Her impossible dragon must have fallen asleep even before Caro had.

"The Enchanter came after the princess, my lord. Married her on the spot."

He nodded sagely, satisfied. "Wise man."

"Steel, Rushford?" Herringham laced his fingers together and settled his hands on top of his briefcase. "I am advising against such an investment."

"Noted, Herringham." Jack slid his gaze along the ridge of stiff-faced men sitting like blackbirds around the conference table in his office at Drakestone. "However, the 25,000 pounds is mine to invest, not yours."

"But sir, Bessemer's invention has yet to be thoroughly tested. British hand-forged iron, replaced by mass-produced steel? Preposterous! What of your own forges? They'll need to be refitted."

"Exactly—and as soon as possible. Here you'll find Richmond's engineering drawings, showing how my factories will be quickly changed over to the new process. We've already begun negotiations to purchase Wright & Sons Tooling. Show them, Richmond."

"Certainly, Jack." Richmond had spent the entire day on his feet, pacing, pointing, commenting. He was Jack's best mining engineer, the very best in the Empire, perpetually charged as if ready to explode. When he did sit, he constructed odd structures out of whatever was at hand. "Rushford Mining and Minerals will not only be the largest foundry to manufacture Bessemer's new steel, we'll also force our competitors to purchase their new machinery from us."

"Refitting the Rushford foundries and factories will cost thousands," Herringham said as he leafed through the report so quickly he couldn't possibly have read it, let alone understand it. "And what if the process fails?"

"It won't," Jack said, weary of the man's dire predictions. Prudence was one thing, but fear of the future would eventually bury the Rushford operation in silt. "I've seen the process myself, from extrusion to finished rails laid down on the roadbed. I've watched rail stock pushed to the limits of speed, with excellent trials and better safety than has ever been possible. Within a few years every rail-bed in Britain will be replaced with Rushford steel."

"Just as every mining operation will soon employ the new Rushford steam-windings," Richmond said, flipping through the report for Herringham, "as I've shown there on page twelve. This is the refitting design for the Glad Heath Works, already under construction. I'm supervising it myself."

Richmond's excitement soon reached the others around the table: a few investors, two geological engineers, Jack's site-viewers, three factory men, and a Parliamentary official. Eventually even Herringham joined, though he looked completely overwhelmed.

Jack leaned back against the bookcase and let Richmond have his due, pleased that Glad Heath would soon be the very safest colliery in all the world as well as the most efficient: a showcase that might bring other mine owners to his side.

He was pleased to his soul that it was Glad Heath that was prospering. His father would be proud of what Jack had accomplished at the mine—the unblemished safety record, and the profits despite it all.

Revenge, Father, he thought with some satisfaction. *A tribute to you.*

The guilt was so much more piercing since Miss Faelyn had come into his life, immeasurably so since she'd brought her sisters to live here. He couldn't fault her love for them; he could only stand in awe of her devotion.

She was an ethereal and inconsistent contraption, and she wore her fragile sentiments on her sleeve, yet he'd never seen a more granite determination. He'd seen little of her and nothing at all of her sisters in the last few days. He'd spent long hours with Richmond finalizing the designs for the refitting, and Mairey was gone to the lodge before he got home at night. Although he had apologized for being a great raging boor with her family, he still felt the distance and the loneliness like a sharp stick through his chest.

He found himself drifting toward the lodge every evening, his heart feeling as wild as the woodlands and the creek in springtime. Sometimes she briefly let him into the hall, answering his questions in her smoked-silk voice with her hand on the door, ready to exclude him from her delicious scents and the sounds of delight just beyond the darkness.

Sometimes she allowed him to sit with her in her little parlor, discussing the Willowmoon Knot or her father's work, but glancing nervously at the ceiling as though she thought her sisters might descend upon them and set him off.

He wasn't ready to meet the children head-on; he was still wrestling with his own shadows, and frightened as hell of such bliss.

Miss Faelyn was digging around in the Tower again today, looking for Cromwell's probate records. Tedious stuff, and he had no doubt that her every move was dogged by Walsham and his coweyed infatuation. Though the woman had denied any interest in the little man, if he ever showed up at Drakestone House with a wad of flowers in his fist, Jack would personally throw him out on his skinny backside. The thought burned a hole in his gut, made him want nothing more than to end this meeting and meet Mairey at the Tower.

He'd never taken honey in his tea, but now he found himself ladling it into every cup because it tasted of her, of her perfectly bowed mouth, her sweet tongue. A fact that Walsham couldn't possibly know! Ha!

"We've already begun the refitting work at Glad Heath." Richmond was standing at the huge map of Britain, which rose nearly twenty feet to the ceiling and spanned the wall from corner to corner. Jack had commissioned it to be painted in the finest geological detail, directly on the wall, behind a set of sliding mahogany panels. His mine works and forges dappled the valleys and ridges, from the Severn to the River Tyne. An inset map showed the sprawl of his North American holdings. All of it his.

The Willowmoon and its bed of silver were there somewhere, winking up at the sunlight, waiting for him. A fortune, a quest for the impossible, and one that was leading to places he could never have imagined.

Because he'd never in his life imagined Mairey Faelyn.

"Show them the new outcropping at Ben Alden, Richmond." Jack joined him at the map, and the others rose to surround him.

"Ah, yes," Richmond said, as he climbed the rolling stairs to gesture at Northumberland. "For those of you who don't know, the new coalfield at Ben Alden is here, three-quarters of a mile from the Newcastle and Carlisle Railway. It will be fitted out from the beginning with the very best in steam technology."

"What about a spur line to the colliery, Rushford?" Ahearne was a diligent but steadfast investor, one of his most consistent. "Have you addressed that?"

Jack clapped the man on the back, pointed to the place where Richmond had his finger. "The right-of-way for a spur line has already been negotiated with the land contract, and the tracks are ready to be laid—new *steel* tracks."

"What exactly do all those black spots mean, Lord Rushford?"

The voice came from behind them all, clear and

morning-bright. Every man in the room turned in unison, bunching and backing away from Mairey as though she were a ghost.

A ghost wearing a small wad of violets in the lapel of her traveling cloak. Jack felt a blast of molten lead in his chest.

Walsham's flowers! He wanted to singe them.

Jealousy. Pure, but not in the least simple.

"Gentlemen," he managed, though his pulse raged in his ears. "I would like you to meet Miss Mairey Faelyn."

He wanted to lift her out of his office and quiz her about her afternoon at the Tower. He wanted to back her into the library and make love to her.

"What are the black blotches on the map, Lord Rushford?" She was lost in her examination of the map, the deep wings of her brows canted in scathing disapproval.

Jack felt utterly chastened by her interest. He was used to digging with his bare hands, with shovels and picks and clamoring mine works when necessary. This digging into paper as she did, into the distant past, was mind-numbing, and it made him feel clumsy and cocksure. Here was the extent of his life painted in brilliant enamels, and it suddenly tasted of rust and salt.

And she smelled of Walsham's violets!

"The black blotches, Miss Faelyn, indicate the coalfields owned by Rushford Mining and Minerals."

She took a step closer to the map, craning her neck and touching her fingers to her lovely lips.

"And the red?" she asked, the worry in her eyes deepening.

"Those are my tin mines, Miss Faelyn, and the blue is lead." He felt like a braggart who'd been caught in an awful truth. The other men were murmuring, approving of the woman or of the extent of Jack's holdings, or his plans. It didn't matter. He wanted to feel proud, but he felt roundly less than that at the moment, and hadn't a clue to the reason.

She turned her glittering gaze on him. "What of silver, Lord Rushford? Do you own any silver mines?"

Jack nearly swallowed his tongue, and came up clearing his throat. What the devil was the woman up to?

"None in England, Miss Faelyn," he said between his teeth.

"Actually, Miss Faelyn," Richmond said, clumping down the ladder to interrupt with his usual enthusiasm, "there are no silver mines in all the British Isles."

"No silver at all?" She still had hold of Jack's gaze. "But what of the work of the ancient Celts?"

"The which?"

Richmond had no idea that he had just become a character in one of Miss Faelyn's fairy stories. Where the hell was she going with this riddle?

"The Celts, Mr. Richmond. Early Britons. I just wondered where their silversmiths had gotten the metal for their artifacts. I'm an antiquarian, and though I see the elegant work of the Celts everywhere, I haven't the vaguest idea how they got their silver.''

"Ah! Well, smelting silver from lead ore is a very old process. A fleck here, a chunk there, melted out of the rock, just as lead and tin are. Silver isn't mined like coal. Not in veins and stockworks. At least not here in Britain.''

Jack decided that the woman had caused enough trouble; God knew where she was leading them all. "What is it you need, Miss Faelyn?''

To be free of you, Lord Rushford. Mairey had never seen Rushford's map before, the grasping hold he had on the riches of the earth. Nor could she have imagined that his holdings so closely ringed the Willowmoon. A chill had come upon her the moment she'd opened the door; it curled around her heart, frightening her to the marrow.

"I'll be right back, gentlemen,'' Rushford said as he took her hand and slipped it over his arm.

He skidded her through the foyer and into the library, scooping her into his arms and depositing her on top of his desk.

"What the devil was that all about?'' he asked fiercely, trapping her with his hands on either side of her legs.

"I only stopped in to tell you that I had returned from the Tower.''

"And stayed to ask about silver mining? *Silver,* Miss Faelyn! And the Celts!''

"I was curious.'' She'd been stunned by the vast scope of his contemptible enterprise, unable to stop her questions. Ripe with splendid news that she couldn't tell a soul, especially not the reprehensible but dangerously attractive Viscount Rushford.

"You picked a bloody bad time to become curious about silver mining."

The very best time, Rushford. "I'd never seen your map before. Where do you hide it?"

"Damn the map! What do I say when those men stop to wonder who you are, and why you would wander into my office unannounced. They're sure to ask why I have an astoundingly beautiful young woman living in my house."

"In the lodge." *Beautiful?* He thought she was beautiful? Well, and that was the problem, wasn't it—all this crackling attraction between them. She kept forgetting who he was; she needed stark reminders of the danger to everyone she loved, to her village. She needed his towering map that bled black with his mines to remind her that he was her enemy.

"The men are your business associates, Viscount Rushford. They will certainly find out sometime that I live on the estate. Just tell them that I am one of those fusty old antiquarians, and that I've engaged your lodge as a place from which to study its history."

"Not bloody likely. You are neither fusty nor old, as every man in that room was patently aware. Not so easily dismissed."

Mairey felt her ears go crimson at the effort to keep from remembering the graze of his tongue against her lips.

"If all goes well, my lord, one day soon we'll find the Willowmoon Knot, and then I'll be gone from your circle and no longer your problem."

Despite all the books and the inch-thick carpets, despite the tapestried drapes, her declaration seemed to echo in the library.

He straightened, a tic dancing along his jaw. He looked angry, frustrated.

"Where did you get these?" He flicked his finger across the sagging violets that her sister had surprised her with that morning.

"From Anna. Why?"

Rushford scrubbed his hand across his mouth, calmed considerably. "They're wilted."

"It's been a long day."

"Made longer by Walsham, I suppose?" He was folding bits of her skirt between his fingertips, watching her.

"He was ... manageable." Mairey hid her amusement; Rushford truly hated the man. She wanted to suspect a heathy dose of jealousy, but that would only rouse too many other suspicions, too many impossibilities.

"Did you find anything?"

Mairey had to look him boldly in the eye to tell him this particular lie. It made her heart feel a little hollow.

"Nothing at all, my lord."

Adam Runville's last will and testament.

"Will you go again tomorrow?"

I'll go to Donowell, as soon as I can get away from you, Lord Dragon.

"That depends. There are other clues to follow." While she bided her time.

"My best to Walsham, madam. My worst to him if he should ever touch you wrongly." He lifted her hand in his, pressed a delicious kiss against her fingertips, and then left her to return to his pillaging.

Left her wanting so very much more.

Jack once again made his way through the twilight toward the lodge, this time carrying a bag of flour. He was running out of excuses, and would have to confess to Miss Faelyn one day soon that he enjoyed her company outside the bounds of their project. Which would sound something like courting. Which made beads of sweat pop out on his forehead.

Bloody hell! He was courting Mairey Faelyn! That explained the gnawing in his stomach and the battering that his heart was giving his rib cage at the moment. Courting!

Hell. No. He wanted to talk to the woman about mining. She'd been interested enough a few days ago to interrupt his meeting; he even had a pocket full of drawings and diagrams to help demonstrate. That he would be gone for the next two days was worth a mention. But delivering the flour from the main pantry . . . yes, this was the best he'd come up with yet.

Near to whistling, he followed the stream till it widened to a pool, his step lighter than it had been in years.

Courting?

"Shhh!"

He stopped at the oddly hovering voice, unable to locate its source. Then came a tugging at his pant cuff. Miss Faelyn's shadow-pale face peered up at him from behind a fallen tree, her wide eyes bright and blinking.

"Miss Faelyn?" he asked, his voice sounding harsh in the cool night.

"Down, Rushford, you'll scare them away." She tugged again at his trouser cuff, the gentle pressure bringing him to his knees beside her.

"Scare who?" He noticed then that her sisters were sprawled like wood nymphs in the giant roots that had once anchored the tree to the bankside. The youngest was draped precariously on a drooping branch, her fingers dragging in the water.

"The fair folk are out tonight," Miss Faelyn said, her words dappled in amusement as she nodded toward the pool. "We're watching them."

"Are you?" he asked, aware of little more than the glint of moonlight on her mouth.

"There's another one, Mairey!" The little voice was bright with awe, and far too loud for secrets. "Look! Look! Do you see?"

"I do, Caro. I see four. Anna?"

"Oh, yes, Mairey, I see them, too."

Jack didn't see anything. Only the woman's moon-bright hair. "Fair folk?"

"There." She pointed at the air above the pond. "Carrying lanterns for dancing at their revels."

Jack saw only the phosphorescence given off by decaying matter in the rushes. "Miss Faelyn, those lights are—"

"*Fairies,* my lord," she said pointedly. He could feel her eyes on him, daring him to contradict her. "What do you call them where you come from?"

"These fairies belong to his lordship." The middle child—Caro, if he remembered rightly, the one who had wielded the poker against him—jumped off the tree to hang off Mairey's shoulder, her round little face between theirs, her eyes sparkling with conspiracy. "They're your fairies, aren't they, sir?"

He looked again at the ethereal illuminations, their feathery lightness matching the stars for acrobatic grace. He remembered his family lying like ragdolls under the open skies, for no other reason than the fact that it was huge and magnificent and they loved each other.

"The fairies aren't mine, Caro," he said, swallowing hard to keep his voice steady, "but they do pay rent to live at Drakestone."

"Really, sir?" He heard Mairey's soft laughter in her voice, and his ears went hot with pride. "What coin do they use to pay you?"

"Well, candy." Jack caught himself smiling at her, and crossed his legs as she was doing and sat fully on the spongy ground.

"Chocolate candy?" The littlest of the girls slid into Mairey's lap and peered into his face, smelling of rose soap and childhood.

The woman was waiting for his answer as readily as her sisters, her eyes sparkling, her mouth dew-damp and stunningly inviting.

"Yes, chocolate," he said, delighting in the grin that she gave him, and nearly jumping out of his skin when she patted his hand.

"Poppy's favorite."

"My favorite!" The squeal of laughter would have sent all the fairies in England back into their holes, or wherever the devil they lived.

"What's in the sack, sir?" Caro asked, poking at the bag of flour he'd set beside him.

"Candy for the fairies?" Poppy leaned down to look.

"For us, too?" The elder, Anna—the flower thief who had pelted him with apples—knelt down beside him, too much the young lady to squeal or poke like the other two.

And still Mairey said nothing, only smiled from behind Poppy's curls and let Jack blunder around and gain his bearings.

"The sack is only full of flour, I'm afraid."

"Fairy flour to make fairy cakes!" Poppy flung herself out of Miss Faelyn's lap and into his, all pointy elbows and sticky fingers, and was circling like a puppy for a better seat.

"Poppy, be careful with Lord Rushford." Miss Faelyn looked pained when she saw where the girl was stepping.

"Jack," he said firmly. "My name is Jack. I feel a hundred years old and a thousand miles away when you call me 'Rushford' or 'my lord.' "

"Are you a hundred years old, Lord Jack?" Anna had taken Poppy's place in Miss Faelyn's lap.

"Are you?" Mairey asked, smiling.

"Thirty-three." He grunted as Poppy dropped into place and lounged against him, a bare foot kicking the fallen tree.

Caro was now hanging on his shoulder, draped over his back, whispering, "I know how to make fairy cakes."

"With honey?" he ventured.

The little girl's eyes grew wide, as though he possessed magic and was willing to use it to better the world. "Then you know, too! Mairey! Can we make fairy cakes tonight? Can we?"

"It's late for cooking cakes, girls," Mairey said, to a chorus of groans. "Aunt Tattie will be asleep."

"We'll be quiet!"

"Yes, I can imagine that happening." She raised a brow at Jack, inviting him to remember the sounds of a household full of children.

"Please, Mairey," Anna said, old enough to rally her patience, but ready to spring away like a gazelle.

"All right. If you're quiet."

Anna snatched up the bag of flour and dashed down the shadowy path with Caro on her tail.

Miss Faelyn got up, dusting off her skirt. "Will you come, my lord?"

He didn't see how he could get away. The realization that he didn't want to came over him in a rush of yearning. Poppy had a hold of his neck, and Mairey had a grip on his heart.

Where else would he go?

"I'm not any good with a cook pot, Miss Faelyn."

"I know." Mairey could well imagine her dragon curled up in her aunt's kitchen, warming his belly on her stove, snoozing after inhaling a plateful of cakes—his mouth sweet with stolen honey. She ought to have sent him back to the main house for safekeeping. But he had managed to stand so easily with Poppy in his arms, and the little scamp seemed extraordinarily attached to the giant.

Ah, Poppy. I know the feeling too well.

"I can't stay long," he said, as though he knew her thoughts. "I need to be off to Cornwall before daylight."

Mairey felt her face go pale, and hoped that he couldn't see in the near darkness. "Until when?"

"Two days, maybe a little longer."

Long enough for a trip to Donowell without him—a prospect that didn't rest as comfortably as it might have a few weeks ago.

"Come, my lord, we've got fairy cakes to make."

"Indeed."

Chapter 9

Mairey made Donowell by late afternoon the next day, and found a room in a small inn on the sea cliff, run by a pair of elderly maidens. She was standing in the nave of Holy Martyr's Church a half hour later.

Rushford was in Cornwall. She had followed him secretly to the train to be sure, then left on a different track. Yet still she watched over her shoulder for him, feeling like a sneak-thief. Her father had spent all his life plotting out the places where the queen's stolen treasury had been recovered. It had taken Mairey less than two weeks to find Adam Runville, his will, and a list of his possessions that meant the world to her cause:

. . . six gilt knives, bonne-handled; one silv'red disk, anciently ornamented; one brass ewere . . .

One silv'red disk, anciently ornamented.

All because of Rushford—the very man who must never see the fruit of all his beneficence. She would spend the remainder of today and tomorrow following Runville's trail, and then return to Drakestone without him knowing that she had ever come.

The deception made her jaw hurt and her heart ache.

But she would persist, for the Willowmoon Knot. For love and devotion, for her village, for the glade, for her sisters and her father.

She forced the chant into her thoughts, trying to rid them of the sound of Jack's close and gentle laughter, and the disarming way it reached down into her chest and lifted the breath right out of her. The way the moonlight made his eyes sparkle, made his fine teeth gleam through his so very reluctant smile.

He'd won Poppy with that smile, and had threatened Mairey's composure when her small sister had slipped her hand into his and dragged him along the path toward the lodge.

He'd looked lost and found again at the same time, and if she hadn't known better, she might have believed she'd seen tears welling like stars in his eyes.

Impossible dragon.

Filling up her mind with more productive images—of slag heaps and gaunt children—she shouldered her bag of foolscap and carbon and went in search of Sir Adam Runville.

Holy Martyr's had once been a priory, its chapel an echo of Canterbury cathedral. In the long centuries since, it seemed that every family in the parish had commissioned a bronze plaque or stone marker to commemorate the loss of a loved one. The walls and floor were nearly paneled with them. She hoped Adam Runville's heirs felt as much dedication to his memory.

She scoured the walls, reading every plaque, walking the length and breadth of the entire sanctuary, deciphering the worn letters in the crypt stones embedded in the floor. She checked the Lady Chapel and the transepts, rounded every pillar, and was about to take her search outside into the churchyard when she remembered the tower.

Two winding stories later, in the middle of the spiraling steps, just below a narrow arching window, she found the name that made her heart quicken.

Adam Runville. Dates, titles, praise, and prayers for his soul. The thieving devil. *Did your queen ever learn of your duplicity? And was that the Willowmoon Knot, Sir Runville—the "silv'red disk, anciently ornamented?"*

Wishing her father were here to share her success, Mairey dropped her hat at her feet, then unrolled a thick piece of parchment and fished around in her bag for a block of rubbing carbon.

She almost wished Jack were here with her. Not the rapacious Viscount Rushford of Rushford Mining and Minerals, but the Jack who had helped her make fairy cakes with her sisters.

By the time Aunt Tattie had come down the stairs, roused from her bed by the unstoppable merriment, everyone and everything was sprinkled with flour.

Griddle cakes, the man had called them, best

eaten with thick maple syrup on a cold morning in the Yukon. Poppy never left his side; Anna was completely in love; Caro had found a best friend; Aunt Tattie was flirting wildly; and Mairey had wanted to cry.

She still did, because there was no cake-making Jack. He was part of her fairy tales. Dragons never won the maiden—she had best remember that.

Mairey fit the parchment against the bronze plaque, squaring her arm and elbow across the top edge to hold it fast against the wall, and started rubbing the block lightly over the page. As awkward as it was, there was no better way to copy a bronze. The block hit the rim of the raised crest beneath and bounced out of her fingers. She muttered, ''Blazing toads,'' as the piece rolled two steps down the spiraling stairs—

And up against a pair of expensive boots, dusty and dreadfully familiar.

''Do let me help you, Miss Faelyn.''

She looked up into Rushford's eyes, feral and dangerous, and utterly cold.

''How did—''

''How did I find you?'' He covered her hand against the wall and the parchment with his own, hot-palmed and huge, invading the cool spaces between her fingers. His eyes were shuttered and as dark as the midnight of his hair, gleaming blue-black in the evening light of the window. ''Your sisters thought I ought to see that you hurried home to them. I thought so, too.''

Mairey couldn't read him at all, he was closed down so tightly.

"You were gone to Cornwall," she said, trying to erase his suspicions with a smile that felt as feeble as it must look.

He put the lump of carbon in the short span between them. "Show me."

"Show you what?" Runville's will? How could he know about it? And what the devil would she tell him?

"Show me how to take a carbon rubbing. Isn't that what this method is called, Miss Faelyn?" His question brushed against her ear as he leaned in to take a closer look.

"A rubbing, yes." Her fingers were cloddish and trembling as she took the carbon from him. "You start like this," she said, feeling his gaze shift to her mouth and then to her eyes. "Hold the carbon flat and . . . and work the edge of the letters."

Her hair was a curling mess after all her travels, her plait fallen to the front, and in the way of her rubbing. But she was caught like a rabbit, unable to shift in any direction without moving against the man.

"Is the Knot here in Donowell, Miss Faelyn?" He lifted her plait off her shoulder and smoothed the curls at her nape, making her breath rattle. "Is that why you came here?"

"I don't know yet where the Knot is."

"But Runville had it at one time, didn't he?" Rushford shifted his length to the same stair as hers, and she was caught even closer, his knee bent into the back of her own, his weight and warmth against her skirt heating through to her drawers and collecting like honey low in her belly.

"Yes. I think so."

"Think so, madam?" His words tucked themselves behind her ear, felt more like a lover's caress than the inquisition she knew them to be. "You must have found his will in Cromwell's probate courts or you wouldn't be here."

"I did." Her confession slipped out like an inevitable sigh, leaving her nothing of her own to defend herself with. "I found it this morning, just after you left."

"Imagine." He said nothing more as she worked at the rubbing, holding the parchment against the wall for her when it would have slipped. She still couldn't read him; kept waiting for him to shake the truth out of her. Her nerves were raw and throbbing when she finally finished.

"Where do your theories take us next, Miss Faelyn?"

Us. There would be no putting him off now; he would be more suspicious than ever. The chessboard was clear again; he would know as much about their progress as she did. Except that, in the end, she knew where the treasure lay. That knowledge would have to keep her going.

"Runville had an heir—a son, John."

"As the plaque reads."

"We need to find the son's will, which could be either here in Donowell or in York—"

"Why York?"

"It depends on which prerogative court proved the will after John died. And from there we follow the trail of bequests until it dead-ends."

"My schedule is clear, madam. Take all the time you need."

Oh, go dig in your coal pit, Rushford!

"It's too late this evening. We'll have to continue in the morning." She rolled up the parchment. "I'm staying at an inn at the edge of town—"

"At the Belle Heather, with the elderly Misses Potterfell. So am I." Without a glance at her, Rushford scooped up her satchel, took her arm, and started down the stairs with her.

"What?" Mairey stopped dead. They'd had only her room left. The other had been full.

"I told them that my dear wife and I had a falling out—" A simple tug on her arm and she was hurrying after him.

"Your *wife*?"

"That I'd been a damned fool, and that I had hoped to make it up to her tonight with flowers . . . and a little old-fashioned romance."

"You *didn't*?" Stunned, Mairey stopped on the stairs again, and again the brute tugged her along after him, lifting her with such ease that she never missed a step.

"Yes, my dear, romance. The ladies seemed quite concerned over the sorry state of our marriage."

"Jackson Rushford, how could you?" The tower door loomed darkly below, and Mairey tried to race ahead to be free of him and his meddling arrogance.

But he held her to him in the well of darkness and spoke his threats against her hair. "I could and did, madam, because I doubt very much that the Misses Potterfell would have approved my sleeping in your room tonight without our being married.''

"You're not sleeping in my room!''

"Oh, but I *am*, Miss Faelyn.'' He was steaming heat against her nape, lifting her hair—and, oh, the blazing stars, were those his lips? "You see, my dear, I'm not letting you out of my sight. Not until we've found the Willowmoon Knot and all its precious silver. Maybe not even then.''

His last threat frightened her most of all. Not because she wanted to be free of his prison, but because—dear God—she'd grown too fond of it.

Everything in the Belle Heather made Jack feel enormous, a fuming, foul-tempered giant in the tree-root home of a pair of ancient, chittering elves—from the low, timbered ceilings, to the small windows, to the diminutive Potterfell sisters themselves. They were fretting over the deliciously cunning Miss Faelyn as though she'd come limping home from Waterloo on crutches, were forcing a biscuit and a cure-all cup of tea into her hands.

"You should have told us of your husband troubles when you first arrived, Lady Rushford. You poor, frightened dear. And so newly married.''

"So *very* newly married.'' Mairey was having her hand patted by one of the sisters and was sending Jack a blistering, narrow-eyed scowl over the woman's bobbing, blue-gray curls. She'd gotten herself into this particular spot. She'd run from him at the first opportunity, with a fistful of information that she had intended to hide from him. He'd had no choice but to find her and keep her.

Keep her? Like keeping a handful of diamond dust from blowing through his fingers. Damn the woman!

"Have you dears any children?" The other Miss Potterfell had toddled over to Jack and was smiling innocently up at him.

"Children?" He'd almost bellowed the nonsensical word, but it had softened in his throat to a breath of air that made him look across the room at Mairey. He remembered her mimed belly at the Tower and the stirring it had caused in his chest.

"Not yet," he whispered through a peculiar tightness in his chest, imagining children with Mairey Faelyn. Bright haired and wild, reckless hearted, like she was. And they'd have all those incorrigible aunts to love them.

Anna and Caro and Poppy. And his own sisters. And a doting grandmother who must have other grandchildren already.

He wasn't very good at keeping the people he loved. Love was trust and devotion. He was careless.

Not like the dragon-hearted woman who, at the moment, looked as though she might castrate him with her bare hands if she could get close enough.

Children? His chest felt huge, and stuffed with hope and fear.

"Sleeping with a robin's egg beneath your pillow helps, or so I've heard," said the first Miss Potterfell.

"Now, now, sister. Children will come to these two in God's time. You see, my dears, neither of us have been married, but we can well imagine the trials of a young bride and the demands of an older gentleman.''

Older? He was barely past thirty.

And Mairey was sneering at him.

"Come, Wife," he said, hunching over to avoid smacking his head into the ceiling beams—though it might serve to knock some sense into him. "You and I have some important matters to discuss."

The leave-taking was a gauntlet of patting and tsking and more fertility suggestions, but Jack finally herded his 'bride' through the Potterfell parlor and up the two flights of narrow stairs to the garret room. She was muttering as he ushered her through the door, but he paused on the landing long enough to give the misses below a final wave before he shut the door and faced the fuming Miss Faelyn.

"Oh, damn you, Rushford!" She drew herself up for a huge blow. "Damn you! *Damn* you!"

"Yes, you're probably right." He locked the door pointedly behind him, hoping to rouse the anger he'd felt that noon when he'd returned to Drakestone early, and *only* because he couldn't stay away. Because even a single night seemed too long. "But once a man is past redemption he really hasn't anything to lose, has he? Now, madam, you will show me Adam Runville's will, and then you will tell me why you skulked away as soon as I was gone."

"I don't have his will. And I don't skulk."

"Runville's probate record, then."

"I only have a copy, and I didn't bring it with me."

"Liar." He could see that well enough in the side shift of her eyes, a glance that swung back full of self-righteousness,

"I traveled lightly, Rushford. I only meant to be here overnight." She stood like a sentinel in the center of the small room.

"You're a brilliant researcher, Miss Faelyn; you would never have left such an important document behind, would never have relied only on your memory. Let me see the copy."

"I don't have it."

He could play her game; he knew rules that she hadn't even dreamed of and had the will to enforce them. "Then take off your shirtwaist."

The woman blushed instantly all the way to her hairline. "What did you say?"

"You heard me clearly. I meant what I said. Now." Jack took a threatening step toward her. "Take off your shirtwaist."

"I will not! And you, sir, will die trying to take it off me!"

He'd die *of* it, of the sheer pleasure. She'd covered her bosom, her hands and arms crossed like wings against a storm.

"Then so be it." He took another, more menacing step; allowed her to dash behind a chair, deeper into the room. The move gained her nothing. It trapped her completely against the window wall and the dying light of the day, and made golden webs of her hair.

"You're a monster, Jackson Rushford." She was

breathing as though he'd chased her down a wooded path.

"And you are a liar, Mairey Faelyn. I want to see the copy of Runville's probate record. I know that you keep your precious notes in there." Jack pointed to the woman's bosom, where her outrage billowed against the wool of her jacket. He hoped to hell that his own cheeks weren't flushed as hotly as they felt, because his imagination was suddenly overfilled with plans for her creamy breasts, as it had been since he'd met the woman. And the room was just too close for that kind of imagining. "I've seen you stash your notes in your . . . between your . . . in your damn shirtwaist!"

Her eyes had grown enormous in her outrage. "You're mad!"

"Perhaps, Miss Faelyn. But if you don't remove your shirtwaist so that I may retrieve this copy from its hiding place, then I shall remove it myself!"

And he would find that place far too enticing. She was too lovely, smelled too fragrant. He'd never had to threaten a woman to remove her clothes, and prayed to God, who had once walked the earth and fought all of its temptations, that the foolish woman would cooperate and show him Runville's record. But he would have it one way or another, if only to make a point that he was in charge and that he would not tolerate secrets between them.

"Very well, Rushford. If you insist. But I am disappointed in you!"

She shrugged off her jacket, revealing tiny pleats

of linen, and rich, round, unstayed bouncing that entreated his hands like just-picked summer pears. And now the foolish woman was reaching behind her neck for . . . what? The buttons of her shirtwaist. . . .

He shouldn't have dared her, and was about to call back his demand when she tugged a silver chain from beneath her crisp collar and slipped it off over her head. A tiny key dangled from the end.

"The copy of Runville's probate record is there in my Gladstone, in an envelope. You're welcome to it. It's nothing more than I told you when you asked."

Swallowing hard, Jack thunked the Gladstone onto the chest at the foot of the bed and managed to fit the key into the lock on his first try. She stood over him as he fumbled past her silky smallclothes and her stockings before finding the envelope and the probate records.

"There, you see," she said, her indignant huff riffling the underside of his jaw. "Just as I told you."

It took all his concentration just to read, " ' . . . six gilt knives, bonne-handled; one silv'red disk, anciently ornamented; one brass ewere . . .' "

"One silv'red disk, anciently ornamented," she repeated, retrieving the note and stuffing it back into the envelope, as though that were the end of it. "The Willowmoon Knot."

"That's all? You came all this way, made this fuss for a 'silv'red disk, anciently ornamented'?"

"It's the Willowmoon Knot, Jack. What else could it be?"

"A fish plate, a pot lid, a coronation medal." He dropped onto the bedchest, utterly bewildered and frustrated to the core.

"I'm sorry, but that is the way and the risk of looking for treasure. Down one trail until it's cold, then up the next. If you find it too frustrating, then maybe next time you should stay behind and leave it to me. I was right not to wait for you."

"You couldn't have been more wrong." He'd partnered himself with a lunatic: a head-spinning, riddle-speaking lunatic, one whom he would and might have to follow to the ends of the earth and back again. "You could damn well have left me a note."

"What would that note have said?" She leaned down to him, her nose an inch from his. " 'Found clue to the treasure. Am going to Donowell to pick it up.' You'd have skinned me for breaching your security."

"You're intelligent enough to have been more cryptic than that." He stood up and she stayed, her chin nearly touching his chest. "My point is that you're a woman. You shouldn't be traipsing around the countryside without an escort. Without *me*."

"It's what I have always done."

"Not any more. Not while you and I are partners. Do you understand me?"

"So very, very well, sir." She circled behind him and dumped the contents of her Gladstone into the middle of the bed. "Now, please, go take a long walk. I'm tired, and I would like to wash up and go to bed."

"Oh, no, madam. I'm not going down those

stairs alone. You'll have to trust me that I will keep my back turned." Jack shoved the chair toward the window and dropped himself onto its flower-flouncy cushion.

"Afraid to face the Misses Potterfell and their questions about our troubled 'marriage'?"

"Terrified, madam."

"So am I." He loved her laughter, loved that she was ever free with the rippling rise and fall of it, whether she was angry, wistful, or plainly amused—as she seemed to be at the moment.

He heard the dash of water in the basin and a rustling of clothes, apparently taking his promise to avert his eyes as gospel.

Not wishing to disabuse her of the notion, he settled firmly into the chair, enjoying the sounds of her, enjoying the soft, evening breeze as it blew in off the blue-dark sea through the open window.

He still didn't know what to make of the woman's artful trip to Donowell, or of her conveniently discovering Runville's probate records the moment he was gone to Cornwall.

She'd told him all she knew of the Willow-moon's history, and was forever regaling him with her Celtic legends. Yet sometimes he felt that his sense of control over the situation was entirely an illusion, concocted by Mairey for his benefit.

He wanted to believe that she was plain-dealing and honorable. But too often he recalled their initial meeting: her outrage and her refusal. And her absurd declaration that she would mine the silver with a shovel if she found it. His partner was as passionately intent upon the treasure as he was; she had been raised up from childhood to see its discovery.

But Mairey Faelyn wasn't a fortune hunter. She was crafty, intelligent, and heroically devoted to her family; her clothes were simple, and she found her pleasure in telling fairy tales to her sisters. He couldn't imagine her sweeping through Paris on a shopping holiday, throwing lavish dinner parties, or buying villas in Spain.

"What will you do with your part of the Willowmoon treasure, Miss Faelyn?"

"Do with it?" She became so silent that he thought she had vanished. He almost turned to see for himself, but then she spoke. "I don't know. I haven't thought that far."

He heard her strike a match, then her corner of the room filled with light. The sea breeze gusted and nudged the window on its hinges, the gentle movement catching her reflection in a single pane.

The glass was old and rippled, making silvery clouds of her nightdress and her hair.

He would have closed his eyes, but there was no rest for him there.

"Thank you, my lord." He heard the bed creak, and he turned slightly in the chair, wondering if she'd meant that she was safely tucked beneath the counterpane and that he was free to move.

"For what?" He stood casually, hoping for the best.

"For keeping your word." She was sitting in the middle of the bed, covered to her waist by a quilt of blue-printed country scenes, bent over one of her field books, making small notes with a pencil.

"What's that you're writing?"

" 'Sleeping with a robin's egg beneath your pillow helps' . . . Hmmm." She looked up at him and touched the end of her pencil to her mouth. "Do you suppose that Miss Potterfell believes that the robin's egg aids in the conception of a child, or that its presence under the pillow acts as an agent to increase passion, thereby bringing the hopeful parents together more fervently?"

Jack knew his mouth was agape, but he couldn't help it until he took a deeper breath. This wasn't a subject for idle conversation.

"I don't know, Miss Faelyn. But I'll be damned if I'm going to go downstairs and ask her."

"I didn't mean you to ask. I should have done so myself, but I was too furious with you at the time." She was looking around the room, studying every stick of furniture. "Where are you going to sleep?"

"On the floor." He'd decided on that strategy the moment he'd seen the bed.

"That's absurd. There's room here." She patted the pillow and moved to the left side.

There was nothing like confession to clear the boards and point out the threats. "Do you know that I'm mad for you, Miss Faelyn?"

She put her notebook down on her lap. "What do you mean, 'mad'? What have I done now?"

"I mean that I feel very much like one of your Oxford swains. Every thought I have in my head right now involves making love to you until dawn."

"Really?" Damn the woman for not being

shocked, appalled, threatened at the very least; for searching his face and then lighting so boldly on the front of his trousers.

"Really. So I am trapped here with you, madam, in a very precipitous state—"

"Hoisted on your own petard." She cocked her head, smiling—actually waiting for a reply—not a bit repentant over her inexcusable knowledge of the male anatomy. What else did she know? And who the hell did she learn it from?

"If we weren't all the way up in a third-floor garret and if the ocean cliffs weren't a hundred feet below—"

"And if the formidable Potterfell sisters weren't just outside our marital chamber, waiting for our reconciliation and news of a child on the way, you'd take yourself off to a dip in the ocean."

"Exactly." The word came out in a strangled heap.

She leaned over to the bedside table and blew out the light, plunging the room into a milky, moon-on-the-sea darkness. She made soft noises into her pillow, sighs that he wanted to feel against his mouth. He was still hard as a rock for her, his fists clenched as firmly as his teeth.

"Sleep wherever you like, my lord. I wouldn't be here with you alone in the dark if I didn't trust you absolutely."

He slept the night on a very uncomfortable rug.

Chapter 10

Mairey woke to the soft sound of snoring coming from the floor beside her bed.

"Balforge," she murmured, rolling quietly to the edge to steal a glance at him. The sight made her blush.

He was dreadfully handsome—even as he lay on his back, sprawl-legged on the blanket, his pillow astray under one knee, his shirttails bunched to his ribs. His stomach was flat, wonderfully rippled, darkly furred against the white edge of his drawers that peaked out of his trousers.

Making love until dawn. She wondered what that would have been like—if she'd confessed a similar madness for him. She'd studied artistic renderings of the act of sexual union: Greek statues, Flemish etchings, lovely pastel-hued Oriental paintings, all with couples cavorting together happily, intricately, the women as ecstatically active as the men.

Hardly the lie-still-and-think-of-England attitude she'd heard rumors about. Jack wasn't the sort to let a lover lie quietly. He was an explorer, a rav-

171

isher, a man of tumultuous endeavors. She suspected they would have been ecstatic together. Until dawn.

Ah, well. It was an overpowering fantasy, the adult part of her fairy tale. But it wasn't meant to be.

She rolled off the other side of the bed, washed quickly under the tent of her nightgown, and then dressed, all the while listening to her sleeping dragon.

He awoke with a roar and shot to his feet, looking as though he'd had a fight with a cyclone. Mairey left him to dress on his own and did battle with the Potterfell sisters, rescuing the man from his own petard.

John Runville's will had been proved in the parish of Donowell, and a list of his household goods had been duly recorded by the archdeacon in the year 1707.

And, bless them, the clerks of Donowell parish could give lessons to the Keeper of the Records at the Tower. The documents were filed with care and precision and kept in a temperate room on the second floor of the city hall. The registrar had been gracious, helpful, and had left them alone with the registry.

Mairey was discovering that sitting beside Rushford was much like living in a hut on the side of a volcano. He thumped the table and rumbled out opinions, leaned over her shoulder and caused her heart to tear around inside her.

" 'In the name of God, Amen,' " he read from

the top of Runville's will, one brow slanted and distinctly piratical when he turned to her. "What is this?"

He smelled of the Potterfells' lemon tarts, and his face was shaved so clean that she wanted to run her hands over his skin.

"In times past, sir, wills all began with a similar divine endorsement. This was a sacred trust. God would condemn those who might try to scuttle the wishes of the deceased."

Rushford turned the page over and ran his finger down the list of John Runville's chattel. "A feather bed, half-dozen trunks, a pair of andirons, spoons . . ."

He stood abruptly, straddling the bench. "By God, it's here!"

The Willowmoon! Every day another miracle, a step closer. She ought to be as wildly happy as Rushford, but there was a converse effect that she didn't want to think about just yet.

Rushford leaned down from his great height, threaded his fingers through the hair at her nape, and brought her mouth so very close to his that she thought he was going to kiss her.

"I like this game of yours, Mairey Faelyn." His voice was low and seeking, that possessive rumble she'd come to adore. He touched his lips to her cheek at the corner of her mouth, but he went no further—only murmured, "I like it fine."

Her skin on fire for him, Mairey turned her head and caught more of his mouth, stole a half-kiss from him.

"Do you, my lord?"

He knew what she'd done and looked devilishly pleased with himself. "It's like drilling into the earth and bringing up bore after bore of worthless basalt or granite. And then one day, just when you're about to toss it in for slag, up comes a shining core glittering with gold, winking at you in the sunlight."

Mairey felt a great hollow open in her chest; heard the warning echo of the dragon stirring there. She was grateful for the reminder. It made it easy for her to pull out of his entangling embrace.

"It isn't a game, my lord." She yanked Runville's will off the table and scooted away to the opposite side of the room, where the light was stronger and the air was less heady. "We're far from done here."

His frown was quizzical, patient. "Yes, I know."

"John Runville might have had the Knot when he died, but he bequeathed it and 'various pagan artefacts' to the Moorlands Museum."

"And where would that be?"

"According to Runville's will, it's in York."

Another day with Rushford in tow, another step closer to the Willowmoon.

"The minster storage vaults hold many a treasure, Lord Rushford, since the museum facilities in Yorkshire are far too small to display everything. But I don't recall ever hearing of a Moorlands Museum."

The minster storage vaults weren't in the minster at all, but in a low building near the deanery, with yards, maybe miles, of shelves, and row after row of boxes.

"We'll have a look anyway," Jack said, convinced that every antiquarian was fusty, rumpled, and stooped. Every one of them but his own Mairey Faelyn.

God, she'd almost kissed him, and would have done so if he hadn't spooked her. She'd smelled of whimsey and violets—still did, though she had closed up tightly for some reason.

Certainly not from maidenly embarrassment. She'd never blinked when he had supported various parts of her as she'd scrambled around on the crates and trunks in the Tower. She'd told him point-blank that she was a virgin. And just last night she had not only invited him into her bed but had also stared unflinchingly at his erection.

And then there was that kiss he'd purloined a few nights ago—that luscious ruse about the honey.

His partner was becoming an unexpected, incorrigible complication. She was also, at the moment, spinning another of her fairy tales for still another enchanted admirer, though this one wore a cassock.

"You see, sir," Mairey was saying, "Lord Rushford has commissioned my father—a London silversmith—to design and cast a Celtic brooch for Prince Albert's birthday. At Queen Victoria's direct request, you know."

"Yes, yes." The curator smiled indulgently at Jack, then went back to smiling at Mairey.

"And since my father was unable to attend his lordship himself, I've been assigned the task of showing him some historical examples of Celtic artifacts. We've been through the British Museum, the Ashmolean, and a dozen others, but his lordship says that he won't be satisfied until he sees *everything*."

She gave the curator a sharp little huff of impatience, with a nod toward Jack, which seemed to satisfy the man that they were dealing with just another persnickety member of the peerage. In a few more minutes they were rid of the curator and alone in another vast vault, oil lamps blazing, and Miss Faelyn's eyes bright with passion for this treasure of hers.

Was it incomprehensible for him to wish they burned as brightly, as enduringly, for him?

"Remember now, Rushford. The Knot is about four inches across and a quarter-inch thick, with serpentine patterns on its face."

"Or so you believe."

She sighed. "Belief is all we've got."

She sent him off on his own quest, making him promise to show her anything at all that might be made of metal, reminding him that silver could tarnish to coal black. Every door and drawer he opened revealed an oddity: stuffed owls, caches of glass beads, or Roman coins.

The woman was in her glory, sharing her discoveries and her laughter with him. She brought life and light to stone statues with her stories of magical springs and great serpents, and gave warmth to the sinuous tracings of bronze.

She was singular and impossible and he was falling madly for her.

"What have you got there, Rushford?" she

asked, fitting her fingers lightly in the crook of his elbow to peer into the coffer in his arms, heating the spot in an instant.

"Arrowheads, it says here." He brought the box down and opened the lid. "Flint."

"Elf bolts, my lord." Her smile was teasing, daring him to doubt her facts.

"My name is Jack," he said. "Will you call me that?"

Her eyebrows twitched into a tiny frown. "Why?"

"Besides making me feel decades older than you, Miss Faelyn, I'd like very much to call you Mairey." Jack felt a telling warmth radiating from his chest. "It's what I call you in my head, how I think of you. And I don't much like having to remember whether I'm talking to you or just thinking about you."

She studied him from beneath those fret-winged brows, a grin at the corners of her mouth. "Are you so easily confused?"

That was neither the question nor the answer he was looking for. "Will you call me Jack?"

More frowning, as though he'd asked her to bear his children. Then a noncommittal "I shall try."

"May I call you Mairey?"

"If it'll help keep your thoughts sorted, I suppose you'd better."

Rascal woman.

The rear of the room was more organized and better labeled. Against one wall was a set of wide, flat, glass-windowed drawers.

They found blue glassware in one, then a drawer

each of tiny stone heads and animal figures. When the next two drawers revealed golden Celtic torcs and silvered utensils, Jack couldn't help but hope for the next one. Its window was obscured by a cloth, and the drawer was unmarked.

"Valuable?" he asked.

"Could be sensitive to light or dust." Mairey cast him a hopeful smile and pulled the drawer to its fullest extension, then lifted the cloth away.

"Phalluses," she said with a little sigh.

"*What* did you say?"

"Phalluses—carved out of stone. Ah, and here's one of wood. All of them Celtic, I believe."

There were two dozen of them, in various sizes and states of repair, but each one in full arousal. She picked up a thick stalk of limestone, carved a few thousand years before, looking every inch its fleshly double. "These are penises, Jack. The male member. Surely you recognize—"

"I'm fully aware of what they are, Miss Faelyn." The woman picked up another and studied its tip with exacting care. "What I can't fathom is how you could possibly know what they are."

She laughed lightly and looked up at him. "The phallus is a fundamental and pervasive symbol in antiquity—as common as flint arrowheads and stone axes. I have a collection of my own in my library."

"Of arrowheads and stone axes." *Please, God.*

"Yes, and of phallic objects."

"A *collection* of them? Good God, Mairey, where did you get such a thing?"

"Post-Roman." She examined another, holding

the perfectly proportioned length of pink-speckled granite to the light, her fingers gripped around its shaft in a gesture so innocently, dizzyingly sensual that Jack thought he might have to leave the room.

"My grandmother started the collection, and became quite the expert, in fact."

"Your grandmother." Of course. Why not? These Faelyns were an eccentric lot.

"My mother enlarged it . . . so to speak"—she smiled—"and now the collection is mine."

Jack hoped to hell she didn't look carefully at his trousers. "I don't know what to say."

"Are you uncomfortable with the subject, Jack?"

"Hell, yes!" The woman's brows shot into her hairline at his bellow. "No! I'm not uncomfortable! What I mean is that—frankly, Miss Faelyn—"

"Mairey. Because you are speaking aloud at the moment, not just thinking—"

"Yes, *Mairey*. It's just that I've never in my life had a conversation with a woman while standing in front of a drawer full of . . . of . . ." Completely drained of words he could use in public, he flapped his arm in the direction of the drawer.

"Ancient stone phallic objects," she offered.

"Exactly." Not that he was intimidated by the specimens in the drawer, or by the one she was fondling. He would measure up against the lot of them quite nicely, thank you. He nearly said as much, but Mairey had gone back to her minute examination, and he was having trouble breathing. "This isn't a subject to be discussed between a man and a woman."

"My parents did."

Jack felt feverish. Sweat ran like molten rivers down his back as the woman handled one ancient but hugely virile penis after another.

"In fact, my father presented my mother with a phallus on every one of her birthdays that I can remember."

"Christ, woman! They were married to each other."

"Devoted." She shut the offending drawer and opened the one below it. "Ah, ha! Just as I expected, Jack. You see, the Celts had a great reverence for their women, too. A belly-goddess."

The figure in Mairey's hand was beautiful and lushly primitive, with large, ripe, pink granite breasts at rest on a belly full of child, and a glistening, hand-polished cleft between her kneeling thighs.

He swallowed hard, his pulse dancing madly, his own phallus as alive as if it were sheathed within Mairey.

"I suppose your grandmother collected those, too."

"Oh, no," she said, smiling fondly at the figure. "But my grandfather did."

Jack threw out his hands. "Well, fine. Fascinating. But it's time we get back to looking for that Willow-knotty thing." He broke away to a place where he could adjust his clothes, grateful for the fullness of his greatcoat.

Jackson Rushford, you're a prude!

Mairey never would have credited it for an instant. But he had turned as red as a beet the moment she had opened the drawer, and redder still with every phallus she'd picked up.

She hadn't meant to tease him, but he was disarmingly handsome with streaks of crimson on his cheeks and smudging his brow.

And all that tight-lipped stammering! The blustering! She'd nearly laughed. But he was a prideful man, and as much as she distrusted him, she would never purposely hurt him.

She had always found the ridges and curves of stone-worked penises elegant and . . . well, oddly stirring. But still, they had only seemed like ancient carved stone to her.

Until today, when Jack had taken such a blushing interest in the stones she held in her hands. They'd seemed heavier with him looking on, vibrant, and warmed through to the core.

Organic. Yes, and alive.

Mairey flushed to the tips of her toes.

Every single, lovely one of them had been Jack's penis! That's where her imagination had gone, running wild in the woods—no wonder she'd been light-headed!

She peeked around the corner of the next set of shelves. Jack was rattling through a cabinet of goblets, scrubbing at his hair and muttering, his coat buttoned to his collar.

What the devil was she going to do with the man? With the days and the weeks and the years stretching out before them? She loved being around him, loved his humor, and the way he smelled of sandalwood soap in the morning and woodsmoke in the evenings. His nightly visits to the lodge had become a precious end to the day.

"Excuse me." The curator came through the doorway, a piece of paper fluttering in his hand. "Ah, Lord Rushford! A telegraph message for you."

Jack took the note from the man and read it swiftly. "My God, no. Not Glad Heath."

"What is it?" Mairey ran to his side, fearing news from Drakestone—Caro falling out of a tree or Poppy lost in the woods.

"A cave-in. Christ." He'd gone pale, his great hands shaking, even as his jaw squared and he looked up at the curator. "Can I get a message sent back?"

"Certainly."

Jack was already scrawling something on the back of the telegram, efficient and furious.

"Tell them I'm on my way," he said, handing the note to the man.

"I'll see to it, my lord." The curator left on the run.

"The Willowmoon will have to wait, Mairey. Come." He grabbed her hand and her satchel and started down the hallway, as though she would naturally agree to follow him anywhere.

Mairey twisted out of his grip and drew away against the cold wall. "Where are you taking me?"

"I've got a ceiling of coal collapsed in one of my tunnels. You're coming with me."

Trouble in your lair, Sir Dragon? "To one of your mines? Where?"

"Two hours by train. I don't know what I'll find when I get there."

Death, surely. And broken lives. A chill shuddered through her. He couldn't force her to go with him. Not to a mine.

"I can't help you, Jack."

He slipped his fingers through hers, brought their clasped hands between them, and kissed her knuckles. "And I can't think of anyone who could help me more."

"How?" Her heart was in her throat: a coward's heart that didn't want to know what kind of man she had grown so fond of.

"Bring your fairy tales, Mairey—the children will need them."

Chapter 11

Glad Heath was a devilish place. Its slag-barren mountain and bristling silhouette of infernal machines was visible for miles before the train thundered out of the dark moors and into the brightly lit station that served the spur line into Rushford's colliery.

The platform was swarming with men running alongside the railcar as it steamed to a stop.

"Stay close, Mairey." Jack was on his feet and stepping down from the private compartment before the car came to rest.

Mairey watched from the top step of the train as he was swallowed up for a moment by a surging sea of coal-blackened miners. They pulled at him, shouting, each one vying for his attention, until he finally lifted himself back onto the step beside Mairey.

"One at a time!" he bellowed in a voice that must have carried itself into the very bowels of the mountain, as surely as it stilled the chaos at his feet. "Where is Stephen Richmond? Stephen! I want my engineers here immediately."

He got a hundred answers at once, waved them all quiet, and pointed at a man. "You, Gadrick! Where's your boss?"

"Inside, my lord." The frantic man shoved closer. "He's one of 'em that's trapped inside."

"Oh, Christ." Jack rubbed his temple but recovered an instant later. "Where?"

"The Shalecross, sir. Number Four, at a thousand feet. And the ventilation shaft with it."

"At the new steam-winding? Bloody hell!"

Jack slammed hold of the handrail and swabbed his face with his sleeve. So, the man's investment had gone awry. No wonder he was angry. He was probably already counting up his losses.

"Who else, Gadrick? How many more?"

"Eight men, sir—as far as we know." General agreement murmured across the platform, then all those faces looked up at Jack again, as though he were their savior and not their bloodthirsty master.

"All right. I'll want names, Gadrick." He swept his arm across the crowd, an iniquitous saint dispensing a costly blessing. "And I want the team bosses to meet me in the schoolhouse in ten minutes."

Schoolhouse? A schoolhouse at a colliery? Of course. There would be children here, hiding out from the nightmare and the terror, clinging to each other, lying bleak-eyed and wakeful in their beds.

Eight fathers trapped in the earth. All at the mercy of the man who was calling out orders and dispatching streams of miners into his pit with picks, to his timber-yard for shoring-stock, sending word to his Strathfield colliery and to London for more engineers and more equipment.

Jackson Rushford was masterful at his disasters.

Above and beyond the rail station, an undulating trail of flickering orange coiled up the side of the mountain and disappeared into a gaping hole that must have been the mouth of the pit. She was trying to make sense of the light and shadows when Jack loomed on the step below her, his eyes shining with intensity.

"Will you visit the families for me?"

She bit back a curse and yanked her hand out of his when he took hold of it. "Which families would that be?"

He sighed, shook his head. "I need someone who can talk with the families of the men who're trapped down there, to let them know what's happening. Will you do that for me?"

He was asking her to represent his villainy, to excuse it to the grieving widows and fatherless children. Now, there was madness. What would her father say?

"I can't. You said fairy tales."

He seemed surprised, disappointed—a look that made her stomach twist. "Please, Mairey. This is leagues outside the bounds of our partnership, but I need you here." He captured her hand and held it this time, unwilling to let it go. "The waiting is hellish for the wives. And so much worse for the children as they wonder if they'll ever see their fathers again."

A shadow crossed his resolute features, lingered within his plea, and made her heart contract.

"I'll do it for the children, Jack." She couldn't refuse him in the midst of a catastrophe—not even one of his own making.

He led her swiftly through the crowded, dark lanes of stone block row houses, past windows and the tiny faces peering out of the pale lamplight. People had gathered in the torchlight outside the schoolhouse, reaching out to Jack as he quickly passed them, seeming so grateful for his nod or a clasp of his hands.

Such misbegotten devotion.

The schoolhouse was a surprisingly tidy, white-washed place, with large windows and a wall heavy with books, reminiscent of Jack's own library. His team bosses broke into a brawl of opinions and facts as Jack made his way to the front.

"Austin, you tell me!" he shouted, and order descended in the echo.

A scruffy-bearded man rocketed to his feet, his hat crushed in his fist. "Richmond took a crew down to inspect the balance pit track, said it didn't look right, it was buckling. Just before the whistle, it was. We've been digging ever since, waiting—"

"Five hours. For me, yes. What else do we know?" Jack continued asking questions sharply, writing with fury and huge strokes on a set of maps, making circles and crosses along tunnels and tracks.

Mairey could only wait and watch him conduct his urgent inquest, while one of the bosses compiled the list of families for her to visit. In the midst of it all, she helped Jack don a set of leather over-trousers and a jacket; then laced and tied his hob-nailed boots as he carried on his meeting.

It felt wrong to be there in the enemy camp, fastening the dragon into his armor while he made plans to minimize his losses. But as the meeting broke up and Jack settled a metal cap on his head, as he cinched a vicious-looking pick to his work belt, she was struck with a sudden, terrifying realization.

"Where are you going, Jack?"

He was dressed like the other miners, and already had a black streak slashed across his forehead that resembled a fatal bruise. "Into the mine—where else?"

"You can't."

"Can't I?" He gave a small, dry laugh, watching her as he clipped a screened lamp onto his belt.

"Jack, it's dangerous."

"It is *now*. Those are *my* people down there, and I plan to bring them up personally—and alive, God willing."

"But—" She had expected him to stay safely above ground, to conduct the rescue without creasing his collar, without breaking into a sweat. Without putting his own life at risk.

Now he looked as fragile as the rest of them—made of flesh and blood and crushable bone.

"Dooley has the list of the men who are missing," he told her quietly, with a grave intimacy that drew her unwillingly into his circle. "I'll send someone to you as soon as I know anything."

"And what do I tell these families?" What

would she tell Anna and Caro and Poppy if their Lord Jack died inside the mine?

He studied her, his mouth firm. "Tell them I'll do my best for them."

His best against a whole mountain!

He turned to go, but she grabbed his wrist and held him tightly. "Be careful, Jack."

He answered with a half-smile and rakish lift of his devil-dark brow, clamped his cap on tighter, then walked into the swarm of miners and out into the night.

"Godspeed," she whispered, praying that God looked after men like Jackson Rushford.

Jack and his team bosses clambered over the rubble, their lanterns casting fitful shadows inside the tunnel.

"It shouldn't have fallen, sir," Gadrick said, craning his neck toward the roof of coal a dozen feet overhead.

"Hellfire," Jack said, sliding his hand along a ridge of glistening new coal, "a new seam."

They were a thousand feet into the incline shaft that had once been the main Shalecross seam, a vein so ancient that it had been opened in the thirteenth century. It had played out centuries ago and now functioned as a faithful friend, holding back the mountain above it to allow the miners to follow the crosscut passageways into other seams. The walls and the roof had been tightly shored up, were minutely and frequently inspected. The shaft was ready for the installation of the new steam-winding system that would drag coal trams up the rails to the main shaft and then into the pit brow more quickly and far more safely.

And now old Shalecross had given up a secret stash of coal she'd been hiding just beyond the shell of rock. Odds were that the stash wasn't large and needed only more supporting, but it had caused a room-sized collapse into the main tunnel—impossible to predict, impossible to shore against.

But the responsibility was his alone, and it made him ill to think of the lives that were at stake.

"Richmond must have suspected it when they were measuring for the new track, sir," Wilson said, leaping out of the way of the brigade of workers who were pulling loose coal and rock away from the fall. "He didn't want anyone but his crew to follow him in here."

How deep this new roof of coal descended along the tunnel, only time and toil would tell. He prayed that Richmond and his men had been far beyond it when it fell in. Even then, without fresh air circulating from the venting system, the coal gas might kill them. There was no time to waste.

"All right, I want every coal tram in the entire colliery on these tracks." Jack tossed a clod of coal into an empty tub. "Then bring everyone you can find into the tunnel. We've no winch, no windings to help us. We'll dig the men out of here the old-fashioned way: loading one tram after the other until the rubble's gone."

Jack gave the job to his best team bosses, then rounded up a crew of young men who had more courage than sense and led them with his maps to a shaft that ran parallel to Shalecross Number Four for two hundred feet before swinging east and diving deeper into the mountain.

"There's twenty feet of solid rock between us and the Shalecross tunnel, gentleman," Jack said, hanging his lamp on a timberpeg. "We're going to dig a connecting tunnel, and with any luck, we'll be shaking hands with Richmond before noon."

God help them if it took longer. Twelve hours was just about how much air the men had to sustain them.

Jack set his muscles and took a satisfying swing at the granite wall with his pick. A fist-sized chunk came spinning off and smacked him in the knee.

The men were grinning at him. "Pretty good, boss," said the youngest, a strapping lad that reminded Jack of himself a decade ago.

"Not bad for an old man, eh?" Jack gave another swing, following through with arms and shoulders that had labored too long at a desk. The impact made him grunt. But he worked steadily with the other men, each doing a five-minute shift at a killing speed, then stretching out their kinks as another man took his place.

Two hours later they had removed less than three feet of stone, and Jack began to despair.

"Lord Rushford wishes you to know that he's doing his very best for you." Mairey repeated Jack's words a hundred times during the interminable night as she went from house to house, giving comfort in his name to the women and children whose husbands and fathers and sons were held hostage by his despicable mine. She had prayed beside the families, embraced the children as fiercely as if they were her sisters, wept and wiped away others' tears.

She had sought proof of withered souls in Jack's colliery, and instead she had discovered not only unflagging faith and bone-bred courage to carry on but also a terrifying acceptance of the risks. Disasters were part of Glad Heath's history, and these people blamed no one, especially not Jack.

"We are blessed to be here in Glad Heath," one woman had said through her tears, clutching her children. "He's a fine man. His lordship won't let us down."

"If any man can find a way to rescue my husband, it's Jackson Rushford."

"There is no man in the world like our Jack."

Their Jack.

The truth was that he'd also become *her* Jack. And she was petrified for him, couldn't imagine never seeing him again.

She'd received three oral messages from him, delivered each time by a different young man. The messages were brief and impersonal, but she'd clung to them like a lifeline.

Yet he was only as safe as his last message, and that had been hours ago—and her heart leaped to her throat every time she looked toward the mine and saw the bonfires on the hillside.

He was down there in the stench and the steam and the darkness, and she couldn't do a thing to help him but pray.

He'd asked her for fairy tales, and so Mairey

gathered the frightened children into the school-house to soothe them with her stories.

And did her best to bring back the light.

Be safe, Jack.

Six hours remaining and at least a dozen feet to go. Jack changed out his crew, bringing on fresh brawn, but he stayed himself until he was forced to meet the train from his Strathfield works.

He wanted to see Mairey—just see her, because he couldn't afford more time than that. She'd been sharp tempered and accusing, as though his reck-lessness had caused the accident.

She'd have to get used to the dangers inherent in mining. He would take the silver from the Wil-lowmoon site in the same way: an open pit as long as it was profitable, and then following the individ-ual veins with a shafts-and-tunnel system.

The streets were nearly deserted, almost peace-ful. The night wind had picked up a laughing mel-ody in its dance through Glad Heath, and not at all to his surprise, he found Mairey at the end of it.

The lamps in the schoolhouse were turned low and sleepy, and all the chairs and tables were pushed to the perimeter. The floor was littered with blankets and children, some soundly asleep in their mothers' arms, most looking up at Mairey as she spun one of her stories.

"Gwynella and the Enchanter." Oddly, the En-chanter had a different name now: Balforge. And he seemed to be a dragon.

They had come miles since he'd first seen her surrounded by so many captivated children. She'd been the irascible Miss Faelyn then; he'd been boorish. Three weeks, and everything had changed: Mairey had become the reason that he rose in the morning, the reason he came home.

He was about to join her when Gadrick caught his elbow. ''Sir, the train from Strathfield will be here in a moment.''

It was for the best. He had work to do.

A half hour later he was supervising the addition of more coal tubs onto the lift chain at the shaft, and soon coal was coming out of the Shalecross at an exhausting rate, bringing hope along with it.

But his place was in the rescue passage. So with the better part of four hours remaining, he grabbed up his pick when his shift came and slammed his vengeance into the solid rock, letting the shock of it echo up through his arms, feeling the sting of the blisters breaking on his hands and building again.

He knew the pulse of Glad Heath as he knew the sound of his own heartbeat. He'd been born in a cottage down the lane, had lived there until the night his father died.

That grisly night had come on the heels of a cave-in—one tragedy following another. Cahill had sent his strikebreakers to make war against Jack's father and the other miners, and his life had changed forever. He might have failed his sisters and his mother completely; he had surely betrayed the promise he'd made to his father to keep them safe; but he'd at least avenged the family's memory.

Glad Heath was his now. It had been idle for ten years before Jack had acquired it from that bastard

Cahill's estate. The man's profane practices, his cruel disregard for his workers, had assured that his mine would eventually fail. And it had, while Jack was in exile in Canada, making his own fortune.

The irony had been vastly satisfying when he'd returned with his wealth to Britain and found Glad Heath on the auction block. No one wanted a derelict mine—no one but Jack. He bought it for a song, and then invested a fortune in bringing the colliery up to his standards of safety and efficiency. He'd doubled the shoring-timbers, engineered innovative ventilation chambering to keep the air fresh, and had installed closed-gear winching and sumps to keep the passages dry. Flame was dangerous, but he found a way to lessen the threat, bringing light and air to the darkness.

He would risk no man's life in the pursuit of profit, so he judged every tunnel and fissure himself. He employed full-time engineers and the best mechanics, who had been instructed—at the peril of their jobs—to shut down production at the first sign of problems.

He'd learned from his father and from his own bleak years at Glad Heath that respect was the key to a man's success, so he sacrificed profits for shorter hours in the tunnels and a living wage for the miners. Even more, he took a wild-hearted pride in sharing his profits with the men who worked for him, and he valued those elected to his advisory committees. His expenses were far greater than any other mining company, but so too were his revenues. His safety record was unparalleled, and he had made enemies of the other owners by hiring any miner who came to him.

And come they did. So many more each year that Jack had opened whole other tunnels, opened new sites for those who wanted to work honestly and with a mind toward the community. Mairey's Willowmoon silver would be one of those new mines. He hoped she would approve.

Twelve hours gone, plus the five before he'd arrived on the scene. He'd never lost a man yet in his tunnels, but time was against them. He prayed as he lifted his pick, prayed as he sweated and strained and drove its steel point ferociously against the bedrock time and again, laboring through his shift and the next. Finally, the force of his own pick broke through to the blackness to the other side.

''We're through!'' he shouted, his heart ready to burst with joy and fear and exhaustion. Three men crowded around the shilling-sized hole. ''Moving air, sir! Feel it?''

The air was moving, but it was rife with coal gas.

''We'll find 'em alive, sir. I'm sure of it.''

But Jack wasn't sure at all. Richmond should have heard the sounds of digging long before this; should have been digging from his side to meet them. He hefted the pick again, and took out his fear and fury on the rock until the hole was large enough to crawl through.

''The risk is mine from here on; I'll go in myself,'' he told his men. ''You've all done more than enough.''

Jack crawled into the blackness, reached back for a lantern, and then started up the narrow incline toward the cave-in.

Please, God, let them be alive.

Chapter 12

Just before noon the colliery whistle began to blow, high and singing. The schoolhouse emptied in an instant, and Mairey hurried along with the women and children, up the sinuous, neatly tended streets toward the pit and its towering tangle of wheels and gears and steel-tackled webbing.

Had they found the men, or was this another horrible cave-in? Rumors had spread all through the night like a field fire, fanned and flaring and dying, then rising again, until Mairey's fear for Jack had become nearly unbearable.

Her heart pounded as she waited with everyone on the pit brow, watched the giant wheel turning and turning. Anything could have happened down there in all that blackness. How many times had she read of rescuers being killed in the tunnel along with the original victims?

Not Jack. Please God, not Jack. Everyone around her must be wishing the same thing for the people they loved.

Loved? Mairey scrubbed that impossible word

from her thoughts. She couldn't love the man—wouldn't.

Everyone grew still as the top of the lift appeared, the cage groaning its way up through the center of the iron frame until it jerked to a stop. There was a shocked silence and then a riotous joy swept the crowd.

The men were safe and stumbling out of the cage! Jack had done it—had rescued them just as he'd promised.

Mairey still searched the grimy faces, her heart frantic as wives and mothers swarmed around the rescued men and pulled them away from the danger and into their arms.

How she envied them all their joy even as she shared it. But Jack wasn't among them, and she'd never been so frightened in all her life. Tears swam in her eyes as the cage descended into the shaft, making seeing difficult.

She pushed closer, found a familiar face—Richmond—the engineer! She recognized him from Jack's office, though he was altogether inky. She caught his arm, happy to see him safe, but terrified for Jack.

"Have you seen Jack? Is he coming up?"

"Ah, Miss Faelyn, isn't it?" Richmond enveloped her hand and shook it with all the glad vigor of a man recently resurrected, grinning with stark white teeth. "We met at Drakestone."

"Yes, yes. But did you see Jack down there? Is he all right?"

Richmond smiled even wider, pointing over her shoulder to the cage rising up again out of the terrible pit. "Looks well enough to me."

Jack! Oh, how she wanted to shout his name and run to him! The lout was safe! And oily black, from the top of his head to his once-crisp white shirttails that now hung out of his stained leather trousers.

Mairey's anger burned as brightly as her relief as Jack made his way toward her. They were shoved together in the tempest of glad-handing and reveling, and he held her tightly, length to length, and grinning

"We saved them all, Mairey," he whispered, his eyes shot with red. "Thank you."

Thank you? For covering for him, for telling his lies, for praying for him, for his people, all through the hellish night?

" 'Glad Heath,' Jack? Is that what this valley was before you destroyed it with your coal pits? A misty, heather-scented moorland?"

He frowned down at her, then slid his hand along his cheek as though she had slapped him there. "It was a heath to be sure, Mairey. But long, long before it came to my hands."

"It's ugly here, Jack."

Something unfamiliar and humbling flickered in the clear midnight of his eyes. He set her from him, a distance that seemed lonelier than winter.

"Glad Heath is a colliery, if you haven't noticed. It's not a spit-clean university. It lacks the clipped hedges and the oak-paneled eating halls. It's grimy, stark, and dreary. The work abrades the skin and blackens the lungs—"

"And it crushes people, Jack." Her panic and anger made her reach for him and hold tightly, made his thick, sinewy arms seem all too vulnerable against the force of a mountain bearing down on him. "Can't you see the danger? Couldn't you feel it while you were down there?"

"I know the risk."

She hated that part of him—the cool mining baron. "I'm sure you do. But the risk is theirs, Lord Rushford, not yours. Their sons and husbands, their fathers."

"And *my* father."

"Oh, and a great risk *he* must have taken every day. Sitting in his fine office in London, worried about his profits, his investment—"

"His *life*." He frowned. "My father had no office in London. I don't know where you get that notion. He labored all his days here at Glad Heath. He died here."

She wasn't sure she had heard him right; she was tired to the marrow and confused by all the celebrating. "Your father died here? How?"

"In a riot during a labor dispute."

"A mining baron, dying at his own mine in a labor dispute? Now there's a switch."

"Mining baron?" He laughed then, throwing his head back to the brightness of the sky, a touch of madness in his laughter. "Bloody hell, madam— my father was a pitman."

"A what?"

"A *coal miner*."

"No." He was lying, trying to make some kind of point.

He cocked his head at her, raising a brow that

was hardly distinguishable from his coal-begrimed skin. "No?"

"He couldn't have been a coal miner. Then how did you—"

"How did I—the son of a poor man—end up with Glad Heath?" He snorted and took the cup of water that a buxom, dazzle-eyed young woman offered to him. He drank it down in a single quaff. "My thanks, Molly."

"And my greatest pleasure, my lord." The brazen woman drew a smile out of him as she sped away with her skirts caught up to her shapely calves.

Mairey's face flushed as a wave of blatant, green-tinted jealousy swamped her. A wholly unworthy and out-of-proportion emotion.

"How *did* you end up with Glad Heath, Jack?"

He glared down at her, swabbing his neck with a red kerchief. It came away black and dripping with sweat. "I bought it from the estate of the man who killed my father."

Another woman came to Jack, the matronly Mistress Boyd, handing him a chunk of bread and a wet rag, leaving him with a motherly kiss and a pat on his backside. His eyes followed the woman fondly before he turned back to Mairey. He seemed righteously proud of himself and so much at home here. "My father worked this mine from the time he was eight years old. He formed a union and led a strike against the unsafe conditions in the pits, shutting down the mine for a month."

"He was killed for leading a strike? Jack, that's horrible. How could that happen?" Feeling roundly possessive, Mairey took the rag out of his hand as he stuffed the bread into his mouth, and she began to scrub the coal off his nose.

"Cahill sent his private army on horseback from the train station, rode them up the hill to the pit, and let them loose against a handful of unarmed men and boys."

"How could he?" Horrified, Mairey scrubbed more thoroughly, streaking the black off his cheeks and forehead, while Jack submitted blissfully.

"Cahill was a bastard who trafficked in human lives. My father was killed right over there." Jack opened an eye and sighted down his inky finger to a lamppost. Its flame burned hotly, even in the blaze of the sun. "He died in my arms."

Her tears blurred his face into a watery gray blotch. "Then you know how dangerous the mines are, Jack. Everything about them, inside and out. How can you in good conscience send people down there to be killed? They depend upon you, Jack. They trust you."

"And by the grace of God I have earned that trust." He took a step backward and frowned at her. "I've turned a death camp into a safe, profitable colliery. Now if you'll excuse me, Mairey, I have a mine to run."

"Ballocks!"

He had turned away, but now he swung back again, the devil in his eyes.

"What?"

"How can you say that your mines are safe, when you've just suffered a cave-in and put all those people in danger?"

"Mairey, some accidents can't be prevented. I would never, ever send anyone down a shaft or into a tunnel that wasn't safe enough for my own father, nor for anyone I loved."

"Ballocks again!"

"I've had enough, woman." He came at her like a bull, head down and charging, and in the next instant he'd thrown her over his shoulder, her backside to the sky, his hand clamped there like a sizzling hasp of iron.

"Put me down, Jack!"

"You've a lesson to learn, Mairey Faelyn." He stomped through the celebrating toward the mine shaft, with its whirling, whining gears and shuddering cables.

"Do you plan to throw me down your mine, Jack Rushford?"

"Tempting, but you'd only gum up the works, woman, and I've just got them working again."

Mairey squirmed just to spite him, knowing that it was useless, that he would only tighten his scorching hold around her legs.

As they approached the shaft, its steel cage rose up again from the bottomless hole into the towering head-frame, then came to a squealing stop.

"Jack Rushford, where the devil are you taking me?"

He stepped into the swinging basket. "To hell, madam."

Mairey's courage fled as he finally released her, sliding her down the length of him as though he enjoyed the contact. "I don't want to go with you."

"We're partners in a silver mine, my dear. It's time you looked at one close up."

Partners—he kept saying that, as though she shared his despicable dreams of silver. They were adversaries.

The lift started down with a shudder. Mairey grabbed his leather coat and hung on for dear life as the cage jiggled down into the darkness.

"Is it supposed to do that?" She was quaking herself, a miserably frightened ninny.

"Do what?"

"That jiggling."

He laughed gently and turned her away from him, so that the layers of rock flew past her nose. "Physics," he said into her ear. "You'll be all right."

Mairey grabbed handfuls of his sleeve where he'd wrapped his arm around her waist. He was warm and breathing steadily, her rock. Her heart was racing with kinetic danger, her pulse thrumming against his fingers where his large hand had claimed her shoulder and the rise of her neck.

"It's windy," she said as a cool breeze blew her hair upwards, a flying, freeing sensation.

"It's supposed to be." He gathered the swirling of her hair into a bundle and held it in his fist. "I've spent a lot of time and money to keep the air circulating through the ventilation shafts."

She had expected stifling heat and the stink of sulphur. But the air was clean, if coal-smelling, and cool.

They stepped out of the lift into a bright chamber, framed like an old Saxon cathedral in tall timbers and crossbeams. A forest on a winter's eve. It had an eerie, underworld beauty. Dark, shiny-faced elves scurried into a second tunnel with their buckets, feeding an ever-rising chain of tubs that carried coal up to the surface.

"That's the last of the cleanup from the cave-in." He put one of the metal caps on her head, a mate to his own, took her hand, and started into one of the tunnels. "I'll show you where we rescued the men."

If she lived, if she ever saw the light of day again, she'd at least have a better understanding of her enemy and his lair. The tunnel twisted and rose, then dipped and straightened. She'd expected seeping walls and crumbling terror. But Jack's mine was clean-lined and stout, and as bright as noon.

"Shoring up the passageways is the key to safety." He stopped at an intersection and slapped his palm against a fat, foot-square timber. "The more bracing, the safer. A great expense, but necessary. I'll take the same care in the Willowmoon tunnels."

You won't get the chance, Lord Rushford.

"We'll use these same double-screened Davy lamps, an added safety feature developed by my engineers. Explosive gasses aren't the problem with silver mines that they are with coal. But light is fundamental to a man's spirit, and I'll bring daylight into the darkness of the Willowmoon Mineworks just as I have here."

Then light a candle for me while you're there, Jackson Rushford. Because I'll be dead before I let you riddle my glade with your worm holes.

"Come." He took her hand again and led her deeper into the mine, past a small culvert and a dark pool, under the great air shafts that dropped sunlight-scented air onto them.

It didn't matter that the people of Glad Heath counted Rushford among their saints. And it mattered even less that Mairey herself had seen too much saintliness in the man this past day.

He could pay each of his miners a thousand-pound wage every year; he could build stately town houses for each of their wives; send their sons to Oxford; marry their daughters off to members of the peerage. But he couldn't bring back the mountain or the woodlands, nor could he restore the streams that had once bubbled up from the springs. And he would never, ever have the chance to do to her village what he and his like had done to Glad Heath.

Agile and sure of himself, Jack moved along the tidy, down-sloping passage with its low ceilings and shadows. He stopped at a short tunnel dug into the stone. It had a hole at the end that emptied into blackness.

"Back there is where we broke through into the Shalecross. We had to cut another, quicker passage. There wouldn't have been enough clean air to last the other way."

"You did all this today?" All the digging and the timbering, as single-minded as ants.

"It took six of us twelve hours, but we managed." He took the lantern and her hand and led her to the end of the rescue passage.

His palm was torn and rough, and she turned it

up to the wavering light. Blisters, broken and bleeding and needing care.

"You helped them dig?"

"When I could. I'm not as young as I used to be, and I'm out of shape."

Hardly. He was huge; had shoulders like a . . . Of course! No wonder he was so broadly muscled.

"You were a coal miner!"

"Like my father." He hung the lantern on a peg above her head. "I started when I was eight, holding open the ventilation doors. I was big for my age, so I was picking coal by the time I was eleven. I worked Glad Heath until the night my father was killed."

He stood close, so very tall and overwhelming. Her metal cap clunked against the thick post behind her and the brim lifted off her forehead like a halo, leaving her to stare up into his breathlessly devilish grin.

"Where did you go then?"

"I emigrated." He flicked his own cap off his head, and it landed with a ringing racket. He stepped closer, still straddling her legs. "I left the country on the next tide, with the law on my tail."

"Jack, why?" The man was a maze of mysteries. The lantern above them planed his features in orange; the coal took the shadows and deepened them. But his eyes were sparkling like diamonds, and made her heart flip.

"Father's strike was illegal, and so was the riot that followed the murders." He threaded his fingers through her hair with tender care, then drew his thumb slowly across her lips, watching all the while, grinning a bit. "I was accused of setting fire to Lord Cahill's offices."

"Did you?"

The corners of his eyes crinkled; his laughter filled up her lungs. "Oh, yes, Mairey. With my father's name on my lips, I did it."

Her eyes pooled again with tears, but she snuffled them away. "Good."

"Yes. Good." They stood hip to hip, her belly to his groin. His erection was a wonder. So grandly different than her dusty old collection: hotly independent, compelling her to squirm, to do something with it.

"Ah, Mairey." He took forever bending to her mouth, touching his fingers to her lips. She rose up on her toes to be nearer, sooner. It wasn't wise to tempt a dragon, especially when one was deep in his den, miles from the sky and the green trees.

"Beautiful, Mairey."

"Jack, I—" Oh, bliss. Oh, gracious. He covered her mouth with his, possessed her absolutely, sweetly, and then with a hungry, diving groan that shot sparks to the ends of her fingers, to the center of her, where his never-to-be-conceived children slept. Tears gathered in her throat, unshed and aching. His kiss was deep, his lips softly searing.

"Worth waiting for, Mairey." Her miner's cap clanged to the ground as he caught her up in his arms and gathered her against him.

"Yes, Jack." Her head spinning with stolen gladness, Mairey climbed deeper into his embrace, ground her hips against his hardness, wanting more of him, as much as she dared in this dark fairy tale of theirs. She kissed him rampantly, traced the planes of his midnight-bristled jaw, brushed her lips across the soft play of his eyelashes. He tasted of soap and fresh bread and a heart-stopping rescue.

He laughed suddenly, his smile as crooked and mussed as his spiky hair. "I've never in my life kissed a woman in a mine."

She liked that a lot. "You brought me all the way down here just to kiss me?"

"I wanted you alone, Mairey. Need you." Another kiss, slanting, slippery, sliding down the front of her bodice, blowing hot through the linen. He shaped his hands beneath her breasts, grazed his thumbs across her nipples, sending a deliciously feverish clenching to the joining of her thighs. "I want you thoroughly, Mairey. In every way I can imagine."

She didn't know what to say, because she could imagine so very much, all of it ending abruptly in heartbreak. He was trembling like the quaking of the earth when he enfolded her in his arms, a caress far more profound than the flesh that still ached for completion.

How simple it would have been to keep on hating him. But he'd taken that from her. He was a man who was doing his best at the only life he knew.

And he did it so admirably, with such easy grace.

She'd survived his horrible mine. He'd kept her safe all the time, just as he'd promised.

What was it that he had said before he'd scooped her up and brought her spiraling down into his netherworld? That he would never send anyone into a mine shaft that wasn't safe enough for his own father. . . .

Or for anyone he loved.

Oh, Jack!

Chapter 13

Mairey was still breathless long after his kiss, long after he'd sent her back up into the light.

Glad Heath was celebrating, and Jack was their hero, though he stayed below, unmindful of the feasting in his name. The town put the mine to rights in eager shifts, having beaten back the devil this time.

And though Mairey looked for Jack all the rest of the day, she didn't find him again until late afternoon. He was leaning back against the lamppost near the pit, only standing because his legs were spread wide with his knees locked, his arms fallen heavily to his sides. His head was tipped back and his face glistened black in the sunlight.

She approached him quietly, thinking at first that he was asleep on his feet. But he coughed suddenly and so violently that he dropped to his knees and bent over, holding himself up on the flat of his hands.

She ran to him, uncertain what to do, whether he

wanted her there or not. She put her hand on his back, soothed his shoulders.

"Ah, Mairey, that feels good," he said, sitting back on his haunches, reeling a little as he cast a sideways, squint-eyed glance at her. "Thank you," he said, with a blink that lasted so long she thought perhaps he'd gone to sleep.

"You're a mess."

"Messy business. But it's done for the moment." He crawled back up the post, planted his feet apart again, and put his hands on his thighs. "I have to be back to London tomorrow afternoon. Still need to stop at the Strathfield Works this evening."

"Not tonight, Jack. You need rest."

He waggled a finger at her, nearly cross-eyed with the effort. "There's none for the wicked, my dear."

The fool launched himself away from the post, looking drunk as he staggered down the hill.

"Jack! Wait!" Mairey caught him around his waist and nearly went down with him in the next step.

"Sorry, sweet," he said, righting them both, leaving her face-to-face with him as she anchored him with her hands round his waist. "You have a very lovely mouth, Miss Faelyn. Honeyed. I'd like to try it again."

She would like that, too. "Not now, Jack."

He must have read right though her evasion—his teeth showed white against his smile.

"To the train, then." He clamped his arm around her shoulder, as possessively as if he had done it all his life. Mairey finally managed to get him to the train, only to find the private compartment noisy with two of his engineers and a mound of paper.

He roused himself as though he'd come fresh from his morning ablutions, and he became the mining baron once again. Mairey fought sleep, but it came anyway, druglike in the rocking motion of the railcar, in the soothing rhythms of Jack's voice beside her.

She was dreaming of labyrinths and confusion, blackness and starlight. A soothing hand against her cheek. Warm, rugged, a saltiness against her lips.

"Come, Mairey." The voice was very nice, too. As nice as Jack's. "My beautiful Mairey."

He was shaking her awake, lifting her hair out of her face. "We're stopping here for the night."

"In Strathfield?" Mairey raised up to look out the window. The sun was gone, leaving only an orange burnish to the slate-roofed buildings. She'd been asleep for hours.

"I've already been there, and finished my business. We're in Dealing, at the junction." His face was cleaner, but she couldn't tell if those were deeply etched shadows or coal dust.

He had already arranged for two rooms in the railway inn, two steaming baths, and two dinners. Separate, alone.

"Sleep well, Mairey." He leaned toward her in the hallway, holding himself off her with his hands above her head.

His lingering, succulent, good-night kiss and

nuzzling neck-nibbling turned to snoozing into her ear, his chin propped against her shoulder.

"Dear man."

Mairey kissed him lightly, which roused him enough to herd himself to his room through the adjoining door in hers. But not before he gave an overly detailed demonstration of the lock that could only be opened from *her* side of the door.

"Completely safe, madam," he said, blinking. Then he lifted one of his brows and strode through the doorway into his room, rattling the knob in reminder after he'd closed the door.

It was only after she was sitting in the tub that Mairey realized she hadn't bothered to turn the key on her side, that he could walk in at any moment—and that he wouldn't.

She scrubbed herself clean and washed her hair twice, to remove the dinge of coal that had collected in every pore. The water was heavenly, warm and drowsing, and she only left it when she caught herself falling asleep.

She tried to ignore Jack's sounds while she prepared for bed, but he consumed her senses. She heard his firm footfalls and the thunk of what could only have been his shoes—first one, and then after a very, very long time, the other. A door opening into the hallway, a stranger's voice and then Jack's, and then a flurry of footfalls and bathwater noises.

She listened to him even as she slipped under the covers, even as sleep tugged at her. She heard the splash of water, then he groaned like a tired mill wheel coming to rest.

A wife would have worked the kinks out of his

shoulders, would knead his ropy muscles, and kiss him wherever he needed kissing. . . .

Mairey woke with a nearby church bell chiming twelve. The doorframe into Jack's room was still limned in bright lamplight, as it had been when she had fallen asleep three hours before.

Odd. He'd been exhausted, ready to drop.

She padded to the door and put her ear against it, listening for a full minute before deciding to knock quietly.

"Jack?"

Silence. Utter silence. Not even the gentle saw of his snoring.

Perhaps he'd fallen asleep with the light on. Or he might have been dragged back to Glad Heath— his life in danger again! She opened the door a crack and peered in. A cold fireplace, an unrumpled four-poster, a writing table with a chair. But no sign of the man, no sign that he'd been there at all.

Her heart pounding in apprehension, Mairey opened the door fully and stepped inside, ready to fetch the proprietor of the inn.

Then she saw him, fast asleep in a long, low bathtub, breathing deeply.

"Oh, Jack."

Her view was straight on and breathtaking. The man's hard-muscled arms were hanging free of the tub, his legs inside, his knees propped against either edge. The soap was unused and sitting on the side table. He'd cradled his head on his shoulder and the back of the tub, the motion of his chest making soft ripples in the crystal clear, belly-deep water.

He was magnificent. Bewitching. He made her pulse hum in her ears.

"I can't very well leave you like this." He might drown, or freeze to death—he'd been in the water for hours. Even if he awoke and promised to bathe himself, she couldn't trust him not to fall asleep again.

She hurried back to her room and donned a robe and a pair of drawers for propriety's sake. Then she went downstairs to the kitchen and ordered two pails of hot water from the matronly cook, who frowned at the lateness of the request until Mairey pleaded monthly cramps and an aching back that was keeping her awake.

Wondering where she'd learned to lie so expertly, Mairey went back upstairs, rolled up her sleeves, then stepped into Jack's room to study the problem.

That problem being that Jackson Rushford was a man.

Dear God, was he a man in every way imaginable! Darkly curling hair lay in a fine sheen across his broad chest, and arrowed its way downward to a dark patch. His penis, his ever-so classically endowed penis, was as stunning and heart-stirring at rest as it surely would be fully . . . engaged.

Was that the word? No. But her thoughts weren't scholarly at the moment. They were tender and burning and made her hands ache to touch him.

Well, then: washing a large, exceedingly male body couldn't be that much different than washing her own. That wasn't quite correct. He wasn't at all like her, he was rock hard where she was soft, and she selfishly wanted to learn every inch of him. To be tender without him ever knowing—because Jack seemed to take his tenderness very seriously.

She answered the knock on her door and took the water pails from the sleepy kitchen girl, tipping her a shilling. Mairey waited for the girl's footsteps to pad away from the door before she carried a bucket into Jack's room and poured the hot water slowly into his bath. She watched him for signs of wakefulness, not sure what she'd do if—no, *when* he woke up.

But he only rubbed at his nose with both fists and then slid an inch deeper into the water, letting his arms come to rest across his hips, just beneath the surface.

Sighing with a shattering longing for her dragon, Mairey added more water until a mist rose off the surface and his skin began to pinken beneath the grime.

Where to begin this purloined venture? He would probably wake up bellowing about improprieties the moment she touched him. He'd been impossibly incensed about the phallus display, so she lay a towel across his groin, masking all that beautiful masculinity—as much for her own sake as for his delicate sensibilities. Then she soaped up a cloth and knelt beside him.

His hands. That's where she would start. Tautly sinewed, blistered and cracked from his labors, and outlined in coal, they had taken the worst damage today, and had wrought such miracles in his life.

Mairey slid his palm across hers, soapy and warm and so very intimate. She caressed the length of his thumb, and he made one of his rumbling sounds very, very deep in his chest.

She was making a careful study of a ragged scar that ran like an extra heart line across the heel of his hand when she noticed that his breathing had gone from deep and untroubled to utterly still.

Immediately wary of what she might find at the other end of all that stillness, Mairey lifted her gaze up the long length of him, from the now-floating towel and his narrow waist, over the muscled ridges of his chest, to a pair of dark eyes that glittered dangerously from beneath a thunderous brow.

"Jack. You're awake." Flushed with guilt as much as with desire, Mairey tried to rise and back away, but he captured her hand with a fluid motion and didn't seem the least bit interested in letting go.

He crooked her closer with a flex of his arm. Nose to nose.

"No, madam, I couldn't possibly be awake. Else there wouldn't be a beautiful woman lounging at my bathside, scrubbing me."

With that, he reached over the side of the tub and hoisted Mairey's backside onto the broad flatness of his hand. Then he lifted her up, over, and into the water.

She landed in his lap.

His very naked, very wet lap!

"Jack!—" Mairey finished the blackguard's name and added a curse inside the sopping prison of his palm.

"Shhhh, Mairey. Can't have the proprietor breaking down the door in the middle of my dream.

It's far too stimulating, and I'm far too aroused to be interrupted.''

Interrupted! "You're not dreaming, blast you!" But her statement sounded more like *Burr nuh deenie, ba oo!*

He tightened his grip and hauled her backward until her shoulders were pinned against his chest. The hem of her nightgown billowed with air, then melted into the warm water.

Mairey tried her best to get away, tried desperately not to laugh, but Jack only clamped his free arm beneath her breasts. He shifted his hips, a great, rolling tide, and arranged her higher on his thighs, groaning like a bear just waking from a long winter's night.

"Another of your folk interviews, my dear?" he whispered beside her ear, taking a bit of the lobe between his lips and sending maddening shivers down her neck. "A highly unorthodox technique. One I hope you don't use on other men, because I wouldn't like that at all. But let me see, perhaps I can help you. Were you going to ask me what the coal miner's word is for arousal? For that's what you feel against your pretty backside. Me, Mairey, and my aching need for you. Do you feel it?"

Oh, yes! She felt him like a rod of fire against her hip. She nodded immodestly beneath his hand, fascinated when she ought to be outraged and flailing.

"That is my phallus, Mairey. Not an ivory carving, not stone, but my hard flesh—which is all your doing.''

Mairey nodded and squirmed a little, thrilled

with the sensation, with Jack's words against her ear.

"So full of your science and your fairy tales. Does it feel as you had imagined?"

Better, better, better! she wanted to say, but his hand was still covering her mouth, though he was drawing his middle finger along the vale of her lips like a kiss. And, oh, all the other places she could suddenly imagine that finger.

"Ah, Mairey, when you wiggle against me like that"—an involuntary shudder seemed to convulse him—"yes, like that, my dear, I'm only roused to want you all the more. Would you like to write *that* down in your field-notes?"

He stirred again, raising her hips with his, setting the swirling hem of her nightgown adrift in his wake. The hand he'd held across her was now gathering up the floating linen, pushing the fabric upward and upward along her thighs toward her hips.

"I'm not made of stone—not like your collection. And I think from your writhing that you're not, either."

Mairey watched in wonder as his dark hand disappeared into the surging folds of linen, in the clear pool where her legs were spread so indelicately, her knees propped wide against his and waiting.

Oh, yes, waiting shamelessly for his magic. She held her breath, disbelieving her anticipation, hopeless with desire for him to do whatever he planned.

His hand swept her curling hair through her drawers, eddies of cool water and then warm, summer sunlight. Sweet anticipation.

He groaned as he cradled his hand over the wild

place between her legs. A riot of wanting, a need to explore further. To take her to heaven, to keep her always.

"Oh, Jack!" He had freed her mouth to delve there with his finger, to trace her lips and play at her tongue as he might at her cleft. He was so damnably near it!

"Stone doesn't quiver, sweet Mairey. Ivory isn't hot. And it doesn't ache."

"I *do* ache, Jack. For you. I ache like fire."

Jack thought he just might explode.

She was arched against him, the antiquarian clad in her proper Victorian nightdress and drawers, her lovely, lean thighs open wide to his hands. She was breathing with little sighs and gripping the sides of the tub in a white-knuckled fury.

"Jack, I, oh! I—Jack!"

He ached to the depth of his soul to part the slit in her linen drawers; a garment so perfectly suited to a lover's fingers. A husband's, surely. But he wasn't her husband—and that was his dilemma, as her springy curls teased at his palm, as her heat coursed up through his fingers.

Had he the right? Had he the will to stop what he shouldn't even have begun?

Married. The word had meant nothing to him for so long, and now it plagued his every thought. He measured it against everything she did, everything she meant to him.

"You need to know, madam, that you can't just walk into a man's room while he's bathing." He'd awakened stirred to the boiling point, dreaming of Mairey. Dreaming of children, Mairey's and his together. She had become his life. He couldn't imagine his library stripped of her curios, of her laughter.

"You were sound asleep, Jack." She sighed against his ear, grabbed for it with her tongue and teeth.

"You can't bathe him without his waking up, wanting you in the tub with him." He caught her mouth with his, played at tongues and teasing.

"You were freezing."

"And you can't fondle penises, ancient or otherwise, in front of him without that man—"

"You. I was with you, Jack."

"Yes, without *me*—reacting just as *you* are now. You feel the ache?"

"In every part of me, Jack." She wriggled her hips, gave a little gasp, and then covered his hand with hers.

Bits of light scattered inside his skull. The split linen parted like a curtain, and he harrowed his fingers through her fleece. "Mairey!"

"Oh, Jack! It's wonderful! I only—" She took a gasping breath as he slid his fingers along her sultry folds and held her, kept her, wary of moving for the storm it would cause in them both.

"You only what, sweet?"

She had thrown her head back against his shoulder, tilting her pelvis into the cup of his hand as though she would consume him. Her nipples were dark points straining at the wet linen.

"Oh, Jack, I—I didn't want you to drown."

"You're too late, Mairey." He was so drugged

with wanting her, he could peel off her gown and take her there in the tub.

But he couldn't—she was made for wedding, for vows, for a marriage bed. Unless he lost his mind completely in the next minute and buried himself inside her.

My God. She was bending, reaching for his scrotum.

"Mairey, please!" He caught her by the wrist and she turned in his arms, floated and then settled on him, her nearly bare skin cool against his fire-hot erection.

"What is it, Jack?" Her eyes were wide, and blinking.

"Have you learned nothing in the last few minutes?"

"Mmmmm . . . I've learned far more than I had intended." The minx closed her eyes and took a startlingly precocious pleasure in rolling his penis against the softness of her belly. "I don't know what's gotten into me—"

Me, my love. I want to be inside you, to the hilt.

"I'm not shy of you, Jack." She spread her fingers across his chest, then slid them up his throat to his jaw, her clear gray eyes filled with desire.

"No, you don't appear to be shy at all."

"Though I'm plagued with curiosity—"

"The scholar in you."

"Now I understand the lure of the phallus through the eons. Yours in particular."

"Mairey!" Jack groaned, then pulled her forward in a single wave of water, covering her mouth with his, claiming her with his tongue. Hungry, so hungry! He should really stop this. But she made tiny, laughing whimpers in her throat and crawled up the front of him, slipped her arms around his neck, and let him plunder and explore.

Until he realized that he was fighting with the third button of her nightgown, that he had breached the opening, then had a handful of lush breast, and his mouth was just bearing down on a ripely puckered nipple.

Mairey's eyes were wide as she watched him, astonished, as though she wasn't certain this was happening to her.

And it shouldn't. Not now.

"Sweet Jesus!" Jack yanked the placket closed, and patted her breast when it was fully covered— out of sight, but not in the least out of mind. *He* was out of his mind! For going this far. For stopping. Hell!

He lifted her hips and stood her up in the well between his knees, staying hip-deep himself. Her gown was a transparent waterfall, her face flushed, her breasts high and round.

"What, Jack?" She looked incensed in her innocence, her hands fisted against her hips.

Despite the raging fever in his blood, he wasn't fit for a night like this. That would be a commitment to something far greater and longer lasting than silver.

"This is a marital pursuit, Mairey. And we're not, are we? Married, I mean."

"No." The word came out wrapped in a weighty sigh, and the next as horrified as if he'd suggested setting her library on fire. "No!"

Unclear why her eyes should be so filled with terror at the mere mention of a marriage between them, Jack decided to shelve the subject until a better time, and send her out of harm's way.

"I think you'd best leave me to my bath, Mairey."

"Oh, no, Jackson Rushford!" She flipped back her hair, the bottom half wet and clinging, then drizzled her opinions across his chest as she wrung out her hem. "I'm not letting you bathe alone. I found you asleep in two feet of water! You're staggering with exhaustion, and I refuse to leave you. Don't move."

He couldn't possibly.

She stepped out of the tub, taking half the bath with her, trailing a stream of water all the way through the open doorway into her room.

"What are you doing in there, woman?" Jack would have leaped out of the tub and gone for his clothes, but Mairey stuck her head around the panel, her shoulder heedlessly bare.

"Cover yourself with a towel while you finish if you want, Jack. I won't look, I promise. But I will be in the same room as you until you're out of the water." She disappeared, and he heard the plop of soggy fabric landing on the floor.

She was undressing. The door was half open, and the woman was undressing!

"I've got three little sisters, Jack. I know a lot about the drowsing effects of bathwater on exhausted children. Poppy gets sleepy the moment she sees the bath."

"I'm not a child, Mairey. I don't need your

help.'' He needed to sort through his thoughts. He needed Mairey.

"And I don't need to find you floating facedown in your bathwater.'' She came through the door tugging a dressing robe around a nightgown. Her feet were bare, and her hair hung like a siren's around her shoulders.

She swabbed up her watery trail, hung the towel over a chair back, and then sprawled across his bed.

"Wash, Jack. Else I'll fall asleep here.''

The woman clearly hadn't understood anything from the last few minutes, that neither of them were made of stone. But neither was she peering into his bathwater any longer.

So Jack scrubbed himself clean, from his scalp to the soles of his feet. The water went milky gray with soap and grime, the clean fragrance rising into his nostrils like memories of home, of scrubbing his skin to bright pink at his nightly baths in the kitchen after a long day in the mine. Privacy had been a foreign notion then, with the rest of his family at the hearth, just out of his circle of modesty. Emma telling stories, his mother plaiting Banon's black hair, Clady fast asleep on his father's lap.

God in heaven, he hadn't allowed such memories for years; hadn't dared, for the grief they exposed.

"Jack?''

"Yes?'' He was standing in the water, his backside bare and dripping with rinse water. He spared a glance at the bed, prepared for the connection of her gaze, for the sharp pang of desire that was becoming as familiar as breathing. But she was tucked up against his pillow, staring at the ceiling, her hands behind her head.

Trust—she was free with it. To be sure, she kept her secrets from him, rationed her Willowmoon lore as if she were a bank manager suspicious of a loan. But when it came to the truth between them, Mairey Faelyn was as constant as the coming and going of the sun.

"Jack, I've been wondering about your sisters."

He welcomed the change of subject and stepped out of the tub to dry off. "What is it you want to know about them?"

"You told me one time that you hadn't seen them for years."

"I haven't." He pulled on his trousers, having nothing else to wear, and certainly not trusting a towel.

"At first I thought you were estranged from them. That . . . well, I don't know . . . that you had offended them somehow in your magnificence, that you didn't think them your social equal, or that you'd married them off to your business associates for the profits they brought into the family estate." She flopped her arms on the mattress, obviously feeling tied to the bed. "May I look?"

"Hmmmm . . . I had no idea your opinion of me was so colorful." He was safely rolling up his shirtsleeve when she sat up and dangled her bare calves over the edge of the bed.

"My opinion of you remains colorful, sir, more so than ever. But the part about your sisters isn't true, is it? You're not estranged; you haven't seen them since the night your father was killed."

She was very good at finding things, uncomfortably so. He wasn't sure he wanted to continue.

"It was earlier that day. At breakfast."

She was quiet for a moment as he rolled up his other sleeve, because it gave him something to do.

"What are their names?"

Are. Not *were.* Leave it to Mairey to understand the tiny morsels of hope that he tucked away for safekeeping. The bargains he'd made with God. He sat down beside her, gripping the edge of the mattress, staring down at the wooden floor, at the long cracks and the fine grain and the swirl of the knots.

"My mother's name is Claire."

"That's very pretty."

"Yes. I hadn't realized—she was my age when I last saw her. Emma was eleven at the time. Banon was seven. And Clady had just turned six." He struggled to get his voice past the lump in his throat. "She'd gotten into the honey that morning. I went up to the strike line with a gob of it in my hair."

"Oh, Jack." There it was in her eyes, in the way she turned to him and enfolded his hand in hers. He didn't have to tell her about the hearth shadows and the ghosts at the lodge. Or why he'd fought so hard to banish her sisters from Drakestone.

"What happened to them, Jack?" Her voice was a little frantic, echoing the panic whenever he wondered the same. "Where did they go? With your mother, surely?"

Take care of them, Jack, my son. He'd done a hell of a job.

"I lost them." He paced away to the open door

between their rooms, where he could better gain a full head of steam. "I was forced into exile by my own mother. God, how I fought her. *I* was the man now, entrusted by my dying father to take care of them. But she put me on a ship bound for Canada, afraid that I'd be sent to prison."

"She loved you, Jack. I would do the very same to protect my son if he were in danger."

There was the motherly sort for you. Missing the point entirely.

"I was thousands of miles from home with no idea where my family had gone. I sold my first nugget of gold and hired a law firm in London to find them, the best team I could afford."

"And you didn't hear anything at all?"

"It's been eighteen years. Nothing."

"That's very odd, Jack. And horribly sad." Her soft brow furrowed. "Has this firm checked parish registers in Yorkshire?"

"Repeatedly." A cool shiver of guilt rode Jack's neck—a recent memory of Mairey and her expert quest through the Tower, through the ancient records at Donowell, turning over every particle of evidence until she had found what she wanted.

He should have fired Dodson.

"There are so many other places to look, Jack. Have they inspected the emigration manifests? Ships leave every day for America, Australia."

Emigration? He'd never thought of that and doubted that Dodson ever had or would.

"This is a law firm, Jack?" She was chewing on her lower lip, her gaze fixed on someplace different and glittering with her interminable tears.

"Dodson, Dodson and Greel." The bastards. One more year and then he'd get rid of them. The decision freed him some.

"Did these same lawyers clear your name, Jack?" She stood suddenly, and her robe loosened like a curtain, completely irresistible. "Or is the constable still looking for you?"

"I am reprieved, madam." *And falling madly for you.* Everlastingly. How could he ever let her go? Quitting breathing would be simpler, or stopping the tides.

"You bought off the legal system?"

"Absolutely." He laughed at himself, at the grubby coal miner turned peer, and it felt very, very good. "I was still in Labrador when I made the New Year's honors list of 1853—an appreciation of my financial contributions to the Empire, so the letter said." He felt better still when he lifted her into his arms, all seven, delectable stone of her, and started toward her room, and was damned pleased with himself when she began to nuzzle his neck.

"So I wrote to the lord chancellor informing him of my regrettable past legal difficulties, and he informed me by return packet, six months later, that my youthful offense had been permanently erased, that I was now Viscount Rushford, and would I be interested in the purchase of old Drakestone House, and three manors in Lincolnshire?"

"Ah, the royal white elephants."

"A whole herd of them." He was quaking again with desire for her, tempted to stay, to join her in her bed, to finish what they'd begun in the bath.

But beginnings were precious, delicate; they

needed strategies and time to plan them.

She puckered a frown at him as he lowered her into her rumpled covers. "Are you leaving the inn, Jack?"

"No. It's two in the morning. I'm going to bed."

She pointed at him and gave an ungainly yawn. "But you've got your clothes on."

"Yes, madam, but I won't as soon as I'm back in my room." He dropped a kiss on her forehead.

"Ah." She was finally blushing, though he couldn't be sure it wasn't a heated flush. "I'm sorry about the bath. I won't do it again."

"Then *I'll* be sorry, Mairey Faelyn. To the end of my days." He closed the door, and listened for the click of the lock that never came.

Chapter 14

*D*odson, Dodson and Greel.

Mairey felt another wring of guilt as she stood in front of the tarnished brass plaque that marked the law firm's chambers just off High Holborn.

She should have at least mentioned this visit to Jack. But he'd been absolutely closed about the subject of his missing family in the week since their return to Drakestone House, so she'd let the matter sink below the surface.

The girls had been so delighted to see Jack when he and Mairey had returned, they had run right past her and flung themselves into his arms, Poppy climbing to his shoulders as if she'd shinnied up his towering trunk every day of her life.

"We took good care of your fairies for you, Lord Jack!" She had the poor man by the ears, bending over to look him in the eye. "The green one's name is Wendell!"

"Wendell? Really?"

"Truly, sir."

If Mairey hadn't been so overwhelmed by the tears that glistened in the dark of Jack's eyes, by his bellowing laughter that rang through the lodge and the smacking kiss he'd put on Poppy's cheek, she might have felt spurned by their desertion. Instead, she was enchanted.

"Sumner helped us plant sweet peas, sir!" Anna waved a seed packet in front of Jack's face, and he'd done his best to follow its bobbing. "And snapdragons!"

"Lookee what I can do!" Caro had come zooming down the banister, on a squealing collision course with the floor. But Jack had plucked her out of the air and stood looking at Mairey helplessly, the giggling girl hanging from his hip like a sack of flour.

"Welcome home, Jack." He was just so very fine.

Her sister's hearts were big, and seemed to know by instinct that he needed their fierce hugs and sticky hand-holdings. Just as Mairey knew that he would lay down his life for them.

As he had done for his own sisters, for his dear mother. How sad that they didn't know how much he loved them, how long he'd stood by their memories. His father would have been so proud of him; his mother must have died inside when she'd sent her son away. Jack still didn't understand why he'd been denied the right to make good on his father's pledge, and probably wouldn't until he had children of his own.

Our children—or they might have been, if this sorrowful tale had been destined to end happily.

No, she couldn't think that. It was selfish and dangerous.

Love was sacrifice, and knowing when to let go.

Yet Mairey held more tightly every day to the man. She sought him out every morning, afraid of the stirring in her heart when she caught sight of his dark eyes. His grief and guilt about his lost family were so close to the surface that she wondered how she'd missed them before.

They'd had no more wild embraces, no tumultuous bathtub romps that left her breathless and wanting. And he'd made no more allusions to marriage. That had been a part of the fairy tale: another time, another land, another princess and her dragon.

But Jack was persistent, and he stole a kiss from her at least once a day, in the most bewitching way. He would catch her in the green woods, or against her desk in the library, in a carriage where she couldn't escape, or late at night in the lodge when it all felt so right.

But the kisses were hardly stolen from her: they were offered, given freely, begged for in her heart and tucked away for the bleak days when he was gone from her life.

She could at least do this one kindness for Jack before she found the Willowmoon Knot: investigate her suspicions of the Messrs. Dodson and Greel. If they had been fleecing Jack all these years, he might not be prepared to hear it. But neither could she let the unforgivable fraud continue. Whether he could see it or not, the man had set his heart aside for all those years, waiting to be loved again.

"So good of you to come, Miss Faelyn. Please sit down." Dodson senior and junior might have been twins if there hadn't been three decades between them.

"Thank you." Mairey sat down on the edge of the chair and smoothed her hands over the fine linen skirt of the suit Jack had ordered for her. She'd come home to a wardrobe full of new clothes and had argued against them, but she'd lost out to his logic.

For visits to Windsor, madam. The scoundrel. She'd lost out to the rareness of the silk that felt like his skin had underwater. But mostly she'd succumbed to his roguish smile.

I'm starved for you, Mairey, he'd said, and then kissed her deeply, sending her off in a great spiral of yearning.

"Now, then, miss, you've come on the recommendation of a Sir Harold Hayward, dean of Galcliffe College?"

"Yes." Hayward's name had been the first to come to her mind when the lawyer's secretary had asked who had referred her. "Dean Hayward said that you'd done some investigative work for a relative of his. Though I'm afraid I can't recall the man's name. A professor at Oxford."

"Oxford . . . Oxford? Hmmmm . . ." The senior Dodson fiddled with the ends of his moustache for a moment and then brightened. "Ah, yes. Blaine, it was. I remember now. A baronet."

Liars! She'd never heard of an Oxford baronet named Blaine.

The younger scooted his chair closer: a well-turned fellow, classically handsome, but with too-regular edges—nowhere as compelling as the man who let Anna put a flower in his lapel every morning, and took extraordinary care to see that it wasn't crumpled by his day's work.

"How can we help you, Miss Faelyn?"

"What I want to know, gentlemen, is how you would go about finding someone that I have lost."

"Lost?" They were a pair of swivel-necked ravens, nodding at each other.

"It's very sad. You see, for reasons too painful for me to discuss in public, my father emigrated with me to Australia shortly after I was born, leaving my mother behind with my three little brothers." A family like Jack's mother and his three sisters, lost about the same time as his.

"A sad turn indeed," the elder Dodson said, leaning back in his chair, weaving his fingers together over his sunken chest.

Warming to her performance, Mairey continued. "Now that my father has passed on, I would like to find my mother and my siblings. They're the only family I have."

"Not even betrothed, Miss Faelyn?" Young Dodson was affecting a rakish brow; God knew what was going on behind those overly blue eyes. Biology, no doubt.

"Not even a betrothed," Mairey said, patting her belt purse. "But I have money enough to retain your firm for as long as you require." She leaned forward. "How long would that be?"

"Well, Miss Faelyn," the younger said, rising like a judge and striding toward the bookcase, his hands clasped behind him, "the duration of our search depends entirely upon how detailed the information is that you give us."

"What sort of information?"

"Dates of birth, place of birth, wedding, uhm . . ."

"Emmigration records?"

Obviously a new thought. "Yes, very good."

"What other records do you investigate?"

"Well, uh . . . many."

"And do you examine these records yourselves?"

"Well . . . no. That is, not usually. You see, our firm deals primarily in wills and estates. We have an operative who investigates claims against inheritance."

"And looks for lost relatives when he has the time?"

"Er, yes, but of course he will *make* time for this," the older Dodson assured her hastily.

"And what is your success rate, gentlemen?"

"Good."

"*Excellent,* Miss Faelyn."

Blue ballocks! The Messrs. Dodson, Dodson, and Greel couldn't find their collective hat if it were nailed to their collective wooden heads. *Damn* them all to the very hottest part of hell.

"You've been most informative." Mairey steadied her outrage and stood. She offered her hand, grateful for her deer-skin gloves, which kept Junior Dodson's fingers from touching hers.

"We shall await your business with the greatest

anticipation, Miss Faelyn. Shall we say next week?''

Say anything you like, sir. ''Next week it is.''

Mairey plunged down the steps and out into High Holborn. She'd never in her life met a more cruel and insensitive pair. ''Bastards!''

Her explosion brought a scowl from a knot of frock coats standing nearby. But she was so near the Inns of Court that the sight of a cursing client bowling out of a law chamber was no doubt as regular as the 5:12 from Dover.

Dear Jack, what they've done to you! Her skin was boiling; she wanted to scream and weep. He had unknowingly hired a company of buffoons. They knew nothing about emmigration registries, or shipping manifests, or factory lists; and they employed an operative who treated Jack's case no better than a hobby!

May their bones turn to salt! They'd stolen eighteen long and unimaginably lonely years from Jack. From a man who needed all the family, all the love, he could find.

He was so very easy to love—her sisters had fallen for him immediately, and Tattie.

And me. Stunned, Mairey sat down hard on a bench to await a hackney.

I love him. It was true! She loved that he had engineered the daring rescue at Glad Heath, and that the people there thought him a prince; she loved that honey made him weep; that when he looked at her she imagined suckling his milk-scented babies and sliding her mouth across his lips.

She loved him, plain and simple . . . oh, and as complex as the dance of the stars and the moon.

Impossible.

She wished he'd never come looking for the Willowmoon; wished he had taken no for an answer and gone about his treasure hunting on another hill, in another glade, another heart. Not *hers!*

She didn't dare let her thoughts wander about Drakestone, the home he'd so grandly made for her family. For they came to rest always with Jack and all the happiness that could never be.

She owed him his sisters and his mother, and she would stand by him whatever the news. But she would keep her search a secret from him, for the sake of his pride and his fragile expectations. To raise them and then dash them would only cause him more grief and guilt, and he'd had too much of that in his life.

She'd discovered from Jack that the heinous Sir Cahill had owned a foundry in Manchester. It was a leap of logic to think that Claire Rushford might have gone there looking for work after her dear husband was killed, but it was a start.

And Jack had waited long enough.

"To the left, Sumner, old man! Paddle to the left!"

"You're in the back, Rushford, sir. You're supposed to be steering!" Sumner missed a frenetic stroke and sheeted pond water back into Jack's face.

"Oh, gad!" Jack swabbed a stringy weed off his

face with his shirtsleeves, then went back to paddling.

The girls were squealing at them from the bankside, jumping like wind-up toys.

"You're wet, Lord Jack!"

"Look! I found a salamander!"

"I can swim good! C'n I show you?"

"Don't you dare, Caro!" They were muddy from stem to stern. Mairey might be amused when she returned from London and saw the mess—she was ever the one to break the rules—but Aunt Tattie was going to skin him alive.

A duck house. Why the devil had he promised to install one in the middle of the pond?

"It's gonna be the bestest duck house in the whole world, Lord Jack!"

That was the reason. Home and hearth and duck ponds. Bless them all. Hope had always frightened him, made him feel weak and unworthy, yet here he was, filled with the stuff, and aching to begin a life together with Mairey. He'd come to the conclusion that marriage was the answer.

"Careful, sir! We're tipping." Sumner was paddling furiously.

He really should have called in Richmond to help in the engineering. "Don't move, Sumner."

The little boat was sitting dangerously low in the water, loaded to its gunwales with rocks that would, in a very few nautical yards, become the foundations for Duck Island, the home of the Drakestone drakes.

"We're taking on water, Rushford."

"Get rid of the rocks, Sumner!"

Unfortunately, they simultaneously chose to toss out one of the stone cannonballs from the same side.

The boat rocked, listed fatally, and then took on water like a burst dam.

"Lord Jack! You're sinking!" A trio of screams came from the bank.

"Hell," Sumner said.

"Damnation."

The sorry vessel dropped out from under them in a single sucking slurp, and then sank to the bottom fully loaded with rocks, leaving Jack and Sumner treading water and the girls in a shrieking panic.

"Welcome to Duck Island, sir."

"You too, Sumner." Jack laughed and swam the twenty feet to the bankside, to the little hands that were eager to help but nearly lethal.

"A towel!" Anna was already racing back from the laundry, her arms loaded down with linens. She dumped a load of them into Sumner's lap and gave the rest to Jack along with a kiss on his eye. The other two fell all over him, wanting to help, buffing his hair into a nest.

They discussed what to do next, and the merits of erecting an island on the foundations of a boat.

"Let's ask Mairey," Caro offered.

"An excellent idea. As soon as she comes back," Jack promised, harrowing the last of the tangles from his hair.

"I'm back now. Is that too soon?"

"Never." Jack's heart gave a thump, and he dropped the towel on the grassy slope. He would have embraced her and set her mouth on fire, but he was soaking with pond water and surrounded by too many people, and she was laughing.

"Oh, Jack! Sumner! You're all wet!" Mairey swiped tears out of her eyes. The others were rolling on the ground, equally demented, echoing their grown-up sister's laughter.

Until they all noticed Aunt Tattie standing at the end of the stone walk, her hands fisted against her hips.

"Uh-oh. She's tapping her foot," Sumner whispered loudly, rising up on his haunches. "I think I hear cook calling me."

"You sit there, Mr. Sumner." Tattie loomed large in the midst of their huddle and took three muddy little hands in one of hers. "Girls, you're coming with me." She kissed Mairey, then raised her spectacles to Jack as he stood there in his dribbling sleeves. "And you, your lordship, ought to know better."

"Yes, ma'am." Jack and Mairey stood silently, hiding from Aunt Tattie in broad daylight, while the others scurried away to their separate corners of the estate.

"It's plain the woman likes you best, Mairey." Jack took her hand and started toward the laundry for a dry shirt, a momentous discussion on his mind.

"The secret is chocolate." She ran her fingers through his hair. He had emptied his boots and taken off his socks, but he still squished water out of the soles when he walked.

Mairey watched from the door of the laundry as

he exchanged a wet shirt for a dry one, a cat smile on her lips. It was too inviting not to kiss, so he did.

"Ooo, your lips are cool, Jack." Hers were warm and her fingers searing as she buttoned his shirt. He would have to live with wet trousers while he strolled back to the house with Mairey on his arm and her scent in his nostrils, while he formed the perfect proposal of marriage.

"You seemed to be enjoying yourself out there, Jack, even when the boat sank. I saw it all."

He was dizzy with happiness, crazy for her smile, and bursting to be alone with her. "You won't tell them, will you? That I'm a sucker for their silly projects?"

"They love you, Jack."

"Ha! They know I'm good for a hobbyhorse ride, or a duck house builder."

"Because you love them."

Yes—that was that whirling sensation in his chest. Being needed for himself. Succeeding where it counted. *Ah, Mairey, what you've given to me!*

"You had a lot of practice, living with three sisters of your own."

"They were a handful. I confess that I see them stair-stepped in Anna and Caro and Poppy."

She seemed distracted from everything but his fingers, opening his hand inside hers and caressing the lines and the hollows. "Time stopped that day, didn't it, Jack?"

And started again with you, Mairey.

"Hell, I'm probably an uncle many times over, yet in all my memories, I'm still fifteen and my sisters are still young. They still have the bony little fingers that knew which of my ribs to tickle until I surrendered the sweets I brought them every Saturday.''

"The consummate brother.''

He snorted. "One who took every opportunity to escape his annoying little siblings. I had discovered women just about then.''

"Ah." She raised a brow that he decided, with great jubilation, was the tiniest arc of jealousy.

"The mating instinct, Miss Faelyn. It's very strong in the young human male.''

"Yes, I know.''

Jack felt the chaotic flush like a fever, borne of this woman and her patience, of the uncommon memories he was making with her.

"And were you successful?''

"At what?" He hadn't the faintest idea what she was talking about, only that she seemed pensive, and intent upon everything he said.

"You and your mating instincts.''

"Ah, that." He caught her around the waist and stopped beneath the wisteria arbor.

"I was bumbling," he said, remembering too vividly, too quickly, to fend off the image of his first time with a woman—which had taken all of fifteen seconds, and hadn't been accomplished until he was eighteen and the first brothel was built in Chantilly. He never went back to the place; he'd purchased his fleeting pleasure with precious gold that should have gone to finding his family. And in the deepest part of him, he had known that the desperate young woman was someone's sister.

"You've grown out of that."

"I'm glad you think so." Her face was turned up to him, her mouth the color of Sumner's prized damask rose, now and forever Jack's undisputed favorite.

He cupped her chin, and tasted her lips with his tongue. Very sweet, soft, scented with honey.

"Jack . . ." She slipped her fingers into his hair and seemed to be choosing her words with unusual care. "Jack, I found something today—"

"Tell me you've found the Willowmoon Knot and we can get down to the real business between us." Marriage. *That* would have been a cloddish opening.

"Not that. But I have found something."

As a man who had forged a career looking for treasures, Jack knew the stomach-churning thrill of discovery. Yet these were grieving eyes that were watching his face.

"Something that makes you frown?"

"I just don't know how to tell you this, Jack." She looked away from him with her bleakness, and the distance left him starved for air.

"Just tell it straight, Mairey."

She swung her gaze back to him, watery and rimmed in red. "When I first took on the task, it seemed quite the most natural thing for me to do. It comes so easily to me."

"So does your riddling, Mairey. What is it?" A premonition rode him. Was she leaving him? Had Walsham or one of the other men whom she charmed so regularly stolen her fancy?

"I've spent my life looking for lost things, Jack.

Digging up burial burrows, capturing folk tales so they won't vanish when all the storytellers are gone.''

"Yes, I know. You're very good at spinning a tale." He didn't think he was going to like this one.

"I can't tell you how dearly your search for your family has affected me. I think about it all the time. My parents have passed away, but I was with them both when they died. And I have my sisters, and can love them, hold and kiss them, every day of my life." Tears were rolling down her cheeks, mystifying him completely. "I couldn't imagine never seeing them again. But if something horrible did happen to them, it would be better to know they were at peace in a churchyard, Jack, than simply lost to me."

That hit him like a slap, an insult to the memories he held so dear. "Not better at all, Mairey. I appreciate your empathy, but I would rather let the subject rest."

"It can't."

"It can if I say so."

"Listen to me, Jack. After you told me about your search, I was incensed!" She threw her outrage at him, the reflection of his own, though better focused and glaring in its brilliance. "Eighteen years, Jack, and Dodson turned up nothing! That's appalling."

"But it's my business."

"Maybe so. But I couldn't just stand back and not do anything. And so I—"

He took her arm, sat her down on the stone bench, and knelt in front of her. "You what?"

She caught her lip with her teeth, lowered her eyes to her fidgeting fingers. "I went to see them. Dodson and his son."

Stunned and wanting to see the truth in her teary eyes, he held her chin. "Why?"

She shook off his touch. "I pretended that I had lost my family—"

"Why, damn it?"

"Oh, Jack." She grabbed his hands, forced her fingers between his, and held fast to them. "I had this appalling feeling that they were. . . . That for all these years they had been—"

"Playing me the fool?"

Her face paled. "Worse than that, Jack. I was sure they had no idea what they were doing. So I asked how they would approach a search for my mother and three brothers. A family much like yours, lost twenty years ago. Oh, Jack, they didn't even know where to begin. They rattled on about their operative who looks through registries *when he has time!* You were the man's *hobby,* Jack!"

Well, then—his suspicions were confirmed. Nothing more than he had already concluded. He stood, avoiding Mairey's eyes, emptier than he'd been before but still whole. He swallowed his outrage so that it wouldn't blaze across the sky.

"Thank you, Mairey." He'd hired Dodson from across the world and trusted him with his business. He'd been foolish not to look for a new firm once he'd returned to England. "I shall take great pleasure in sacking them tomorrow morning. They aren't my regular staff of legal advisors; I only used Dodson for this single issue."

His anger was burning brightly, but he didn't want to focus too clearly on its meaning. *Treacherous bastards*. He needed to walk for a while, needed air.

"There's more, Jack." She slipped her hand into his.

"More? Did you find them embezzling from me, too? Impossible—I have a whole staff of lawyers and accountants who protect me from incompetence."

She held his face between her soft hands and made him look into her eyes, though they were still streaming with tears.

"Jack . . . I found your mother."

His heart went wild and leaping. Heat seared the back of his eyes before Mairey's words settled into the air between them.

"What did you say?" He held fast to her arms, wanted to see and hear her words because she couldn't possibly have said what was ringing inside his head. Sunbursts of hope, star-pinned wonder filled his chest. "My mother? You found her, Mairey? My God, where is she?"

He wondered if he would recognize her after all these years, and why she hadn't come with Mairey.

"Oh, God, Jack, how do I tell you this?" She kissed his palm and held it to her lips, to her damp cheek. "Your mother died, my love, a very long time ago."

"You're mistaken, Mairey." He pulled his hand out of hers, standing stiff and disconnected. That wasn't possible. He'd promised his father he would take care of her; he only needed to find her and his sisters and then he could start. He'd bought this house for them—

"I found the registry of her death, in the parish church just outside Manchester." Her fingers quaked as she handed him a folded sheaf of paper. "I made a copy of it, and a carbon rubbing of her gravestone. Jack, I'm so sorry."

His limbs were numb as he took the bundle, tucked it under his arm, and looked out across his estate, counting all the freshly painted corner posts in the fence that bordered the herb garden. He was waiting for his throat to clear of the volcanic sob seething there, waiting to breathe again without aching.

"When did it happen?" He swallowed back the molten heat, and let it burn its way down his gullet.

"She died in Manchester on December fifteenth, 1842."

Eight months after he left Glad Heath. All those years of imagining that his mother was waiting on the porch for him to come home, bread-scented and smiling, holding back the wriggling tide of his sisters. Lost to him completely.

"Jack, you have to know this, too." Mairey reached for his hand and took just his fingertips, as though she thought he would lash out at her. "Your mother died in childbirth. And the baby with her."

That couldn't be! A stunning tide of relief washed over him. He threw the offensive papers on the ground between them, utterly astounded that Mairey would put him through this horror for nothing, without checking her facts.

"You've found the wrong woman, madam! My

mother was not pregnant. She would have told me. Father would have.''

Mairey was shaking her head, sternly denying his happiness. ''She probably didn't know herself, Jack, not until you were gone. But she was delivered of a full-term, stillborn son.''

''No.'' No. No. No! ''It wasn't her, damn you! I will find her!''

''His name was Patrick.''

Oh, God! His father's name. An unchecked sob roared out of his chest, became a howl of shame, of loss. Now his brother was a casualty of Jack's neglect, too—his father's request turned to ashes from the first.

''That's where I was today, Jack. In Manchester.''

She touched his arm, and his stomach reeled. He shook her off and grabbed up the strewn papers, dry as death, crackling like ancient autumn leaves.

''You did all this *today?*''

''In just a little over an hour from the time I arrived at the railway station. I did nothing extraordinary, Jack. The parish register was available; the old vicar pleasant and helpful; your mother's name and the details written quite clearly, and exactly as I would have expected.''

He'd always safely entombed his guilt in the knowledge that he had engaged the best agency that money could buy, that Dodson and his lot were as relentless in this quest as he. He'd relied upon men who had made a mockery of his fidelity and a farce of his crusade.

But in the end, that highly polished veneer of

diligent pursuit and familial devotion had been stripped away by a single, disposable hour in the life of Mairey Faelyn. He had hired her to find him a silver mine, not to flay open his life and turn it out to the sun so that he had no course but to stare at its ugliness. Would the very capable Miss Faelyn next find his sisters lodged in a whorehouse?

"Damn you for meddling."

"Meddling?" She backed away, her eyes flashing silvery hot. "How can you say that, Jack?"

"I didn't ask you to interfere."

"But I have. And it's done. I know it hurts, that it stings your pride and scrapes your stomach raw. But you've lost eighteen years, Jack; don't lose another day. Let me help you find your sisters."

"*No!* You've already done enough, Miss Faelyn."

She caught up his sleeve when he turned to leave, bracing her palms against his chest in her angry defense of him. "It wasn't your fault, Jack. Don't you see that?"

There was the flaw in her logic. So bloody plain he wondered how she could have missed it.

"Dodson might well have been using me, Miss Faelyn, but not half as expertly as I was using *him*."

He left her while he still had breath, before he made a monster of himself and an enemy of the misguided woman that he adored.

Chapter 15

 ❧❧❧

Supper tasted of sawdust to Mairey. The girls were fretful, wanting to run free in the woods. Jack had been gone since yesterday, God knew where. He'd ridden out of the stable like the madman he was.

Loneliness and despair did that.

She'd never seen a man in such anguish. And she'd caused it: rammed a spear though the slit in his spiny armor, found his huge, defenseless heart, and then, because she was prying as well as pushy, she'd given that spear a good, solid twist!

He had cried out in his agony—a horrible lament that had torn open her own heart. But instead of letting her explain, instead of seeking her comfort, instead of staying to plan with her to find his sisters, the scoundrel had gone barreling off, dragging her shredded heart along after him.

"The stone-headed, ungrateful churl!"

"No word from his lordship, love?" Aunt Tattie seemed to be the only one of the family not affected by the runaway wobble of the earth; she seemed happily content with her humming as she padded through the parlor, turning down the lamps.

"I can't very well expect to hear from him." Mairey snuffled back another plague of tears so they wouldn't smear any more of the notes she'd been making. "I told the lout something he didn't want to hear."

"Ah, men." Tattie sat down on the settle and rubbed Mairey's back in great soothing circles. "Was it something his lordship needed telling?"

That his mother was dead? And that he'd had a brother he would never meet? That they'd been dead for nearly eighteen years, and he could stop looking for her; stop waiting for his life to begin? "Oh, yes, he needed telling."

"Well, then he'll understand."

Tears erupted from Mairey's eyes again, dragging huge sobs from deep in her chest. "I don't think he ever will."

"He doesn't blame you, whatever you've told him. Not really. And certainly not for long. Not the way he loves you."

A whirlwind propelled Mairey off her aunt's shoulder and made it almost impossible to focus.

"He *what*?"

"Don't tell me you haven't noticed. I've never seen the like." Tattie winked and thumbed a tear off Mairey's lip. "Never since my own Perry."

"Jack doesn't love me." He *mustn't*!

"Well, he does. Which is quite the nicest of happenstances, since you love the man to distraction."

"I—" Mairey simply nodded, resigned to the plain facts. She'd never known any man like Jack.

Wise and reckless, compassionate and granite-headed.

Hopefully not angry enough to track down the Messrs. Dodson and Greel and beat the daylights out of them. Though if he had, she'd have gladly given her entire collection of elf bolts just to watch and would have sacrificed her stone axes to add a punch of her own.

She went to the window and looked out on the moon-blanketed woods, cursing this feeling of helplessness.

"Where the devil are you, Jack Rushford?"

Jack leaned up against an elm at the edge of the dark woods. Mairey's woods. Cricket songs and rilling water, that sweet smell of green. The lights of the lodge winking at him.

He'd let her family swarm over Drakestone willy-nilly, even encouraged the intrusion; let the household routine become disrupted; and like a fool, let them all into his heart—that great big murky chasm.

Shored up with stout timbers, crossbeams and struts. Indeed, *heart*wood. Sturdy stuff, impregnable, unbreakable. Best when hollow and echoing and insulated from unthinkable truths by ghosts and shadows.

Dodson, Dodson Greel and *Rushford*. *There* was a partnership. Conceived long ago in the conscientious pursuit of Jack's lost integrity, dedicated throughout its term to the cherished memory of a valorous father, and, in the end, executed by all parties with contempt for both truth and honor.

The truth was that Jackson Rushford was a coward. Afraid that if he allowed anyone, himself included, to search too efficiently for his family, he would discover that he had done too little and was years too late. All of them slipping away from him, falling, drowning, just beyond the reach of his fingertips.

He'd ridden hell-bent to the rail station and, still denying the truth, had gotten halfway to Manchester before he had realized where he was going. He had to see for himself this eighteen-year-old grave. His mother's name. And this other child—his brother . . . Patrick.

But as he had stepped down from the darkened platform, he realized that he still didn't know where she was buried; he'd been too clumsy in his thinking to ask Mairey in which churchyard he'd find his mother's grave.

He hadn't learned a thing, though Mairey had tried to teach him.

He'd been a damn fool. Blaming her for holding up a mirror to his deficiencies, for loving him; and then tearing away from her like a maniac. His pride tasted like metal, chewed like a handful of nails. But he had swallowed it all, though it took him a full day to do it.

He wanted her to know that he wasn't a lunatic or a brute, that she had courage where he had none at all. He wanted her wisdom, her help to find his way back. He wanted her to know his heart, all of it. That crowded, madly thumping vessel in the center of his chest, the one that had always seemed so empty but now was full to bursting.

So here he was, lurking outside her house like a lovelorn dolt, holding fast to the monumental decision he'd made this evening.

The lodge was dark save for a single light high in the gallery window. Nine o'clock. The girls would be gone to bed by now, Mairey's bedtime tales tucked under their pillows to sweeten their dreaming. Tonight's tale and last night's would surely have been of fire-breathing dragons and purloined princesses.

And that dragon's name would rightly be Jackson Rushford.

He wondered if the trellis beneath Mairey's window would hold him.

"It's Lord Jack! Look, Poppy! I found him!"

They leaped at him out of the understory, flying toward him in streaks of white gossamer and clouds of giggles and streaming hair.

"Anna Faelyn, what are you doing outside in the middle of the night?" He knelt on one knee to corral them, and they fell on him in a clump of arms and legs, landing fairy kisses that would probably leave purple bruises. "Ouch! Caro, does Mairey know you're all out here?"

"No, she'd skin us!"

"Where have you been, you mean old Jack?" Poppy found his neck and clung there, a bare heel in his crotch until he shifted her to his hip.

"We were looking for you."

"Here, in the woods, in the dark?"

"You made Mairey sad when you left." A belly-blow from Anna that had nothing to do with her sharp little elbows.

"I didn't mean to. I made myself sad, too."

"Do you promise never to run away again?" Anna had her sister's persistence and sense of order, and was far too perceptive for her years.

"I promise to do everything I can to make her the happiest woman on earth."

"She'll like that."

"I certainly hope so." This was no place and no time for a conference. "And I don't need to be looked for any longer. You found me; I'm home." At least near it. "Which is where you should all be. Now, be off before Mairey finds you gone."

But even as he gave the warning, the door to the lodge clicked open and Mairey stepped out onto the wooden porch in her nightgown, a candle held high, searching for something beyond the glow.

"Trouble," Jack whispered, wondering how the hell he had become a confederate to three changelings. He was smiling grandly, finding it difficult to hold in the belly laugh that was brewing in his chest.

The four of them became part of the shadowed brambles and the ferns, huddled in a conspiracy of silence as they protected their collective hides and rode out the danger of discovery.

"You should marry her, Lord Jack."

"Sh!" He clamped his hand over Caro's mouth, felt her silly grin in the middle of his palm.

Marry Mairey? Oh, God, yes! Tomorrow if she'd let him. His heart filled up so fast the tide of it jostled him off balance, and a twig snapped under his knee.

Mairey turned sharply and took a step toward

them, held her candle higher, and leaned forward in her glowing gown and spun-glass hair. She stood for a long time, peering directly at their fear-frozen tableau, before she pinched out the flame and gazed up at the bright moon.

"Come home, Jack." Her whisper or his wish, or a soughing breeze. She was there, and then she was gone. The door closed, and everyone collapsed but Jack.

"Off you go, young ladies! Now! And I mean go straight into the house or I'll see that Mairey knows you were out here."

"Yes, sir, Lord Jack." Anna was giggling.

"Don't say a word about me, or we'll all be in trouble."

"Cris and cross our hearts!"

Then they were gone, bare feet shushing across the small yard and through the side door of the kitchen.

Not a minute later, their small, smiling faces and waving hands appeared at the garret window.

Ghosts. No, not ghosts—hoarded remembrances, cherished and enduring. Maybe that's all he would ever find of what-might-have-been. And maybe that would have to be enough.

He let the gouging grief hurt this time, and the lost years; let them sting the back of his throat and fill his eyes to overflowing.

He waved Godspeed to his phantoms and hello to the three little girls who had won over his heart the moment Anna's well-aimed apple had hit him in the shoulder.

He left the woods for his cavernous house, a man with marriage on his mind and Mairey in his heart.

Unsure what whimsy had drawn her outside earlier, but suspecting the foolish moon and Jack Rushford, Mairey went back to her restless idling. She dusted the curios on the mantel, read for a time in the parlor, then soaked for an hour in the tub until she was prunish and pink. She made the rounds to the girl's rooms and left kisses on their foreheads, wondering how each of them had gotten bits of mulberry leaves in their hair. Her three dancing princesses.

She tried her best to sleep, but the crickets were in full voice tonight and the breeze that caught at her curtains was too sweet, and soon she was pacing down the stairs in her night rail.

The Willowmoon and its knot-work were on her mind, a maze inside a maze; Jack's life and hers woven together intricately, recklessly. She couldn't leave Drakestone until she'd found the Willowmoon Knot. She couldn't stay for the ache in her heart.

Finding the Knot quickly was the logical solution. The sooner she did, the sooner she could extricate herself and her family.

Which would cause great tides of grief that would drown her every day for the rest of her life. But it couldn't be helped; she had promises to keep. She would start bringing her work home to the lodge, and separate herself from Jack a little at a time until she could manage perfectly—perfectly wretchedly—without him. *No time like the present,* she thought, trying to convince herself of the urgency.

The twenty-volume *Gazetteer of Ecclesiastical Antiquities* had been delivered to Drakestone's library earlier today among the properties that the Royal Family were to give to the new museum at South Kensington, and she hadn't found a single moment to study them. She would do so now.

After donning a long walking-coat over her nightgown and slipping into a pair of garden boots, Mairey left the lodge and made her way toward the main house.

A rustle of guilt stirred the air in her lungs and tainted the sweetness of the night. Not because she had stepped out of the bounds of their relationship and proved Jack's lawyers as devoid of honor as they were of resources. He needed that jolt of truth, whatever it had cost him in agony.

Rather because he was the most honest and trusting man she had ever met—which left Mairey feeling caddish and hollow. She was in the business of deception, and Jack was her helpless mark. Even if he read his way through all twenty volumes of the *Gazetteer of Ecclesiastical Antiquities,* even if he memorized every word of it, he would still be confounded. He needed Mairey to make sense of the passages and to lead him to the Willowmoon Knot.

And that made her great, bellowing dragon vulnerable to her slightest falsehood, the ones she created every day to keep him off track. Big, sloppy red herrings, drawn so easily across his path.

With the weight of the ages pressing on her shoulders, Mairey let herself into the dark library, feeling her way along the familiar textures to her workbench, surprised that Jack's eloquent scent of leather and soap was so strong and so evocative though he'd been gone for more than a day.

She lit the lamp on her worktable, then lugged volume one of the thick gazetteer to her desk and flipped open the cover.

This Volume, intended as a Gazetteer of Minor Collections of Antiquities, is Respectfully Dedicated to the Most Honorable, the Viscount Norbury, Lord President of the Council of Antiquaries, 1778.

The Willowmoon Knot hadn't been in York; she and Jack had returned to the storage rooms in the minster and had found nothing of Runville's pagan collection, no mention of its ever having been cataloged. It might have been stored there unremarked for decades and then been traded to another parish, or sold to a museum or even to a private collector by one of the minster's deans.

1778. Nearly modern. It was the most tantalizing resource yet. Inefficiently indexed, and compiled from many sources, it would be a long, hard read. She should have been thrilled at finding the *Gazetteer*, but success had tasted bitter recently.

"If you were to search for my sisters, Mairey, where would you begin?"

"Jack!" Her heart wild with relief, Mairey searched him out in the shadows that stuffed the corners of the library. She had sensed him in the darkness after all, she'd heard his breathing, felt his heat and his scent. She wanted to run to him and hold him through the night—an accidental friend, an inconvenient colleague . . . and oh, yes, a lover.

"Your sisters, Jack?" she asked instead, trying to assess his mood across the distance between them. "That would depend on what more you could tell me about them."

"Everything, Mairey." His desk chair creaked, and she heard him rise. "I would tell you everything. You can have Dodson's file full of lies and distortions, for all the good it will do you." He teetered in place, caught his hand fast around the back of his chair.

The lout had injured himself, or he'd been drinking. Which didn't seem at all like the Jackson Rushford who planned and controlled the workings of his rigid life to the nearest inch.

"Jack, where have you been?" Concern for his recklessness made her voice far more chafing than she meant.

"Out."

"More than out, Jack. You were gone a night and a whole day." His delicate mood be damned. Mairey grabbed up her lamp and set it on the table beside him, then stood back to examine him as he flinched from the light, squinting down at her. He looked tumbled.

"Were you worried about me, Mairey?"

"Worried? How about terrified, good sir?"

He smiled sideways, too charmingly bashful for this hour of the night. "I didn't mean to worry you."

His hair was standing every which way, finger-combed and drooping damply into his eyes. She reached up and ran her fingers through its silky blackness.

"Your hair is wet."

He was jacketless, collarless, with his sleeves rolled to his elbow. "I took a bath, Mairey. I think I fell asleep again."

"You think?" He looked half-asleep still.

He leaned down lazily and pulled her close to whisper in her ear, "I didn't have you there to rescue me."

A very good thing, because she wouldn't have had rescue on her mind.

"Sit here, Jack, before you fall." Mairey wrestled him into the high-back chair. He landed with a grunt and a grimace. "Have you been fighting? Did you kill Dodson?"

"Christ, Mairey, I wanted to take on every Dodson and Greel I could get my hands on."

"And did you, Jack? Did you find Dodson and beat him to a pulp?" Hoping he had, Mairey knelt between his spread thighs and took pleasure in the intimate smoothness of his beard against her palms while she turned his jaw to examine him for injuries.

He hadn't even a scratch on him, save for the cut he must have just gotten from his razor.

"I would have, Mairey. But I didn't want you to hate me any more than you do."

"I don't hate you, Jack." Lunatic. He didn't know that she couldn't possibly hate this part of him, the lost boy who was searching for his family. Not when she wanted to *be* his family.

He tilted his head, and squinted at her through

one wickedly smiling eye. "Not even when I'm an inconsiderate ass?"

"Not even then, Jack." What the devil had gotten into him on his wild pilgrimage? He certainly hadn't been drinking; he smelled of soap and starch.

"I'm exceedingly glad of that, Mairey."

"Well, then, sir. If you were not out looking to bludgeon Dodson for his crimes against you, where did you go?"

"I was hunting for ghosts." He looked quite serious, the way a headmaster might as he was explaining the tidal effects of the moon. "I felt like a damned ghoul, last night and all the day long, tromping through every graveyard in Manchester."

"You went to Manchester." Mairey smiled hugely, relieved that he'd found at least a little hope tucked away in his outrage. "You really hadn't spent the day stalking Dodson."

"Bastard—he's not worth the trouble. I had a more precious mission."

"Your mother." Her heart swelled and grew lighter for him, though it still ached. She bundled his hand between hers. "Oh, Jack, you're wonderful—"

"Don't, Mairey." He brought their clasped hands to his lips and set a kiss on her fingers, his gaze fastened fiercely to hers as it so often was of late. "And don't beam at me like that with your eyes all misty, as though you believe me to be the perfect son and protector. I am not."

He needed sleep—or something. But getting the enormous man up the stairs and into his bed was going to be a mighty challenge. Leaving him there—alone—might prove impossible.

"Jack, you *are* a perfect son *and* brother. I know of no one who could have been a more exemplary protector, given any circumstances."

"Do not indulge me, Mairey. I've been a damned fool."

Oh, how she could count the ways—and be at the task for weeks! But Jack had never been anything but honorable and courageous in his devotion to his family. He had been their battle-ready champion from the day his father died, and long, long before that, if she knew the boy as well as she knew the man.

"Whatever you say, Jack." The man was not ready to admit to his goodness; battering him with it would only make him more stubborn. She left him and went back to her worktable. "I only meant that I was glad you saw your mother's grave."

"I didn't." He thrust himself out of the chair, stuffing his thumbs into the back of his trousers and pacing the room in his giant's stride. "I couldn't find the bloody thing."

Her spirit sank into the mud; she leaned against the table. "At St. Simon's Chapel?"

"You didn't say which church." He sliced her a self-directed indictment as he paced past her toward the bank of windows.

She followed him, feeling guilty. "I'm sorry, Jack—"

"Don't you dare, Mairey!" He abruptly turned back to her. She ran into his chest nose first and stayed there to sniff a little of his starchy tang.

"The fault was mine—all of it. I should have damn well asked you where she was before I went storming off. Instead I raged at you like a feral beast, accused you of . . . what was it I accused you of?"

"Nothing that matters, Jack." Nothing mattered but his shamefaced smile and the shadows that planed his jaw. "I understand—"

"You couldn't possibly." He planted himself on the edge of her desk, leaving Mairey standing between his spread knees. "But I am belatedly and enormously grateful for your trying to knock some sense into me, and entirely unworthy of your persistence. And I'm damned sorry for being a jackass, though it won't be the last time. I'm notoriously stone-headed."

"Indeed, you are." But he had a heart of bread pudding, sweet and soft and impossible to refuse. "As for Dodson, I would have kissed you if you had given him a good wallop."

"Kiss me now, Mairey." His voice was rough, filled with longing, and he tugged her closer. He gazed at her mouth as though he'd been lost in a desert and she was a cool oasis. A kiss wouldn't be very wise, not with the way her hands were trembling, the way her heart was pounding. He was leaning forward, had cocooned her nearly completely in his arms as he rested his hands on his knees. His cheek was soft, scented with citrus.

He was whispering feathery things to her. "Home, Mairey. Beautiful Mairey. Forgive me, Mairey."

"I do." If she didn't kiss him soon and be finished with it, the kiss would become his, and outright volcanic.

He was so very close, nudging her ever nearer, stealing her pulse and the air between them, until she found his mouth and covered it with hers. Oh, such a soft and impatient place.

He made a sound like her name, a plea, an exaltation that made her want to sing. Then he was growling low in his chest, his breath shuddering past her lips.

"God, Mairey, I want you." He plowed his fingers through her hair, tilted her face to him and plundered her mouth. "I want you forever."

Forever? *Oh, yes, Jack!* She wanted him completely, wanted to stay and stay, wanted children with him and to putter in his garden. But his life was mining and hers was already claimed by secrets and silver and that blasted village that she loved, and her lovely and sheltered family.

It isn't fair, Papa! But it was fact. And as dreadful as death.

Mairey scrambled to her feet and backed away from him, her arms aching from the need to hold him.

He was shaking, his grip on his knees a white-knuckled clench, and his breathing like a horse after the Derby.

"You're exhausted, Jack Rushford."

He straightened from the desk in all his rumpled, quaking wonder. "I was."

"You need to be in bed." Mairey bolted away from him and ran a few steps up the spiraling iron stairs that led to the mezzanine—and then across to the back door of his room.

"*We* need to be in bed, Mairey." He stood in the middle of the library, a glint-eyed, unsated dragon looking too pleased for his own good.

Her heart was racing, thrilled when his ringing footfall hit the landing a few steps below her.

"That wasn't my meaning, Jack."

"Oh, but it is mine, Mairey. I want to make love with you in my bed. *Our* bed, if you please."

"Ours?" What was the man talking about?

"Or in the lodge where you keep your heart." He started up the stairs relentlessly, his eyes fixed on hers, making her pulse thunder against her throat. "Or in the woods, or here in the library."

"You didn't sleep at all last night, did you, Jack?" That was the reason for his intimate confessions—not a passion for her. Certainly not love, as Tattie had suggested. Jack had said nothing about love.

She'd be lost completely if he ever did.

"I did sleep, Mairey," he said, closing in on her and her very illogical idea of getting him safely into his bed. "Dreaming always of you and the priceless gifts you've given me."

Odd, but she couldn't remember a single one. "How much sleep did you get?" She spun away and scooted up the stairs, five steps ahead of him. Then only two.

"I got enough."

She stopped at the mezzanine and turned to him. An even greater mistake. "Enough for what?"

He scooped her up in his next stride and started

toward his room. "Enough to make love with you till next Tuesday."

"Jack!"

"Till Wednesday, then, if you like."

She liked Wednesday too, too much.

"Jack, put me down."

"No."

His chamber door loomed—immense, shiny mahogany, and a fat brass latch that opened too easily to a room bathed in the dim light of slumbering lamps. She saw starry glints of gold and emerald and ruby glittering in the periphery. His bed was as huge as he was, tall, oak framed, and four posted, heaped with pillows and overlain with an undulating sea of autumn-hued counterpane.

Heaven on earth—a place to sprawl, wild-limbed, and collect his kisses wherever he cared to lay them.

"You wanted me in my bed, Mairey."

And everywhere else, Jack!

"Well, here it is." He let go of her legs and caught her up against the length of him, so warm and so vibrantly hard in so very many places. "Here *I* am. And damn me, if you're not wearing your nightgown."

His smile was loose and tilting and far too charming; and he was watching her through half-lidded eyes, with a pulse-pounding, possessive hunger that she had *badly* mistaken for exhaustion.

"Jack, I just came to the library to get a book. And I really shouldn't be . . . oh. Oh, yes." Mairey sighed long and deeply as he trailed his beguiling mouth and then his tongue down the column of her throat; she watched in dizzying expectation as he slipped his splendid fingers past her coat and into the neck of her nightgown, then lifted it aside, exposing the yearning hollow of her throat to his spice-steamed breath and the fevered tracing of his mouth.

"Ah, Mairey, I missed you. Wanted you. Wanted this." His huge and gentle hand cradled the underside of her breast through the linen of her gown. But she might as well have been as naked as the dewy morning for the bliss he caused, for the exquisite aching between her legs as though his hand was toying there again.

He was besieging her nipple like licking fire, and Mairey climbed to meet him. He nipped her and touched her deeper, and plied his excellent torture through the linen of her gown. She suddenly wanted to be free of her coat and her nightgown, skin to skin with him.

"Oh, Jack, you . . . oh!" She wanted to be possessed by her very own dragon, but it was imminently dangerous to her secret strategies against him. Baring herself to him like a common jade, delighting in his growls of adoration, taking tiny little gasps inside her throat, grabbing his shirttails and urging his hips and his feral hardness against her belly wouldn't help her cause, either.

He'd get a wholly wrong idea about her intentions.

She was getting a wholly wrong idea about her intentions!

Mairey closed her eyes and banished the voices that warned her to run from him, from the man she loved, who made her laugh and rented his woods to the fairies. She let her stolen joy and Jack's scent fill her.

He was her phantom kingdom, a sanctuary where dragons were princes, where there was no such thing as the Willowmoon Knot, no silver mine or slag heaps or open pits.

"Did you mean it, Jack?"

He backed away a step, leaving an aching confusion of drafts between them. His shirt hung open where she'd freed the buttons, white against rippling bronze.

"Did I mean *what?*" His breath tore out of him and his thick arms flexed beneath his sleeves, his hands clenching as though he'd been checked in the midst of a fistfight.

"That you wanted to make love to me tonight."

He shook his tousled head slowly, grinning slyly. "I meant *every* night, my love."

Oh, my. "Then make love to me, Jack. Please."

Wasn't that what fairy tales were for?

Chapter 16

Abolt of raw, fire-tipped lust jolted through Jack, nearly driving him backward with its power. He'd been fighting to hold on to common sense, a window of sanity, while he put together the right words to propose. Assuring her that he had the most honorable intentions would take careful thought and finesse—and at the moment he was lucky to be thinking at all. His heart was galloping, pumping molten blood through his veins and into his groin, but not a drop was going to his sodden brain.

He'd taken refuge in the library in order to dissuade himself from breaking down the door of her room. Yet somehow he'd conjured her in her bedclothes, this guileless apparition who had turned his life upside down.

The belt at her waist had come loose, and her coat hung off her shoulders as though it wanted the floor. She was covered to the cleaving of her breasts by her nightgown, and standing in a too-big pair of muddy boots. Boots and bare feet and a plain, plain gown—and still the magic swirled around her.

"God, Mairey, you're beautiful."

It was a diminishment of all she meant to him, but she laughed kindly and gave a bashful assessment of her slumping clothes.

"This old thing?" Touching that hollow between her perfect breasts, she turned him a coy hip and a side-bent knee.

His brain seized up. "Every inch of you, Mairey."

"These too?" She jiggled one boot off and then the other; stood in her bare feet on the leaf-strewn design of the carpet.

"Especially those." He was utterly undone, ready to take a boring of this precious mine, to sink a shaft and lose himself inside her. "But"—he hung onto the shredded remains of his sanity—"I ought to take you back to the lodge while we're still dressed and able."

She put her hands out as though to stop his words; shook her head as though she didn't want to hear. "No, Jack, no. I want this. I want tonight to last forever."

Forever. Beginning here and now, my love, not a one-night roundabout. He would peel her of every stitch, find delicate inroads, secret pathways to the treasure she had become to him.

"Forever it is, then, my love."

She watched him from under her exquisite lashes as she shoved the coat off her shoulders and let it fall to the floor. Her fingers absorbed him as she unfastened the pearly buttons that ran down the front of her pale nightgown to the joining of her thighs—one button and then the next, and then two more, till the gown was hanging off one shoulder, teasing him, taunting, till he couldn't stand the wait.

"Let me." He threaded his fingers through the tumble of her hair and made love to her mouth, then stepped back to slide her gown down her arms, to simply stare. He'd watched her breasts tease against her shirtwaist for so long that he knew them intimately, loved them dearly. They were marvelous, creamy, high and lush, rose-tipped and just full enough to cradle in his hands, to crest with his thumbs.

"Oh, Jack, that's—" She inhaled hugely, and threw her head back. Her upward motion pressed her closer, allowed him to catch a budding nipple between his lips. She gasped and impatiently shook off the prison her gown made at her elbows, then clutched the back of his head, tugging him closer. "Yes, *there*. How wonderful you feel to me."

"And this too?" He pulled the sweet morsel into his mouth, between his tongue and teeth and set her to mewling, reaching for handfuls of his hair. Her mouth, her breasts, her belly. She writhed and danced against him, and he held her hips to keep them still, then took her mouth again to keep himself from dragging her to the carpet and filling her with his seed, with his hopes.

Marry me, my love. Be my wife, tonight and always.

"Jack, I want you closer." Her gown was still caught up on the fine bones of her pelvis, soft contours of alabaster, hiding that sacred font he would kneel to worship before the night was over. Even as he loosed the maddening thought, even as he was kneading the span of her waist, she covered his hands with hers and guided him over her hips, pushing the bunched-up linen off the gentle slope to drop to the floor in a puddle.

She was lamplight and ivory, sleek and rounded, dazzle-eyed and blessedly eager, peeling him out of his own shirt, tasting across his shoulders, his collarbone, the hollow of his throat, leaving him breathless and grunting like a boar.

"God, Mairey!" He shrugged out of the other sleeve, then filled his arms with her splendor, lifting her off the ground and against him.

"Ah, much better, Jack. Your chest to mine."

"Your heart and mine."

She wrapped her legs around his waist and held his face between her hands, tracing the abundance of her mouth across his eyelids and against his lips.

Sweat beaded his forehead and ran down his back while his hands were laced together beneath her bare and quivering flanks, forced by physics into idleness; supporting her when he wanted to be teasing at the seductive cleft pressed so sublimely against his belly. There were still barriers between her sultry heat and his raging urgency, wool and linen and cotton aplenty. But his sense of memory was crystal clear—the exotic fragrance of her on his fingers, soft folds and slick heat.

His serendipitous lot was to just stand there and take it, to count backward from a hundred while she rocked against him and made rampant love to his mouth, murmuring something about secrets and dragons and longings.

He'd been in a nearly perpetual state of arousal since he'd met the woman. He was currently, everlastingly, rock-hard and throbbing, on the verge of some good old prurient thrusting.

"Your trousers, Jack."

Oh, excellent—she was a mind reader. "What about them?"

"Take them off, please." She spoke against his ear, with tongue and teeth and no small amount of humid heat.

God in highest heaven, he'd found a treasure. Naked and open and more precious than all the gold in the Yukon. He carried her to the edge of the bed, almost mad with the need for her. Her fingers were already on top of his, brushing them away from his own buttons.

"Let me, Jack." She sighed as she smoothed her fingers across the fabric at his groin, which bulged, barely holding back his erection.

He grabbed her wrist, kissed her palm. "Too much exploring, love, if I'm to last long."

"Please, Jack." She was looking up at him, an unclad sprite with deviltry on her mind. "I won't touch until you say I can."

"Hardly a comfort to me, Mairey. I'm already this aroused for you." His unsubtle sprite smiled, and he took in a breath that cleared his head. "You may help."

Her fingers were quick and sped ahead of his down the front placket. She freed the last button. "There!" Then she sat back on her hands, as though she expected his penis to spring from his pants and dance for her. She looked perplexed and very impatient.

Before her virginal but very accomplished hands could find him inside his drawers and work her wiles too quickly, Jack shucked the works: trousers, drawers, socks, and shoes, while she looked on from her backward-sprawling, provocative pose on the edge of the bed, roundly appraising and waiting for him.

Mairey was sure she had died. And she was in heaven, assigned her very own angel. The man was extraordinary, his skin golden in the soft light from the lamp at his bedside, his smile as husbandly as it was draconian. Hungry and adoring.

His penis had been spectacularly rigid all along, provocative while concealed and now blissfully displayed, thick veined and pulsing. The grand prize in any collection. Blue ribbon quintessence— and it needed much closer examination.

But he was bearing down on her, bracing himself with one hand beside her hip, and all she could see was the blazing dark of his eyes.

"Were you looking for the moon at the lodge tonight, Mairey, or for me?" He planted a kiss on her belly.

The moon? His question finally penetrated the cloud of heat. Jack had been at the lodge tonight; must have seen her on the porch. Oh, that made her happy, made her meet his fingertips as he glided them upward from her stomach. "That was you? The noise in the underbrush? Why didn't you say something?"

"We—I was terrified."

"Terrified of? . . . Oh!" His touch dizzied her, tantalized. So deliciously scandalous and unscholarly, making her nipples crimp and pucker. He teased them, encouraged the spectacular crimping with his fingers, squeezing lightly, licking, lighting a wick deep inside her.

"Terrified of *you*, my love."

Mairey doubted that. He was so large and so tender as he leaned down to kiss her mouth. So maddeningly restrained—almost leisurely, as though he had a lifetime to spare.

"You are spectacular, Mairey Faelyn." He cradled the back of her head, kissed her ear, then the hollow of her throat, sowing a field of his glittering starlight across her shoulders. "Have I ever told you that?"

"I would have remembered, Jack."

"I plan to make it a habit." He was bedrock and she was flecks of gold; precious and ever a part of him.

Her entire life had been built upon a promise, an often bruising and always desperate promise she'd made to her father—the very same promise that her father had made to his father, that her grandfather had made to his father, and so on, and so on until her head dizzied and she wanted to scream.

She wanted Jack, wanted him forever; but she would have to settle for tonight—despite the consequences to her heart.

She knew where children came from, and had been calculating the pertinent dates and cycles since she'd found Jack downstairs in the library.

She couldn't possibly conceive tonight, according to every source she knew from cotters' wives to modern physicians: she was in the wrong part of her monthlies to conceive a child; this was her first time; the moon was full; she was sure there were no robin's eggs under Jack's pillow . . . there were any number of converging reasons against her conceiving any of Jack's unborn children.

Which made her stomach ache with grief. But tonight would be her fairy tale, remembered in her heart to last a lifetime.

There was no one but her in this kingdom of Jack's, her huge, naked-haunched dragon. Bronze above the waist, only a little less below. Thick muscles and compact cords and appealing whorls of dark hair that she wanted to follow with her tongue.

But she would have to wait her turn while she leaned back on her elbows, her legs spread indelicately, impossibly wide over the side of the bed; while Jack, her extravagant, amazing Jack, braced his weight with one arm against the mattress, nuzzling her throat, making his way toward her breasts and then further downward.

How far down, she didn't dare guess. She felt as ripe as a summer peach, warm and fleshy and ready to burst. His thewy arms were quaking on either side of her hips, and he was breathing like he'd been running cross-country through the woods.

And then he was kneeling between her legs.

"Jack, what are you doing?" Mairey sat upright to see his broad hands slide down her torso to slip round her backside and drag her closer to him. Closer!

"I'm not doing anything yet, my love."

Then why was she nearly fainting from lack of air? Why was her imagination outpacing him? And why was he lifting her ever so slightly off the bed, kissing the inside of her thighs, and then the hollow that joined her leg to her hip?

"But, Jack, you're—"

"I have a tale to tell you, Mairey."

"Now?" When his every word danced across her belly like a steamy, mischievous cloud, to froth against her curls, to drift them with his breath and toss them in his storm. And all so very lightly that Mairey thought she would go mad, *had* gone mad with the wanting.

"Oh, yes, now is the best time to tell my tale, my love. While I have your attention."

"You have just about all of me, Jack!"

"Not yet. Not nearly enough." Her dragon's black hair glistened against the paleness of her legs. At the joining of her thighs! Damp curls that he shouldn't even have been looking at, let alone—

Sweet yellow saffron, he kissed her! Lightly, sweetly, and with his tongue, on that vague boundary between her belly and her sex.

"Once upon a time—" The indescribable man was fingering his way further down, sifting through curls, teasing where she was wet and fully awakened. He had held her there once before, and she had felt possessed. But this was—

"Ohhhhh!" Mairey sighed out the breath that

had been caught in her throat for the last five minutes. "Soooo wonderful!"

"Ah, the rest of my story is even finer, Mairey."

How could anything be finer than this singular intimacy? But she was determined to listen to his every word, to *feel* his every word!

"Are you taking fieldnotes, Mairey?"

"Oh, yes, Jack. Memorizing everything you say. And everywhere you say it. Please, *please,* go on." And on! "Oh!"

He was parting her with his fingers, seeking something from her, finding the telling hot dampness that had been gathering like a summer storm. Fueling the fire that burned in her belly.

"Once upon a time, my sweet, my *tasty* Mairey"—he kissed her tenderly, altogether chastely where his fingers played—"there was a fusty, old dragon."

"An irresistible dragon," she said. Another of his intimate kisses, deeper yet, probing. An unladylike gasp came whistling out of her chest.

"The creature was melancholy, my love."

"Oh, *Jaaack!*" *That* was the tip of his tongue! His *tongue!* A hot, slick bolt of lightning that wedged itself inside her cleft and then retreated. But just like lightning, its blazing blue artifacts stayed to flare and lick its way into the core of her. She reached blindly for the hand that was kneading her hip, wanting something of him to hold onto, something to keep her from soaring away.

"Yes, madam?" He caught up her hand, kissed her fingers and then the inside of her knee, then

led his ravishing tongue along a trail toward still
another of his intimacies.

"I doubt this dragon was melancholy, Jack."

"Why is that?" Another kiss.

"Oh, Jack! Because . . . Dear God!" His tongue
was everywhere, and his fingers, too; sliding and
slipping, nuzzling her as though he were kissing
her. "Because dragons are usually fierce, yes! Yes,
oh, my, yes!"

"Are they, love?" He sounded grandly amused
by all her squirming. But she couldn't help herself.

"And they're relentless!" She grabbed the
astonishing man by his hair, bringing him closer,
and pinned her heels against his shoulders to beg
relief from his enchantment, to beg for more of it.
"Oh! And big, Jack! Dragons are enorrrrrmous!
Oh, Jack!"

He tugged and teased until she was bucking and
grinding, ready to explode.

"But still and all this dragon was sorrowful, my
dear—"

Her throat was sore from all her groaning. "Was
his name Balforge? It must have been."

"If you'd like it to be."

"Oh, I would!" Balforge was *her* dragon. The
one who had coiled himself around her heart, the
one whose tongue was laving her as though she
were dessert, the one who called her his love.

He nuzzled her once more, then left that place
of startling wonder, left her aching and twisting and
unfulfilled, and carried her further onto the bed and
against the pillows.

"You see, Mairey my love, this Balforge lived

and worked all alone in a drafty old cavern.''

She clung to his neck, to his mouth. "Did he have wings?''

"Unfortunately, no." Jack stretched out above her, kneeling between her thighs, braced on his elbows, looking even more hungry than before he'd sampled her, his stalk dazzlingly large and inviting. "Because if he had, he wouldn't have spent so much time on the train, traveling between his . . . other caverns, and he wouldn't have been so ill-tempered.''

She fit her arms around his broad back and kissed him, thoroughly bewitched by her storyteller and his irresistible theatrics. "A very modern sort.''

She was about to prompt him for more when he snuggled his penis against the nest he'd so attentively feathered for it, and Mairey nearly fainted with pure pleasure.

"There's more, my love.''

"Oh, yes, a *lot* more, Jack!" She raised her hips to collect the thrilling length of him, to slide it here and there. "You are wickedly large, my lord. Hot, too.''

"And you are willful, madam." He shook himself like a waterdog, then gulped in a huge breath of air before he focused his eyes on her again with a half-grin. "I meant, my sweet, that my story has a princess.''

"I was hoping so." His hips were wonderfully planed, his backside carved in shifting marble and just as hard.

"She was beautiful, intelligent, enchanting." He

practiced his sorcery with every word, moving his hips and his flesh, pressing her into the mattress as though he couldn't get enough of her.

"And he was wonderful." She caught his mouth and kissed him thoroughly, memorizing the taste of him, dancing her tongue with his.

"Ah, but, Mairey, the princess was his downfall."

Guilty tears sprung to her eyes, hot and heartaching and kissed away by the fine man who loved so fiercely. "I'm sorry for that, Jack."

"Oh, trust me, love—you've taught me happy endings." He slid his hand down her belly, followed afterward with his mouth, and just when she thought she'd go mad, he entered her with his finger. "And we will have one."

"Oh, Jack!" Mairey tilted her hips to meet him, gloried in the feeling of possession, in the lush flickering of his tongue, as he delved with two fingers, filling her marvelously but not nearly enough.

She wanted *him*—all of him. Wanted him to hurry with his story, to take her to his place of happily-ever-aftering. "What happened to the princess and her dragon?"

He was maddeningly slow, dazing her with a blinding stroke of his fingers, and then a nibble on her breast, an ardent tugging that made her feel ripe and sun-warmed, spinning his tale with silken strands that tugged her pulse in a thousand and one directions, but ever upward toward a place she couldn't quite reach.

"The uncivilized fellow imprisoned his wanton captive in one of his caverns—"

"She was wanton as well?"

"Mmmmm . . ." he hummed huskily against her belly, making her light-headed with his fondling. "Balforge was a very lucky dragon, though he didn't know it and made her work for him day and night."

"His housekeeper?"

"His very own antiquarian. A beautiful collector of folktales, a finder of lost dreams."

"I like your story, Jack, love the way you tell it!" With his tongue and his mouth and—"Oh, yes, finally!" He pressed the broad tip of his penis against her—a star-splintering fit that made her wrap her legs around his hips and coerce him forward with her heels. "There, Jack."

"Not yet, my love. We've much farther to go."

Mairey couldn't imagine any more of his extravagant torture. Though she opened her legs wider and begged him come, he ignored her graceless hints, though hard-rippling tremors shook him and made him struggle for air.

She wanted to confess that she loved him, that she wanted to stay and stay, but there was too much danger in that. Even here in this fairy tale where most anything could happen.

Anything.

"I want to touch you, Jack." She reached between their bodies, slid her hand down his lean-muscled trunk, across his flat belly, and closed her fingers around the most brawny shape she'd ever had the pleasure of touching.

"Mairey!—" Jack swallowed a howl and made a grab for her hand. But she was already there in the steamy hollow between them, her innocent fingers encircling his shaft in faultless, fluting links, her hands making grand forays even as he shot to his knees in pure reflex.

"You're so lovely, Jack." She was sitting up, fondling the length and breadth of him as she had those others in the drawer. "Warm and hard—and soft, too! Beautiful!" Her words of admiration broke against him, warm and moist and too close.

"Blazes, woman!" He hadn't been prepared for her adventuring; wasn't expecting delicate fingers scribing the details of his anatomy and exalting them, sheathing him thoroughly with her masterful hands, taunting him with that instinctive, pounding, pulsing rhythm and taking him too near the edge before he could stop her. He should have known that Mairey would astound him in this, too.

"A kiss, Jack?"

"Almighty God, yes!" But he caught her hands before she could bestow one and drove her back into the pillows, pinning her wrists above her head.

"Why didn't you let me kiss you as you did me?"

"Another time—" Though that promise only hardened him further, if that were possible. Their quintessential parts were heated and poised and throbbing, Mairey's legs clutched round him, ready to take him completely. "I'm crazed for you, Mairey. I want to plunge and thrust in you."

"Then do." She laughed and tucked him closer, expertly now, and harrowed her fingers through his hair.

"I don't want to hurt you."

"You couldn't possibly."

Jack had never in his life waited for anything with such visceral, tethered yearning; he was in her heart and in her eyes; he could see the wonder so plainly, so perfectly. He wanted to be soul-deep inside her, straining with her till the sky fell out from under them. Her exotic bouquet was in his nostrils and on his fingers, in the blending of their mouths.

Here was his miracle, making tumultuous love with him, urging him to pillage her, whispering her silky treasures to him, coiling her hips in wide undulations, taking him against her, pressing and pressing him ever deeper till he met that tender barrier he'd found with his fingers.

Virgo intacta. "You're very tight, love."

Her brows knitted, worried for them. "We'll fit together, Jack." She arched her hips and shoved at him with her heels. "There, do you feel the place?"

"God, yes, Mairey. Stop!" He shuddered with the effort of not plunging forward into all that exquisite heat.

"Then, please, Jack!" His wanton princess had found him again, her eager hand fitting him against the silky wetness he'd drawn from her. "Let me take you inside me. Let me hold you, Jack."

An irresistible tide shoved at him. "As deeply as you can bear, my love."

"Then all the way to my heart, Jack." Sighing against his mouth, she tilted her hips and took the tip of him as far as she could, then kissed him. "The rest is for you, my enormous dragon."

"Oh, my love!" Like a man possessed, he thrust fiercely, mindlessly, breaching her swiftly, the pleasure exquisite and propelling as she closed tightly around him, taking him deeper and more fully with each sharp sigh.

"Ohhhhh, Jack, oh, yes! Please, please, do!" Until he was buried to the shank and quaking, and his nymph was stretched languidly beneath him, her eyes streaming with tears and not quite focused, as though she were trying to recognize a beloved scent on a summer breeze.

"I hurt you, my love. I'm sorry." He kissed her eyelids and struggled not to move.

"Oh, no, Jack. I'm restored—filled with you. Happy now."

Happy. This delighted him beyond belief. "Then *I'm* happy."

She wriggled her hips, stunning him with her earthy lust. "So you are, my lord." She kissed him hungrily, then began to rock gently, finding the rising rhythm of his heartbeat and hers.

Jack steadied his breathing and met her deeply measuring strokes, taking leave of her and then returning only when she clutched at his hips and begged, laughing with her as they came together again in ever-ascending fury.

"Whatever happened to Balforge and his princess?"

Jack held his weight on his elbows, keeping her close to him and sheltered, just the two of them and their driving need to have union. "Oh, love, he lost his heart to her."

"Did he?" She gave him a willowy sigh and a

fierce embrace that locked her ankles around his backside, and drove him to the brink with her rocking.

"From the first moment he saw her."

"Oh, my enchanting dragon!" She was breathless beneath him, praising his clever marauding, taking his ravenous kiss as an offering, bestowing her own at his temples and on his mouth, while the tempest rose and raged around them. Exuberance and adoration, and all the swirling forces of nature caught up in a firestorm.

"Tell me your happy ending, Jack. I can't stand the wait."

"Neither can I, my love." He was reeling with restraint, and all of it for Mairey, for her pleasure, for her love. He slipped his hand between them where she was wet and ripe for him, where they were fused together and grinding toward the same slivered sunlight, the same everlasting bliss.

A simple touch, a skiff, and then Mairey's throaty, "Ohhhh, mmmmy! Jaaaack!"

The searing force of her release shattered him, came roaring out of nowhere to overtake him in its whirlwind. But before he succumbed to the fragmenting glory, before he lost himself inside her completely, she needed to know.

"You have my heart, Mairey, my soul."

His heart! Oh, Jack—! Mairey was still soaring from the splintering, skyrocketing pleasure that he'd brought her to, still clutching him against her and riding his thermals up and up into the brightness. The crests came and went and came again, catching her up like a gadabout feather, with Jack the wind and her wings.

Her marvelous dragon reared up, nostrils wide and scenting, his sinew and flesh glistening bronze with sweat. He bellowed her name, caught up her bottom into his splayed fingers and then plunged into her, far, far deeper than he had been before, hotter still, and again and again and again. Then, with a convulsive groan, he filled her with a rapturous, spilling heat; his seed, a gift she would cherish but grieve over. It would find no purchase in her womb tonight.

And she wept.

Like a great, spent beast falling back to earth, Jack lowered himself to his elbows, snorting air in huge gulps, his muscles still quivering, his hips still pulsing into her. He whispered, "This, Mairey, my delicious love, is what happened to Balforge and his princess."

She kissed his mouth, where he tasted of salt and their own erotic fragrance. "You mean she gave herself to him like a wanton?" Mairey clung to his priceless, quixotic romance, not wanting it to end. Not ever.

"Oh, yes." He was still inside her, less full now but a tumid congestion that made her want him again. Right now. "They made love through the night—"

"I'd like that, too."

His dark eyes had taken on a brilliant and determined gleam. "And, much to the joy of everyone in their kingdom, they were married the next day."

Mairey's heart ka-thumped, and then somersaulted; terror and joy mingled as sizzling steam.

"Married?" He couldn't be thinking that! Wasn't! She tried to sound scholarly, but he was sliding his huge hand between them to cover her breast, finding her nipple with his fingers. That delicate twist, a husbandly fondness that made her gasp. "A princess can't marry a dragon."

"Oh, yes you can, Mairey." He was making slow and devastating love to her ear, to the ridges and the valleys, with his teeth and with his tongue.

"Me, Jack? Why would I marry a dragon?"

His eyes glittered darkly when he turned her chin. "Because you love me as madly as I love you."

Panicked, but slowed by languid limbs and an overwhelming love for him, Mairey tried to scramble out from under his weight, but he was as solid as a mountain, lazing on her like a sun-sated lizard. "I don't like the way this story ends, Jack."

"It's the only possible way." He shifted onto his elbow, his breathing still ragged; still dallying with her nipple, a tether between them that she couldn't break for the budding pleasure that was stirring her hips to move again. "You didn't think I would take your virginity and then leave you?"

"You didn't take anything from me, Jack; I gave myself to you willingly."

"Brazenly, my dear." She felt a dreadful loss when he shifted his legs and slipped out of her. A plea was on her tongue to call him back, but he replaced his fullness with his inflaming fingers, and she was filled again with the shock of bliss.

"Oh, Jack!"

He laughed gently against her ear. "Another reason that I love you, Mairey."

And, shameless bandit that she was, she took his stroking as she had his shaft, her hips meeting and matching him, crying out his name only a moment later, clinging to him, thrusting against him until she was exhausted and breathless, and more in love with him than she could ever imagine. And sadder than she'd ever been in her life.

"There, sweet. You love me."

"Sexual urges," she managed between close-caught breaths that threatened to be sobs.

"In some, perhaps, but not in you, Mairey—else we would have consummated our heady alliance weeks ago." He was nuzzling her neck, her throat, a sated beast toying with a mouse. "Under your desk and mine, in the greenhouse and in the broom closet at Windsor. But I wouldn't do that to you, Mairey, and you wouldn't do that to us. Not without love; not without commitment."

"It's impossible. I can't marry you." Mairey wriggled out from under him and up against the bank of pillows at the headboard, frightened of his certainty and of the vistas that he offered. "Please, Jack, don't ask me."

"I already have, my love. And I do again. Marry me, Miss Faelyn."

"No."

He was braced on his elbows, and her legs were spread on either side of his shoulders, knees bent, his face between her thighs and fire blazing in his eyes. Her pulse was still primed for whatever magic he planned, her heart a tattered wreck. But he reached beneath her and the pillows and dragged out a fistful of pristine, white sheet. With indescribable tenderness he wiped the dampness from her thighs and her belly and the place they had joined together.

"We are alloyed, Mairey." The sheet was wet and blood-streaked, the stark evidence of a fairy tale gone terribly awry. He bent his head and kissed her belly; held her with the whole of his hand, his palm pressing against her as though to keep his seed from leaving her. "You and I, and the rest of our lives."

The Willowmoon was her life, apart and separate from Jack. It had to stay that way. She loved him too dearly to hurt him, and that's what would happen in the midst of some distant happiness. They would find the Knot and she would have to leave him, stealing his children and his dreams from him when all he had wanted from her was love.

"I love you, Mairey. We have children to make together. Can't you see that?"

She *could* see it, and it made her weep.

He left his splendorous kiss between her breasts and on her mouth as he rose up on his knees and carried her onto his lap. She took him inside her again gladly, let him increase and come and spill himself into her, until he was kissing the tears from her eyes and off her breasts. "There, now. We'll marry tomorrow—"

"No, Jack. I can't!" Mairey shoved at him, taking unfair advantage of his still-fevered embrace to scramble away, across the bed and over the side. "Don't say that! I can't."

He looked so endearingly confused, confessing his love so plainly, his plans for a splendid marriage and even more splendid children.

"Why? Do you have an appointment in the morning?"

"Yes."

Jack was confounded by Mairey's refusal of his perfectly honorable proposal, and vastly in love with the lunatic. She was standing in the middle of the room as gloriously naked as the day she was born, lying to him about some damned appointment that she thought would get in the way of their wedding day.

"Consider it canceled, sweet. You and I are getting married tomorrow morning." He swung out of bed himself and turned up a lamp to better gauge what Mairey was thinking in her addled head.

"No!" She put her hand out and backed away, as though that would stop him. "I can't marry you at all, Jack. Not ever!"

He walked forward toward her. "Why can't you marry me?"

She countered his steps backward, wringing her hands. "Actually, I'm—"

"Already married?"

"No!"

He'd been joking, but he was relieved to hear her furious denial. She was a complicated creature; had contrary views on life that few other women would ever entertain. He'd gained three steps on her while she stood fox-frozen in place.

"Then why, Mairey? Are you in love with another man? Sir Dithering Walsham of the Tower, perhaps?'' This one made his heart stop as he waited.

''You can't be serious!'' The very best answer in the universe; loaded with satisfyingly appalled horror. She bumped up against his tall-winged reading chair, took a backward step up onto the seat, and stuck her heels into the cushion.

''I'm not serious about Walsham, Mairey. But I am certain that you love me.''

''I don't.''

''You do. And I love you.''

''It won't work between us.''

''It already has.'' He was wreathed in her scent.

''No!'' She laced her fingers, pleading, her nose so close to his he could feel her exhaling. ''We're different people: I'm a scholar and you're a viscount.''

''Then wedding me would make you Countess Scholar, I believe.'' He knelt in the chair, enjoying the view as lamplight played on her bobbing breasts, the sight making him hard again and aching for her. ''We'll change the Rushford escutcheon, my love. Add a phallus *rampant* and a willow leaf *environed.*''

''This isn't a joking matter, Jack.''

''I've never been so damned serious in all my life. You *are* my life.''

''What about the Willowmoon?'' She closed her arms under her breasts, which only pushed them higher, nearer. ''It's . . . I've got work to do.''

''And so have I.'' He hadn't expected to have to convince Mairey to be his wife, but he would meet the project head on. ''But the Willowmoon has nothing to do with marrying and raising up children together.''

That launched her into a full-flight panic. ''It has *everything* to do with it!''

He hadn't noticed the fear in her eyes before, couldn't imagine where it was coming from. Mairey wasn't prone to female jitters in any form.

''How does a silver mine have anything to do with us?''

She opened and closed her mouth a few times, before she snorted and threw out a laugh. ''I'm your employee.''

''You're the woman I want to spend all my days with.''

''No! We're partners.''

''Indeed.''

''I don't love you. I *don't!*'' *Protesting too much, my dear.*

''Ballocks, madam.'' She looked small and lost, goose-fleshed and shivering from head to toe. He wasn't sure what was frightening her about his proposal, but he'd be damned if he gave up without a fight. ''Tell me why we shouldn't be married. One reasonable reason might satisfy me, though I'm confident that there are none. Debate me with your cons.''

''I . . . I don't have to tell you anything.'' Her lower lip stuck out in a weepy pout.

''My turn, Mairey. The pros: I am irrevocably in love with you. I am obscenely rich, and well-behaved *most* of the time. I love your Aunt Tattie and your hat, and the fact that you wised me up to my follies, and I am mad about your precocious sisters. Who, by the way, unanimously agree that I should marry you without delay.''

She closed her hands over her mouth, her eyes wide in horror. ''You discussed our marriage with them?''

''Briefly, at their instigation. They are very wise. And you are my life, Mairey. To the end of my days.''

''No, Jack.'' That faint keening of his name, that plaintive whimper, tugged his heart up into his throat. Then huge tears suddenly pooled in her eyes, soupier than before, spilling over her cheeks in a great wash. She sobbed, her whole sweet face crumpling and working, her shoulders hunched and quaking.

Hellfire! This wasn't going at all well. He lifted her into his arms and held her tightly, fortified by her clinging. ''I refuse to say that I'm sorry I love you, Mairey. I won't. It's the bloody truth. If you'll just tell me how I offend you—''

''No, Jack, you don't! It's just that—'' A hiccoughing belly-sob shook her. ''You're . . . you're just too . . . too—''

''Too what?'' He was ready for the worst.

''Too *wonderful*.'' She was howling again in her inexplicable anguish.

''I'm too—'' *Wonderful?* Not greedy or pigheaded, not an unredeemable monster? Wonderful he could work with. Irresistible might take a few days.

''So—'' A hiccough. ''So—'' Another sob. ''So, you'd better just forget about meeeee.''

Jack tucked her chin over his shoulder and held

her close, letting her tears fall while he tried his most *wonderful* to soothe her.

"Ah, Mairey, if I've learned anything in eighteen years of waiting for my life to begin, if I've learned anything from you at all, it's that I must champion my family with my bare hands and that I must love them relentlessly, as I love you."

Which only brought on more weeping, and led finally, blissfully, in the wee hours of the morning, to a fevered bout of lovemaking that set Jack's ears ringing and had Mairey crooning his name in a most encouraging way.

Chapter 17

❝❝I**mpossible,** arrogant, *pig-headed* man!❞
Mairey stood in the parlor of the lodge,
stuffing her most recent notes from the *Gazetteer*
into her work-satchel, and snuffling away the tears
that seemed to burst forth in floods of biblical proportions whenever she thought about Jackson
Rushford.

Which was so *bloody* constantly that she'd not
only picked up the man's cursing but she'd also
lost the ability to put one thought in front of the
other.

Six weeks ago the man had resolved that they
should be married, and since then he had led an
unflagging campaign toward meeting that resolu-
tion. Leave it to him to be honorable and persistent
after he had deflowered a virgin.

Marry Jack? Ha! *There* was a cautionary tale to
be collected and cataloged.

Viscount Jackson Rushford was her greatest enemy in all creation. Even now he was dogging her
tracks, eager to accompany her on today's trip to

the British Museum, sniffing after the ripening scent of the Willowmoon Knot, no longer confused by the scent of red herrings.

To make matters worse, he was damnably cheery, ruthlessly loving, and paid no attention at all to her rebuffs. Which, she had to admit, in recent days had become downright indistinguishable from encouragement.

She couldn't help it. He was masterfully cunning in his crusade. The girls crowded him with their love, charmed him out of a pony for each, and he took it all in his stride, like a huge old hound who didn't mind having his ears pulled, but who would tear out the throat of anyone who tried to harm his family.

His family: that's what they all had become to him. Not a substitute for the one he had lost so long ago, but a new beginning which, as he had stated, he was pursuing relentlessly.

She couldn't deny him a minute of his newfound happiness. It would be cruel of her; would haunt her for all her days if she did. Just as he haunted her nights. She hadn't been sleeping well lately, flopping around in her bed until her nightgown was sweat damp and her head was spinning in circles.

A spinning that sometimes tilted the ground even in the middle of the day.

Her stomach gave a rolling lurch, breakfast bubbled and squeaked for a moment, and settled only when she sat down and gripped the edge of the table to stop it from whirling.

"He's here, Mairey, dear." Tattie came trilling through the arch, beaming at whoever was following her—as if Mairey couldn't tell who *that* was. "His lordship has come for you."

Jack filled up the doorway with his height, and her heart to the brim with his courting smile. Relentlessly.

"Good morning, my love," he said, as though they were intimately alone and the world belonged just to them and her aunt wasn't glancing eagerly between them, patting her hands together, ready to applaud, or pray, or both. "You look good enough to eat."

"Jack!" Mairey frowned at him, but flushed to the tips of her breasts, which had become tender and weighty since that night she'd spent in his arms.

Jack's smile grew lazy and wicked as he leaned against the jamb, obviously aware of the crimson blush staining her cheeks—and proud of who'd caused it.

Aunt Tattie only giggled—not a dignified sound from a woman of her age and refinement. "Doesn't our Mairey look pretty today?"

"More lovely every day, Tattie. She puts the sun and the moon to shame."

More giggling from a woman who had been perfectly sane and a dangerous she-wolf of the highest rank when they'd first arrived at Drakestone.

Now Aunt Tattie was Jack's chief promoter. "Doesn't his lordship look fine today, Mairey?" Maybe even a bloody conspirator.

"He's dressed well enough for a trip to the museum." Damn the man for his persistence. And bless him. "We'd best get going. It's nearly eight."

"Shall we, *Mairey?*" He proffered his proper elbow.

"No," she said, answering his artful pun sharply, but receiving a patient, boyish grin in reply. She took his arm, treasuring its warmth, painfully aware that she was playing with fire.

Jack always looked uncomfortable in London's private hackneys. They were never tall enough for his head, nor was the foot-well wide enough for his legs. Whether he sat beside her or across from her, riding with him was an intimate affair. Today he lounged in the seat opposite, his knees outside hers, his gaze attentive and too loving.

"I missed you yesterday, Mairey."

I miss you always, Jack.

He'd been in Manchester again, systematically combing the parish registries and orphanage files. Mairey had gone with him the first time, to show him his mother's grave. He left a fistful of flowers that Anna had picked, quiet tears that made her ache for him all the more, and a stalwart promise to find his sisters.

He had fired Dodson with an amazing amount of restraint.

"If I kill him, Mairey, I'll go to jail," he'd told her. "I'll never find my sisters, and I'll never be able to take you to wife. The bastard isn't worth it."

Then he had taken up his own investigation with

all the fervor of a zealot newly come to a demanding God.

In truth he was very good; he had a memory for names and dates and places that made him dangerous—because unfortunately, he had transferred this newfound skill to the investigation of the Willowmoon Knot.

Now she replied, "I'm sorry I couldn't go to Manchester with you, Jack. But you found a name that might lead you to Emma." He had come home to the lodge elated but wounded by his efforts, and needing a family to share in his joy. Mairey had slipped into his embrace without thinking and had stayed far too long.

"A slim lead. I still can't believe that it's come so quickly." His grin was so natural and hopeful. "I've drafted letters to three manor houses, asking to see their employment records. The letters went out in this morning's post."

"And you did it without me." She hadn't left him stranded.

"*Because* of you, Mairey." He leaned across the cab and took her hands. "Marry me today."

"I can't."

"And you can't tell me why not, when I can think of a million reasons for us to share our lives, starting with the love we feel for each other. Unrestrained and honorable, passionate, and a hell of a lot of fun. Then there is Anna. Caro. Poppy. Your aunt and our unborn children. Family. And your damned phallus collection."

"Jack." He found her smile and made the most

of it, nuzzled her chin and then planted a row of kisses along her jaw.

"Then, my love, there's our nightly bath in the same tub. We've more duck houses to build for Poppy and riding lessons for Caro, not to mention fending off the sweaty-palmed young men who will soon be courting Anna in the parlor."

"She's only ten."

"Oh, love, time goes by so quickly." He was so reasonable, so plausible in his dreaming. "And of course, stretching out as far as we can see, is our search for the Willowmoon Knot and all that silver. Partners, remember?"

He might as well have hit her in the stomach. Mairey shoved at his shoulders and sat upright, banging her head against the little window behind her. She tried not to look his way, tried not to care that she had injured his pride once again.

"All I ask, Mairey, is that you give me one reason why we shouldn't be married. Do that and I'll stop asking."

He stared at her and waited for the answer she couldn't speak. So she turned away and watched the lorries go by.

I can't marry you, Jack, because I love you far too much.

The expansion of the British Museum was only eleven years old, and already its storage vaults were bursting at their seams with new artifacts arriving weekly from Egypt and the Orient, the priceless and the profane crammed into every square inch of space that wasn't used for display.

With the aid of the *Gazetteer,* a stiff-nosed curator, and Jack's Moses-like letters of patent, they were once again in a cool, airless basement, alone with some of the greatest treasures of civilization.

Mairey had prepared a false set of notes for Jack and had sent him whistling off to a vault around the corner from where she had intended to look.

If the astonishing theory that she had formed from the *Gazetteer* was correct, if the Knot had somehow managed to make its way from Yorkshire into the possession of the amateur archaeologist Sir Edmund Larkenfield sometime before 1778, then it might well have been sold to the British Museum in 1810, along with the rest of Larkenfield's collection of antiquities—which had remained scattered through this warren of rooms, virtually unpacked and uncataloged, for nearly fifty years.

She had only come this far because of the man in the next room. She had never felt so wicked, or so angry. She loved Jack as she loved her life, and all this deception was beginning to drown her.

As Mairey studied her own encrypted notes, she was struck by a wave of deceit that made more of those fat tears form in her eyes, made her stomach pitch again with regret.

Deception.

She was an expert at it now. She could have gone on the stage, would have been the talk of London with her sleight of hand.

Deception. Letting Jack believe that they were working toward the same goal, when in actuality she was planning to steal the Knot before he even knew that she had found it.

Let him go on looking until his hair grayed and his shoulders stooped, and the light in his eyes had dulled. Mairey would be long gone with the Willowmoon, living secretly in her village, where she'd have to exist on the sweet memories of her handsome dragon.

Yet there was something in all this convoluted deception that she had never considered, probably because finding the Knot had never seemed so possible before: what would happen *after* she had rescued it, after the disk of silver was tucked safely away in the glade?

What then?

A little bell of jangling, implausible joy began to ring in her head. She'd been thinking in all the wrong directions.

What if she *did* find the Willowmoon, and what if Jack *wasn't* with her at the time? What if he never actually saw it? Then he could never identify the markings, never even know that it had been found. Therefore—and this was the glory-cloud miracle and the happy ending—he could never use the map as a source to the silver.

A marvelous pantomime was mounting itself in her brain. Gaslights, costumes, lots of singing. And a pair of lovers whose stars might just become uncrossed.

Let's say that she opened this random drawer in front of her and found the Willowmoon Knot lying there, winking at her, saying, "Good morning, Miss Faelyn and isn't it a fine day." After she picked herself off the floor, all she'd have to do would be to pocket it and say nothing to Jack.

It would be gone—just like that. As though it had never been a threat.

Oh, Lord, the Knot would burn like molten lead. But at the end of the day, after *pretending* to look for it, after combing through the catacombs with Jack, his partner, his love, the mother of all his unborn children would just leave the museum, clinging to his steadfast arm, savoring the weight of the Willowmoon as it jostled against her thigh.

She would feast on the sunlight as Jack escorted her down the wide stairs and into Great Russell Street. She might even stop him on the steps and kiss the daylights out of him. Yes, she would definitely do that. In fact, she'd make love to him on the way home in the hackney, and then demand that they be married on the spot.

He'd like that.

Then when Jack went on another of his treks to Manchester or to one of his mines, she would take a quick day-trip to her village, bury the Knot where it would never be found again, and make it home to Drakestone in time to have dinner with her husband.

A fairy tale come true! Why hadn't she thought of it before? Once the Willowmoon Knot was discovered, it merely had to vanish without a trace. There was nothing in the Faelyn family pledge that demanded she entomb herself with the Knot like one of the pharaoh's servants. She didn't have to hide out like a bandit, because no one would ever know that she'd taken it. Once she had rescued it and its map was removed from public memory, then her job was done.

And her life with Jack could begin.

Mairey stood in awe of this pantomime. It was very good.

It was flawless.

But only if Jack never *ever* saw the Willowmoon Knot. That was the trick, the sleight of hand that would make all the difference. Whether she found the Knot here at the British Museum or at the Ashmolean or in Queen Victoria's stocking drawer, she could *never* let Jack know about it.

For that would be the end of it—her dreams and his. The children that they would never have.

He was as rich as Croesus, contented, titled, and he had no need at all for a silver mine. Once the Knot was safely buried and Mairey was in complete control of its destiny, they could spend years, wonderful years, looking for it together. A hobby. A family game. The Rushford legacy.

She still couldn't risk a marriage to him, though; not until she had found and hidden the Knot. Because if she failed, if he should ever see it, then she would have to steal away into the night; she would have to disappear with her sisters and Jack's children, and retreat to the safety of her village as though she had never existed.

And that would destroy him completely.

There was one path to their happiness, and it was up to her to find it—quickly.

All this heady excitement had winded her. She must remember to breathe more often; she was dizzy again, and not quite right in the stomach.

But she was certainly well enough to rescue her dragon from his lonely cave.

* 　 * 　 *

Mairey's notes made no sense to Jack. Hellfire, nothing she'd done in the last six weeks had made any sense to him. He asked daily for her hand, confessed his uncompromising, unconditional love for her.

And daily he heard, along with a deluge of weeping, "I love you, Jack, but I can't marry you! I can't! No matter how often you ask."

But the baffling woman consistently followed her refusal by throwing her arms around his neck and making love to his mouth.

Only last week she had vehemently refused him and then proceeded to seduce him immediately afterward in the greenhouse. She'd pushed him onto a bench, lifted her skirts, unfastened his trousers, and sat down on him.

Blazes, the memory of her sighing ecstacies still made him hard and quick, even now. And more resolved than ever to prevail. They belonged together, he and Mairey; they deserved a life with the girls and Tattie and all the children that would come from their remarkable union.

This damned Willowmoon Knot was at the root of all her apprehensions, which made no sense at all. They were after the same thing. His interest was the silver, plain and simple; success brought him privilege and opportunities. His title allowed him to demand action, which was more vital now that he had taken back his search for his sisters.

But Mairey's obsession with the Knot had never sat right with him. Disproportional loyalty to her father? A symbol of her independence? Wealth of her own? Pride?

The only course was to find the blasted thing. The truth would be there in its mysterious knot-work. A truth that Mairey would have to unravel for him.

The *Gazetteer* hadn't specifically cataloged a silver crest of pagan design, or anything named Willow or Moon or Willowcrest, or any derivation thereof. Despite all logic to the contrary, his stubborn, faultless mentor with the silver-flecked eyes seemed to think that the Knot might have at least been here in the museum at one time, and stored with a collection of twelfth-century Scottish plate-ware.

He had learned a great deal from Mairey about the fine art of detection, despite the heady distractions of her rose-scented hair when it slipped out of its prison of pins and pencils, despite her earthy laughter and his perpetual state of arousal whenever she was within sniffing distance. He was indeed learning to read through the lines of a text and form a whole image out of its mismatched parts.

Which was why some boxes labeled ''Larkenfield'' had caught his interest when he'd arrived this morning. The *Gazetteer* listed the man as a collector of ecclesiastical antiquities. The name was memorable to Jack in that Larkenfield had been not only a minor figure in British archaeology during the last century but also a Yorkshireman *and* a canon of York Minster for fifteen years. Odd that Mairey hadn't noticed the connection.

Had Larkenfield been a petty thief? Had he pilfered the storage rooms at the minster close over the years and come up with a collection of long-forgotten antiquities to grace his mantelpiece? Barring that intrigue, Larkenfield might even have purchased the pieces from the diocese.

Well! A theory! And he'd devised it all on his own!

Mairey would be quite proud. And best of all, if they found the Knot she'd have no reason not to marry him.

"God willing, Mairey Faelyn, Sir Larkenfield will bring us together." Jack tucked Mairey's confusing notes into his jacket pocket and found her where he'd left her, diligently sifting through fat drawers of wood shavings cushioning singular items of Celtic enamel work.

"I have a theory, my love."

"Jack!" The eyes that found him were feverish with an elation that seemed to have startled her. Despite the breadth of her grin, her cheeks were chalky and her hands were as damp as though she'd just washed them.

"Have you found the Willowmoon then, Mairey?" He kissed her forehead, fearing that she was ill. "Can we go home and be married?"

"No, Jack! But—" The woman held the rest of her sentence inside her smile, then hooked his neck with both hands and planted a sultry kiss on his mouth, following it with a dozen more all over his face.

"Very nice, my love. Very, *very* nice." Jack just stood there, enjoying her assault, knowing better than to ask where she'd found such happiness.

She finished abruptly and stood back to study him, as though she hadn't seen him in years. She sighed, so blissfully that Jack's hopes soared.

"You said you have a theory, Jack? Something to do with the Scottish plateware?"

"No. With an archaeologist named Larkenfield."

"Who?" The question was more a forlorn hooting sound, a baby owl lost in the woods. The chalkiness increased to gray. She sat down hard on a tall stool.

"That's it. You're not well, Mairey." Jack stooped to pick her up. "We're going home."

"No! I have to stay." She twisted out of his embrace and pushed away. "I'm just tired, Jack. Tired of everything." There came the tears again. "I'll rest while you tell me your theory."

"Then sit." Skeptical, Jack handed her his kerchief and watched her carefully as he detailed Larkenfield's many possible connections to the Willowmoon, expanding on his earlier theory, puffing out his chest because it all sounded as plausible as any theory they'd followed yet.

Mairey listened raptly, patiently, as she sat on the stool, her fingers white-knuckled and laced in her lap. She wiped at her brow twice, but by the time he had finished, she looked much improved and was ready with her questions.

"That's very good, Jack. Where do you plan to look first? In the Yorkshire registries?"

"I'll start in here with you."

"Why?"

"The name Larkenfield, for one. It's on labels all over these rooms here."

"Really! I hadn't noticed." She read her way across a shelf of boxes. "Why, you're right, Jack. Mmm . . . to save time, why don't we each take a room, and then we'll know it's done."

"You'll be all right in here alone?"

"Why wouldn't I be?"

"Because you look like you've seen a ghost."

"I haven't been sleeping well."

"Neither have I, love. And you know why." He kissed her cheek again; satisfied that it was cool and dry. Her mouth was wet and ready for him, and she was tugging him closer, her fingers making inroads through the buttons of his waistcoat.

If she was going to run hot today, he was going to make damn sure she knew that he was just as hot. He clamped his hands over her backside and pressed her belly against his erection.

"Jack, you're—"

He stopped her hand from slipping between them. "Yes, I am, madam." He inhaled cool air through his nostrils. "But this is a museum."

"I love you, Jack."

"Marry me then."

Her eyes were awash with those tugging tears again, and he could hardly credit his hearing when she said, "Someday, Jack. With just the right miracle."

"Someday?" His heart swelled. He nearly crowed.

She didn't say "no." She said "someday." Someday could be next month or next Tuesday.

Jack decided to leave the subject hovering there between them. He tipped her chin to better kiss her, delved deeply, and then left her sighing.

If she wanted a miracle, he'd give her one.

As he opened overstuffed drawers and dangerously stacked cabinets full of close-packed effigies and musical instruments made of dried gourds, and well-endowed wooden icons from some warmer clime, he realized that the Larkenfield collection hadn't been uncrated because it was nothing more than an eccentric's nest.

Clay whistles and seedpod rattles and feathered headpieces, all of them musty and inscrutably sorted: by alphabet, or color, or size, he couldn't tell.

Unwilling to give up on a perfectly good theory, though he was sorting his way to the bottom of a large trunk, past hefty pieces of stone gargoyles and brass bosses, when his heart took a shuddering leap.

These things were Celtic! Ha! Definitely Celtic. The serpentine interlacing, the unsubtle patterns of nature that turned and turned back and forth upon each other. Mairey had taught him the elements; he'd even begun to see them in his sleep.

So there *was* an order here in Larkenfield's collection. Ecclesiastical *and* Celtic. Exactly what might have come out of the catacombs of the minster at York.

He picked more carefully through the trunk, looking for Mairey's silver disk. There was knotwork aplenty, but only in wood and stone and ivory. Thoroughly disappointed, and glad that he hadn't called Mairey to come look, he repacked the items, nearly forgetting the flat, ironbound coffer that he'd set aside when he'd unpacked the trunk.

When he lifted it, the coffer rattled with a weighty mass that slid back and forth inside.

He popped the little hasp and opened the domed lid. More bird's nests, but used for packing, it seemed. Delicate hummingbird's nests, by the size and shimmer of the feathers still poking from the intricately woven grasses.

He lifted the three nests away, expecting more bosses or the myriad cloak clasps that littered the halls of antiquity.

Indeed, there were two more gold-encrusted cloak clasps. And below them—

A silver disk, beautifully Celtic. Intricate and undulating with all its asymmetric tendrils, each of which ended in long narrow leaves. The willow. A ridge of chevrons. And the four phases of the moon.

And if all that hadn't convinced Jack, hadn't made his heart race with joy, when he turned the disk over he saw that some long-ago hand had written in equally curvilinear script,

The Willowmoon Knotte. Source unknowne.

"Mairey!" He shouted her name and whooped, stuffed the precious knot into his jacket pocket, and the clasps and the nests back into the coffer.

"Bloody blazes, woman, come quickly!" She ought to be here with him. She ought to have been the one to find it, the first to hold it, to feel its coolness on her palm. This conquest was hers; he was only her grateful, awe-struck apprentice.

"Mairey!" He listened eagerly for the footfalls that should have come flying into the room already. He couldn't wait to see the joy light her face when he reached into his pocket and unfolded the Willowmoon to her.

Bright silver and triumph: that would be the hue of her eyes today. Tonight, they would be the smoky gray of a married woman, or at least a betrothed one.

He stuffed everything back into the trunk so that no one would be the wiser, fighting the forces of nature that had expanded the contents to twice their original size.

The Willowmoon Knot. Just a step in the direction of the old Celtic silver mine. But it was the most important step of all.

He slid the trunk back into place, then sprinted down the hall toward Mairey, calling her name again and again. He reached the jumbled room at a run, expecting to find her distracted by her notes and her burrowing.

"Mairey!" His heart slid to a stop, then dropped into his gut.

She was lying face up on the floor, her limbs bent like a string puppet's and her face sickly white, an enameled bowl fallen from her hand.

"My God, Mairey!" Jack scooped her into his arms, raw panic surging through him. He couldn't lose her to some stray illness. Her arms hung limp as a rag while he bent to listen to her heart.

"Thank God!" It thumped solidly against her chest, a blessing from the heavens. He cuddled her against him, brushed her dry lips with his mouth and stayed to feel her warm, strong breath against him.

"Mairey, wake up!" The woman had fainted dead away. But she was already blinking awake, wetting her lips with her delicate pink tongue, and making sighing, good-morning noises in her chest. She yawned broadly and stretched, as contented as a fairy princess roused by her prince's kiss.

"We really shouldn't be making love here, Jack." She reached up and ran her fingers through his forelocks, twirled a hank and pulled him closer with it, whispering, "Not in the basement of the British Museum."

Light-headed with relief, Jack stood with her in his arms. "We weren't making love, Mairey. You fainted."

"I don't think so. I must have been overcome by your kiss. Snow White in reverse, my prince." She wagged her finger at him. "I know my fairy tales."

Undoubtedly, but at the moment she was in no shape to diagnose her own condition.

"A healthy woman doesn't just faint without reason. You've looked ill for a week."

"I feel perfectly fine now, Jack. You can put me down."

"Not on your life." Taking no chances with his lady love, Jack carried Mairey and her satchel up the stairs and out of the museum. He gladly suffered more of her kisses on the step, but didn't set her down until he had dropped with her into the seat of a hackney, where she seemed intent upon finding a way into his trousers.

"Doctor Timson, in Kensington," he called to the driver. "Quickly!"

Jack listened outside Timson's examination room, his ear stuck blatantly to the panel. Timson's murmuring monotone. Mairey's clear voice, made unintelligible through two inches of oak and the swooshing of blood in his head.

Though he'd known Charles Timson since returning to England, the doctor had steadfastly refused to allow Jack in the room while he was examining Mairey. Certainly Jack trusted him, one of the few in the British Empire who was both a physician and a surgeon. Jack had consulted with him on the destructive health effects of mining, and together they were working on a bill to put through the Commons.

But hell, Jack had seen every inch of Mairey without her clothes. And she was the least modest woman he'd ever met. He just wanted to know what had been plaguing her and how he could help.

He rapped on the door with his fist. "Hurry up in there!"

Silence. He paced the labyrinthine pattern in the oak floor, glared out the window, studied the roadway of blood vessels on the ghoulish diagram on Timson's wall, then stuck his hands into his pockets.

The Willowmoon Knot! Bloody hell, he'd forgotten! He fished the piece out to study it, but he was too wracked with questions and worry, and the symbols were gibberish to him. Mairey would have to translate.

Mairey. He paced some more while he carefully wrapped the Knot in his kerchief and buried it safely in the bottom of his deepest coat pocket.

He'd surprise her with it when this was all over. Tonight, after dinner at the lodge, when everyone was asleep and they were alone in the parlor.

The latch clicked and Timson came through the door, drying his hands on a towel. Jack peered past the man's shoulder, fighting the urge to shove him out of the way. Mairey was sitting on a padded table, her small, straight back to the door. She turned and met his gaze, wide-eyed as a doe in a meadow.

"She'll be out in a minute, Jack." Timson shut the door, closing him off from Mairey.

"Damn it, Charles! What's the matter with her? What do I need to do? Will she be all right?"

"Eventually." Timson removed the spectacles that hid his gray eyebrows and buffed the lenses with the corner of the towel.

"What the hell does that mean?" Jack's stomach reeled with apprehension. Mairey sick, suffering. "Tell me now!"

Timson stuck his spectacles back on and peered owlishly at Jack over the end of his nose, relishing a secret of some sort. "It means, Jack, old man, that you're going to be a father."

"I'm—" The whole blessed world stopped on its axis while Jack held his breath and waited for the humming of his heart to settle. "What?"

"Miss Faelyn is pregnant."

A father! And a husband. "Ohhhh, yes!"

A surge of joy drove him through the doorway

of the sunlit examination room. Mairey was standing in the middle of the room, shoving her arms into her jacket.

"Mairey, my love!" As sylvan and beautiful as the woods she adored, the rhythm of his pulse and the meaning of his life.

"Jack. I'm—" Her eyes were brilliant stars and lit with wonder; her cheeks glowed. "We're going to have a baby."

"Yes, my love, we are." He couldn't help his grin, or his belly laugh as he gathered her into his arms and drew her scent to the center of him. Here was where he wanted to spend his days. He was truly inside of her now, his blood and hers mixed and making everlasting magic. "Ah, Mairey, I love you."

"Jack?"

He held her tightly, not wanting to hear her objections, knowing that they would not stop him from protecting his child, or this woman that he loved. "You'll marry me, madam. Today. Our child will know its father."

"Oh, Jack, I—"

He raised her chin sharply, never so serious in all his life, for his dewy-eyed Mairey and the flower that was budding inside her were everything to him. "I've lost one family to my carelessness, Mairey; I'm not going to lose another."

Mairey's heart reeled with her love for Jack, for the silken thread that connected them. He wasn't a careless man; he was principled, and his love, imperishable.

"Well, madam?"

I'm sorry, Papa. But the Willowmoon will have to stay hidden for now.

She couldn't risk looking for it. Not with her husband and their child to protect. The Knot had been safely gone for two centuries. And though she was filled with a dark foreboding, it would have to keep while her children grew, while her marriage bloomed.

"Marry you, Jack?" She put his warm hand on her belly, where their child was sleeping, then slipped her arms around his neck, met his spectacular kiss, and gave him all her dreams. "In a heartbeat, my love."

Chapter 18

"**A**re you a princess now, Mairey?"

"She's my *countess*, Caro." Mairey's intoxicating husband, the vastly handsome Viscount Rushford, looked more like a sagging Christmas tree decorated with squealing little angels than a titled bridegroom freshly home from a hurry-up wedding.

Caro was in his arms; Poppy was perched on his shoulders, her arms caught round his head like a mane; and Anna was stuffing a fistful of daisies into every hole in his jacket.

She'd never seen a man so brimming with peace. Mairey felt it, too. The moment they had married, a great calm had swept through her. The driving wind stopped, and all the voices. Leading Jack away from the Willowmoon would be critical in the next few years. He would grumble his frustration, but he would follow her lead.

And if she did find it in the bottom of some forgotten barrel, her pocket would provide a safe refuge for it until she could take it safely home.

Jack would never know.

His grin filled his face and lit his eyes.

Aunt Tattie was beside herself with happiness. "Lord Rushford married your sister, Caro. That makes him your brother-in-law."

"I have a brother!"

"A *big* brother," Anna said, giving Mairey a bouquet of daisies and a buss on the cheek.

"Just imagine: the pair of you sneaking away today to be married." Tattie dabbed at the corners of her eyes. "Pretending you were off on one of Mairey's humdrum trips to the museum, when you might have had a celebration."

"I'm sorry, Auntie." Mairey gave the woman a guilty hug and looked at Jack across the parlor. "Perhaps we'll have a reception later. You can plan everything."

"I suppose that will do."

"In the meantime, Mairey and I will be spending tonight at the main house." Jack's eyes never left Mairey's, even as he let Caro to the ground and disengaged Poppy's arms from around his neck like a grinder and his long-armed monkey. "The rest of you must stay here and pack."

"Are we moving away?" Anna looked stricken.

"Into the main house." He planted a kiss on top of the girl's head. "In the morning."

That set off a wave of jumping and whooping.

"Now upstairs with you, girls." Tattie winked at Jack and raised her brows at Mairey, then gave them a little shove toward the door. "You two go along, as well."

Leave-taking took a bit longer and included the

story of the *Princess and the Pea* in which Mairey
was the princess and Jack played the pea and
everyone ended up on the floor in a laughing
tangle. But as soon as the lodge door was closed
and they were safely in the yard, Jack lifted Mairey
into his arms.

"I can walk, Jack."

"Yes, my love, but not fast enough." He was
already on the wooded path, his shoulder deflecting
the overhanging branches while Mairey hung on to
his neck.

She tucked his hair behind his ear to better tease
the delicate ridges with her tongue, taking full advantage of his inability to fend off her teasing,
which made him sigh and squeeze her closer.

"Are you in a hurry then, sir?"

"Indeed. To plow you thoroughly, my countess."

Mairey liked being carried by her husband. And
she liked his plow. "Your seed is incorrigibly po-
tent, Jack. Probably a boy."

"A son. God bless us, Mairey." He swung off
the main path and charged through the understory.

"A shortcut, husband?"

"Privacy. I want to kiss you before I burst."

"An admirable idea." The woods were dewy
with the coming night, the highest branches still
gilded by the sun and the pale gentian violet of the
sky.

Mairey knew the place he was taking her to: the
streamside with the enormous, fallen beech along
the bank, one side on dry land, the other in a few
inches of brookwater. The thick roots were heavily

branched with sinewy twists and tucks. Its smooth gray skin was springy with moss.

He had already kissed her here twice before. Once at twilight, when the girls were out in the stream catching fairies. That had been just a chaste buss against her cheek, and she'd dreamed about it for the next week. They had been alone for the second kiss, which was longer, deeper, toe-curling.

"Now that we're married, Mairey, I can confess that I have imagined you entirely naked, alone, and waiting for me right here in this very spot. On that very tree."

"Truly?" All that imagination from a man whom she once thought only understood digging holes into the earth.

He set her on her feet, bent down, and picked up her stockinged foot. "What happened to your shoes?"

"I lost them down the trail."

He kissed her fully but too briefly and then let her go. "I'll get them. Wait here."

"I promise." Jack disappeared through the brush, his greatcoat slapping at his calves, off to rescue her shoes. Her very own dragon. Let's see, that would make his child a dragonet.

Though she shouldn't care, Mairey hoped for a boy, a strapping young lad who would grow up to be his father's reflection. And besides, Jack would indulge a daughter's every whim, and she would grow up hopelessly spoiled.

"Did you really picture me naked here on this tree, Jack?" she called.

"Entirely naked, madam," he called back to her from somewhere down the path.

Mairey grinned and swiftly began working the buttons of her shirtwaist, applauding this imagination of her husband's. Hers was more risqué and might shock the man to his socks, but she doubted he'd complain.

She tossed aside her shirtwaist and her camisole.

"What exactly am I doing in this imagination of yours?" The air was chilly and nipped at her bare breasts. "Just standing there?"

He stopped his brush rattling for a moment. "You are recumbent on the trunk, my love. Waiting for me."

"Ah!" *Recumbent.*

Mairey tried not to laugh too loudly as she stepped out of her skirt, petticoats, and drawers all at one time. She listened carefully to Jack's tromping as she rolled her stockings off and dropped them on the pile of clothes.

She felt wickedly beautiful, a wood nymph awaiting her satyr. Elfin revels. All the sensuous delights of the late summer forest—dappled shadows and bright water and dancing breezes. Jack's hands, oh, his mouth. Despite the hint of an early autumn, Mairey's skin felt as warm as if the sun were playing on her.

"Exactly how am I recumbently awaiting you, husband?"

"Lounging exotically, my love, an arm here, a leg there." He was on his way back, all twig-snapping footfalls. "And skin, Mairey—lots of your lovely skin."

"It sounds complicated, Jack. And uncomfortable." She draped herself just so on the fallen tree, an arm lounging exotically along a jaunty root, a leg bent demurely, coyly. *Lots* of skin and other features that she knew Jack would enjoy.

Her unsuspecting husband came crashing through the underbrush. "I found both shoes, Mair—"

He came to a full, jolting stop.

"Recumbent like *this,* Jack?"

He blinked. Shook his head. Blinked again. And then his eyes grew huge.

"Mairey!" Her shoes hit the ground, forgotten. He was with her in a roaring twinkle, straddling the log and her thighs, his greatcoat a glorious tent that trapped his warmth and his spice.

His kisses fell everywhere, expansive and tongue-wet and branding. He coiled her hair in his fist, collected it and scrubbed it over his face. Mairey moaned in her glory as he suckled at her breasts, now so deliciously tender and receptive. He formed his hands like a cradle and murmured against her belly, spoke of precious treasures and miracles.

"Our babies, Mairey."

She opened to him as a moonflower, moaning against his mouth.

She was free to be open with him now, and she was truly laughing for the first time in a very long time. Jack's powerful coiling, his wreathing her with his love, hadn't bound her. It had made her free. Free to love him, free to be loved by him.

He smelled of a night ride through the woods,

his shoulders dusted with bits of moonlight and silver weed.

She started working at the buttons on his trouser front, hoping he wouldn't notice. Surprise was the order of this amazing day. Surprise strategies. Surprise babies and weddings.

His buttons were nearly free, and he was bulging against the top of his drawers. So eager. So marvelous. Her hands ached to hold him.

He raised up from where he'd been laving her breasts, her very hungry-eyed husband.

"Good God, Mairey, have you any idea what you do to me?"

"I do." The last button, and he sprung free. Aching to explore him to the fullest, Mairey took all of that long, velvety thickness between her hands, bent over his hips, and took him directly and firmly into her mouth.

"Ohhhh." Jack thought his brain had shot out the top of his head. He braced his arm on the tree behind him and jammed his heels against the soft ground, which bucked his hips upward and drove him deeper. "Mairey! I want—"

He wanted her to stop—to wait until—no!

"Oh, yeeesssss!" He held his breath and tried to see more than darting stars and Mairey's moonlit hair in his lap. But she had her hand inside his gaping trousers and had scooped up his scrotum; was playing and fondling there while she suckled and tasted and encircled him with her lusty fingers. Oh, the heavens, and the bounteous earth.

"Enough, Mairey."

She sat up and kissed his mouth. "I've been

thinking about this part of you for too long, Jack.''
Then she went back to her cavorting.

She thinks about my penis! He wanted to hoot
but all he managed was a strangled growl while his
wife drove him to lunacy.

''Enough, enough, Mairey!''

He lifted her face between his hands and steadied
his breathing while she asked, ''Is this what you
imagined, Jack?''

''I never, *never* got this far, Mairey. Not
nearly!'' His commonplace imagination had
stopped on the blunt edge of reality, his erotic fantasy arrested by the classical painters of reclining
nudes. Lamentable painters with only their art to
move them, lacking the smokey fragrance of moss
crushed by Mairey's rosy bottom, the silky sleek-
ness of her skin beneath his hands, the feel of her
tongue—

''Oh, Jack, I love you!''

And those miraculous declarations of her heart
riding on the night wind.

Never had he imagined that he'd find a wife who
would tease at his senses in the woods. But that
was what came of marrying a nymph.

Mairey had draped her legs over his thighs, leaving her open to him, to cradle his erection and let
him tease there, while he made love to her mouth.
She unbuttoned his braces at the front and tugged
his trousers down his hips.

''Here in the woods, Jack?'' She took him into
her hands again, made him growl again and shudder. ''To celebrate our marriage?''

"You'll have me baying at the moon, love, and waking everyone up."

She laughed. "Just starters then, and the rest of our wedding night at home, in our bedroom." A tilt of her hips and she had him poised against all that luscious slickness, on the brink of thrusting himself into her. He spanned her slender waist with his spread fingers, his arms quaking with restraint. But he had to tell her, to make sure she understood.

"I'm so damned happy, Mairey."

"You look it, Jack." She cozied her hands around his waist inside his coat.

"Are you happy? You didn't want this marriage."

She caught her lip, and tears sprang to her eyes. "Oh, but I did, Jack. I did with all my heart."

"The child changed your mind?"

"You did. I've never been happier in all my life. Never felt so loved."

"You are."

"Nor quite so naked." She glanced down her length, then up into his eyes.

"You're cold, love. I can see it here." He covered her breast with his palm, hungry for the hard little nipple and its shadowed boundary. He leaned down, drew its twin into his mouth, and warmed it, rolled it.

She sucked air between her teeth and wriggled beneath him, pressing him closer with her enticements.

"Not cold at all, Jack. Just wanting you to come join me in my fantasy."

"I am astounded, madam, how our thoughts entwine."

Laughing brightly, her eyes catching all the sparkling grays of the twilight, his unconventional wife laid her hands on top of his and slid them down to fit around the perfect curve of her hips. Then her warm hands disappeared beneath his greatcoat and his shirttails, to seize his bare haunches and give a beckoning shove with her heels.

And she took him just inside her. Just. A suckling pressure around the end of his penis that overwhelmed him and shattered his resolve to take his time.

He hauled her into his arms and propelled himself into her until she sat astride him, her legs hitched up around his waist. He was deeply engulfed, struggling to keep his sanity and his seat, while her muscles played him as her fingers had.

"Oh, that's much better." She trembled like the willows that hid them as she gripped his upper arms, rocking on his lap, arching backward and then pitching forward, as though he were a swing and she had plans to soar to the moon.

He wanted this ecstasy to build forever, to fly on the same trajectory as his love—preposterous, then undeniable, then absolute and timeless.

"I want your skin against mine, Mairey."

"In our wedding bed." She was clinging to his neck, breathless and sweat-slick, whimpering against his mouth.

"Oh, yes." He found her with his fingers, feverish and damp, her portal filled with his thickness. Her eyes got smokey, her voice sultry and low.

"Oh! Jack! I'm—oh!" She drove against him, arched like the pale crescent moon, her hair streaming silver down her back, her gaze fastened to his. His nymph, his naiad. "I love you so!"

"Ah, wife!" Jack came unraveled and his release thundered through him along the length of his rod. He thrust deeply, and Mairey took him to the shank. He cocooned her in his arms as he pulsed into her, gushing out his passion.

Mairey felt every long and straining inch of him. Peace came as deeply seated as he was, and all she could do was cling to him, hoarding the last of his shuddering, already feeling the loss that would come when he wasn't inside her.

"The happiest night of my life, Jack."

"And mine." He held her tightly as he kissed her, rocking gently with her in the moonlight, whispering of all the many nights ahead.

He was just beginning to harden again when something rustled in the brush.

"What was that?" Mairey hung on around Jack's neck, and he closed his coat over her. He pulled out of her and half stood, lifting her up with his arm beneath her backside.

"I am Viscount Rushford, the master here. Come out of hiding, immediately!"

"Blazing toads, Jack! What if it's the girls?" she whispered.

"Impossible—with all their chattering, we'd have heard them a mile away." He pulled a coin out of his pocket and hurled it into the underbrush. "Show yourself!"

A great fluttering and flapping shook the brambles, and a blurring phantom launched itself out of its shadows right at them.

"A hawk owl!"

"Bloody hell!" Jack clamped his hand over Mairey's head and dove to the right, pitching them into the stream.

Jack shifted as he fell to take Mairey's weight, landing with a growl on his back. Mairey bounced off his chest and then rolled into the calf-deep icy water.

"Heavens, that's cold!"

"Mairey, are you all right?" Jack sputtered, reaching for her as she clambered to her feet in the gravelly bed.

"I'm fine. But you're going to be sore."

"God, you'll freeze, wife. From lack of clothes, from this water—what's so funny, madam?"

But Mairey was laughing too hard to reply. He was hardly more than a shadow in the pale twilight, and shaking off the water like a hound, hitching up his trousers and fastening them when they wanted to cling to his knees.

He lifted her off her feet and sloshed to the pile of clothes she'd left near the tree. *Their* tree. "Do you often sport about naked in the woods, madam?" He draped her shoulders with his coat, wet but still warm from his heat.

"Only the occasional bath in a stream when I can't get a room at an inn. Why?"

"I thought as much." He found her shoes and

stuck one on her foot. "But no more stream bathing, Lady Rushford, unless you're with me."

"It wouldn't be fun any other way." Mairey stood up when she had both shoes on and stepped into her petticoats and skirt, her hair dripping all over the ruffle like little faucets.

Jack displayed her drawers and then stuffed them into his pocket. "I like the idea of you without these under all those skirts." His grin caught the moonlight as he lifted her into his arms and carried her the rest of the way to the front steps of the main house.

His hair was wet and his clothes were still dripping water and flecked with moss. Mairey's own hair was twisted ropes and leaf-strewn.

"Welcome to our home, Lady Rushford."

Jack carried her through the door to Drakestone with pomp and majesty, and a whole lot of kissing.

They met Sumner coming down the stairs, frowning at them like a disapproving father. "Good evening, sir."

"You mean good wedding night, Sumner. I'd very much like you to meet the Lady Rushford. We were married today."

"Well, finally." He winked at Mairey, then wrinkled his nose at their clothes. "I shall have bathwater drawn."

Jack left Mairey to their chamber and bathed in the laundry. "Much quicker," he'd said, "and I welcome the cold water, madam."

Mairey soaked up the heat in her bath and scrubbed until she was glowing and scented with orange blossoms. Then she tucked herself into their huge bed to await her husband.

His counterpane was lush, and the pillows, deep. She was warm and sleepy and so contented that she could feel her thoughts drifting toward dreams.

A dragon lived there. A man-shaped one, but with a dragon's heart—as impenetrable as it was predatory. She'd cowered from him at first, afraid that he would tear her family from her. Instead, he held her as though he thought her infinitely precious. He had kind eyes, and an honest soul, gave her his child to care for. And when the child came, he would be there to soothe her, to call her name—

"Mairey." Mairey, Mairey. He seemed to like her name, liked to whisper it against her mouth, to follow it with his tongue, in the same way he liked to kiss her.

He was big, weighty like sunlight on a wheat field. And his hands were so able. Oh, yes, able to, *liable* to, do most anything. He could turn a hillside to rubble with a simple gesture, and that still frightened her. But most of all he loved her, loved her family, and gave her children.

Mairey's dream fused seamlessly with her waking.

"I love you, Mairey." Jack was leaning on his elbows, claiming her leg with his, tugging at her breast with his lips—little nips, little tugs, and she was making little whimpers to match his rhythm, circling her hips to bump against all his astonishing nakedness.

"You are particularly pliant when you're asleep."

"And you are ever-hard, husband. Ever ready."

"Are you?" He found her slickness with his fingers. "Mmmm, you are." He parted her legs with his hands and caressed her until her breasts were ripe and wanting, her hips riding the clouds where Jack's tongue played her, sought her. She rose with his tides, joined in his joyful, raucous surges, until they were both wild and straining against each other and the world was spinning.

Yes, this was life and hope. Jack was her fairy tale come true.

She lost herself in the bliss of their wedding night. Her husband pleasured her for hours and gave her fathomless peace and the whispering of his heart in the quiet.

It was in the deepest night, while she was cocooned within his arms, that Jack shot up on his elbow, a wild rejoicing in his eyes.

"Bloody hell, Mairey! I forgot!" He kissed her soundly and leaped off the bed. "I can't believe I forgot!"

"Forgot what?"

"Where the devil did I put it?" He took a twice-around tour of their wedding bower, lifting damp clothes and sorting through the mess they had made in their abandon.

"What are you looking for?"

"Ah, yes!" He was a hunter sniffing the air as he started toward the dressing room. "My wedding gift to you."

"You're wearing it, Jack." She couldn't help but laugh when he stopped mid-stride and turned a crimson-cheeked grin on her and then on his own half-risen penis.

"That'll have to wait, Mairey." Though *that* didn't look as though it was of the same opinion. "Don't move, wife."

Mairey fell back against the pillows, deliciously married, profoundly in love, and admiring her husband's flanks as he bounded into the dressing room. Hard-shadowed flanks and all that masculine equipage. No wonder it was so difficult to keep her hands off him.

He burst back into the bedroom a moment later, stabbing around in the pockets of his soggy jacket.

"I've had no time to wrap it up in a velvet bag, Mairey."

"Your wet jacket will do—though I can't imagine how you slipped away from me today to find a wedding gift. Unless you divined our baby and planned our wedding for today."

"My hindsight is excellent; I should have seen the signs: my rosy wife and her ripening breasts and a waist which is just a bit thicker than I remembered."

"I was neither your wife nor amenable to your fondling."

"Ha! Not amenable? That's not my recollection."

Mairey blushed, aching for him, because everything had turned out so very right.

"However, Mairey, my stupendous divination talents do run to coal and lead, and, with your help—" he pulled a wadded handkerchief out of his pocket, tossed away the jacket, and planted himself in front of her on the bed, a huge, astounded grin on his face.

"Give me your hand, Mairey."

A wedding ring? The absolutely dear man—it must be. Though the object wrapped up in his wet handkerchief wasn't at all wedding-ring shaped . . . more like a small, thick saucer. The gladness drained out of her heart for a moment and flew away in fright, leaving her stomach flipped on edge and her head light. Her palms were damp and fisted into her lap.

The baby again—already making itself known as forcefully as its father, interrupting her every thought.

"Your hand, my sweet wife." Jack was jubilant, his dark eyes gleaming the brightest she'd ever seen them while he waited impatiently with his gift.

"All right, Jack." Mairey smiled back at her marvelous husband and gave him her hand, trusting him. He took it to his lips, kissed her fingers and her palm, then held it flat against his bare chest, where his heart pounded as though it would fly away from her.

"Full circle, Mairey. We were meant to find each other."

She hoped so; prayed that she hadn't stolen this moment of happiness. "I love you, Jack."

"Which makes me the most fortunate man in the world." He put the kerchief and its weighty contents in her palm and closed his hand over the gift.

This odd prickling across her scalp *wasn't* a manifestation of her pregnancy. It was fear, dark and cringing; an inexplicable foreboding having something to do with Jack's wedding gift.

"For you, Mairey. For us."

It came again, a great winged terror that swooped over her head and made her flinch, made her clutch her fingers around the round object. No! Not a disk. It couldn't be!

. . . one silv'red disk, anciently ornamented . . .

"Jack!"

His eyes were so guileless and proud, so eager with his harrowing secret. "Open it, Mairey."

No, please. Not the Willowmoon. Impossible! She didn't want to risk it all, didn't want to know. They could throw it into the fire, and it would be gone.

The piece in her hand was unbearably heavy, a murky darkness inside the crumpled linen. Her fingers shook in her dread, though she tried to hold them steady as she peeled back one corner and then the next, catching the sob in her throat before Jack could hear it.

"A crest of silver knot-work, Mairey," he breathed. "No larger than my palm."

The linen fell away like the petals on a spent poppy. It was beautiful and wicked and molten hot in her hand.

The Willowmoon Knot.

She would know it anywhere. The sweeping spirals of willows and the cycles of the moon. The shale slopes of Nevisfell and the meanderings of the Stoney, the heart of silver and the tiny valley where her village slept. As fine a map as any that Moule could have drawn.

Oh, Papa, what have I done?

"Of course, my love, the achievement is yours."
Jack was bent over the Knot, his cheek next to hers,
grazing her with his mouth and his fine whiskers.
"You led me right to it—I merely picked it up.
Though I haven't the faintest notion what all those
markings mean."

The end of us, Jack. Not a disk, but a lethal arrow, pointed directly at everyone she loved. Aim
it anywhere and precious blood would spill. Mairey
wrapped the hateful thing in the kerchief and set it
on the bed beside her.

"I'll have to study the design myself, Jack."

"But not for days yet, Mairey. We've a marriage
to begin."

He was such a fine man, immeasurably decent.
She grasped at that tiny shred of hope and logic.
He loved her. And that being so, wouldn't he, in
his enormous capacity to understand, also love
what she loved? Wouldn't he see the infamy in
scraping away the willows to mine a cold-breasted
metal that had no meaning to anyone? Wouldn't he
see that not all treasure can be held in the hand?

"When did you find it, Jack?"

He looked sheepish, a scoundrel caught doing a
good deed and liking it too much. "This morning,
in one of Larkenfield's trunks. Can you imagine my
luck?"

Yes—and all of it cruel; ill-timed and far-
reaching.

"You've had the Knot since this morning, Jack,
and you didn't tell me."

"No time, my love." He lifted her chin, studied
her eyes. "You fainted, Mairey, if you recall. And

then there was our baby''——he spanned her waist
with his hands——''and a wedding at the registrar's
office. And we've been making love every moment
since.'' His easy smile devastated her. ''Priorities.''

''Yes.'' They fell into place too easily. A pledge;
a promise to keep. One of them older and bred in
the bone. A daughter's duty to her father, as deeply
felt as a son's. Jack would have understood——if
she'd been able to explain to him all the reasons
she had to leave him tonight.

''I thought you'd be a little more excited,
Mairey. After all, I've done a rather miraculous
thing.''

Her miracle. She couldn't move for the grief
bearing down on her. ''You've overwhelmed me,
Jack.''

He feigned injured pride with one of his roguish
brows. ''I've seen you overwhelmed, my love, and
you make a lot more noise than that.'' He leaned
her backward against the pillows and began his
tender crusade to steal what little she had left of
her heart. ''Let me see if I can do better this time.''

To embrace him once more, to last through all
their lives——long into those empty years when she
would reach out for him and he would be but her
dearest memory.

''I love you, Jack!''

''You are my heart, Lady Rushford, forever
more.''

She took him into her, and, in the same exquisite
moment, she found the Knot beneath her hip, cold
and exacting. Furious and already grieving, she
shoved it over the side of the bed, unwilling to

share her last embrace with its shadows. It landed with a leaden clunk, a sound that echoed through her heart.

Jack looked up from his nuzzling, a brow cocked. "Not going to sleep with the Willowmoon Knot under your pillow to help you dream about a silver mine?"

Her wayward dragon, who would never learn his own strength, whom she loved more than her own life.

"Oh, Jack, I'd much rather dream of us." Mairey gloried in his touch, wept through every caress, and spent her passion for him through that final release, while the moon in its infallible course crept across the counterpane.

Jack was deep into his untroubled dreams when she left him.

Without another breath, for fear of collapsing into sobs and slipping back into the bed beside him, Mairey retrieved the Willowmoon Knot and stole out of Jack's life forever.

Chapter 19

❦❧

"Wake up, Anna!" Mairey's hands were icy cold and shaking badly as she untucked the covers from beneath Anna's chin. "Sweet? You've got to get up now."

Anna stretched and yawned, then blinked up at her through the dim predawn light of the garret. "Mairey? What's wrong?"

"Nothing, sweetheart. We're going away." Mairey hadn't shed a tear since she'd gotten to the lodge—couldn't, because there wasn't time, and the girls would panic. She had to get them out before Drakestone House began to stir and Jack found them. She feared that most of all.

"Going where?" Anna sat up. "Where's Lord Jack?"

Lost to us, love. "He's sailing away to Canada on the morning tide, to see to an emergency in one of his mines."

Anna scooted out of bed. "Lord Jack went to Canada without us? Without *you*, Mairey?"

"He wants us to live in the country while he's

344

gone. You remember our old village—the one we used to visit sometimes when Papa was alive. We're going to wait for him there.''

''He'll come and get us?''

Oh, how this wicked knot had tangled their lives!

''Of course, he will. Come now, sweet. Dress in these.'' She helped Anna into a pair of knickers and a shirt that were miles too big but would serve as a disguise. Jack wouldn't be looking for three little boys and a young man in a stableman's hat; he'd be tearing up the world for his wife and his child, for three little girls whom he loved. He'd said it plainly enough: that he'd lost one family to his carelessness; that he wasn't going to lose another. Because he loved too deeply, and without end.

''Should we wake Aunt Tattie now, Mairey? She takes hours to dress.''

''No, Anna.'' She couldn't risk Tattie's questions. She wasn't a Faelyn; had never heard of the village that was tucked away beneath the Willow-moon glade. Tattie would never accept Mairey's story of Jack's drowning at sea. She would return to him at Drakestone, very much alive and seething in his anguish, and he would descend on Mairey and her village with all the devices of hell.

Her heart broken to bits, Mairey fumbled with the buttons on Anna's coat and sniffed back tears that clung to the insides of her chest. ''Auntie's staying here at Drakestone to look after the lodge while we're gone.'' Jack would surely take care of her; he'd need her support, her devotion.

''For a whole week?''

"Maybe a little longer." How long was a life-time? And how long could a heart grieve? Mairey wound Anna's hair into a knot, then settled a woollen cap onto her head.

They roused Caro, who had great fun dressing up in lad's short pants and coat, charged with adventure and caught up in the whispering.

Poppy slept on, completely unaware, as Mairey dressed her and carried her past Aunt Tattie's dear snoring and down the stairs. They took little with them, just enough for a long day's ride on the train. They would make the village by sundown and begin a new life, but a far lesser one, without Jack.

Mairey and her three little loves left Drakestone through the quiet woods, following the deer trails and leaving new, trackless ones as they went, Jack's child and the Willowmoon hidden close against Mairey's heart.

I'll love you always, my valiant dragon. My Jack.

"Mairey!"

Jack woke in a blind, groping panic, a biting fear gnawing in his gut and his heart trying to tear out of his chest.

He was in his room, *their* room, in their marriage bed. But something was vastly wrong.

Mairey was gone. Her scent, her clothes. He slid his hands over the mattress and into the hollow of her pillow, but even before he'd felt the chill of long-empty sheets he knew that she had left him hours ago.

For the lodge, surely. Out of habit—to check on

her sisters. They rose before the sun to do their mischief. Jack's pulse settled as he counted up the reasons why Mairey would have slipped out of bed.

To study the Willowmoon was the very first— the most probable. She had seemed so unaffected by it last night. He'd presented her father's legacy to her on a platter, and all she could do was to stare at it as though it bored her. A testament to the intensity of their love-making, he supposed, to the newness of their marriage—and the child.

He looked around for the disk, but it was gone from where it had fallen the night before.

That was the answer, then. She'd awakened with the birds and was now in the library, hard at work deciphering the bewildering tracings—her wedding gift to him, an equal exchange.

Such diligence. He nearly laughed at her timing. He pulled on trousers and a shirt and then left the bedroom for the library mezzanine, intending to entice her back into their bed. He would lock the door this time and never let her go.

"Mairey! Have you unraveled it yet? Have you found me my silver mine?"

But there was no answer as he descended the spiral of stairs to the main floor, not even an echo of his own voice. The library looked just as it had for the past few months: a harmonious blend of stuffy mining baron and eccentric antiquarian.

But Mairey wasn't there, nor was she in his office. Sumner hadn't seen her, and neither had cook. He set off toward the lodge, trying to balance his growing anger at having to chase her down again with the baseless panic, the paralyzing fear that had settled in his bones when he'd found her missing from his bed.

He arrived at the lodge to find the door standing forlornly open and Tattie flying down the stairs in her night-robe and curl rags.

"Tattie, have you seen—"

"Your lordship, my little ducks are *gone!*"

Jack's heart stopped. "What do you mean, gone?" He raged up the stairs and went from room to room, Tattie on his heels, but found only empty beds and a terrifying loneliness.

"We have to tell Mairey, sir! She'll know what to do."

Jack caught the woman's arm. "You mean she isn't here? You haven't seen her?"

"Not since you took her off to your honeymoon last night."

"Christ!" Jack tore apart Mairey's bedroom and the library looking for clues, then roused the household to search the grounds and the woods.

It wasn't until mid-afternoon that he put all the pieces together. They glittered and danced before his eyes, blinding him with their dazzling clarity.

Silver. It had been the treasure all along. A brilliant hoax, concocted by him, but executed to the finest detail by the very talented Mairey Faelyn.

Tales of fairies and giants and dragons. Enigmatic riddles. Kings and loyal queens and caravans of jewels.

All for his benefit. Whatever it took, she had been ready for him. Costumed in scholarly innocence, bountiful with her false love and her practiced tears. She even dangled her little family in front of him—his family, too—long enough to distract him from her artifice.

And he had believed every part of her tale—because she had made him love her.

But she would get nowhere with her dreams of silver. Let her study her Celtic map and sell its secrets to the highest bidder. He would know the moment that ground was broken on a new mine.

And she would soon discover that she had stolen one treasure too many.

She had stolen his child.

"I've never seen so many trees, Mairey!" Caro threw great handfuls of willow and maple leaves into the air and let them rain down on her head.

"I thought you'd like it here, Caro."

Once upon a time, the glade of the Willowmoon had been Mairey's favorite place in all the world, with its seasons of high color and brilliant drama as the silver-trunked willows' leaves turned from fresh green to gold.

But now her peace felt like a gray-walled prison with too much sky. Though her sisters frolicked and the sun shone down on the cusp of summer and fall, these three days away from Jack had been bleaker than she could bear.

What a terrible price she had exacted from the man she loved. Dear God, the mess she'd made of his life and hers. She'd left not a note nor a hint of where they had gone. He was a good man and would only suspect betrayal at the very end, denying it in his heart as he employed every resource to track her down. She was exhausted, weary from running, her energy sapped by the baby's need to make her sleep all the time and by the grief that overtook her constantly.

"When is Lord Jack coming to get us, Mairey?"

Sweet, Poppy, you'll have to settle for a less dizzying height than our Jack's broad shoulders.

"I don't know, Poppy." Oh, what an unblinking liar she had become.

"I want him to come home today." Poppy's lower lip stuck out wretchedly as she ambled from tree to tree, giving each of them a hug, as though she thought her Lord Jack might feel her embrace from across the phantom sea.

"I'd like that more than anything." Here was a fairy tale that needed telling: the dragon come to rescue his princess from the malevolent treasure she was guarding. The world gone topsy-turvy and magically right.

"Will he come by Christmas, do you think, Mairey?" Anna had found one of their grandmother's flower presses in the attic of the old house and was collecting an assortment of leaves to start a specimen book.

"It's a very long way to Canada," Mairey said, sitting down on a low outcropping of shale, "and an even longer way across the country."

She would have to tell the girls some day that he wasn't coming for them—fabricate some agonizing tale about a shipwreck and their beloved Lord Jack drowning at sea. What a horrible day that would be! Killing Jack to make them forget him, so they wouldn't go looking for him one day. Wicked lies and tender hearts.

She had buried the Willowmoon Knot the morning before; had come here to the glade and found a perfect and lasting place to hide it. She had prayed for her father and mother and given thanks for all the Faelyns who had gone before, who had sacrificed so much. It was over now, and her village was spared the fate of a crushing mine works.

There was no turning back on this promise—no returning to her husband to beg forgiveness. She would find her joy and contentment in raising Jack's child, and live out her days in the peace of the village, where she could watch her sisters grow to womanhood and then leave her to seek the wide world.

"What are you doing, Poppy?"

Her sister was spinning like a top, her arms outstretched and her chin lifted to the sun. "I'm wishing for Lord Jack to come home from the sea."

"Wish him home for me, Poppy."

I love you, Jack.

The girls began throwing handfuls of leaves at each other and then turned the barrage on Mairey, until everyone was squealing and laughing and falling all over each other.

"Not fair! Three against one!" Well, two, Mairey thought, touching her hand to her belly.

I'll take care of your child, Jack. He'll know what a fine man his father was. No better man in the world.

Mairey scooped up a skirtful of leafy ammunition, ready to toss it at her sisters, but they had stopped, frozen in their battle stances and staring at something in the woods behind Mairey.

Something wonderful, by the looks of wide-eyed awe on their little faces. A heron perhaps, pausing in the treetops.

"Lord Jack! Mairey, it's him!"

"Jack!" He'd found her, here in the glade! A sob of relief and joy and absolute terror wrenched from her chest; made her turn and stare, and gather her sisters close. He was her world, her life, and he'd come to destroy her.

He was framed in the gray trunks of the willows, huge in his fury, silent and flinty as the winter, capable of tearing the trees from the ground with his bare hands. The sharpness of the sun pierced the canopy and dappled his shoulders and his great-coat in emeralds, turned his black hair to ebony. His eyes gleamed with demon fire, possessive and hot, and made her heart yearn for him.

The willows shook as he started toward them, a hunger in his gait, a bloodlust. Mairey tried to hold the girls back, clutched at arms and hands, but they wouldn't be held as Jack approached.

"Take us home, Lord Jack!"

"Don't ever go away again!"

She watched them stumble over each other in their headlong dash to meet him. He lifted them into his arms as he walked, took their kisses and their hugs, and returned them fiercely, but all the while he was looking at Mairey, the glint of obsid-ian in his gaze.

"See, Mairey!" Poppy laid her cheek next to his and squeezed him in delight. "Lord Jack came back when I wished him! I told you he would."

You wished too hard, Poppy. He hadn't come for

them, but for his bloody silver. She had stolen his treasure, and dragons didn't like that. He was danger and delight. The end and the beginning of her happiness. The father of her child, a man whose duty to family ran as deeply as hers.

She had long ago lost her fear of looking into his eyes; she had found so much splendor there. But now they were searing black and his gaze as unrelenting as his long strides that brought him deeper into the glade. She backed up a few steps, seeking a place to take her stand against him, where she could better gather her sisters behind her—once she'd disentangled them from him.

"Did you go to Canada already, Lord Jack?" Caro was rifling his pockets as she hurried to keep up with him. "Did you see a *bear?*"

"You didn't go, did you, Lord Jack?" Anna had captured one of his hands and looked up at him with her heart in her eyes, a lamb taking comfort in the arms of a lion. "It takes more than three days to sail to Canada and back, doesn't it?"

He stopped two yards from her, a seething dragon come to feast upon her heart. Little hands had rumpled him, from his dark hair, to the smudge of dirt on his waistcoat, to the leaves in his trouser cuffs.

"Is that what you told them, Mairey?" His voice came from somewhere distant, filled with bitterness. "That I had sailed to Canada?"

"Jack, I—"

"Kiss him, Mairey!" Caro was behind Mairey, shoving her closer. "We already did!"

He was waiting for her answer, his chest rising

and falling in his unleashed wrath. Nothing she could say would mitigate the situation between them. He would have his silver now, and she would do her best to thwart him in his ravaging. A great storm was brewing here in the glade; she couldn't allow the girls to suffer its fury.

She gathered Anna away from Jack. "Anna, sweetheart. Would you take Caro and Poppy to the house and help Mrs. Russell with lunch?"

"Oh, yes! Can we have a picnic?"

What a fitting tribute before Jack could turn the beauty of the glade into a slag heap. "Of course you may. But later, Anna."

"Oh, goodeeeee!" Poppy scrambled out of Jack's arms and ran after her sisters, their skirts and their laughter flying out behind them, kicking up a flurry of leaves.

Mairey's stomach churned as she watched them run down the path that led through the woods and across the wheat-golden fields beyond, past the winding glint of the Stoney to the slate-roofed cottages of her village.

How long would it take Jack to befoul it as he had Glad Heath? The unstoppable mining magnate—he owned the world; why not her village? Resentment flared and sizzled down her spine and she swung around to glare at him.

"How did you find me, Jack?"

"Madam, if you believe that I wouldn't track you to the ends of the earth, then you misunderstand your worth to me."

"My weight in silver? How flattering."

"Damn you, Mairey! I want the Willowmoon Knot."

It was such a devastating echo of a long-ago time—before he'd stolen her heart; before she'd stolen his, and his baby and all his dreams.

"What does it matter now?" Shamed to her soul that she had failed both her father and her husband with the same duplicity, Mairey took two steps backward but met a fat maple tree and had to look up at him. "You already have it all."

"All?" His eyes glittered with molten fury, were red-rimmed and haggard. And still he was her coiling dragon, sinuous and unbridled, advancing on her, no sense of propriety to keep him from pressing his hardness against her belly, his mouth against her temple and then the hollow of her neck—an intimacy she craved and met, a richly scented memory that swept her along with the beating of his heart.

"Whom did you sell the Knot to, madam? Tell me, damn you!"

It was the silver he wanted. What did he need with the map when he was standing on top of his bloody treasure?

"I didn't sell the Knot, Jack."

"It's mine, Mairey. *You're* mine. My faithless wife." He cradled her head with the greatest of care, though his anger shook him. "Whatever is yours belongs to me. Your books, your collections, and the goddamned Willowmoon Knot."

"Jack, please!"

"You remember the Knot, Mairey: I found it and gave it to you on our wedding night." His mouth came down roughly on hers, made salty by his grief, filling his throat with a desolated moan that made her weep. "You took that from me too, Mairey. All my love, my trust. So I'll have the bloody map from you—as I will have the mine and all its silver when I find it."

When he finds it? Mairey's heart battered at her chest, her thoughts flying backward through the last few minutes. That meant he didn't know that they were standing right on top of his damnable mine! If he would only give her a clear moment to think, maybe she could lead him away from it.

Oh, love, we have a chance!

"How did you find me, Jack?"

Jack had wanted nothing more than to hate her, had determined to shut her out of his heart as easily as she'd shut him out of hers. He had expected to follow her glittering path to the Savoy, and from there to the fashionable salons of Paris, to a woman ablaze with diamonds and laughing at her success, at him. The antiquarian who had bested the mining baron at his own game.

But he'd found his Mairey standing in a sylvan glade, magnificent in her simplicity, her eyes bright with a pain that echoed like thunder in his heart. She had leaves clinging to her hair, harrowing tears pooling in her eyes.

"You taught me too well, wife. I followed a trail of births, marriages, and deaths. Your father is buried in the churchyard below us, in the parish of Lynne, in the North Riding of Yorkshire. Your mother is here, too."

She pushed lightly against his chest. "Please, Jack—"

"And who couldn't follow the trail of three little girls and an overly protective young woman, all of them dressed up as stable hands?" Sweet God, she smelled of the autumn, of smokey resins, spicy and vibrant, caught up in the curls at her temple. "It's difficult to hide such gilded tresses as yours, my dear. They make men think of climbing impossibly tall towers, and slashing through forests of thorns to impress you with their great love for you. Well, I have such a love for you, Mairey."

She was sobbing, clutching her arms around her waist and shaking her head. "I'm sorry, Jack. You can't know how much I love you. I didn't want to hurt you."

"But you have—you've wounded me as no one else in the world could."

"Please!" She twisted out of his arms and he let her go. "Jack, I'm sorry it turned out this way."

"This way? Which way is that, Mairey?" He caught her shoulders and turned her. "That you betrayed me for another man's treasure?"

"I didn't! There's no other man! How could you think that?"

"For your own, then? Have you bought your pick and your cart or will you wait until you have found your silver? Damn it, Mairey. There is nothing right about this whole enterprise. I *know* you. I know your heart and all of its splendor. I know its fullness, because I've been there, Mairey. I'm *still* there, inside you. In here." He spread his hand over her belly, his heart aching with all that she'd

stolen from them. All their hopes, their happiness.
For what? "Tell me why you ran from me."

"I can't, Jack. I never should have loved you."

"But you do love me, Mairey. You belong with
me."

Yet she also belonged here in this glade, among
the willows and the maples, where the sun wove
its rich traceries into the paleness of her dress. Was
she homesick for this place—for her father and
mother? For a peaceful village far from the likes
of Drakestone House?

He had crossed the same river three times to find
her. He had followed a steep trail through a fragrant
meadow, climbed a hillside to these woods. Her
woods. And her home, it seemed. The shale hills,
too, as they rose like the dorsals of a serpent into
the brilliance of the sky. The sort familiar to him,
because at their roots, they would be rich in lead
and tin and—

Silver.

Oh, God. A winding river, a chevron of hills, a
forest of willow. His pulse surged with recognition.

"Christ, Mairey. This is where the Willowmoon
led you."

She gasped, paled, and caught hold of a branch.
"Don't be absurd, Jack." But she laughed too
brightly, falsely. She paced away through the trees,
touching the trunks and fingering the yellowing
leaves. "I would have engaged an engineer to meet
me here, if I suspected that there was silver
hereabout."

"Like hell you would have." He found a likely
spot near an outcropping of shale, then knelt down

and yanked away the moss, then dug in the sweet-scented earth.

"What are you doing, Jack?"

"I'm looking for my silver mine." Three inches further, and he was scraping at solid, crumbling rock.

"Stop it, Jack!" She was on her knees beside him, had a fierce hold of his wrist. "*Please* don't. If you love me, you'll stop. We can start over again."

But he was already pinching a raisin-sized rock between his fingers, holding its dark, sharp-edged tarnish in front of her. Holy hell! He'd pulled many a nugget from the rivers of the Yukon, but none were ever as pure as this.

"Silver, Mairey."

He'd never seen a face so filled with defeat. She hung her head, her shoulders drooping. "Yes."

"You knew where to find the silver from the moment I handed you the Knot. While you lay there in our marriage bed. You recognized the river and this hillside of willows."

She said nothing, but rose wearily and turned away from him to look up at the hills.

"You made plans to leave me, and then you made love to me." He stood, wishing for understanding. "For auld lang syne, Mairey?"

Her prideful shoulders shook with a sob. "Because I love you. And I would miss you."

She hunched over her knees as though he had beaten her, as though he would.

He had his answer, and yet something deep inside of him knew that the answer was wrong. This was Mairey, not some greedy industrialist, not a social climber. She was the clear-hearted woman who loved him, who loved their child and her sisters. Who loved the woods and the innocent places. Who had gone to heroic lengths in her devotion to her family and to her father's memory—

Her father. There it was, splendid and bright.

Erasmus Faelyn was buried in the village below. This was Mairey's home, not a coincidental place she had discovered by following an ancient map.

"My God, Mairey. The Willowmoon wasn't legend to you; it was fact. You wanted to find the Knot because it would lead someone like me to the fortune in silver lying just beneath the ground."

"Please don't spoil my village." The sun lit her face, making shimmering streams of her tears. "Don't let this beautiful glade come to be like Glad Heath. Let me keep my promise to my father and to my grandfather."

"And to all the Faelyns who have ever been? Is that it, Mairey?" Christ, his fierce-hearted wife was a champion like none he had ever known. She hadn't stolen the Willowmoon Knot; she'd only returned it to what she knew to be its rightful place, driven by promises far older than his own. No wonder she had known his heart so well.

"Please, Jack. I can't stay here to see it happen."

"I don't imagine you could."

Sweet Mairey. She wasn't a deceitful, dishonorable thief, but an indomitable warrior, prepared to sacrifice her own life to protect her family—an incomparable woman who would love him till the end of time.

"Who owns this land, Mairey?"

"The Crown." She stood her ground, her chin firm but her face streaked with tears. "It always has."

"And the name of your village?"

"It doesn't have one. Our family kept it off the maps that way. An unremarked part of Yorkshire, overlooked for its plainness."

"But loved for its beauty?"

Another shattering sob wracked her, and he loved her for it.

"Please, Jack, don't bring your blight upon my village. Think of Anna and Caro and Poppy, our unborn child—"

"Oh, Mairey, my love." He gathered her into his arms, letting her sob her tears into his waistcoat where they warmed him to the marrow. "I think of them every minute, as I think of my own sisters. I think of the fortune I would gladly give if I could have them back. You see, I always believed that if I opened more mines, one day I might find them."

"Jack, you can't open this one—"

"Oh, but I could, love. More simply than I had imagined, if this is indeed Crown land. No greedy dukes to include in the royalties—"

She shoved him away, his lady lioness. "I will fight you, Jack! With every weapon I can find!"

"I'm sure you would, Mairey."

"I'll raise a strike against you—I'll burn you out! I'll speak to the prince consort!"

Jack didn't dare smile, let alone laugh, though it bubbled up inside him.

"Speak to the prince if you feel you must, Mairey, but I think I'll speak to the queen herself."

"Throwing your power as always?" Her chest rose and fell, and her breasts shifted as he loved them to do.

"I hope it works this time, Mairey." Choosing between Mairey's love for him and a hillside rich with silver was the simplest thing he'd ever done.

Mairey was breathless with fear, and even more alarmed by the sudden change in her husband. He was smiling. No. He was grinning devilishly as he came toward her.

"So, madam, what will you name this village when it belongs to me?"

A heartless question. "I hate you, Jack."

"No you don't." He was stalking toward her, looking confident and horribly pleased with himself. And why not? He had his mine. She had handed it to him on a silver tray.

"I'm going to fight you, Jack."

"No you won't, my love. You'll be too busy raising our children." He lifted her into his arms and kissed her madly. "And I'll be too busy keeping the secret of the Willowmoon."

She pushed against his shoulders, misunderstanding his words for the rushing of her pulse against his. "Keeping the secret from your competitors, while you exploit the hillside."

He shook his head. "This is your home, Mairey. I don't need another silver mine."

Hope made such a clamoring noise in her head

that she wasn't sure she'd heard him right. "What did you say?"

"I already have two. And if another means losing you, my love, I don't want any part of it."

There were joyous bells this time, and Jack's laughter, and the erotic swell of his melody as he made love to her mouth.

"Look, Caro! Mairey is kissing Lord Jack again!"

They were at the edge of the woods, coming fast.

"We're not alone, wife."

"I love you so much, Jack."

"I know." Mairey felt his smile as he closed his mouth over hers; heard the rumble of his laughter. "Does your cottage have a private room for the two of us?"

"Oh, yes, my love."

"Good. Because I plan a good deal of princess-plundering tonight."

"Come plunder, my dragon. I am yours forever."

Epilogue

Drakestone House
Eighteen months later

"**Y**ou are a darling tyrant, Lady Rushford." Lady Arthur shook Mairey's hand vigorously and started down the front steps of Drakestone House, remarkably agile for a woman of more than sixty.

"We have to be relentless, Lady Arthur, if we're going to change the laws to protect the health of miners and their families." Mairey followed the woman to her phaeton, delighted that this afternoon's meeting had gone so smoothly and had been so well attended by the wives of peers and parliamentary ministers. "The mining barons certainly aren't going to spend their profits on research into black lung and poor diet and lack of sunshine unless we force them."

"No, indeed. May all the mine owners in Britain beware." She added with a broad wink, "Your own husband included."

"Viscount Rushford is foursquare behind the British Women's Colliery Health Standards Commission." Mairey would defend her husband's honor with her bare hands if necessary. "He's spent thousands already!"

"I know, dear." Lady Arthur's grin was filled with affable mischief. "I was referring to the fact that his beautiful wife wraps him so easily around her little finger. Good girl."

Mairey couldn't help her flush or her smile. Her dragon had been wrapped around more than her little finger last night—and early this morning, before their son had awakened for his breakfast.

"Jack does indulge me now and then. He would have joined us today, but there was an important meeting he had to attend." Jack's meeting was with little Patrick, and the agenda included diapers and pram-strolling and all those irresistible cooing and smooching noises Jack made to him.

Hardly a fitting reputation for Britain's most influential mining baron, but a matchless reputation for a father and husband.

"Parade your husband for us next time, dear. He's sinfully handsome, and quite the gentleman." Lady Arthur waved as her carriage sped away.

Mairey loved her new crusade and was committed to the fullest, but she had missed her son and his father terribly these last three hours. She gathered up her notes from Jack's conference table, and left his office for her desk in the library. A picnic would be a fine way to spend the rest of the day.

The warm afternoon light streamed in through the library windows, scattering rainbows across the room. Her search for father and son ended on the sun-washed carpet. Jack was lying on his back, his head propped on a cushion and his son sprawled loose-limbed across his chest, his long, bronze fingers splayed possessively over Patrick's diaper-thick bottom.

They were both snoozing blissfully.

Mairey felt like weeping for the boundless joy they brought her.

Jack was never far away from her these days. She had assumed that after a chaotic year of negotiating his way past three little girls and a new wife, and now a son, all of whom adored him, Jack would have grown immune to his family, weary of their demands. But every day he seemed to draw them even closer.

He encouraged the girls in their pursuits, supported Tattie in her tussles with Sumner, and joined Mairey in her causes.

And now he held her village and the silvery peaks from the Crown, a landlord with all the powers of the State behind him. He'd kept his promise to keep the glade of the Willowmoon a secret between them, reserved and protected forever under the control of Rushford Mining and Minerals.

"I love you so, Jack," she whispered. Patrick stirred, wriggled his nose and his fingers and his toes, and then settled his little cherub cheek against his father's heart, and Mairey's breasts reacted on cue. He would be bellowing for a snack in a moment, waking his dear father from a much-needed nap.

"Come, my little one." She scooped her baby

into her arms, but he slept on, undisturbed even as she settled him into his cradle beside Jack's desk. Jack looked irresistible, too handsome not to kiss while he slept. She knelt to do so, only to feel her husband's familiar hand sifting through her skirts, brushing lightly along the inside of her thigh. She gazed down at his eyes, glistening beneath his dark lashes.

"You were sleeping a moment ago, my dragon."

"Dreaming of you, my love . . . of this, of your scent." His eyes turned smokey when he found the breach in her drawers, and darkened when she met his questing hand and moaned.

"Oh, Jack! You're incorrigible. And wonderful."

"And you, my love, are delicious." He slipped his free hand behind her neck and pulled her close to kiss her. "You finally finished with your meeting?"

"Oh, yes." She grew light-headed from his exhilarating caress, but encouraged his exploring. "We voted to petition Parliament for a hundred thousand pounds to establish a visiting medical corps. Oh, my!" She took a sharp breath when he dipped his fingers inside her, and another when he stayed to play.

"And then what, sweet?" The devil.

"We had tea—"

"And?"

"Then I told the ladies that I had a burning need to make love with my husband, and so I shooed them out, and came looking for you."

"And here I am, my love."

"You certainly are!" The rogue knew just how to make her sigh and gasp; and a long, breath-stealing moment later she was thoroughly sated, and tucked against Jack's shoulder.

And their son slept on in his cradle, as Jack described in detail how brilliant Patrick was—and only nine months old, mind you—and Mairey listened with all her heart, until Patrick woke up starving and wailing.

Jack wondered how happiness could make his heart ache. Stuffed full, he guessed. Even watching Mairey nurse their son was enough to sting the back of his eyes; the feel of the boy's hand wrapped around his finger sent him soaring with pride and filled with love.

Patrick finished his noisy meal and grinned up at his mother with all the besotted joy that Jack felt.

Could a man be more blessed?

"I was thinking, Jack, of a picnic." Mairey was fastening the two ingenious little openings between the copious pleats in her shirtwaist that allowed modesty while she was nursing.

But Jack was very good at gaining access when his son wasn't busy there. . . . "I was thinking, Mairey, of retiring with you to our bed."

Her smile aroused him in an instant. She stood with Patrick on her hips and offered her hand to Jack, promising a splendid afternoon as soon as they could get the boy to sleep.

But then the library door burst open, and Poppy dashed into the room.

"Michaelmas cakes!" She was carrying a plate of lumpy baked goods. "See!"

They were the oddest cakes he'd ever seen. Plump with whole acorns and crumbling oats, spiced with bits of sea green moss, bristling with golden straw and glistening with honey.

"Are these people cakes, Poppy?" he asked, hoping they weren't, wondering how he would pretend to eat one without injuring her feelings.

Poppy giggled. "For the horses, silly!"

"I see," Jack said, forgiven for his gaff.

"Are the cakes cool enough yet, Poppy?" Caro asked as she came skipping through the door in her riding clothes, older these days, and mad for her new nephew, who seemed to think his young aunt was the funniest thing in the world. She nuzzled his nose with hers. "Hello, my baby duck."

Patrick whirled his fists at her and bounced on Mairey's hip.

"I'm going to jump the pony today!"

Jack's stomach lurched. Mairey shared a look of horror with him, but smoothed her fingers through Caro's hair. "You mind your teacher, Caroline Faelyn."

"Lord Jack!" They heard Anna long before she came clattering through the door in a pair of wooden garden clogs. She would be twelve two months from now, but was fast adding grace to her girlish beauty, and would soon be trailing gangly young men in her wake. Just now, though, she was wearing homespun gardening trousers and a huge, mud-caked shirt.

"For you, Lord Jack." She handed him a thick,

battered envelope that had suffered far more than her finger smudges.

The mail came to Drakestone twice a day, and company correspondence flowed up and down the drive like ferries on the Thames.

This was not that kind of mail.

"What is it, Jack?" Mairey touched him, shifting Patrick into her arms.

San Francisco. Addressed in a firm hand to "Jack Rushford, London." A simple envelope, but his heart was in his throat.

He had discovered recently that an Emma Rushford had emigrated to America in the spring of 1844, sailing around the Horn to California. His own Emma would have been fourteen, but the manifest hadn't listed ages, so he had sent inquiries to his contacts in San Francisco.

He had learned to hold tightly to his hope.

"Where did you get this, Anna?" he asked.

"I was out at the end of the drive, and a boy came by with it."

"Did he say anything?"

She blushed through her sunburned cheeks. "Not about the letter. I told him I would deliver it to you straightaway."

"Thank you, Anna." His hands shook as he sliced the envelope open. He felt Mairey's eyes on him, and absorbed the love that she wrapped him in.

"Were you expecting a letter from San Francisco, Jack?"

Where was the line between expectation and hope?

"Every day, my love." Because Mairey had taught him to love relentlessly.

Dear Mr. Rushford. He could hardly see for the tears that welled in his eyes.

If you are my brother, as your handbill at the San Francisco post office says, you'll know these pictures as well as I do.

Mairey fit her hand through his arm. The girls were crowded in. And all the world stood still.

The next page was a pencil drawing of a cottage on the side of a hill. The next was a rickety wagon—a child's. And then a hearth seat with a carving of a daisy.

"Who drew the pictures, Lord Jack?" Caro asked.

He looked up at Mairey, a huge sob clutching at his heart.

"My sister drew this, Caro. Her name is Emma."

Mairey's eyes were starry with astonished joy, her cheeks streaming with her lovely tears, and her mouth, when she kissed him tasted of all the miracles she'd brought him.

"Happily ever after, Jack." She nuzzled his chin and gazed up at him, while Anna and Caro and Poppy clung to them both, and their son chortled and blew little bubbles between them.

Jack kissed Mairey soundly, his treasure, his dearest heart. "Oh, my sweet love, now and forever after."

Dear Reader,

It's so difficult to finish a book you love—you've had the chance to live in their world, and to fall in love with the hero…just as the heroine does! If you were swept away by the Avon romance you've just read, I invite you to be just as enraptured by some of these other upcoming love stories—only from Avon.

Readers of historical romance won't want to miss Linda Needham's *The Wedding Night*, a powerful and sensuous love story from an author who's a rising star of romance. Jackson Villard, a rich, ruthless lord has sealed off his heart from life—and love…until he meets vibrantly beautiful Mairey Faelyn. But he doesn't know that Mairey is out to betray him…

Scotland conjures up images of misty highlands, men of honor…and the women who love them. Lois Greiman's latest in her *Highland Brides* series, *Highland Enchantment*, is an unforgettable love story between a daughter of a laird and a man of honor. Don't miss this page-turner from an award-winning writer.

What if you're an attractive widow, respectable, above reproach, attending a London ball with the height of English society. Then, across the room, your eyes lock with those of a tall, mysterious stranger…only he's not a stranger to you—and he's capable of exposing your wildest secrets. This is just the beginning of Susan Sizemore's lushly sensuous *The Price of Innocence*.

And for readers of contemporary romance…everyone once fell in love with Peter Pan, the boy who wouldn't grow up. Now, talented newcomer Mary Alice Kreusi creates a wonderful spin on this story in *Second Star to the Right*. It's a richly delightful story, all about the power of love and the belief that dreams really can come true.

Be swept away—all over again! Enjoy,

Lucia Macro
Lucia Macro
Senior Editor

AEL 0498

Avon Romantic Treasures

Unforgettable, enthralling love stories,
sparkling with passion and adventure
from Romance's bestselling authors

❃❃❃❃❃❃❃❃❃❃❃❃❃❃❃❃❃❃❃❃❃❃❃❃❃❃❃❃❃

Avon Romances—
the best in exceptional authors
and unforgettable novels!

THE MACKENZIES: PETER   by Ana Leigh
79338-5/ $5.99 US/ $7.99 Can

KISSING A STRANGER   by Margaret Evans Porter
79559-0/ $5.99 US/ $7.99 Can

THE DARKEST KNIGHT   by Gayle Callen
80493-X/ $5.99 US/ $7.99 Can

ONCE A MISTRESS   by Debra Mullins
80444-1/ $5.99 US/ $7.99 Can

THE FORBIDDEN LORD   by Sabrina Jeffries
79748-8/ $5.99 US/ $7.99 Can

UNTAMED HEART   by Maureen McKade
80284-8/ $5.99 US/ $7.99 Can

MY LORD STRANGER   by Eve Byron
80364-X/ $5.99 US/ $7.99 Can

A SCOUNDREL'S KISS   by Margaret Moore
80266-X/ $5.99 US/ $7.99 Can

THE RENEGADES: COLE   by Genell Dellin
80352-6/ $5.99 US/ $7.99 Can

TAMING RAFE   by Suzanne Enoch
79886-7/ $5.99 US/ $7.99 Can

Experience the Wonder of Romance
LISA KLEYPAS

STRANGER IN MY ARMS
78145-X/$5.99 US/$7.99 Can

MIDNIGHT ANGEL
77353-8/$6.50 US/$8.99 Can

DREAMING OF YOU
77352-X/$5.50 US/$6.50 Can

ONLY IN YOUR ARMS
76150-5/$5.99 US/$7.99 Can

ONLY WITH YOUR LOVE
76151-3/$6.50 US/$8.50 Can

THEN CAME YOU
77013-X/$5.99 US/$7.99 Can

PRINCE OF DREAMS
77355-4/$5.99 US/$7.99 Can

SOMEWHERE I'LL FIND YOU
78143-3/$5.99 US/$7.99 Can